Cleanup Crew

Stefanie DiDominzio

CLEANUP CREW

Copyright © 2024 by Stefanie DiDominzio
All rights reserved. No part of this publication may be reproduced, distributed, or transmitted in any form or by any means, including photocopying, recording, or other electronic or mechanical methods, without the prior written permission of the publisher, except in the case of brief quotations embodied in critical reviews and certain other noncommercial uses permitted by copyright law.

ISBN: 979-8-9916335-0-5 (Paperback)

Any references to historical events, real people, or real places are used fictitiously. Names, characters, and places are products of the author's imagination.

First printing edition 2024.

Dedication

To everyone I met on my journey through life. We met for a reason. We had an impact on each other, even when we didn't notice.

Prologue

The clouds are getting heavy in the distance as the sun begins to set, spreading vibrant shades of pink, orange, and purple throughout the sky. Sunsets have always brought me a sense of peace. Unfortunately, they quickly fade away. I stand here a bit longer, watching the sky grow cold, dark, and lonely. I take a deep breath and push away the negative energy that is trying to breach the surface. Today is the last time I'll watch the sunset from this porch. This house on the edge of the lake will no longer be in my family after tomorrow morning. Maybe I should take a picture, it'll last longer.

"Amazia?" a voice behind me requests my attention. "There you are."

I don't turn at first knowing it's Cassandra, the realtor. She walks up and looks out over the lake. The sunset has already faded, grayed out of any color. "I'm not sure if anything is real anymore," I admit. Cassandra isn't really a friend, but I burned all the bridges I had when I decided to run away from this life. Cassandra is the only person left in town that I speak to. She understands why I want nothing to do with this town after what my family did.

"You can't keep blaming yourself for an accident," Cassandra whispers kindly.

I look over at her, trying to read her intentions. "Do you really believe it was an accident?"

She sighs and looks out over the water for a moment longer before looking over at me to respond. "The court says so. I have no reason to doubt their investigation or decision."

She seems genuine, and she has no reason to lie to me. She is two years older than my brother, making her four years older than me, and she didn't know either of us in high school. "I hope you're right. I hope the investigators got it right. I just wish Matteo hadn't gotten behind the wheel that night."

"He wasn't drinking like you thought. His toxicology screenings proved that," Cassandra reminded me.

"But why did my father and my uncle have to die? Why did the universe take away the people this town loved most?" I ask rhetorically.

"I wish I had the answers you seek," Cassandra says before pausing. She looks to be contemplating what she'll say next. "Have you been to see him?"

I look down, knowing she thinks I should try to connect with my brother before I leave town for good. "No, I can't see him like that. He doesn't even remember me. It's best that I just leave him behind like everything else I know," I say, gesturing around the house.

Cassandra sighs, knowing I want nothing to do with this former life of mine. I already packed all of my remaining belongings. I moved most of my stuff to my new house months ago once I found a place near my new job in a city far away from my past. The last of my things were necessities I left for while I was here to close on the sale of my family home. My brother was never going to function enough on his own to use it. The rest of my family was dead. My father left everything to me, almost like he knew my brother wasn't going to be the same after the wreck. The doctors say he'll likely never regain his memories from the head trauma. The doctor promised me that moving away wouldn't hurt him or his recovery since he had no idea who I even was. I paid for the medical bills and memory care facility with the money my uncle left me, which was a surprisingly large amount of cash. I had no idea he was, well, rich. I promised to use all of those funds for my brother's care. If he was ever released to society, I'd hire someone to run his finances from the accounts I set up. Beyond that, I wanted nothing but a fresh start.

"I wish you luck, Amazia," Cassandra was genuine. "I couldn't survive the city life," she jokes.

"I think I love it simply because it's so different than the rural small town where everyone knows everything about everyone else," I admit.

"Listen, just be careful. I know you're a strong and independent female, but the big city is full of horrible people who will lie and cheat to get their way." Cassandra could have easily become my friend if I stayed in town. She is the only person here that I've spoken to since the wreck that took my family away. Of course, there were other casualties in town that I force myself to forget about, knowing it's too hard to think about all this town has lost.

"I promise to be careful," I say with a forced smile.

"Okay," she says turning toward the house. "Ready to lock this place up one last time?"

I look around, taking it all in, knowing after this I will never return to my family home or the hometown that no longer feels welcoming to me. "Let's do it."

1

New York City really is a whole world in itself. It's been a year since I sold my family property in small town Arkansas. I left everything behind to start a new life in the big city. It was terrifying, but the adrenaline of it all kept me sane. I was able to get a job with over the phone interviews before officially moving here. Of course, commuting into the city everyday really does suck. My house in the suburbs is significantly more affordable than the city, and the train station isn't far from home. The other flip side is that if there are vacant rooms in the hotel, I can always stay the night, especially during snowstorms that shut down the city.

I look up at the forty-story building in front of me. The Rush Hotel and Conference Center is a new five-star hotel a few blocks from Broadway and Times Square. A year ago, I was hired to work at the front desk. I knew I needed more, but I wanted to get settled into the city before applying for higher paying jobs with better long-term benefits. Within six months, I was promoted to rooms control supervisor. I worked closely with the front of house management, as well as the conference center team, to be sure all room blocks were properly made for incoming conferences, weddings, events, and of course VIP visits. Most of our VIP clients are guests on popular morning shows or late-night talks shows. They always request suites with private access, letting them come and go without anyone knowing they were even here.

"Amazia!" I hear someone yelling down the dimly lit employee hallway that runs between the guest halls and freight elevators.

I stop, knowing who it is and wishing I could disappear. "Seth," I say turning to face the banquet setup manager running up behind me. "What can I do for you?" I ask, hoping it'll be business related. We're alone in the hall, my least favorite situation because he'll probably try to ask me out again.

"Hi," he starts, coming to a stop in front of me, carrying a clipboard which is overflowing with an unorganized pile of papers sticking out at all angles.

"Is there something urgent, because if not, I have a meeting to get to," a lie, but he doesn't know.

"Oh, yeah. It's not, I mean it's not really. I was just wondering what you're doing for the weekend?" he awkwardly stumbles over every word he tries to get out.

"I work weekends, Seth," I say in a dismissive tone.

"Oh, yeah, I forgot you do that. You know as a supervisor you don't have to anymore," he awkwardly continues.

"Seth, how about you let me worry about my department and my schedule, okay?" I really don't have the patience for him today. He's always so socially awkward, but he tries to ask me out anytime he can corner me in a deserted employee hallway. Sometimes I wish that I worked in security or engineering and could escape to a nearby immediate work order to get away.

"Okay, but on your next weekend off, maybe we could grab a drink or coffee? I mean, I'd prefer dinner, but you don't seem to like the dinner option, and I really can't wait any longer."

"Seth," I say, interrupting him. "Stop asking me out. It's not going to happen, okay?" I stand and wait for his response, but all he does is stand there looking like he saw a ghost. "I have to go," I say, glancing at my watch. After another awkward moment with no response, I turn and walk away, disappearing into a stairwell before he could muster up the courage to say something else or worse, follow me.

* * * * *

The rest of the day went by like any other ordinary day. I finalized the next schedule for my employees, and I met with all department heads to finalize the next set of upcoming room blocks and events. We have a school group coming in for a chess tournament while also blocking out rooms for an undisclosed VIP wedding. Normally, this would be two simple room blocks to separate, but due to the lengthy list of demands for the VIP guests, certain party goers need to be separated onto different floors to avoid any added confrontation. I'm going to be sure to schedule myself to be off the weekend they're in house.

I left work without seeing Seth again. I mentioned something to my friend Pete in security about an employee I'd been having trouble with. I didn't want to give names at first, but Pete insisted, saying there were other similar reports about some banquet staff members. I finally caved, and Pete said he wasn't surprised and that he'd take care of it. I didn't want Seth to get into any trouble over asking me out, but he might not give up so easily on someone who doesn't know how to turn him down if he corners them.

As I walk out of the employee entrance on the side street, a strong gust of wind rolls through. I hug my winter coat tighter around my shoulders, glad I decided to grab it instead of wearing my hoodie today. Thankfully, The Rush does all of the employee uniform laundry for us. It makes it way easier in the winter, especially once the snow starts making a mess of the street and sidewalks. I feel a few drops of rain flying in the gusts of wind bending its way through the streets of the city. Thankfully the subway station isn't far from here, but I do hate making this walk during the winter months.

As I make my way down into the subway station, I'm thankful that I only have one train change to make it into the suburbs. As I make it down to the platform, I look around noticing the number of homeless people hanging around has doubled now that it's grown colder out as winter approaches. Most of them keep to themselves and don't bother you, but that isn't always the case. It's important to keep your eyes peeled, especially when you're alone. It's the one thing I hate about having to travel back and forth to my house in the suburbs, the trains.

Once I arrive at the suburban train station, I'm glad to see that several other passengers are exiting at the same station. It always makes me feel better when I'm not the only one walking out to my car this late at night. I've tried having a roommate a few times over the last year. I was hoping someone from the hotel would take me up on the offer so I'd have someone to travel in and out of the city with. Most of them wanted to be in the city full time, and none of the roommates ever worked out. I did like the security of not having anyone else in my house, especially on days I worked, but I do miss the company sometimes. Though, in reality, I prefer to be alone.

I don't let myself have many friends and I don't date. There are too many creeps in the city. Klarissa is the only person I'd truly consider a friend, but she understands my limits on friendship. She knows I prefer to keep to myself. I have no social media accounts to occupy my mind and burn into my soul like the rest of society. I wouldn't even have a cell phone if it wasn't necessary for communicating with others throughout the workday. Of course, this means I have two cell phones, which is even more annoying to be honest. I do occasionally load books onto my personal phone to read on the train rides to and from the city.

Once I get into my car, I turn it on and blast the heat, trying to warm it up before my teeth crack from all the shivering. I look at the temperature projected onto the screen in my car. Thirty degrees, it's below freezing, great. It takes a while for the car to begin to warm up. I would have been home already, but I decided to let the window fully defrost with the heat rather than having to scrape the frost off the front windshield in this cold. I'm not entirely ready for winter just yet. Once the front windshield is clear, I set off down the road towards home. Thankfully it isn't a long drive because I am ready for a quick, hot shower and my warm bed. I pull up to the house and into the driveway, which is large enough for three vehicles total. There is no garage or carport, which I regret this time of year. I'll add it to my wants list for the house. The house itself is a small, light gray house that matches most houses on the street. They're all small lots with neighbors on all sides. My backyard has a chain link fence on the two sides and a wooden privacy fence at the back, though I can't see much of it in the dark. The older gentleman that lives next door is taking his trash out as I climb out of the car and rush toward my door.

"Hey, Mr. Brownstone!" I yell as I pull my keys out of my bag.

"Oh, hi there Amy!" he yells back before slowly walking back inside with help from his cane. The poor man was a bit hard of hearing and never understood that my name is Amazia, not Amy. I just let him call me Amy, the poor old fella.

Once inside, I check that all the doors are secure before making my way upstairs to my bedroom. I drop my coat on the coat rack and look at myself in the mirror, seeing my red cheeks from the cold outside. My dirty blonde hair is a mess of tangles in the thrown up messy bun. My makeup has faded throughout the day, especially the eyeliner which is smudged in a few spots, making it look like it was a rough day. I reach up to rub my red cheeks, feeling the dry and irritated skin, probably a bit of New York City wind burn. I'll put on my deep moisturizer before bed.

I turn on the TV and flip on the late-night news to check the weather forecast before taking my shower and climbing into bed. The meteorologist pretty much says that he's surprised to see a sudden collection of clouds in the area which might bring snow during the afternoon hours tomorrow. Great, our first snow and it isn't even December yet. So much for long term forecasting skills. This morning there was no sign of precipitation, especially snow, in the forecast for at least ten days. Liars. It's going to be a long winter.

2

Another week goes by, bringing us to the last weekend before Thanksgiving, and the big undisclosed VIP wedding is here. It's going to be the most talked about winter themed wedding of the elite in New York City this season, according to all of the tabloid magazines. Plenty of the tabloids already have rooms booked for this weekend, but a lot of new requests have been pouring in as we approach the big event. Of course, I got roped into working overtime due to some mistakes the front desk agents made as some of the guests checked in. A few guests asked to be moved to other locations and a new front desk associate didn't read the clear directions that say staff is not allowed to move any of these guests without management. So, here I am doing as much damage control as possible. I was able to redo some of the rooms before other guests checked in. It was perfect before, now it's as good as I could make it under the time constraints and unforeseen circumstances.

"Did you hear about Banquets?" Klarissa rolls her chair over to my office door to ask. Klarissa isn't technically my assistant, but she takes on a lot of assistant type duties for me, so I moved her to the cubicle immediately outside of my office door.

"What about it?" I ask, not even looking up from my work to hear her latest gossip.

"They demoted Seth," Klarissa says while sounding like she has more to tell. I look up at her, waiting to see if she'll spill the rest without me asking.

"Really?" I ask curiously. "What did he do?" I go back to working on my room blocks for the wedding, double checking any reservation that hasn't been checked in yet to be sure I avoid as many conflicts from the request list as possible.

Klarissa stands up and walks into my office, coming close enough to whisper so no one else hears what she has to say, which only intrigues me more. "Apparently, there have been several employees who came forward with allegations of inappropriate behavior. Security tried to speak to him about it and get his side of the story, but he flipped out. The security managers had to come down from their office to handle the situation. The only reason he still has a job is because there's no proof, at least that they could find."

"What kind of proof?" I ask.

"All of the people who came forward said that he never approached them in areas with security cameras," Klarissa continues.

"Interesting," I think about the few times he cornered me. I don't recall there ever being a camera in those areas either. "Were there any allegations of physical contact?"

"I can only speculate," she shrugs. "Security was told to back off of him. Apparently, they were rotating keeping watch to try to follow him. The hotel manager said it was a waste of resources but to continue to keep an eye out for video footage. I heard they couldn't find anything though, which is why he gets to keep his job in banquets for now."

"Sounds like a PR nightmare waiting to happen," I say, returning to my work.

"Hopefully it doesn't come to that," she says before turning to walk back toward her cubicle.

"Hopefully whoever from security spilled all the beans to you won't be spilling the beans to anyone in the press," I add, noticing her rolling her eyes at me before she leaves the office.

Seth is annoying and he was always trying to get me alone so he could ask me out, but what if there was more to it? What if I was just smart enough to keep a distance between us and to immediately turn him down. Hopefully this is all over exaggerated and everything remains calm. I'd hate for Seth to cause problems or do anything to ruin the wedding this weekend.

"I'm printing the changes for the rehearsal dinner," Klarissa yells from her cubicle. "It appears they've added five more rooms to the rehearsal staff block of rooms."

"What could you possibly need five additional staff member rooms for, for a simple rehearsal dinner?" I ask under my breath.

Klarissa brings the papers in, clearly hearing my snide remark. "Apparently it's a three-person band and two band staff members."

"Adding a band… to a rehearsal dinner… the night before? God it must be difficult to make such dramatically necessary decisions. What a rough life these people have," I say sarcastically.

"Says the one who secretly has plenty of money set aside," she side eyes me.

"That's a bit different than rich society people who flaunt it just because they can. None of this is necessary. And there is zero reason to add a band to the rehearsal dinner, the day before."

"How are you so cynical?" Klarissa laughs as she walks out of the office again.

My hometown in Arkansas helped make me the cynic that I proudly am today.

*   *   *   *   *

"Amazia, the band is here," I hear the front desk call from the opposite end of the long check-in counter. I was able to magically find them five rooms together in the hotel. They'll be closer to the chess kids, but hopefully they're not a rough type of band that shouldn't be near kids.

"I'll check them in," I say as I walk over and take over the computer from the new front desk worker, the same one who moved some of the wedding guests yesterday.

"He's checking in all five rooms," the front desk associate says, nodding towards the guy standing directly in front of me.

"Thank you," I say with a sassy smile and an overly dramatically eye roll which I immediately regret when I realize the guy standing there saw all of my reaction. "Sorry," I say before putting on the customer service face necessary for the front desk. "I don't typically work face to face with customers these days."

"Seems like a good decision," the gorgeous guy in front of me says with a smart tone.

"Are you in the band or what?" I ask, ditching the customer service voice after hearing his attitude.

"No, just day of event planning for the entertainment part of the rehearsal," he says dryly. I look up and really take him in as he scrolls through something on his phone. He is clean cut and well put together. He has a very neat, classic tapered crew cut hairstyle that looks perfect even with the high winds outside. He's wearing black jeans and a black t-shirt under his black leather jacket lined with a dark gray hooded sweater. I stop while looking at his face, mesmerized by the perfectly placed features. He looks up and catches me staring. At first, I don't look away. His blue eyes meet mine and we stand there just looking deep into each other's eyes for several moments, as if he could see directly into my soul, until he interrupts my day dream. "Did you need something else to get us checked in? I was told it was all taken care of."

I shake off whatever just happened, not understanding what about him pulled me in so dramatically, especially with his clearly uninterested attitude. "I assure you it is. I took care of the reservations myself when the request came through last night."

"So, if I hate the accommodations, you'll be to blame... Sorry I didn't catch your name for my future complaint card," he says, looking down and texting on his phone.

"You won't be complaining," I say knowing that these rooms are far better than what he's expecting of this weekend.

He looks up as if he's trying to read deeper into my response. "Your confidence is... interesting."

"Thank you?" I respond awkwardly, not sure if it's a compliment or not. "The name for your room?" I ask while typing away into the computer.

"Jared Wright," he says, looking down as if there is more to what he's saying. Maybe it's a fake name.

"Do you have an ID Mr. Wright?" I ask, noticing he looks surprised at my request.

"Do you need one for everyone in the band getting a room?" he asks curiously.

"Just yours will do," I say in a dry tone, trying to match his from earlier.

He pulls out his wallet and pulls out an ID, handing it over to me. As I reach out to take it, his finger grazes gently against the palm of my hand. I can't help but notice two things: one he twitched slightly at the contact of our skin, and two I felt a huge electric surge at the slight graze. Not the normal electric shock after walking on carpet, but a stronger electrical current. By the way he looks up at me, he felt something too. "Thank you," I whisper awkwardly, trying to pry my eyes away from his.

I type in all of his information and copy it to all five of the band rooms. As I make two sets of keys for each of the five rooms, I explain that he'll need to be available with his ID if anyone needs access to the room without a key card, unless they each want to stop by with an ID to get their name specifically registered. "If anyone gets locked out or loses their key card, you're the only one who can get new keys or have access through security. You can have each guest check-in with their ID if you want them to be able to have access without you."

"That won't be necessary. The less information in the computer about the band, the better," he says as I hand him the room keys.

"Is that why you were added so last minute?" I ask without thinking. I feel the look of shock on my own face as he responds as if there is nothing to it.

"This band wasn't the first choice of the bride," he says sternly.

"Sounds like you brought a great wedding present then," I joke as I hand back his ID.

"Hardly," he says, picking up all of the room keys. "Did you need anything else?" he glances over at me briefly while waiting for my response.

"No. Have a good weekend at The Rush, Mr. Wright," I say trying to remember the required send off from the desk.

"Thanks," he replies in his usual dry tone before immediately looking back down to his phone. He types several messages, pausing to hit reply or read other messages as he makes his way back out of the lobby doors and towards the check-in parking lane out front.

"Strange fella," the front desk associate says, stepping back toward her desk.

"You don't say," I reply, hardly acknowledging her. I can't take my eyes off of him until he's out of view. Something about his attitude is intriguing and I can't figure out why. Maybe it was simply because he was steamy hot or maybe it was the strange reaction we had as our skin brushed each other's. Either way, I likely won't see Mr. Wright again during his stay anyways.

3

"Where's the banquet staff meeting?" Klarissa asks as she follows me from the office, toward the conference area.

"Back hall behind the ballroom, I think," I reply as I lead the way. The last of the rehearsal dinner guests and staff arrived before two this afternoon. Now that the front desk should be back to normal check-ins, Klarissa and I head towards the Conference Center to see if any of the event managers have any issues or complaints about rooms that we can try to resolve before the rehearsal dinner gets underway.

Klarissa and I arrive in the back hallway just in time to see the all-hands meeting breaking up into smaller department meetings. We walk through the banquets team and head towards the event managers in the middle of the large crowd of employees.

"Afternoon, Ms. Franklin," Seth says to me in passing.

"Hello, Seth," I politely reply in a professional manner as I continue walking.

"Did creeper Seth just talk to you?" Klarissa whispers to me once he's out of earshot.

"Yes, it's a daily thing if he can find a way to run into me," I explain.

"Gross," she says making weird grossed out noises.

"He isn't so bad if you just turn him down and not lead him on," I say with a shrug. I don't want to stand up for Seth and whatever he's done to some employees, but I also don't like talking about it in crowds of employees either. I see the event managers walking into the ballroom just ahead and I rush to catch up. They stop once they see Klarissa and I heading their way.

"Amazia, Klarissa, it isn't often that we see you two out of the office these days," Amanda, the department head says, coming over to greet us.

"Big weekend, big clients, big loads of extra work for everyone," I laugh before unlocking my tablet. "So, are there any issues or complaints about rooms or locations that we can try to resolve before the rehearsal dinner begins?"

"You guys finish up, I'll be right along," Amanda says to the other event managers, so they'll leave us. Once they're gone, Amanda takes out her notepad, "Actually, there is a strange request."

"How strange? Wait like, is it about these odd family separation groups because redoing all of those blocks last night was terrible," I confront Amanda.

"Mr. Berlusconi, the father of the bride, has been handling all of the drama over the room placements personally. Those won't be an issue for you. He is keeping control of the family and advising that the hotel is simply following his wishes,"

Amanda explains. "The strange request has to do with the rehearsal dinner band."

"What is it about this last-minute band?" I ask at a whisper, knowing they're loading in their gear nearby for their sound check.

"If you can keep a secret, they might be *the* wedding band also," Amanda says out of the corner of her mouth.

"Hopefully they don't suck," Klarissa adds.

"Anyways," Amanda continues, "their event planner is requesting either all five rooms be moved closer to the conference center, or one large suite be available to them, closer to the event space."

"They are a demanding bunch of last-minute musicians," I reply.

"Their event planner said he meant to ask during check-in, but he was distracted at the front desk," Amanda explains.

"Yeah, real distracted," I whisper.

"Didn't you check him in, Amazia?" Klarissa asks.

"Yes Klarissa, yes I did," I reply with an angry smile. Sometimes she just speaks without thinking.

"That was you?" Amanda asks, looking intrigued.

"Yeah, why?" I ask.

"That makes a lot more sense," Amanda starts. "He suggested it was the new girl's desk, but he had a lot of good things to say about the check-in process."

"He did?" I ask, surprised.

"You were always the top front desk associate when you worked down there, so it's no surprise that you were able to customer service him into a positive comment about the front desk," Amanda says. "His only complaint was that you didn't provide your name so he could properly compliment you."

"That's surprising. He was very dry and awkward to deal with," I tell Amanda briefly.

"Well, whatever you did, keep it up. I passed the compliment on to Mr. Berlusconi, and he was thrilled to hear such positive comments before the celebrations even begin," Amanda suggests.

"I can't move all five rooms, but I have a nearby suite available. One band suite coming right up," I say as I click away on the tablet to book it to the wedding block before someone tries to upsell the room. "I'll grab some room keys and get them delivered to Mr. Wright. Does he want his name on that room as well?"

"That is what Mr. Berlusconi has requested," Amanda replies writing another note on her pad.

"Are they about to do sound check?" I ask.

"They are," Amanda says checking her watch for the time.

"I'll grab keys and head back before they're done. We'll see you for the rehearsal dinner," I exit, leaving Amanda to do whatever else is on her to do list before the events begin.

*   *   *   *   *

I leave Klarissa in the office to listen for any issues that need to be addressed while I run the suite keys back to the band before they finish their sound check in the banquet hall. As I arrive back in the conference area of the hotel, I duck into the back service hall and walk the long way around, glancing in each room along the way, looking for the band. I can hear the sound check continuing in the banquet hall, but finding Mr. Wright might be more difficult.

As I round the last corner, I see him standing halfway down the hall. He isn't far from the stage door, leaning up against a piece of equipment in the hallway while texting on his cell phone. Does that man ever stop texting?

"Mr. Wright?" I say as I walk up to him.

He looks up to see who is interrupting him. He looks pleased to see it's me, but also uninterested. "Jared," he says in his dry tone.

"I just came to drop off the suite keys," I say, pulling the key cards from my pocket.

"Oh! You were able to provide us with a closer space?" he asks, standing and sliding his cell phone into his back pocket.

"Couldn't move all five rooms closer but I had a nearby suite available instead. I hope that'll work," I say as I hand the keys to him, trying to keep my grip firm as I feel my palm getting sweaty in his presence.

"As long as a few of us have closer access to the banquet hall, it'll do perfectly," he says, smiling as he retrieves the suite keys from my hand. He looks different when he smiles. I wonder why he's so dry and serious all the time. His smile shows that there is clearly another side to him. This time, as he reaches for the key cards, he is careful to be sure our skin doesn't brush against one another's.

"Well, there is the access you requested Mr. Wright," I try to say in a dismissive voice so I can walk away.

"Jared," he again says dryly, the smile already faded away.

"I'm sorry?" I ask, missing what he said.

"Please call me Jared... and you are?" he asks, trying to make eye contact with me.

I find myself staring back into his blue eyes and I do my best to not get completely pulled in. "Franklin, Amazia Franklin."

"Amazia. That's unique," he says, still staring back into my eyes.

"Thank you," I say, hoping someone will interrupt our moment before the tension rises too high.

"All done boss," someone walks up behind me, pulling us out of whatever moment we were trapped in.

"Did we get the rooms moved?" another musician asks.

"No, but we have access to a closer suite now," Mr. Wright explains to the band as they come off stage with a load of questions.

"I'll leave you all to it," I say, bowing out.

"Until next time, Amazia Franklin," Jared says before I can walk far enough away to hide my inner fears. His tone didn't seem as dry as I've become accustomed to either, maybe he does have a soul hiding in there.

4

Once the ballroom was set up, all of the event staff got their dinner break while management did a final walk through with the family. Amanda asked that I accompany them, saying the family was impressed with the positive remarks from the band's event manager. Apparently, the family hired Mr. Wright for the weekend to manage the band for them. During the walk through, the family did explain to Amanda that the band will be staying to play at the wedding reception tomorrow as well. Good thing I booked their rooms, including the suite, for the entire weekend, just in case. That news also seemed to please Mr. Berlusconi, who reeked of power and authority.

The walk through is wrapping up as we all convene in the ballroom lobby. I'm thinking that I will get the chance to sneak away for the rest of the night, but I'm surprised to hear the last request from the family. "Is there anything else we can do for tonight?" Amanda asks.

"We do have one strange request," Mr. Berlusconi begins, glancing over at me. "My wife would like Ms. Franklin to be present for the rehearsal tonight."

"Amazia, is that a possibility? Are you available for the evening?" Amanda asks.

"Amazia? What a beautiful name," the mother of the bride speaks for the first time.

"Thank you, ma'am," I acknowledge her before looking back at Amanda. "I'd be happy to stay." This is a bold-faced lie, but I wouldn't dare say no to the family hosting the wedding of the season, especially since they know who I am now.

"We'd be happy to provide a room if you don't want to commute home late after the festivities are over," Mr. Berlusconi adds.

"That won't be necessary," I begin, waving them off.

"It is the least we can do. You never know what kind of help may be needed at one of these events. Unforeseen circumstances always seem to arise in events this large," Mr. Berlusconi says, almost like he knows something we don't.

"Well, that's all set," Amanda begins. "You two go and get ready for the rehearsal. We'll see you shortly."

"Thank you both," Mr. Berlusconi says, glancing at me again before he puts his hand on the small of his wife's back to lead her away towards the guest rooms.

Once they're out of earshot, Amanda comes to stand next to me as we watch them walk away. "This event just gets more and more curious with every meeting I have with that family."

"You owe me one, by the way," I tell her.

"For what?" Amanda asks curiously.

"For agreeing to stay. I've been here since five this morning and need to be back at five tomorrow too," I admit.

We turn and walk back towards the employee service hall so we can grab dinner with the others before the conference center cafeteria closes for the night. "I honestly didn't think you'd say yes. Sorry they put you on the spot like that."

"I know how important this event is to you and to the hotel. We can't afford to disappoint them by me turning down their request to stay."

"Well, I do appreciate your sacrifice," Amanda laughs as we enter the service hallway.

"Did you also get the feeling that he knows more than we do about tonight?" I ask, curious to see if Amanda caught on to what I did.

"I've been spending a lot of time with this family over the last few months and most of the day today. They are very… odd. They are polite and professional, but also very mysterious and secretive. I honestly don't know what to think of them. I really have no idea if what he said about what problems might come up is a threat, a warning, or just a prediction from always dealing with large events." Amanda shrugs before we walk into the cafeteria to grab our dinner as most of the staff is heading back to the banquet hall for last-minute preparations.

* * * * *

The rehearsal dinner starts off without a hitch. I stand with Amanda at the banquet hall doors to help her and the security staff check everyone into the dinner. Guests have to be on the security list to be allowed in. Part of this was to keep the tabloids and media out. Part of me thinks it's also to keep something secret, but who knows what.

"Ms. Franklin," the temporary banquet manager comes up behind me.

"Yes?" I turn towards him.

"Any chance you're free to lend a hand?" Max asks.

Amanda turns towards him, "Why? What's going on?"

He gestures for us to step aside with him, which we do. Once we're out of earshot of the doors he begins to explain. "You know I just took over for Seth?" He waits for us to nod before continuing. "Well, I've been letting him help me run everything. This is a huge event, and I cannot afford to mess it up."

"Okay..." Amanda says, looking at me, but I shrug in response.

"Seth didn't show up after dinner break," he explains.

"What do you mean?" Amanda asks, looking surprised.

"Once the hall opened, I looked everywhere. No one has seen him since dinner."

"That's odd," Amanda says. He's never late and this isn't like him to disappear.

"Do you think he's trying to sabotage everything because he got demoted?" I ask.

"He doesn't seem the type," Amanda shrugs.

"Either way, I need help," Max explains.

"I can call in a few people," Amanda shrugs.

"No, I've got it. If I have to be here, I might as well pass the time by putting in some labor hours," I say.

"Are you sure?" Amanda asks, sounding bad for putting me to work.

"Yeah, I got it," I say brushing it off as a minor inconvenience. In reality, I don't want to stand around all night. I'd rather do something useful to pass the time. "Don't worry about me," I wave Amanda off while following Max into the back hall.

* * * * *

Once everyone has arrived, Mr. Berlusconi begins the evening with a rather long speech while we serve the tables. I took over Max's tables, the bride's family, while Max worked Seth's in the middle of the room. Max was too nervous to serve the family, saying he was afraid of the Berlusconi family, especially the father of the bride. Thankfully, while I serve the table, the father is making his speech. His wife did ask me if there was anything in the hotel that I wasn't good at.

Once his speech is over, a short video plays showing photos of the bride and groom as they enter the ballroom from the stage. They remain on stage for a moment after the video to introduce the band. I can see Mr. Wright standing at the edge of the stage clapping along with the crowd as the band begins to play. I wait for the bride and groom to sit at their table, front and center, before delivering their meals. The groom kindly nods in thanks as the band begins. I see Mr.

Wright eyeing me from the wings of the stage before I see him disappear from sight.

Once the bride and groom are set, I sneak to the side of the room to the doorway leading to the back hall. I see Max standing in the corner, leaning against the door frame. I join him in the doorway, leaning against the opposite door frame. "The band is pretty good," Max says.

"Especially for a last-minute addition," I add.

"What do you mean?" he whispers back.

I nod for him to enter the service hall with me. "They were only added yesterday. Apparently, they're playing the reception tomorrow now too."

"That's curious," Max replies, looking back out into the hall. "This is one strange wedding."

"You're telling me," I laugh. "I'm apparently a room control, front desk, banquet associate now."

Max laughs, "Well, you're wearing many hats this weekend. But this family seems to like you for some reason."

"I sure wish I knew why. I didn't do anything special."

"Not a bad place to be," Max shrugs.

"Makes me a bit nervous though. Feels like they want something more from my presence."

"We might never know what the truth behind it all even is," Max says with a shrug. "Time for refills," Max says as he rolls a table of pitchers toward the service door. We all grab a pitcher and begin to make the rounds to refill drinks while the bus boys come in to begin clearing empty plates. Meanwhile, the band continues to play.

5

The band continues playing until the bridal party comes up to do their rehearsal speeches. The band stays on stage behind them to play again once they're done. While the speeches go on, the staff clears all of the tables to prepare for dessert and coffee. The speeches begin to come to a close as we finish serving dessert. The groom gets up last to thank everyone for being there for their special weekend. He thanks the bridal party for their speeches. He thanks the staff for all the preparations and help with the event. Lastly, he thanks the band and requests they play a few more songs to close out the evening. I walk around to fill the last of the coffee cups before the band begins to play again. I'm stopped by Mr. Berlusconi.

"Ms. Franklin," he says to me as I fill his coffee cup.

"Yes sir?" I reply at a whisper, stopping behind him.

"Is there anything at this hotel you can't do?" he asks with a smile on his face, which I haven't seen before.

"Not that I'm aware of sir," I kindly joke back.

"Well, we're glad you decided to stay this evening. It appears I was correct in assuming they'd need an extra hand with the dinner."

"You're very wise to be prepared for all scenarios," I reply kindly.

"Thank you, Ms. Franklin," he replies.

"Amazia, please call me Amazia. I'm not a huge fan of my surname if it isn't necessary," I smile politely, hoping this isn't crossing the line with the family, but knowing it'll be a long weekend if I have to listen to them constantly calling for Ms. Franklin.

"Amazia it is," he says before turning back to the table.

I stop at the bride and groom's table to fill their coffee cups as the groom sits back down. I glance up at the stage as the lights dim and the band begins again. I don't see Mr. Wright anywhere around. In fact, I haven't seen him since the band first came out at the beginning of dinner. Curious for a day of event manager, isn't it?

I spot Max waving for me from the back hallway. I make my way over to see what the fuss is all about. "What's wrong?" I ask.

"Someone forgot to keep the band's dinner up here in a hot box," he starts, sounding in a whisper panic. "I can't leave to go find it. The hot box got moved downstairs to the cleanup hall. It's three floors down near the kitchens."

"Do you need me to find it?" I ask, a bit concerned I'll even know how to find it. This area of the conference center is a mystery to me.

"Would you please?" he pleads. "I'd go myself, but I can't leave them without a supervisor. And I trust you to handle this more than any of these part time staff members I hardly know."

I sigh, wondering if this responsibility is too much for me. I turn and look into the banquet hall. The family seems to be set; they'll hardly notice if I'm gone for a few minutes. "Okay, what am I looking for?"

"Okay, it's in one of the rolling hot boxes. It's a short one, not one of the six-foot-tall ones. The laminated page on the front will say 'the band' or 'band's dinner' or something along those lines. It should have six full meals in it, we always make one extra."

"Okay, I think I can figure that out," I say wearily.

"You'll have to bring it back in the elevator, but it'll take a minute to wait on it during this busy time. I suggest taking the stairs down. Go down three flights then when you exit into the kitchen, the hot boxes should line the wall between the stairs and the freight elevator. Hit the elevator button before you look so you can get back up here before the band finishes their set. I'll have someone set everything else up outside the green room. Do you need a hand setting out the meals once you get back?" Max explains in detail.

"No, I can handle that. Can I borrow your key set?" I ask, knowing I won't have access.

"Yeah, here you go," Max says handing me his extra set. "These were Seth's, so I still have my set if I need them."

"Perfect," I take them. "Wish me luck."

"Break a leg!" he says as I walk away.

Once I'm out of sight of the ballroom, I turn a corner and jog down the hall towards the stairwell door. Once I get there, I burst through it assuming the stairwell would be empty but quickly realize I'm mistaken. I shove the door open, striking someone on the other side. "Oh, shit, sorry!" I say before realizing who it is. I reach out to steady them, but quickly stop myself when I see it's Mr. Wright. "Are you okay?"

He looks up, noticing it's me for the first time since I smacked him with the metal door. "Amazia?" is all he says at first. He removes the hand he has against his nose to reveal a small amount of blood.

"Mr. Wright, I'm so sorry! I didn't mean to... I mean I didn't think anyone would be here," I ramble feeling stupid for this inconsiderate mistake. This could change the family's view on me if they find out. "Your nose. Shit, is it broken? I'm gonna get fired for that one," I continue to ramble.

"Amazia," he says so gently I stop to stare at him, thinking this voice isn't his. It's not dry or monotone like usual. Once I look up at him, he continues, "Amazia, relax." He reaches a hand out to gently touch my arm, bringing an odd sense of peace as his hand gently holds my upper arm. "It's just a bloody nose. And you're definitely not getting fired," he laughs at the end, which seems so unlike his nature. After a few moments of me not responding, he shakes my arm gently, "Amazia?"

"Hmm?" I can't speak, so I force out a reply.

"Breathe…" he looks me in the eye, bringing me deeper into his gaze. I let out the breath I didn't know I was holding. "Good. Breathe with me." I match his breathing while he continues to stare into my eyes, as if he's trying to read my mind or something. "That's better," he says as he releases my arm. "Where are you off to in such a hurry?" he asks curiously.

"Oh, shit!" I say, remembering what I'm supposed to be doing. I brush past him, forgetting to keep my distance. I feel a strange sensation as I pass him, different than when he had his hand on my arm.

"Amazia?" he calls after me. "Where are you going?"

"Sorry about your nose!" I yell back at him. "Time sensitive errand!" I say as I disappear down the stairs, running as fast as I can without falling. Part of me is trying to hurry up and find this food and the other part of me is trying to run away from whatever strange interaction I just had with Mr. Wright.

I reach the banquet kitchens and sprint down the long hallway to the freight elevators and hit the upward call button. I turn around and sprint back down towards the half size hot boxes, reading the labels until I find the box for the band. I quickly unlock the wheels and begin to push the cart towards the freight elevator. I need to make up some time. Thankfully the elevator magically arrives just as I get there with the hot box. I use Seth's old key card to force the elevator to go directly to the ballroom level. I try to catch my breath as the elevator goes up, knowing there is a huge possibility that I'll run into Mr. Wright again in or around the greenroom, especially since one of these meals is for him.

As the elevator doors open, I see Max looking concerned near the ballroom service entrance. He bends his head in the direction of two people in a deep conversation at the opposite side of the hall. I look in the direction he indicates while slowly walking the hot box down the hallway towards the greenroom entrance. As I approach, I realize it's Mr. Berlusconi speaking sternly with Mr. Wright. Crap. I hope that has nothing to do with me. I calmly walk past them, trying not to draw any attention to myself.

As I get close enough to hear, I think I hear Mr. Wright say, "The blood is mine, minor nosebleed, probably the cold air outside."

"As long as everything else went as planned," Mr. Berlusconi said in a calm voice, noticing me about to pass.

"Yes, sir," Mr. Wright discreetly replies, realizing I am well within earshot.

"Ah, Amazia!" Mr. Berlusconi turns to say, thrilled to see me for some reason. "I was just wondering where you disappeared to."

"Just trying to get the band's meals to the green room before they finish their set, sir," I advise with a smile.

"Jeri..." Mr. Berlusconi begins, but stops himself, "Jared will assist you in getting everything set for his band."

"Allow me," Mr. Wright says, trying to push the hot box for me.

"Mr. Wright, that isn't necessary," I begin.

"Oh, but it is, Ms. Franklin," Mr. Wright says in a tone sounding final, back to his normal dry and monotone voice.

"Thank you for staying this evening, Amazia," Mr. Berlusconi says. "I'm glad you were the one taking care of the family tonight." He turns and slips back into the dining room before I can reply.

"My pleasure," I whisper while rolling my eyes. I regret it again when I notice Mr. Wright watching my reaction. "You weren't supposed to see that."

"Your secret is safe with me," he replies in his dry tone. "But…"

"But, what?" I ask as we reach the door to the green room.

Mr. Wright opens the door and looks inside. He steps back into the hallway and looks in both directions to be sure no one else is around. He nods for me to enter the green room as he pushes the cart in before us. As the door closes, he steps up next to me, very close but doesn't allow any contact between us. He leans forward to whisper in my ear, "But never let them catch you rolling your eyes. Not this family. Trust me." His tone is serious, not as dry as his normal tone, but there is something threatening about the way he says it. He takes a step to the side, adding distance between us.

"Whatever you say, Mr. Wright," I reply, not knowing what else to say.

"How'd you get on his radar, anyways?" he asks me.

"No idea," I admit.

"What did he mean when he thanked you for staying?"

"He requested I stay for the rehearsal dinner tonight when we did the final walk through. Said you never knew when extra help would be needed at a large event, or something like that."

"Yeah," he huffs, "you never really know."

"You still want dinner in the greenroom?" I ask, hoping to find a way out of the narrow hallway we've been standing in.

He looks up at me, clearly understanding why I'm trying to get out of this awkward situation we're in. He's acting like he did when he checked in, with his dry and uninterested tone. He isn't like the guy who got his nose smashed in by a door just minutes earlier. I'm not sure if he's bipolar or hiding something about this family. Either way, I can't break our eye contact now that he's looking right into my eyes again. I don't know if I'm supposed to be scared by his threatening warnings about the family or if I'm supposed to feel safe and secure in his presence.

"Amazia…" he starts, back to his gentle voice.

"Mr. Wright?" I reply softly, trying not to hold my breath again.

He laughs, "Why do you refuse to call me Jared?"

"What?" I ask confused by his question in this tense moment.

"Please… call me Jared," he says at a whisper as he closes the distance between us again.

"Jared… what are you doing?" I whisper back, looking up into his blue eyes. My heart is racing, and I'm sure he can hear it with how loudly it's thumping away in my own ears.

He takes another step closer, leaving the tiniest space between us. He reaches one hand up, slowly towards my face. He stops himself once his hand is near my neck, searching in my eyes for me to stop him. When I don't, he continues to slowly move his hand towards my face. His fingers gently graze my cheek, as if he's afraid any contact will cause his fingers to burst into flames. I feel a shudder as the soft skin of his fingers ever so gently brushes against the skin on my cheek. He slowly and gently brushes his fingers back along my cheek until his thumb reaches my cheek and his fingers uncurl to gently rest along my jawline. He holds his fingers there while his thumb gently caresses my cheek as he continues to maintain eye contact. His thumb gently grazes over my lip before resting on my cheek as he slowly leans forward, and I feel myself trying not to hyperventilate.

His face slowly moves in closer as he watches me closely, as if still waiting to see if I stop him. I'm not sure why I don't, but something about every move he makes is so natural, gentle, and kind. For some reason, I'm overcome with trust that I can't understand. I trust him. He moves his hand to gently lift my chin up towards his face. I can feel his breath on my face as he stops just beyond my reach. I think he's about to take that final step to connect when the crowd in the ballroom erupts in applause as the band ends their final song. He sighs, letting go of my chin and resting his forehead against mine instead of connecting his lips to mine.

"Shit," he whispers, still breathing heavily. I can't tell if he's complaining about the band being done with their set or if he's mad at himself for what just happened between us.

"The band is pretty good," I awkwardly say, trying to break the tension.

He laughs before taking a deep breath and taking a step back, away from me. He looks toward the stage and avoids making eye contact again. "Yeah, they aren't too bad." He looks off toward the stage for a moment, then down at the hot box cart. "Come on," he says while looking at the cart. He continues to avoid making eye contact. Instead, he takes the hand he was holding my face with and reaches out to hold my hand. He gently wraps my hand in his as he pushes the cart into the green room with his free hand. He gently pulls me along behind him until we reach the opening to the room. He lets go to turn the cart further into the room and around a corner.

"I've got it," I interrupt the silence. "You can go deal with the band or whatever it is you need to do."

"Are you trying to get rid of me?" he asks, still not making eye contact.

"Not exactly," I reply honestly. I crouch down and open the hot box, pulling out one tray at a time. I lift one up and place it on the table next to me. I quickly notice that Jared standing next to me. I glance up and he's looking right at me.

"My job is to take care of the band. I'm doing my job," he whispers, gently reaching over my arms to take the tray from me. He breaks eye contact to carry the tray to the opposite end of the table as he takes off the lid to help set everything out.

I crouch back down and take each tray out one at a time. As Jared returns with an empty one, I return it to the inside of the hotbox. Jared finishes setting out the final tray while I unload the box of drinks sitting on top of the cart. We finish just as the band walks into the greenroom.

"Oh, perfect! I'm starving!" one of them says as they walk in. The fourth person who walks in, the other person not in the actual band, walks up behind Jared and pats his back, "Great work, today."

"Thanks," he says in his dry tone, clearing his throat before glancing up at me. Something about this glance looks like another warning. I simply look away, placing the last empty tray back into the hot box and rolling it back towards the hallway leading to the employee halls. "Thank you, Ms. Franklin," he says as I exit the room.

I briefly turn back and smile, "You're welcome, Mr. Wright. Let Amanda know if you need anything else," I say before quickly turning to leave the room.

* * * * *

We continue to clear tables throughout the rest of the event, hoping to have most of them cleared before the event ends. Some tables request additional coffee or bar drinks until the last call. Most of the extra guests said their goodbyes to the family before leaving for the night once the band finished. Shortly after, the family is assembled in the center of the room for the actual wedding ceremony and reception rehearsal. The event management team walks them through each step for tomorrow while the server staff members continue to quietly clear the room. I help Max supervise the clean-up. We can't remove any tablecloths or tables until the family leaves, so we do as much as we can while the rehearsal continues. Max and I stand at the service doorway watching most of the time. At one point, I notice Jared on stage helping the band readjust some equipment for tomorrow's setup. He avoids looking my way, but I caught him looking at one point when he didn't think I'd notice.

Once the family finished with rehearsal and retired for the evening, I helped Max get the banquet set up team started on what needed to be moved tonight. Most of the table linens and decor would be added in the morning. Once they were wrapping up in the ballroom, Max and I check with Amanda at the fountains where the ceremony would be held.

"Amazia? You're still here?" Amanda asks.

"Yeah, I got invested. Max needed a second hand in keeping everything in order," I answer.

"She's literally my new favorite person," Max jokes. "She not only took care of the family, she got the band's meals set up, and saved my ass a few times tonight."

"No surprise," Amanda replies before looking at me. "I hope this means you're taking up the families offer to stay the night at the hotel. You don't need to travel out of the city alone so late, especially when you need to be back so early."

"I'll probably just pass out for a few hours in my office," I admit.

"That's hardly acceptable," Amanda says in a demanding tone. "Just stay in my suite. The family insisted I stay on site this weekend. Add yourself to the reservation, Room 622."

"Thank you, Amanda," I say accepting her offer.

"See you soon, I'll be heading that way myself after I lock up the office," Amanda says.

"Goodnight," Max says, waving as he walks back toward the back hallway.

"Goodnight," I say waving to them both as I head back to my office to grab my emergency overnight bag and add my name to the reservation.

Once I add my name, I make a key at the key machine in the office and head to the guest rooms via the employee freight elevator. I'm happy to see Amanda getting off the guest elevators as soon as I enter the hallway from the back hall. "Thanks again," I say.

"Please, it's the least I can do. And you really don't need to sleep in your office when I have this entire suite to myself," she says unlocking the door. She turns on the lights and we step inside. I instantly realize they booked her one of the two-bedroom suites on the extended stay list.

"Dang. They went all out on you," I admit, taking it all in.

"It's like pocket change to these people, and I won't complain. It's not often clients pay for us to stay on site when they request 24-hour event management," she says as she grabs a water from the full-sized refrigerator. "Help yourself to anything in the kitchen. You can use the bedroom on the right, no one else has been in there since I checked in yesterday."

"Sounds good, thank you," I say.

"Goodnight," she says entering her own room and closing the door.

I grab a bottle of water from the fridge and head to my own room. I quickly change for bed, ready to pass out, knowing tomorrow will be a longer day. I unpack my overnight bag and decide to just stay here tomorrow too, especially with the snow showers forecasted for the entire weekend.

When I climb into bed, all I can do is wonder what it would be like to be loved by him. Am I really thinking about Jared Wright right now? Is it crazy to even have these thoughts? I just met the guy. I can't stop thinking about the kind smile or how handsome he is, well… how hot he is. Then I remember the dry and monotone version of him with the resting bitch face. Even then, he was gorgeous to look at, even with his infuriating attitude. "Get yourself together," I tell myself out loud. I'll probably never see him again. This weekend is going to be crazy, and I likely won't be anywhere near the wedding tomorrow. It's unlikely I'll run into him again after this weekend. This city is huge and he's clearly freelancing.

Then, as I'm on the edge of sleep, I remember the connection we had in the greenroom hallway. I remember my heart racing as he came closer. He was slow and deliberate with his moves, but carefully watched for my reactions the entire time. He clearly was ready to stop if I told him to. That makes him more of a gentleman than the personality he put off in his usual demeanor. Then there was the moment he relaxed me in the stairwell after I almost broke his nose. I feel myself toss and turn as my mind replays all the different versions of him. Dry and monotone versus kind and gentle. Eventually, the tossing and turning stops as do the thoughts about Jared. Eventually, I fall asleep.

6

"Amazia! Room Service!" I hear Amanda yelling from the kitchen as I'm finishing getting ready.

"Coming!" I yell back as I double check that I am ready to leave. I feel like I'm forgetting something anytime I get ready from my overnight bag at work. I turn off the lights, grab my ID badge, and head out towards the kitchen. When I exit my room, I see Amanda sitting at the bar along the kitchen.

"Apparently, wedding day comes with room service," she says.

"You order all of this?" I ask.

"No, Mr. Berlusconi sent it. He sent two cards with it," she says pointing to the room service cart in the kitchen.

I walk over to where she's pointing and look down at the cart. I see my name on an envelope and am surprised. "Did we each get a card?" I ask, picking it up.

"Sure did," she replies between bites.

"How did they know I was here?" I ask, glancing at Amanda while I open the envelope.

"No clue," she replies before taking another bite. "Either way, I could get used to this."

I open the card and read:

Amazia,

We are so thankful for your assistance at the rehearsal dinner and we hope to see you again today. Please enjoy this breakfast as a small token of our appreciation for your sacrifice and help this weekend.   - Mr. Berlusconi

"What is with this family?" I ask Amanda.

"They are too rich to handle, honestly. Either way I'll take the extra cash and free breakfast while I can," Amanda says, standing up and grabbing one last slice of toast before picking up her bag to leave. "You staying again tonight?"

"Yeah, if you don't mind," I reply.

"I'd be thrilled to have you. Less creepy when I'm not in this huge suite alone," she replies as she heads to the door. "See you later, hopefully not in banquets."

"Let's hope!" I yell after her before she closes the door.

*   *   *   *   *

A half hour later, I'm settled into my office when the front desk manager calls with an issue upstairs. I ask why she can't just deal with it, but all she says is that they're requesting Ms. Franklin's assistance. I can hear a strange tone in her voice as if she wants to say something more but can't. I agree to head up to the lobby. On the way, I send her a text on her work phone, trying to get to the bottom of what I'm walking into. Unfortunately, she doesn't respond.

"Ms. Franklin!" she yells as soon as I enter the lobby area. She begins running towards me from the opposite side of the lobby to meet me before I can reach the desk. She smiles and whispers through her teeth, "The bride's family is requesting to speak to you."

"Why didn't you just say that on the phone," I say, rolling my eyes, then wishing I hadn't after Jared's warning last night.

"I'm terrified of this family," she whispers, trying to laugh it off.

I laugh at her to put a smile on my face as we approach the desk. "Probably a great idea to feel that way."

"They're right over here," she leads the way to the desk they're waiting at. As if I couldn't see them already. It's Mr. Berlusconi and another male I've seen following him around. The other male was seated at the table next to the family yesterday with a bunch of other mafia looking dudes.

"Ms. Franklin!" Mr. Berlusconi says loud enough to make everyone in the lobby glance my way.

Don't make a face, don't roll your eyes, don't turn red, I try to remind myself with all the eyes on me. "Hello Mr. Berlusconi," I greet as I step up to the computer they're waiting at. "What can I do for you this morning?"

"I'm sorry to request your presence this way. I was told your office isn't accessible to the public," he says.

"That is correct," I acknowledge.

"In that case, there are two reasons I've called you down here. Firstly, we wanted to thank you for your assistance and hospitality yesterday evening. Several of our family's staff members noted your professionalism during dinner, especially once we told them you don't even work for banquets."

"Thank you, sir. It was the least I could do given their short-staffed situation."

"So sudden," he says, waiting and watching for my reaction.

I shrug, "Happens all the time in the hospitality industry." I'm not sure what he is testing me for, but I feel like honesty is the best policy.

"I hear that is true of these industries," he begins, looking satisfied with my response. "The other reason we're here, is to request a few rooms be added to the list for housekeeping to skip. The front desk wasn't comfortable with the request since we asked for it to begin today."

"That's easy. What rooms?" I ask while signing into my rooms control page.

He lists off the rooms he wants to add to the list. I also open a chat with the housekeeping director to be sure we get these added to today's list immediately. As I add the rooms, I send the message down to the housekeeping manager to be sure we're all on the same page with the changes. The director immediately acknowledges, as he's also here working overtime for this extravagant event.

"Okay Mr. Berlusconi; I have all of those rooms added to the list for housekeeping to skip. I've been in contact with the housekeeping director so he can be sure they all get skipped today as well. Do you need any extra towels delivered to any of the rooms today?" I explain.

"No, I think we'll be fine," he answers.

"The housekeeping manager is going to provide a cart of towels near the staff door at the end of the hallway in case anyone needs a few more and doesn't want to wait for them to be delivered," I explain.

"As always, Amazia, we appreciate your hard work and attention to detail. The Rush is lucky to have you employed here."

"Thank you, sir," I acknowledge, feeling proud that someone notices for once. It also makes my stomach turn. Why is Mr. Berlusconi so fixated on me and my customer service. Hopefully I'm just over thinking everything. "And Amanda and I were grateful for breakfast as well."

"That was Mr. Vittori's idea," Mr. Berlusconi points to the man standing next to him. "He's my assistant, my right-hand man really. He was confused when he couldn't find a room in your name last night. We were worried you hadn't accepted the offer to stay."

"Amanda offered so she wouldn't feel so lonely in her suite," I explain, also being sure they aren't mad I didn't accept the offer. Jared's warning coming to mind.

"We're glad you stayed. I'm sure today is a busy day for everyone. If you need anything else, please let Mr. Vittori know. We hope to see you at the wedding?" Mr. Berlusconi asks, watching carefully for my reaction.

"I'm not sure where I'll be needed today. Have a few department related issues to deal with this morning," I try to avoid telling him that I want nothing to do with the wedding or his family.

"I'll leave you to your work," he says before he turns to walk away. Mr. Vittori nods to me before turning to follow Mr. Berlusconi toward the escalators. They take the escalators to the next level, likely going to check on the ceremony and reception areas before getting ready for their day.

"Amazia?" a nearby front desk associate is trying to get my attention.

I shake off my daze and look over and see the front desk associate speaking on the phone.

"Yes sir, I'll advise her immediately," the associate says before hanging up.

I log out of my rooms control system and walk over to the associate. "What is it?"

"A gentleman on the phone requests your presence at the coffee bar," the associate advises.

I glance over to the coffee bar behind the escalators, but cannot see anyone watching or waiting. "Thank you. Did they mention who they are?"

The associate shrug, "Sorry ma'am."

I sigh, "That's okay, thank you." I begin to walk away, passing the manager on the way, "Strange weekend."

"You're telling me," she replies as I walk toward the coffee bar as discreetly as possible. I walk around, looking for anyone familiar.

"Ms. Franklin," I hear a newly familiar male voice.

I glance to my right, to a man leaning against the wall with one foot propped up against it in a dark corner. "Mr. Wright," I say as I walk up towards him, ducking into the same shadow.

"Didn't I tell you to be careful around the Berlusconi family?" he asks in a seriously dark, whispered voice.

"You did, and I'm doing my best to follow that direction," I reply.

"Good," he says, relaxing slightly at my acknowledgment.

"Is there a reason we're speaking in a dark corner?"

"For your protection," he replies vaguely in his normal dry voice.

"Should I ask for an explanation?"

"No," he replies in a conversation ending tone. After a few awkward moments of silence, he speaks up again. "Why did you accept their offer for a room if you're trying to follow my direction?" he's looking down still, avoiding any chance of eye contact.

"I felt it was safer than rejecting their offer outright," I explain, unsure why I'm being interrogated by a stranger. A hot and sexy stranger that I wouldn't even consider an acquaintance at this point.

He huffs at my response, "Probably the best idea."

"How did you know about that?" I ask.

"Amanda mentioned to the band that you two were staying on site for the weekend," he explains.

There is an extended silence between us as if neither of us knows what else to say. "Was there something you needed other than to interrogate me?"

He laughs and stops leaning against the wall. He steps closer, his demeanor melting into his gentler self. "I was just needing a favor."

"And what is this favor?" I ask, nervous at what he might say next.

"I need the suite to be on the no housekeeping list."

"Anyone at the front desk could have done that for you."

"I know. That was my plan, but then I saw you down there speaking with Mr. Berlusconi."

"So, you avoided the lobby?"

"Precisely."

"For my protection?"

"Exactly," he says, looking up at me for the first time, instantly making eye contact.

"Any specific reason?" I ask curiously.

"The band will be in and out of the suite all day. Just better if they're left alone," he explains.

"That's not what I meant…" I begin.

"I know," he interrupts as he closes the space between us, reaching out to take my arm, pulling me further into the shadow.

"You're going to tell me to not ask questions, aren't you?" I whisper, feeling my breath catch as he closes the remaining space between us as he backs up to the wall, pulling me closer to him.

"If you already know, then I don't have to tell you," he whispers back, maintaining eye contact.

"Jared?"

"Yes?"

"Should I be worried about something?"

"Just avoid the wedding, if at all possible," he says, gently reaching out to brush the hair back off of my shoulder. His eyes follow his hand for a moment before slowly tracing their way back up to my eyes.

"I don't get much choice in my job duties."

"Just try to avoid getting involved, if you can."

"What if I can't?" I ask, wondering what my backup plan needs to be.

"Then be sure to avoid Mr. Vittori and myself," he explains in a stern voice.

"Why you?" I whisper, leaning in closer to him as if gravity is pulling me there.

"You don't want Mr. Berlusconi or Vittori seeing us together, for your protection," he says as his fingers graze my cheek just like yesterday. He again moves his fingers back until he wraps them around my jawline. His thumb softly brushes against my lips. "Just trust my discretion."

"I'll do my best. I don't plan on being anywhere near the conference center today," I slowly whisper back.

"Good," he says, taking in a deep breath as if contemplating his next move.

"Jared?" I ask, resting my hand against his chest softly for balance.

"Yes?" he responds curiously as he wraps his other arm around me, holding me closer.

"Are we this close for a reason?" I ask, unable to think clearly while this close to him.

"That depends…" he starts.

Then my phone rings, interrupting our moment. "Shit," I whisper as the phone makes me jump with surprise. I pull out the phone and check the screen, seeing Klarissa's name. "Sorry," I say to Jared before answering. "Hello?" I answer while maintaining eye contact and physical contact with Jared.

"Amazia, where are you? I need you in the office! Now!" Klarissa sounds overwhelmed.

"Okay, I'm coming. Is everything okay?"

"It will be once you get down here," she replies vaguely.

"Okay, I'll be right there," I reply before hanging up, still holding eye contact with Jared.

"Until next time Ms. Franklin," he says, releasing his hold on me with his dry tone. The arm which was wrapped around me loosens as he releases me slowly. His other hand remains on my face a moment longer as his thumb gently rubs my lips again before he drops his eyes down and slowly drops his hand from my face, looking disappointed.

"Mr. Wright," I say in a tone giving away my own disappointment. I step back, watching for his reactions. When he doesn't move, I take another step back to leave, looking around for anyone who noticed us before I go to walk away. "I'll take care of the housekeeping with the suite."

"Thank you," he gently whispers as he leans back against the wall, looking both overwhelmed and disappointed as he refuses to look back up at me.

I turn to walk away, and feel his eyes look up and follow me as I go. What the hell is going on between the two of us? I shake it off and take the long way back down to the office.

* * * * *

As soon as I scan my badge and open the door, I notice a small crowd outside of my office. "What the hell?" I whisper to myself as I pause in the doorway for a moment. I take a breath and begin walking.

"Oh! There she is," Klarissa says, pushing through the crowd to get to me.

"What's going on?" I ask.

"Amanda's looking for you," Klarissa answers.

"And there are ten other people outside my office, why?"

"You guys get back to work," Klarissa yells to them as we walk past her cubicle.

"Why are they all over here?" I ask as I see what they were all looking at.

"It's an original Ivy Matthews painting!" Klarissa shrieks.

"It's worth about a half million dollars," Amanda says, stepping out of my office, where the painting is now hanging.

"And it's in my office, why?" I ask, at a loss.

Amanda shrugs, "Apparently, it's been donated to the hotel by the Berlusconi family. They requested it be hung in the office of Ms. Amazia Franklin."

"Jesus Christmas!" I exclaim.

"Jesus Christmas?" Klarissa asks.

"It's better than yelling Jesus Christ! Isn't it?" I shrug.

"I think either are appropriate, under the circumstances," Amanda says.

"What's the catch?" I ask, getting nervous that this doesn't end with an extravagant painting.

"You have to work the wedding," Amanda explains.

"Say what?" I ask, feeling defeated.

"Mr. Berlusconi didn't explicitly say anything about if you refuse, but I don't really want to find out what happens if you refuse," Amanda replies honestly.

"I don't know," I start, my mind racing. "I had planned to stay far away from the entire ordeal." In fact, I practically promised Jared I would stay away from the wedding. What advice would he give under these circumstances. Is it better to be cautiously involved or to suffer the possible consequences of rejecting the request.

"I'm not sure that it was really a request," Amanda says in a tone advising she's feeling the same way about not wanting to see what consequences follow if I refuse.

"Any idea what I'm requested to do?" I ask.

"You're not going to like it," she smiles awkwardly.

7

"Are you ready Ms. Berlusconi?" I ask the bride.

"As ready as I'll be," she replies shyly. "And please, call me Elena."

"Cold feet?" I ask, trying to make gentle conversation as we walk from her room to the private elevators.

"Not exactly," she begins. "My family is a bit... particular."

"Does your family not like your fiancé?" I ask as we step into the elevator.

"Oh, they do, they do. In reality, they introduced us many years before we started dating. I just don't think they did it so we'd marry one another," she continues. "His family isn't as rich or... well... connected, the way mine is."

"Mind if I ask... what about that is worrying you?" I ask cautiously.

"I'm not sure I even know," she laughs. "I just want to be happy, safe, and secure in my own life."

"Do you see that happening with your fiancé?" I ask as we step out of the elevators and walk down the hall toward the fountains.

I see her smile light up her face before she has the chance to respond. "I do," she glances up at me to say.

"Then that is all that matters," I smile back at her as we step up to the door leading to the last hallway to her wedding ceremony.

She surprises me by throwing her arms around me in a hug. "Thank you Amazia! I'm so glad it was you that my father allowed to escort me down!" She lets go and looks back up at me. "He wanted some guy I don't even know named Domenic to do it! It felt so impersonal, if that makes sense. Anyways, he said he had one other option he'd feel comfortable with. It surprised me when he said it was someone from the hotel. He isn't usually so trusting of people he hasn't worked with."

"I hope that's a good thing, to be trusted by him?" I ask.

"It's a very good thing. As long as you stay on his good side, you're set."

The door in front of us opens as we hear a male say "Elena, we're ready for…" the voice pauses as he looks up and notices me standing with the bride, "you."

"Thanks again Amazia," she says, hugging me one last time before stepping through the door to meet her bridesmaids, her maid of honor holding her bouquet out to her.

Meanwhile, I never break eye contact with Jared. After a moment, the bride has joined her wedding party and is paying no attention to Jared or myself. Jared glances back at them to be sure no one is watching as he closes the door so that we are again, alone. "What happened to staying away from the wedding?" he asks in a hushed, but clearly frustrated tone.

"That was my plan," I harshly whisper back. "He didn't give me much choice!"

"Well, shit Amazia! You escorted the bride? On your own?" he continues to urgently whisper.

I gesture around, "Clearly!"

"Please tell me that's all you're doing today?" he asks, back to a voice with a touch of his gentler tone.

I make a face that gives away my response before I even say, "I don't want to lie to you," I say with a shrug.

*   *   *   *   *

The ceremony was beautiful by the fountains. After Jared suddenly stormed off without me, I followed my directions to stand by between the fountains and the banquet hall until cocktail hour was to begin. Once the ceremony finished, the couple, Mr. Berlusconi, and Mr. Vittori immediately left the area. Once they passed, the guests were allowed to mingle at the cocktail hour set up in the fountains area just behind the ceremony set up. Once cocktail hour began, I was to assist with closing down a few areas of the hotel for the photographer to capture several wedding photos. Jared is also here but kept his distance and refused to look at me.

As the hotel liaison for the photographer, I answer all guest questions that arise as we have to provide detours or other information about restaurants and such within the hotel. I use my customer service skills to focus on the hotel guests so I can try to forget about Jared, especially the times

I have to stand near him to speak to guests. I still don't understand why the event manager for the band is escorting the wedding party around like this.

Once the photographer is finished, Mr. Berlusconi releases Jared to check on the band and me to check in with Amanda and the banquet staff. Jared leads the way towards the banquet's back stairwell, and I follow, knowing it's the easiest way to get there. By the time we make it to the stairwell, Mr. Berlusconi, Mr. Vittori, and the newlyweds have all disappeared from sight. I see Jared glance back just like I did before he opens the door to the stairwell and quickly grabs my arm and pulls me inside with him.

He closes the door behind us and immediately begins pacing on the landing. "This is getting complicated," he whispers to himself in his seriously dry tone.

"Can you maybe explain what the issue is?" I ask, stopping him in his tracks.

"I honestly don't know. *That* is the problem," he states, looking down at the ground and refusing to look up at me.

"Jared…" I say, unsure of what to say next but knowing I need to get his attention. When he doesn't respond I take it upon myself to force him to look at me. I step in front of him and gently place my hand under his chin to force him to look up. "Whatever it is, we'll figure it out," I say as he continues to avoid making eye contact.

"It's not that simple," he whispers, looking both defeated and torn.

"I can handle it. I can handle myself. I can handle today. It all ends after this wedding anyways," I say, trying to convince him as much as myself.

He finally looks up and into my eyes. He moves his own hand to cup my cheek. "Amazia, I really hope you're right. I hope it all ends after the wedding and you never hear from the Berlusconi family again."

"Why is the band manager escorting the couple around with their photographer?" I randomly have the courage to ask.

He huffs a laugh, "It's way more complicated than that."

"Then tell me," I urge, wishing I wasn't so damn confused.

"It's safer for you if I don't," he explains.

I let go of his chin, dropping my hand. "Why is that always the answer."

He gently places his other hand on the other side of my face, "Because it's the truth."

"What's next for the band after the wedding?" I ask.

"No idea."

"Then it'll all be over after tonight," I say in my own final tone.

"It'll be over after tonight," he repeats back.

"Now, we have to go before anyone starts wondering where we are," I say.

"You're right," he says, dropping both of his hands from my face. He uses his left hand to gently grasp my right hand to lead me down the stairs, "Come on." We walk down the two flights of stairs that lead to the same landing where I almost broke his nose yesterday. As we reach the door, he stops and turns to face me, letting go of my hand. "I'm sorry."

"For what?" I ask, curiously

"My actions haven't made sense to me, so I know they have to be confusing for you too," he admits.

I laugh, "Yeah, definitely confusing."

"I'm sorry for that, but I've never been this person before."

"What does that mean?"

"I don't have feelings or emotions, not ever."

"What changed?"

"You did," he says as someone opens a door above and starts walking down the stairs. Jared nods towards the door we are at, opening it, and stepping out into the banquet back hall. There are lots of people working nearby, so again, our conversation is cut short. "Until next time Ms. Franklin," he says as he turns to walk to the greenroom to check on the band.

"Amazia! There you are," Amanda says as she practically runs over to me. "Here is your jacket," she hands me a lightweight navy-blue blazer.

"Really?" I ask in an annoyed voice, looking over at it.

"It's part of the requirements of this event. The family paid for all of the blazers to match perfectly." Amanda gestures to her own.

"I see," I look around and realize everyone has one on.

"Come on, you have to get in place before the doors open in a minute," Amanda says, helping me slide the blazer on.

"How did I get stuck serving Mr. Berlusconi again?" I ask.

"His request... or well, demand... remember?" Amanda asks.

"Right. Why did I have to be good at my job and make a good impression?" I rhetorically ask.

"No good deed goes unpunished," Amanda says while ushering me toward the ballroom. "There are your four tables," she points them out.

"No bride and groom?" I ask.

"Mr. Berlusconi advised that the band manager would be handling their meals personally," Amanda explains.

"That band manager has a lot of odd jobs," I laugh.

"Apparently, he is more of a freelancer for the family for large scale conferences and such. He does day of event planning, or something along that line of work," Amanda continues as she checks off tasks on her to do list. A timer on her phones goes off. "Here goes nothing."

* * * * *

The entire wedding reception goes off as planned. I serve my four tables without incident. Mr. Berlusconi and family are happily consumed with the festivities and almost entirely ignore my presence. When it came time for the bride and groom to dine, I assisted Mr. Wright as he was busy backstage with the band getting ready to perform. The bride was overjoyed to see me again. I congratulate her briefly before returning to my assigned tables.

Shortly after dinner, the normal wedding reception events take place while we work to clear tables. The dessert is served shortly after the father and daughter dance which slowly adds all of the married couples in the family, then in the entire room. By the time they make it back to their seats, the dessert is served, and coffee is poured.

The guests eat dessert while the bride and groom smash their cake into each other's faces. Then the clean-up begins as some guests retire early. Others dance the night away for hours. The open bar remains open until the party comes to an end just before midnight. The band plays one last slow dance for the couple as the remaining guests lined up for the couples send off. Once the sendoff begins, the band exits the stage. I briefly notice Jared walking around on stage and helping to quickly pack up equipment.

"It all ends tonight," I whisper to myself as I watch Jared from the opposite side of the ballroom.

Once the guests all leave the room, following the newlyweds, we close and lock the ballroom doors and immediately switch on all of the lights for clean-up. We finish clearing tables so another group can stack chairs, send tablecloths off to laundry, and break down tables. The banquet set up crew comes in to remove everything as Amanda, Max, and I move to the back hall to get control of the process so we can all get some rest. I glance at the stage before leaving the ballroom, but it's already cleared out and empty. I glance around in the back hallway, but still see no sign of Jared or the band.

Once the back hallway is cleared and put back in order, Max and Amanda start letting people go for the evening until everyone is gone but the three of us. Amanda grabs three champagne glasses and fills them with the remaining open bottle from the bar. "Here's to a wild weekend with lots of twists and turns!" Amanda says.

"Here's to getting a promotion at the worst possible time!" Max adds.

"Here's to me never working banquets again!" I laugh.

"Cheers!" we all say in unison as we tap glasses together and drink.

"That was, well… let's never do it again, eh?" Max says, setting his glass down and walking away. "Goodnight, ladies."

"Goodnight, Max," Amanda and I say as he walks off.

"Ready to crash?" Amanda asks.

"Absolutely," I reply, following her back to our room.

8

Almost a week later, the Berlusconi family finally checks out. The bride and groom immediately left for their honeymoon, but a large portion of the Berlusconi family stayed until Wednesday. I was sure to hide out in my office during the day and immediately head home once I clocked out. It was nice staying in the hotel on those late nights, but I'm thrilled to be back to my 7 A.M. to 3 P.M. schedule. I never did see Jared again. He and the band checked out in the middle of the night after the wedding. Of course, I never thought I'd see him again after the wedding, but I didn't expect him to just disappear either.

Wednesday afternoon came quickly once the Berlusconi family checked out. I was sure to avoid Mr. Berlusconi after the wedding and was surprisingly successful. I did receive a nice letter from the bride herself thanking me. She also gave me her contact information in case I ever needed anything. She said she'd be glad to provide any assistance if I ever requested. I'm not sure if I'll ever need her for anything, but it doesn't hurt for a rich person to owe you a favor.

After I clock out, I wait for Klarissa, Amanda, Max, and a few others in the employee center lobby. After the week we had with Mr. Berlusconi and his family, we decided to celebrate at a local bar hotel employees frequent nearby. We weren't the only ones with this idea. As we arrive, we realize the bar is full of people from the hotel, all blowing off steam and celebrating the official completion of the Berlusconi wedding.

"Did you know that Mr. Berlusconi paid for several of the security cameras to be blocked during their visit?" Pete, the security guard asks as we're sitting at the bar.

"I mean, it's not the first time we've blocked cameras for certain guests," I reply, sipping my drink.

"True, but the number of blocked cameras caused a lot of problems for us in security. In fact, it's part of the reason we weren't able to track Seth down anywhere on camera after the staff dinner the night of the rehearsal."

"That is curious," I reply, never thinking Seth taking off was such a big deal. He likely wanted to quit after being demoted. Maybe he thought he could ruin the big event if he took off just before it began. Unfortunately, I didn't let that happen by stepping in.

"But they're all finally gone," he says raising his glass.

"I'll drink to that," I say. "Cheers!" I say as we tap glasses and drink.

"Hey Amazia?" Klarissa yells. "Help me win this next round of pool against Engineering?"

"Sure, why not," I shrug and head over to the pool tables.

*   *   *   *   *

"Come on Amazia!" everyone cheers, hoping I can make this shot and win the game.

I pick up the pool stick and take a deep breath, hoping I don't fuck this up for Klarissa. A lot of people are betting on me, and I definitely am feeling the pressure of needing to win. I make a lap around the table as I try to determine the best move. "Corner pocket," I declare as I come to a stop on the long end of the table and begin to second guess myself. I begin to lean forward, as if I'm ready to line up my shot, but pause, feeling someone behind me. I don't turn to look, knowing someone is closer than they should be. I take a breath and can sense who it is before they even speak.

He leans into me, reaching around me to help line up my shot. "This is how you win," he whispers into my ear. He moves with me as I follow his lead to line up my body as well as the pool stick to take the shot. Our breathing becomes as one as I feel him match each breath I take. "Are you ready?" he whispers.

I nod, knowing I'm unable to answer verbally in our current situation.

"Three, two," he says, while moving with me to prepare for the shot, "one." Together we hit the pool stick against the eight ball on the table. The ball moves in slow motion as it rolls towards the corner pocket. It bounces off the edge before delicately sliding all the way around the edge before finally sinking into the pocket.

Everyone watching erupts with cheers, almost like they never saw the man come up behind me to make sure I won the game. A few people exchange high fives and toasts, a few chug the last of their drinks. They all walk away, some heading toward bathrooms and others lining up at the bar to purchase their next round.

"Mr. Wright..." I say aloud without turning around.

"This isn't a workplace," he whispers into my ear, still close behind me.

"Jared?" I ask.

"Amazia," he begins, in a gentle whisper. "Didn't think I'd run into you in a place like this."

"Didn't think I'd run into you, ever," I reveal.

He reaches out to take my arm in his hand. He gently turns me to face him. He's close, too close. Like back in the greenroom hallway all over again. "I was working in the area."

"The band playing nearby?" I ask.

He laughs, "No. I don't work with the band."

"What were you doing last weekend?" I ask.

"Part time event manager, for the family. Never worked with the band before that event."

"So, you work for that family?" I ask in a confused tone.

"Not exactly," he says looking into my eyes and pulling me into a familiar trance.

"You seem very complicated," I admit.

"You really have no idea," he replies in a serious tone. After several moments of silence he asks, "Can I ask you a question?"

"I guess," I shrug, wondering if I really have a choice at this close proximity.

"Can you handle complicated?" he looks deeply into my eyes while he waits for a response.

"I guess that depends on the level of complicated," I answer honestly, not sure if I can answer that question without further details.

"Would you be willing to try?" he asks.

"I'm not sure what you're asking me," I reply, not ready to give an answer to a vague question.

He sighs gently, breaking eye contact to look down for a moment. "This is unconventional. None of this is like me," he whispers.

"Jared, just tell me what you're talking about."

He looks up at me again, surprise in his eyes. "There is just something about you…" He pauses, but his phone dings before he gets the chance to continue his thought. "Shit, hang on," he says before reaching for his phone, checking in, and sending a quick reply, all without moving away from our close proximity. He puts his phone back in his pocket and looks back at me, searching for eye contact. "Where was I?" he asks in his normal dry tone.

"You were going to tell me what the hell you're trying to ask me."

A smirk grows into a smile. "I'm not entirely… normal."

"Okay..." I start, waiting patiently for more of an explanation.

"I'm complicated."

"Please tell me something I don't already know," I ask for something more.

He smiles again and glances down. "I don't know how to do this. How to do the normal human interaction stuff."

"Jared..." I say, waiting for him to look back up at me. Once he does, "Normal is overrated. Can you do me a favor and tell me what's on your mind?"

"I don't want to scare you away," he admits.

"Are you a serial killer or something?" I ask as a joke.

"No," he laughs.

"Are you referring to your usual... demeanor?" I ask, thinking of his usual dry tone.

"That's part of it."

"Why hide behind a false personality?"

"That's the thing. That is me. That is my personality. The person I am around you is what's different. You brought something out of me that I've never seen before, never felt before. I can't explain it, but I'm terrified that you'll fall for someone who isn't... me."

"You think I'm gonna fall for you?" I ask, genuinely.

"The new side of me, yes. I think you'll fall hard, but I can't control that side of me. I can't turn it on unless you're around. I can't figure out how to proceed."

"Jared, are you asking me out?" I jump to the point of all of this.

He smiles and relaxes slightly. "Amazia, would you consider taking a chance on someone as complicated as me?"

"That's a complicated question," I laugh, not meaning for it to come out as such a joke. "What do you have in mind?"

He glances at his watch, noticing the time. "I have to run. That was one of my bosses on the phone." He pulls out his cell phone and clicks a few things before handing it over to me. "May I start with your number?"

I take it from him wearily and type in my name and number and hit save before handing it back.

"That was easier than expected," he says as he takes his phone back.

"So, you running into me here wasn't an accident?" I ask.

"No, that was an accident. A happy accident. I just promised myself that if I ever ran into you again, I needed to stand my ground and figure out how to handle these newfound emotions and such."

"You are a very curious creature, Jared Wright."

"You have no idea," he says as he leans toward me again, but stops before he gets too close, again.

"Don't you have somewhere to be?" I whisper.

He sighs, "Why do you do these things to me?"

"You'll have to be more specific," I ask for specification.

"Sounds like a discussion for another day. Dinner? Tomorrow?" he asks.

"Um, sure. Alright," I answer out of surprise.

"Great. I'll text you," he says before quickly rushing away.

"Complicated alright," I whisper to myself as I turn to watch him go. The thing is, when I turn around, he's nowhere to be seen. Was he really even here?

Right on cue, my phone dings, revealing a text from a new phone number. "Glad you'll give complicated a chance- Jared."

"What have I gotten myself into?"

9

The next morning, I wake up to find another text from Jared. "Are you working today?"

"Yes, it's my Friday," I reply before even getting out of bed. Thankfully I'm not the type to feel hungover after just a few drinks, but I'm still exhausted from staying out so late. Shit, I'm still exhausted from the overtime last weekend. I lay my phone back down on the nightstand while I have breakfast and get ready for work.

After I have my shoes on, I grab my backpack and keys before going back to the bedroom to grab my phone. When I pick it up it vibrates, indicating a message. I unlock the phone to find another message from Jared. "What time can I pick you up from The Rush?"

He plans to pick me up, okay. I smile, feeling the butterflies flapping in my stomach at the thought of someone putting in the work for a dinner date for once. Most guys in New York City just expect you to walk and meet them at the restaurant. I grab two outfit choices and fold them delicately into my backpack. I can have laundry services steam them for me during the day. I'm scheduled until 4 P.M. but I usually don't leave on time. I'll give myself an hour to change and finish up. I can always finish up after I get dressed if necessary. "I should be able to leave at 5 P.M.," I reply.

"Perfect," is his last reply.

Once I park at the train station, I check my phone, curious to if I'd have another text, but find no messages. I board my train and continue to read a book on my phone while we travel into the city.

* * * * *

Once I'm settled in the office, I pull out the two outfit choices to get Klarissa's opinion.

"What are those for?" she asks as she walks in to check what I'm up to.

"I have a dinner date tonight, and I need your help," I reply, trying not to smile.

"Amazia Franklin has a dinner date! Damn girl! I was starting to think you'd never give anyone a chance," she hoots, drawing way too much attention from the rest of the room control cubicles.

"Shhh, stop," I say swatting at her arm.

"Sorry," she says, understanding that she embarrassed me.

"So, which one?" I ask directly.

"Any idea where you're going?"

"Not a clue."

"Hmm," she starts, holding her chin in thought as she glances back and forth between my two choices. "I say go big, be bold and sexy. Wear the dress."

"I don't have a jacket formal enough for that," I say, pointing to my winter coat. "Needs to be formal enough to not clash but casual enough for whatever he has planned for dinner."

"I know someone in laundry that can help," Klarissa says before snapping a picture and walking away.

"Why is everyone walking away from me before finishing a conversation?" I say aloud to myself.

* * * * *

"Come on! Get out here!" Klarissa yells at me from outside the laundry service fitting room.

It's just after 4:30P.M. and Klarissa got laundry services to not only steam my dress, but to provide an appropriate jacket and shoes. "Okay, I'm coming out," I say as I unlock the door and step out.

Klarissa gasps as I round the corner, "Oh my God, Amazia! You look smokin' hot!"

"What? Really?" I ask as I walk closer to the laundry door where the full-length mirror is. "Damn," I say, looking back at myself in the mirror. The maroon, long sleeve, ruched bodycon, short dress hugs my curves perfectly. The knee-high brown heeled boots and elegant dark gray peacoat complete the outfit perfectly. "Holy crap."

"Yeah girl. You're hot stuff!" Klarissa explains. "Whoever is taking you out is gonna die in awe."

"Thank your friend, then meet me back down in the office before I have to leave," I say, trying to pull my own eyes away from the mirror. I'm not looking forward to walking past so many co-workers. I should have brought my stuff up here with me instead of having to go back to my office.

"Amanda is meeting you there with one last accessory," Klarissa says before I walk off.

I look back to ask what she means, but she's already ducking into the laundry services door. I turn towards the office wondering what accessory she has for me. When I get to the office, Amanda had already come and gone but left a note with the bag on the desk. "This should match perfectly. It was a conference gift at one point which I've never had the chance to use." Under the note is an oversized handbag with a long, skinny shoulder strap.

"Perfect," I whisper to myself as I decide what necessities have to come with me. Keys, phone, wallet, eyeliner, lipstick, mints, perfume, and tide pen. Everything else can stay here for the weekend.

A moment late Klarissa walks up, "All set?"

I sigh, looking around. "I think so."

"Can I walk you out?"

"I kind of wish you would," I admit. "At least part way."

"Don't wanna walk the employee tunnels alone and watch everyone pass out gawking at you?"

I laugh with her, "Something like that."

I check my phone before we head towards the employee door. "Looking forward to our evening."

"I'm looking forward to getting to know Mr. Complicated," I reply in an attempt to be sassy.

"Be careful what you wish for," he replies.

"This is where I leave you," Klarissa says, pulling me back to the present. We're at the last door before the lobby.

"Thanks for everything," I stop to look at her.

"Knock him dead," she says with a wink before she walks back towards the office.

"Here goes nothing," I pep talk myself before reaching for the door.

My phone dings. "I'm pulling up to the main lobby now."

I push the employee door, exiting into the main lobby, hoping to walk past the front office staff without anyone noticing me. I step up to the doors, pausing to take one last deep breath before I push open the exterior door. As I do, one of the bellmen pulls the other open from the other side for me. Thankfully, he doesn't mention anything if he recognizes me. Though, my pulse is racing, so I might not have noticed if he had. I step out of the second set of doors, which are automatic, and look around.

I spot only one car parked along the hotel's two-lane portico. As I look that direction, someone is exiting the car. Before he turns around, I notice his black jeans, dark gray boots, and medium gray short coat. As he turns around, I know for sure that it's Jared Wright climbing out of a brand new 2024, metallic blue, Chevy Camaro. Something about this moment makes him even more sexy, if that's at all possible. His face is neutral, like the dry work version of him, as he buttons his coat before closing the door and turning toward the lobby doors. Once he notices me, his expression changes immediately to a gentler one. As his eyes look me over, he even looks impressed.

He walks around the car to the sidewalk, meeting me at the edge. "Wow," he says while looking awestruck as he looks me up and down again. "You look… amazing!"

I try not to blush, but I'd bet I'm failing miserably in this moment. "Thank you. You look…" I can't say sexy, can I?

"Amazia?" he asks, looking at me curiously.

"You look sexy, alright? There I said it," I spit out before thinking.

"Not what I was expecting, but I accept your evaluation," he says with a smile. "Shall we?" he asks, walking toward the passenger door. He opens it and patiently waits for me to climb in before closing the door. His car smells like a mixture of new car smell and sandalwood. He walks back around and quickly unbuttons his coat to climb back into the driver's seat. "Sure is cold out there today."

"I was not ready for this cold weather just yet," I admit.

"But you look nice and warm," he says as almost a question.

I laugh, "Yeah, thanks to help from my assistant and laundry services with this coat."

"Well, I think it looks great. You look great," he says, smiling over at me before putting on his seat belt and starting the car. "You ready?"

"Yeah, it's too cold outside to give up now," I joke, making him smile again.

"I'm glad to see your sense of humor on full display," he says while driving out of the portico.

"What do you mean?"

"I can tell when you hold back. Your customer service voice is believable, but I can tell when there is something more under the surface."

"Oh, can you?"

"Yes, Ms. Franklin," he jokes.

"You think you have me all figured out?"

"Mainly, but not completely."

"Okay, prove it."

"What? How?"

"If you think you know so much, prove it."

He glances at me several times between watching the road as if deciding what to share. "Okay... when I was checking into the hotel, you thought me a stuck-up musician. Then, later, when you tried to break my nose, you thought I was a lost visitor. Then, I confused you even more in that greenroom."

"I did assume you were part of the band, but I most definitely did not try to break your nose in that stairwell. Clearly, you were somewhere you shouldn't have been. If you were with the band, like you were supposed to be, that never would have happened."

"So, it's my fault you hit me with a door?"

"One hundred percent."

"I see you avoided the greenroom part of the conversation."

I blush again, remembering my pulse racing as he invaded my personal space. "There's nothing to talk about," I pretend to shrug it off.

"We'll table that conversation for later than," he smirks.

"How'd you get into the portico at the lobby?" I ask, quickly changing the subject.

"I have connections," he vaguely advises.

"And you'd tell me more, but then you'd have to kill me?" I joke.

"Something like that," he replies, in his dry and serious tone.

"Where are you taking me?" I ask, trying to change the subject before it gets awkward.

"You ever been to Gotham's Restaurant?"

"Gotham?! You got reservations… at Gotham?" I ask, shocked at the development.

"I have a contact who has connections," he shrugs.

"Of course you do," I reply without thinking.

"You're very sassy for a first date."

"Thank you?" I question.

He smiles, "I like it."

"That's good, because if not I'd tell you to just drop me off at a subway so I can get a train home," I joke.

"Train?" he asks.

"Yeah, I take the train out of the city."

"Suburbs?" he asked, sounding surprised.

"Yeah. Way more affordable."

"Even with the added commute expenses?"

"Yeah, even with."

"Interesting."

"Based on your expensive car, I'd say you're pretty well off."

"Not exactly, but I work a few jobs to pay the bills and afford the things I want."

"A few jobs?"

"The event planning, band management, it's just a freelance gig for extra cash."

"How many jobs do you have?"

"Three or four."

"How do you have time for yourself?"

"Higher paying, part time gigs. Then I can schedule work around my life and what I need."

"Interesting."

"I didn't lie when I said I was complicated."

"Just a mystery for me to figure out," I say, thinking about all the secrets he has.

10

Of course, Jared used his connections to get a reserved parking spot right in front of the restaurant. I'm starting to get suspicious about who all these contacts are. Once he's parked, he gets out to walk around and open my door for me. He holds out a hand to help me gracefully climb out of the car. The streets of New York are covered in a thick slushy mess from the recent snow. The sidewalk in front of the restaurant is clear and free of slip hazards.

Once I'm out of the vehicle, Jared closes the door and holds an arm out for me. "Shall we, Amazia?"

"Of course, Jared," I say, gently looping my arm through his. He smiles and leads us into the restaurant. I try to ignore the magnetic pull I feel with my arm through his. He's too close and I can hardly control my heart rate as we walk into the restaurant. Once the host brings us to our table, Jared even pulls out my chair for me like a gentleman.

The host offers something about wine and thankfully Jared orders because I was in a daze until after the host left the table. "Are you okay?" Jared asks.

I smile, shaking off my inner thoughts. "I'm great, just overwhelmed, I guess."

"So, I did some research... on our situation," he begins, looking unsure of how to proceed.

"Our situation?" I ask with a giggle, unsure of where he's going with this.

"Are you laughing at me?" he asks in his dry, serious tone.

I try not to smile as I reply, "No, Mr. Wright. Not at all."

"Ms. Franklin... as I previously advised, this is not a work affair."

"I'm sorry, Jared," I smile.

"Are you?" he asks, looking intently at me for the truth.

"Yes," I say, reaching out to touch his hand. "Now what were you saying?" I ask before taking my hand back.

"Here we are," the host says returning with the wine. He pours each of us a glass before leaving the bottle on ice nearby. "Stephen will be your server," he gestures to the gentleman next to him.

Stephen steps up to introduce himself and to take our order. Once he leaves, I try to catch Jared and make eye contact, but he's avoiding me.

"Jared?" I ask, still waiting to catch his eye.

He looks up and I catch him, pulling him in as he gazes back into my eyes, back to trying to search them for the answers to all of his problems.

"Tell me what you were going to say," I say in a serious tone.

"I was going to try to explain how I did some research to understand how this is all supposed to go," he admits.

"You mean, a date?" I ask.

"Amazia, don't…"

I quickly interrupt him, "I'm not doing anything but asking a serious question. Is that what you're referring to?"

"Yes," he maintains eye contact, but also maintains his dry tone.

"Why did you need to know how this is supposed to go?"

"Because I don't want to mess it up."

"You really want this to go well, don't you?"

"I really do. I've never done this. I've never wined and dined someone. You're different Amazia, I told you," his voice grows gentler as he goes.

"What makes me so special?"

"I wish I had words to describe it," he answers in his softer voice.

"Care to try?"

He sighs, breaking eye contact for a few moments before looking back. He reaches out one hand, grasping mine within his gently. "I'm a workaholic, to an extent. I work hard, I plan, I organize, and I keep myself busy. I don't waste time on others, if that makes sense. I never saw myself as a boyfriend or husband or whatnot. I just never wanted those things. I never understood the need and want for those things. I was content with my life going the way it was, and then I met you."

"Me, of all people made you rethink… everything?"

"Yes, Amazia, you're the reason I'm feeling real emotions for the first time."

"Emotions? Like any emotions?" How could he not have experienced emotion.

"I lost my family young. I know there were emotions, but when I was working through the grieving process, it was easier to just turn them off, I guess."

"But something changed?"

"I met you."

"Was it when I hit you with the door, because this could all be trauma induced?" I try to joke.

He smiles and laughs it off, "No, not trauma related. It was before that, back in the lobby when you were checking me in."

"The infamous band manager, too busy on his phone to pay me any attention."

"Until I made the mistake of looking up. Then I wanted to give you all the attention in the world, especially once you sass talked me."

"So, it was my attitude you fell for?"

"It was your attitude that got my attention," he clarified.

"Then what kept your attention?"

"Your beauty."

"Me? Really?"

"And that was before I saw how gorgeous you look today."

I try hard not to blush, but again feel myself failing as I try not to smile.

"Amazia, your energy, your attitude, and your beauty caught my attention. You pulled me in and never let go. Then you hit me with that door, and it was a wild coincidence that we even ran into one another."

"Then the greenroom happened."

"I felt this strong need to protect you. I needed to warn you to be more careful. You never know who is watching, especially after you rolled your eyes at Mr. Berlusconi."

"You always protect people while that close to them?"

"For you, yes. I want to be as close as possible. That is the best way to protect you."

"Why were you that close?" I ask, hoping for an answer this time.

"I couldn't help myself. You were somehow pulling me in."

"Like a magnet?"

"Yes, exactly."

"I felt it too," I admit.

"Then you understand the pull and the need?" he sounds thrilled to not be alone in this feeling.

"I do, but not why you got so close to just walk away yesterday," I remain honest.

He looks down, breaking our eye contact. "I told you I had to research our… situation. I want to do everything right, but I don't know how to do that."

"How to date?"

"Exactly."

"You've really never done this?"

"Not once," he admits, looking back up at me.

"Then, I'm thrilled to be your someone special."

"Are you?"

"Definitely," I say as the food runner arrives with our first course.

*   *   *   *   *

We chat throughout our three courses. I help start off most conversations with questions like "What's your favorite color" and "When is your birthday?" I'll have to try to remember his in the spring, if we make it that long. He relaxes more and more as we go through dinner. He is naturally smiling and laughing with me without holding back like he was in the beginning. He seems like a perfectly normal person. I'm not sure why he feels like he isn't worthy of me, or anyone. He's clearly both nervous and determined. I wish I could bring that nervous side to the front, to help him overcome whatever has tormented him in the past. It's adorable for someone so hot and sexy to be this nervous throughout a simple dinner date.

After all the courses are through, he pays the tab before getting up and walking to my side of the table. "Ms. Franklin," he says, reaching a hand out to me.

I take his hand and stand. "Thank you kindly, Mr. Wright," I play along.

He lets go to pick up my coat and hold it out for me to slide my arms through. He gently helps lift it onto my shoulders before holding his arm out for me to drape mine through.

"Have a good evening," the host says while opening the door for us to exit.

"I still can't believe you got reservations at Gotham so last minute," I say as we approach the car.

"Sometimes it pays to have friends with connections," he says in his dry tone, sounding uninterested in that line of conversation.

As we approach the car, I notice it's already running. "Remote start?"

"Of course," he says with a smirk. "How else do you survive these cold ass winters?"

"Are you secretly rich?" I joke.

"Rich is a stretch. I just work hard to earn enough to live how I want to."

"I like a man who's good with his finances," I say as he opens the passenger door for me to climb in.

"I'll be sure to keep my finances in order then," he smirks before closing the door and walking around. He climbs into the driver's seat and fully starts the car before securing his seat belt and glancing over to be sure mine is also secure. "So, where did you say you live? Manhattan? Queens? Upper East Side? Brooklyn?"

Eventually I interrupt him with a shy smile, "Not in New York State."

He looks over at me, "Wait, a suburb. That was what you said. So where?"

"Um… Connecticut."

He looks surprised, "Really?"

"Yeah," I say with a shrug.

He smiles, "Well then, we have quite the adventure ahead of us."

"Oh, you don't have to drive all the way out there. I can just take a train like usual."

"No way am I ending our first date by dropping you off at a train station." He pulls his cell phone out of his coat pocket and hands it to me. "Put in the address."

"Are you sure?" I ask, thinking it's too far.

"Absolutely. Plus, now we can continue to get to know one another. Isn't that important in dating or relationships or whatever?"

He's so adorable when he asks questions about basic human emotions or dating. "Yes. That is an important component," I say with a shy smile. I type my address on Shippan Avenue in Stamford into his phone and hand it back hesitantly. "If this isn't too far."

"That isn't even that far!" he looks content with the distance. "I've driven further for a freelance four-hour job before," he shrugs.

"An hour is far to drive if you don't have to."

"Only if you don't want to," he says with a smile as he pulls out of the parking spot and heads towards our destination.

*　　*　　*　　*　　*

I start to get anxious as he pulls onto Shippan Avenue. I can't believe he drove all this way. I guess now we get to see what his research said about how to end a first date.

"Home sweet home," he says through a yawn as he pulls into my driveway. "Where's your car?"

"Parked at the train station," I shrug. "It's okay, the bus stops at the corner and goes to the station. I take it sometimes in nicer weather during the summer when the sun is out later."

"That is unacceptable," he says in a serious tone.

"Okay Mr. Protective," I smile. "You can't shelter me from the world."

He sighs, "You're right."

"Did you admit defeat?" I jokingly ask.

"Hardly," he says in a serious tone before looking back up at me. He shuts off the car, "Come on. Let me walk you to your door."

I smile, knowing he probably read this is customary while researching how tonight should go. Now, the question is, is he finally going to kiss me? We've gotten plenty close several times now. He comes around and opens my door while I'm considering the possibilities.

After he closes the car door, he holds out his arm again for me to drape mine through. I follow his direction and slide my arm through his. He leads me toward the front door without a word, but he looks deep in thought.

As we reach the door, I let go and reach into my bag for my key. "Thank you for a wonderful evening," I say as I pull out the key and look up at him.

He looks to be contemplating something. "I had a great time getting to know you more tonight." He's looking down and avoiding eye contact again.

I reach out and touch his arm, wrapping my fingers gently around his wrist. "Jared? What is it?"

He looks at my hand before looking up. "It's just you. Making me into someone I never thought I could be."

"What do you mean?"

"It's like I'm a real person around you," he whispers, almost like he doesn't believe it.

I step in closer, leaving little space between us. "You are a real person," I whisper.

"But I've never felt that way before you," he admits, sounding genuine.

"Then I guess you're stuck with me if you want to keep feeling this way," I whisper as I feel my pulse racing with our close proximity.

"I want to keep you around," he jokes through a yawn.

"You're exhausted," I say.

He gently rests his forehead against mine, "I worked pretty late last night," he said before yawning again.

"I know this seems forward of me, but please stay."

"Amazia, I can't even kiss you on the first date."

"Says who?"

"My…"

"You don't have to believe everything you read on the internet," I joke.

"I just want to be sure you're taken care of and appreciated. I'll never take advantage of you, Amazia."

"I appreciate that, and I trust you."

"Are you sure you should?"

I reach up and gently touch his cheek. "I can feel it down to my very bones. I can trust you. You'll never do anything to hurt me."

"I've wanted to kiss you since that moment in the greenroom," he admits, at a whisper.

"Then why didn't you?"

"It wasn't the time or the place."

"What is the time and place?"

"I'll know it when we find it," he says as he lifts his forehead from mine before looking up and gently kissing my forehead.

"I'll be waiting patiently," I whisper back, feeling both relieved and anxious. I feel the magnetic pull to him. I feel my lips needing to taste his as they meet for the first time. But I control myself, wanting to respect his wishes to wait until the time is right.

"I don't want to push boundaries," he begins.

"Well, fuck boundaries," I say before moving my hand to the back of his neck and pulling his face down to mine and kissing his lips with as much passion as I've been bottling up since the greenroom. He tries to resist for a moment before gently leaning into the kiss. He gently wraps both of his arms around me and pulls me closer as he deepens the kiss and returns the passion that I've known was plaguing him. After several wonderful, passionate moments pass, he gently pulls back, and we both try to catch our breath. Our hearts race as one as he leans his forehead back against mine. He gently moves one hand to cup my cheek and gently rub his thumb along my cheek.

"I didn't mean to…" he starts, but I interrupt.

"I meant it and I know you needed that too," I confess.

"But I…" he starts again.

"You didn't do anything wrong. We are both adults and we both wanted the same thing."

"You're not wrong," he smiles.

"Now, please accept my offer to stay. I have a spare bedroom you can sleep in. Completely acceptable for a first date."

"I am not sure if I can say… acceptable," he advises.

"Why don't we start by going inside before we freeze to death," I joke, knowing we are both on fire with the heat between us.

"Whatever you say, Amazia," he whispers before gently letting me go.

I unlock the door and hold it open for him to follow me inside. He smiles kindly before closing and locking my door behind him.

11

I wake up feeling my tight muscles relax as I stretch out under my soft covers. After a few moments, I reach over for my phone to check the time. Today is my favorite day of the week, the first day of my weekend. I still can't help but wake up at the crack of dawn though. I toss off the covers and drag myself out of bed before my brain catches up and remembers last night's date. Oh crap, Jared is asleep in the next room. I suddenly panic, crossing to the closet to find something casual enough to walk out into my living room wearing on a day off. I quickly choose something both casual and comfortable before racing to get ready. I do my best not to make a sound in case Jared is still asleep. Once I'm ready and presentable, I exit the bedroom cautiously, listening for sounds showing Jared's awake.

At first, I hear nothing, so I proceed down the hallway toward the living room and kitchen. As I get closer, I smell something delicious before I see Jared moving about in the kitchen. I shake off the anxiety and walk into the kitchen, smiling as I watch him. I lean against the door frame and stand there watching for a minute before asking, "Did you make me breakfast?"

He jumps and turns, clearly startled. "Shit! Amazia! Didn't anyone ever tell you not to sneak up on someone?"

"Well, considering you're in my house, shouldn't you have been prepared for my presence?"

"Well, yeah, but I didn't think you'd be intending to scare the shit out of me first thing in the morning!" he says in a serious tone. He isn't mad, just startled.

I smile and walk towards him. "I'm sorry. I really didn't think I'd have that effect on my great protector." I walk up next to him and gently kiss his cheek.

He smiles in return as he moves breakfast onto two plates.

"I'm impressed," I admit. "Got up before me, found everything in my kitchen, and made breakfast all before I made it out here." I walk toward the coffee pot realizing it hasn't been touched, "And all without coffee?"

"I avoid caffeine at all costs," he shrugs.

"Interesting fact," I admit before turning on the machine and brewing a single cup. "I, on the other hand, require my morning coffee to function."

"Noted for next time," he says.

"There's gonna be a next time?" I ask in a smart tone.

He looks serious as he stops and says, "I sure hope so."

I smile at him, which instantly relaxes him. "Me too."

"Good," he says, breathing out. "You had me for a second."

"Did you honestly think I'd have invited you to stay here if I didn't want to see you again?"

"Honestly, I don't know. Remember, I've never been in this situation before."

"Well, keep up the good work. A woman could get used to this," I say, nodding to the breakfast he prepared.

"In that case, let's eat," he smiles as he walks the plates to my kitchen table.

*   *   *   *   *

After breakfast he drives me to my car at the train station. He offered to bring me back into the city, but I told him I avoid the city on my days off. He said he didn't blame me and to be careful driving back home on the slippery roads. Snow fell again overnight, adding a layer to the previously slick surfaces. The streets are brown with slush mixed with sand. New England winter is officially upon us.

Once I'm back home, I make a cup of hot chocolate and curl up by the electric fireplace with a book I've been trying to read. Occasionally, I manage to read a few chapters. Most of the time though, I'm so lost in thought about Jared that I realize I was not really absorbing anything from the text. After a few hours, I'm startled by a knock at the door. I put down the book, wrap up in a sweater and go to the door.

As I open the door, a young lady is standing there with a bag. "Amazia Franklin?"

"Yes," I reply wearily.

"Your Doordrop order," she says handing me the bag.

"Umm, thank you," I say kindly, knowing I didn't order anything.

"Have a nice day!" she says while turning to run back to the warmth of her car.

"Be safe!" I yell back, knowing the roads look a mess.

I close and lock the door, checking the receipt on the bag, but finding no clue to who sent it. Just then I hear my phone ding in the kitchen. I walk into the kitchen and place the bag down before reaching for my cell phone. I unlock it to see a text from Jared. "I wanted to be sure you didn't go out in this weather. Enjoy one for lunch and one for dinner."

I smile, not trying to hide the blush growing on my cheeks. I reply, "Just putting a delivery driver in danger instead?"

"I wish them the best, but it's you that I am concerned about."

"Thank you, Jared."

"Anything for you."

*   *   *   *   *

I spent the rest of the weekend in the house. I finished reading the book and cleaned up a bit. I also pulled out my Christmas decorations and began to set everything up for the holiday, even though it is something I usually refuse to do before Thanksgiving. I didn't grow up with big Christmas celebrations. It's something I started doing on my own to be different from how I grew up. It always seemed a bit of a waste to decorate for myself, but I do enjoy the change in décor for the month of December. Setting up a little early this year can't hurt with the long holiday season at the hotel ramping up over the next few weeks when families visit New York City for Christmas.

Throughout the weekend, Jared sent me texts between jobs. He said he had a long weekend ahead with several different part time jobs taking up his time. He is sure to text as often as possible to continue to get to know me. We set another date for dinner and a movie the following week. After that dinner and movie date, we never stopped seeing each other whenever possible.

12

For the last month, Jared and I have been getting to know one another. We've scheduled a date every week and have regularly stayed up far too late texting at night. Klarissa has been giving me a hard time for refusing to share many details about my secret someone. She's been nagging at me for details since the first date. Now that it's been a few weeks, I ask Jared to accompany me to our yearly hotel staff New Years party, which he wearily agreed to. He wanted to spend Christmas with just me as an even trade, which I agreed to. He also wanted to schedule a very important pre-Christmas date, though he won't tell me anything about what he has planned. I've told him all about how Christmas wasn't anything special for my family growing up. He doesn't understand how anyone could grow up without knowing the magic of Christmas. He constantly talks about the magical Christmas lights in the city. He understands how growing up in small town Arkansas isn't the same as experiencing Christmas in New York City. I was still new to the area last year, and avoided the crowds at all costs, simply going to and from work. I didn't truly experience Christmas in the city last year. So, Jared promises to show me the true spirit of a New York City Christmas on our date tonight.

He picks me up at the hotel in the evening, as soon as he can get there from work. He was worried he'd be late, but I told him not to rush and that I had plenty of work to complete until he arrived. Of course, as soon as he said he was on his way to get me, the butterflies instantly began, and I found myself rushing to get myself ready. It doesn't matter how often we get together or how much time we spend together, I can't stop this anxious feeling. I made sure Klarissa left on time today so she wouldn't be around to ask me a million questions about Jared. I thought it would help me keep calm, but it might have made it worse. She is usually a good distraction while I'm waiting for Jared.

The portico staff are all becoming far too familiar with Jared. He still gets in because of his connections, but even without it, the portico and valet staff would let him in as long as it isn't too busy. Unfortunately, they've also put two and two together, seeing me leave with Jared several times now. One of them asked Klarissa, who returned to the office very angry that the portico staff know more about the mystery date than she does. As soon as Jared pulls into the portico, I rush out and quickly climb into the car before the valets have a chance to go and talk to him. They wave when they see me and go about their business, thankfully.

Jared starts out by driving north and taking us to the New York Botanical Gardens where we walk through the Glow event, all lit up for the holiday. The walk itself is about a mile and a half long and a great start to our night. It doesn't take long for Jared to reach over and take my hand into his, holding my hand while we walked through the gardens. Once we're done, Jared drives us to Central Park, where we walk to a waiting horse and carriage. Carriage rides in December are booked months in advance, but of course, Jared used a connection to get us our own private carriage and trip route. Once in the carriage, we find a basket holding a thermos of hot soup and breadsticks. The carriage takes us into Central Park before stopping to allow us time to eat before continuing on with our private adventure.

Jared puts his arm around me and pulls me close under the thick blankets as the carriage takes us through Central Park before making its way towards Washington Square Park. Once we arrive, we get out to take a photo under the Christmas tree at the landmark arch. The carriage driver takes our photo, our first photo together, before helping us back into the carriage. We quickly depart, heading down towards Broadway, Time Square, and 5th Avenue, before taking us in a loop around Rockefeller Plaza. The Rockefeller tree is giant, and much larger than expected. None of the photos of Rockefeller in the winter do it justice. After making a loop, the carriage stops to let us off at the Rockefeller ice skating rink.

"You ready?" Jared asks as the carriage departs, leaving us on the sidewalk.

"For what exactly?" I ask, worried that he's going to force me onto this ice-skating rink, and of course I'd do it for him.

I just won't tell him how terrifying that sounds, especially in front of all of these strangers.

"I'm taking you ice-skating at the most romantic ice-skating rink in the city," he says with a huge smile on his face. Who could say no to that.

"The most romantic, huh?"

"That's what…"

"Your research says?" I laugh as I finish his sentence for him.

"Come on," he says, taking my hand and pulling me along with him towards the booth to pick up skates.

"You're really going to make me do this?" I ask as we stand in line behind another couple.

He pulls me in front of him as he wraps his arms around me, looking right into my eyes as he says, "One hundred percent." He leans in and kisses me gently for just a moment before the employee behind the counter clears their throat to get our attention now that it's our turn.

We get our rental skates and head toward an open bench to slide them on and lace them up before Jared holds out a hand for me to take before standing. "I've got you," he says as he helps me up and I begin my death grip on his hand. He leads me out onto the ice, and I can feel the anxiety building in my chest as I notice how many people are scattered all around the giant ice rink.

"I don't think I can…" I start, anxiously looking around.

"Amazia…." Jared interrupts me, trying to pull my attention. "Amazia. Look at me," he gently pushes, trying to get all of my attention on him. I eventually give in, looking right into his eyes as he holds both of my hands in his as we stand together on the ice.

"I can't even go out there," I say, trying to find an excuse.

"Babe, I hate to break it to you," he starts, glancing down for a moment, "but, you're already doing it."

I look down, curious to what he means. I see we're both standing on the ice, but it takes a moment to realize we are slowly gliding along the ice as well. "Whoa," I start, feeling myself losing my balance, but Jared already has my arms in his hands, holding me up somehow.

"You're doing fine, but you need to relax," he gently instructs.

"Am I though?" I ask nervously.

"Yes. Yes, you are," he laughs.

"Are you laughing at me?" I ask.

"Yes, I am," he says, pulling my attention off of my feet and back up to him.

"That's… rude," I say in a serious tone, unsure if I mean it.

He smiles, "I'm sorry."

"I might forgive you later," I joke, keeping my eyes on him as I realize he is no longer holding my hands, but has his arms around me like we are slow dancing. I don't dare look around as I try not to focus on my wobbly feet.

"Can you forgive me now?" he gently whispers.

"Not until I survive this ice-skating experience," I whisper back, feeling calmer by the moment within his arms.

"I've got you, babe. I'll keep you safe," he continues to whisper.

"Can you keep me upright while making sure no one else pokes my eye out with their toe pic?" I ask sarcastically.

"I'm absolutely positive that I can," he says genuinely.

"And you're going to magically teach me how to skate too?"

"I've already done that," he says in a proud voice.

"What?" I ask, feeling confused at his confidence.

"Amazia, look around," he says, looking up and around. "You're skating just fine."

I give in and look around, quickly realizing we are no longer at the edge of the rink but moving slowly towards the far end. Jared is slowly moving us with other skaters scattered all around us as we go. No one is watching us, which helps relieve my anxiety some. I look down and see my feet moving along with Jared as he gently moves his feet to keep us both going. "Jared…" I whisper out in surprise.

"Yeah?"

"You're pretty incredible. Did you know that?" I ask what's on my mind without thinking.

"I've never been told that before, but it sounds pretty nice," he replies with a smile before pulling my face up to his and kissing me passionately as he pulls us around the rink.

*   *   *   *   *

Jared and I continue to skate for well over an hour as I slowly become more and more comfortable. It isn't long before Jared is only holding one of my hands as we skate together, laughing and smiling as we go. He pulls out his phone to take several photos of us as we go. We even stop and get someone to take a photo of us skating with the Rockefeller tree in the background. It was more of a magical evening than I ever expected. I never had a magical memory of Christmas, but Jared has changed that for me forever.

Once we finish at the skating rink, we change back into our shoes and I find the horse drawn carriage is back to pick us up. Jared really pulled out all the stops tonight. After we climb into the carriage, Jared hands me an insulated tumbler full of the most delicious hot chocolate I've ever tasted. We sip on the hot chocolate as we ride back through Christmas lights. Jared snuggles closer and wraps his arm back around me as we ride back toward Central Park. Once we begin to pass through the entrance of the park, I gently lean my head over to his shoulder which only makes him pull me in closer. The carriage eventually comes to a stop right next to Jared's blue Camaro. He quickly uses his key fob to start it so it can start warming up as we climb down out of the carriage. Jared has a quick word with the driver, thanking him for the evening I'm sure, before he leads me over to the passenger side of his car and opens my door for me.

Once I'm in, he walks around to climb into the driver seat, and he begins to head out of the city. "So, did I help change your mind about Christmas in the city?"

"That is a loaded question," I honestly reply. "But… you have definitely changed my ideas of what Christmas could be."

He smiles, clearly happy with my answer. "Well, I'll be sure to make this Christmas one to remember."

"I think you already have," I admit with a shy smile.

He glances over to smile back at me before reaching over to hold my hand in his as he drives us out of the city.

I'm exhausted before we even leave the city, therefore I am beyond ready for bed once Jared pulls into my driveway.

"Come on, I'll walk you in," he says as he climbs out of the running car.

"You're crazy if you think I'm letting you drive back into the city this late," I say as I unbuckle my seatbelt and reach over to turn off his car.

"Babe, I'll be fine," he says with a shrug before closing his door and walking around to open mine.

As soon as I get out, I step right up to him, dangle his keys in front of him, and whisper, "But... you're staying," before walking towards the front door.

Jared closes the passenger door and turns to grab my arm before I can walk too far away. "You know I won't cross any boundaries. You know how seriously I'm taking this," he begins.

I step into him, looking up at him without making any contact. "I know that. You know that. I also know that my guest room is nice and cozy, or at least I hope it is."

"Amazia..."

I interrupt him, "Jared. Please, just stay so I know you're safe."

He sighs heavily before replying, "If that's what you want."

"It is," I reply with a smile before turning towards the house and digging for my key.

I hear Jared open his trunk and retrieve something before following me up to the porch. I have the door unlocked by the time he reaches me. I look over and see a backpack over his shoulder.

"You came prepared this time?" I ask.

"I wanted to be sure that I had a change of clothes for work if you forced me to stay and make you breakfast again," he jokes.

"How thoughtful of you. Why yes, I'd enjoy a home cooked breakfast in the morning," I tease as we step into the house, locking the door behind us.

* * * * *

Jared drives me into the city the next morning so I won't have to take the train. I explain that it was no trouble, taking the train. He insisted on driving me since he had to get back to the city anyways for the day. He apologizes for having to stay away for the next few days, stating he has a ton of small jobs to finish before the holiday arrives, including Christmas Eve. He promises to save Christmas Day for me and only me. On Christmas day, he comes over early and we share brunch while exchanging gifts. He brought over movies that he researched to be the best Christmas movies. We watch The Santa Clause and Elf while sitting together on the couch, his arm around me, holding me close. We've grown close over the few short weeks, and I couldn't ask for more.

Jared is the perfect gentleman, and he never crosses boundaries. It took me two weeks to get him to feel comfortable enough to kiss me, without me making the first move. He always would say he was afraid to mess something up. Eventually, I asked him why he always said that, and he replied that research shows that making a move too early is statistically shown to mean shorter relationships. Although I doubted him, he swiftly proved it by showing me the articles he read. It may be a partial truth, but it isn't a whole truth.

As he cuddles next to me through several more Christmas movies, I feel more at home than I've ever felt in my life. I can only imagine that he feels the same way. He smiles down at me in a way that I never imagined possible when I first met him in the hotel lobby. He was so stern and monotone through our conversation before he asked for my name for when he filed a complaint. Apparently, that wasn't actually his intention, but I fell for it due to his demeanor. Thankfully, I almost broke his nose, leading to the next stage in our strange love story. Love story? I can't love him yet, can I? No. I can't feel that way just yet. Maybe I am, I think as I look up at him and smile. But either way, I'll wait for the right time and place to admit it to him.

13

A week later, I'm in my office finishing up the last of my yearly paperwork when Klarissa bursts into my office. "Amazia! Why aren't you dressed yet?"

I look up and find Klarissa in a long red dress with a slit up the side and a deep back line. "Well, hello there," I smile, seeing her dressed up for the first time.

"Shut up! I won't look nearly as good once you're dressed up and ready," she sighs, leaning onto my desk.

"Wait. What time is it?" I ask, glancing down at my phone.

"Time for you to already be dressed and ready for your man," she says in a smart tone.

"Shit! When did it get that late?" I ask, closing my computer and grabbing for my dress hanging behind my door.

"You have time," Klarissa says gently. "I had laundry steam your dress, so it's wrinkle free and ready to go."

"You did?"

Klarissa nods as she follows me into the hall.

"You're amazing! I wish I had the power to pay you more and officially make you my assistant."

"Me too girl, me too," she laughs as she follows me into the bathroom between our office and laundry services. It has a large dressing area separate from the bathroom stalls for added convenience for those of us who use laundry regularly for uniforms.

Klarissa leaves me alone while I change, knowing small talk only adds to my anxiety. Once I walk out, her silence quickly melts away. "Amazia! Gold is definitely your color!" she says, sounding in awe.

"You don't think it's too much?"

"For New Years in New York City? Hell no! You're not in Kansas anymore!"

"Arkansas," I correct her.

"Same difference," she brushes it off as a minor mistake and comes over to help fix my hair into a simple updo for the night.

I touch up my makeup and double check that I feel presentable before turning to face Klarissa. "How do I look?"

"Amazing, but first…" she says, reaching into her bag and quickly pulling out a bottle of perfume and spraying. "And now you smell as good as you look," she winks.

"Thanks," I say, waving the perfume out of the air.

"You're welcome. Now, let's go. It's time for me to get a sneak peek at this fella you've been keeping away from me for over a month now!" she says, ushering me back towards my office so I can drop my belongings and grab my phone.

I quickly check the messages and see that Jared is just now arriving. I should have just enough time to walk to the conference center before he makes it that far.

* * * * *

"Meet me by the fountain," Jared texts as we're both enroute to the conference center from different directions. Apparently, he used his connections to get free valet parking at the hotel. Of course, he did. At least it'll be warm for our drive back to Connecticut.

As I approach the employee doors close to the fountain, I can hear Klarissa talking, but I can't make anything out over the pounding of my heart.

"Amazia!" Klarissa yells, slapping my arm.

"What!?" I stop, turn to her and ask as I reach to rub my arm.

"Were you listening to anything I just said?" she asks, crossing her arms dramatically.

"No, not really," I admit with an embarrassed smile.

"Damn, you must really like this guy. He's still making you nervous all these weeks later."

"Shut up!" I say, swatting at her crossed arms.

"Oh, come on! It's adorable!"

I groan dramatically. "Why are you making me blush before I have to go out there!?"

"Because you're going to blush once I obnoxiously introduce myself anyways," she says as she pushes through the doors exiting the employee hallway into the fountain lobby.

I follow her through, trying to breathe through the anxiety she built up inside of me. It doesn't work at first, but once I pass through the door and see Jared, it all melts away into pure happiness. He turns and immediately spots me, a smile growing on his face as he takes me in. It reminds me of how he looked at me on our first date.

"Hello beautiful," he says meeting me halfway and kissing my cheek gently as he wraps one arm around me, pulling me close.

"Hey babe," I say, not sure if I've ever called him that before, and it makes me blush immediately.

"Well, hello there mystery man," Klarissa says, further embarrassing me.

"Jared, this is Klarissa. Klarissa, Jared," I introduce them as casually as I can possibly fake under the circumstances. Klarissa got me all worked up on purpose, I know it.

"Pleasure," Jared begins. "I've heard a lot about you," he continues in his dry, professional tone.

"Funny, because I have heard almost nothing about you, sir," Klarissa replies like the smart ass that she is.

"Okay, stop. You're not going to interrogate him right now," I try to get Klarissa to back off.

"Okay, but I'm going to get something out of him before the end of the night," Klarissa threatens.

"Don't you have a date to go find?" I ask her, trying to get a moment alone with Jared.

"Fine. I'll leave you two alone, for now. Hopefully my date showed up this time," she says as she walks off toward the banquet hall.

"What was that about?" Jared asks, looking confused.

"She uses holi-dates," I explain.

"Holi-what?" he laughs.

"It's like a fake date that you use for the holidays," I shrug.

"Glad you didn't need to use one of those," he says with a smile as he pulls me close to his front and he places his hands on my hips.

"I wouldn't have bothered," I admit.

"You would have come alone?" he asks, sounding surprised.

I shrug, "I wouldn't have come at all."

"Really?"

"Yeah. It's never really been my thing. Big, extravagant parties."

"Well, I'm about to change that about you," he says as he wraps his arms around me and pulls me closer.

"Oh, really? You enjoy these large parties?" I ask as I wrap my arms around his neck.

"I didn't used to, but I have to go to a lot of them for work. I've learned to make the most of it and enjoy them."

"For work, huh?" I ask.

"Sometimes to work the event and sometimes at the request of my boss," he shrugs. "Sometimes working for rich people means showing up to random events you're invited to."

"Sounds like a rough life," I say in a smart-ass tone.

"It really can be," he smiles, pulling me closer as he leans in to gently place his lips on mine. The kiss doesn't last long, but it easily melts away any anxiety I had about spending the night at this party. "Come on," he says as he releases me to hold my hand.

I smile back at him, "Here goes nothing." I let him take my hand and lead me towards the banquet hall where the party is taking place. It isn't often that hotel employees are able to attend the large New Years party, but, of course, Jared has connections. He was even able to get Klarissa her ticket, plus one.

As we reach the lobby of the banquet hall, we see a number of people gathered around in small groups. It seems the lobby area is set up for a quiet space compared to the loud music coming from inside. There are high top tables scattered all around and a large mobile bar set up along the far side of the lobby. Avoiding people that I know will be nearly impossible.

"Is that Jared?" I hear a nearby voice ask.

"Jared?" I hear a familiar male voice yell.

"Oh shit," Jared whispers before turning towards the voice. His demeanor immediately changes and goes back to the dry and serious person I met all those weeks ago.

I follow his gaze as he turns toward the voice. Two tables away I see Mr. Berlusconi and his assistant Mr. Vittori. Shit is right. I distinctly remember Jared's comments about this family and them not seeing us together. I decide to take the customer service approach and smile widely, as if I'm thrilled to see them. Jared takes my hand and pulls me along until we get close.

"Mr. Berlusconi," Jared says, reaching out to shake his hand before quickly wrapping his arm back around my lower back to hold me close.

"Jared! I thought you requested the evening off?" Mr. Berlusconi asks as he looks over at me. "Amazia! What a wonderful surprise! Amanda told me that you were lucky enough to be off duty tonight."

"Perks of being a supervisor," I smile with my customer service personality on full display.

Mr. Berlusconi looks pleased with my answer before turning his eye suspiciously on Jared. "Now I see why you've been less available the last few weeks."

"Clearly you remember Amazia from Elena's wedding," Jared says in his monotone voice again.

"How could I forget? She graciously took over when the banquet staff needed help with the event. And, of course, Elena still hasn't stopped talking about her assistance before the ceremony," Mr. Berlusconi and Jared exchange curious glances while he reminds us of our last interaction. "Is that where you two originated?"

"No, no," I reply. "I hardly remembered him being here that weekend."

"She almost didn't believe me when I told her I was here," Jared adds stiffly, playing along.

"How curious," Mr. Berlusconi continues as he looks back and forth between us. "How did this little interaction begin then?"

"We ran into each other a week or so after," I vaguely reply.

"What a small world," Mr. Berlusconi adds strangely. "I'm honestly surprised to see you here Amazia, and with Jared of all people." He keeps his eyes on Jared as he says it, as if he's trying to read Jared's mind.

"It was a curious event," Jared adds.

"Happy accident really," I add with a smile, looking up at Jared.

Jared breaks eye contact with Mr. Berlusconi just long enough to look down at me with his gentle eyes. "Happy accident," he says in his dry tone but shows me how he really feels in our eye contact, and I can feel it warm me up inside.

"Well, I'll leave you two to it then. I hope you enjoy the festivities," Mr. Berlusconi says.

"Nice to see you again," I add in my customer service voice, lying easily to him.

"Oh, and Jared..." Mr. Berlusconi says as we turn to walk away. "I'm glad to see you taking some time for yourself. You can't be a workaholic forever, right?"

"Right," Jared laughs dryly back before turning with me to walk toward the bar. Jared seems concerned as we silently walk towards the bar. Something about the way Mr. Berlusconi said he can't be a workaholic forever bothers me, but I can't figure out why.

"Don't turn around," Jared whispers as we approach the bar.

"What can I get you?" the employee behind the bar asks, eyeing me suspiciously.

"Sprite and whatever she would like," Jared says kindly to the employee as he leans against the bar top.

"Same, please," I add.

The employee nods before stepping away.

"Why is he here?" I ask, looking over at Jared and leaning into the bar close to him.

"That's a wonderful question," Jared replies in a suspicious tone.

"Is it?" I ask, trying to figure out what's going on in his head.

"It's... suspicious, that's all," Jared replies, looking over to me. He looks down into my eyes as if I can blink away whatever is bothering him.

"Well, I say we avoid him the rest of the night and pretend he isn't here," I smile up at him and gently rub his arm, trying to pull all the anxiety I can see him holding in his shoulders. He slowly relaxes over several moments.

"Here you are," the employee says, dropping our fancy glasses in front of us.

"Thank you," I say without taking my eyes off of Jared. "Shall we?" I whisper.

Jared only nods as he reaches for his glass, without looking. I do the same until he turns and holds his arm out for me to wrap my arm into. "Here's to a good night with my beautiful Amazia Franklin."

"However kind of you, Mr. Jared Wright," I tease back, making him laugh. We walk away from the tables and towards the banquet hall.

"Can I ask you something?" he asks, stopping me at the banquet hall doors.

"Of course, Jared," I reply, unsure of what he's going to ask.

He looks around, making sure Mr. Berlusconi isn't in sight, I assume. "Maybe I should have done this sooner, officially that is."

"Jared…" I say, feeling nervous about what he's referring to.

"It's okay, Amazia. It's not a bad thing," he smiles as I see his gentler side coming back out for me, and me alone. "I want to be sure it's okay, before we are in that situation again. I want to ask if you're okay with me calling you, my girlfriend." He looks so sweet and genuine as he asks that I can't help but smile.

"Jared… I'd like that very much," I say through the huge smile I can't hide from my face. I'm sure my cheeks are red as well from the blushing.

"Aren't you proud of me?" Jared starts, pulling me in close again. "I did that on my own, without any research," he says as he leans in and kisses me passionately, pulling me closer for several moments before reluctantly letting me go.

"I'm very proud of you," I smile. "Now, you need to keep those lips away from me so we can focus on the party until midnight," I joke.

"Good point," he says. "No more kissing until midnight. Got it."

"I didn't say all that," I say.

"Nope. It's too late. You can't talk me out of it," he teases. "I got to call you my girlfriend before the year ended. Next step, make the stroke of midnight memorable." He gently releases me before turning to walk away, further into the banquet hall, without glancing back to be sure I'm following.

"Jared, wait! That's hardly fair," I says as I rush to catch up to him.

*   *   *   *   *

We enjoy dinner with Klarissa and a few other co-workers to try and avoid Mr. Berlusconi as much as possible. We see him at a distance several times early in the evening, but he seems to quickly disappear once dinner is over. Jared comments as to how typical that is, for him to show his face at an event before performing a disappearing act. Jared claims that the only reason he stayed late for the entire wedding was due to his daughter's request. That is also apparently why Mr. Berlusconi added so much last-minute staff to the event, including the band and their very own event manager for the weekend. I wanted to ask how they chose the band at the last minute, but I decided against it, sensing Jared didn't want to talk about it anymore than he had to.

Klarissa tries to ask Jared a million questions, and he gently answers many of them before I finally cut her off. Klarissa doesn't remember him from the Berlusconi wedding, and I'd rather keep it that way. Amanda intercepts me on my way into the bathroom at one point in the night to interrogate me about my newfound relationship with the infamous band manager. I told her the same story I told Mr. Berlusconi, that we ran into each other after the wedding and hardly remembered one another from the wedding event. Amanda seemed satisfied with my response before telling me how hot she thinks he is. I try not to blush, but know I'm failing, especially when she says she's happy to see me getting out more. She's known me since I started working here, back when I didn't know anyone. She even had lunch with me a few times until I felt more at home. I also think she put in a good word for me when I was up for my promotion, which I'll never complain about.

After dinner, Jared and I danced the few slow dances that the DJ played. We mingled with random co-workers and acquaintances to pass the time until the main event comes on and the countdown begins. The desserts were brought out around 11 P.M., bringing most people out towards the lobby area to mingle in a quieter space over coffee and desserts. Jared and I sip on some coffee to stay awake, knowing we're both usually in bed long before now. We make our way back into the banquet hall with everyone else at 11:50 P.M. as the party hosts make a few announcements. They thank the staff and party goers for making the event a huge success. Not only is the event an employee involved event, but also a hotel wide fundraiser for local education. The hotel raised over two million dollars at this year's New Years event, which is outstanding. I have a feel Mr. Berlusconi had a hand in the acquisition, but I don't dare bring it up. I'm just glad he disappeared and never came back to bother Jared again. I did see Jared check his phone a few times after the initial interaction, and I can only guess it has to do with that family, but I trust Jared and I know he'll talk to me when he's ready.

"Come here, girlfriend," he says, holding a hand out for me to take. I smile, taking his hand as he leads me away from the crowd as the three-minute countdown begins.

"Where are we going?" I ask, following him through the banquet hall.

"A better spot, that's all," he vaguely replies.

"Jared, we only have a few minutes," I say, feeling confused.

"Exactly," he says while leading me out of the ballroom and quickly away from the lobby.

"Where are you going?" I ask as I check my watch. We can hardly hear the announcer in the banquet hall as we get further away.

"Somewhere special," he says as he stops in front of the giant Christmas tree that stands between the banquet lobby and the nearby fountains.

"Somewhere special?" I ask as he turns to face me.

He shrugs, "Somewhere more private, and a little more special."

"Christmas is over," I say, glancing over at the tree.

"Christmas ends at the stroke of midnight as we ring in a new year."

"I never expected you to be so into Christmas," I laugh.

"You never expected a lot," he gently says, reaching forward and brushing a stray strand of hair from my face, tucking it behind my ear.

"You've got that right," I slowly whisper back, feeling breathless at the gentle gesture.

"I just wanted to ring in the new year with you, and you alone, by my side." His voice is at a whisper as he looks into my eyes, speaking from the soul.

I feel my heart rate increase as my cheek naturally flush. "I couldn't ask for anything more," I whisper back as we hear the countdown begin in the ballroom.

"Ten. Nine. Eight. Seven. Six…"

"Amazia, thank you for opening your heart to someone as complicated as me this year," Jared adds during the countdown.

"Five. Four. Three. Two…"

"Jared…" I begin.

I am interrupted as he gently places a finger over my lips to shush me as we hear everyone in the ballroom erupt.

"One! Happy New Year!"

The rest happens in slow motion, almost like a romantic fairytale. As the song to ring in the new year plays in the banquet hall, we can hear the deep eruption of fireworks outside from time square several blocks away. Jared smiles with genuine happiness in his eyes as he leans in for a magical new year's kiss, sealing our fate for the new year as he makes silent promises that are left unspoken while his kiss grows deeper and more passionate by the second. He has never initiated a kiss this serious before. He was still always very hesitant around me until I'd make a move, never wanting to cross a line. This is the first time I feel he completely took over and led the way as I feel his hands cup my face for several moments before he wraps his arms around me to pull me in closer. I follow suit and wrap my arms around his neck, pulling him deeper into the passionate kiss we are sharing as the new year rings in from the banquet hall nearby. Time around us seems to slow as we get lost in one another. After a minute of being lost, reality comes back as we hear the song end as the crowd roars with applause from the banquet hall.

Jared gently releases my lips as he tries to catch his breath, leaning his forehead down against mine. We're both breathing fast as we try to adjust to normal air again. The magnetic force between us is still strong as he tries to slowly pull away. He lets me go to wrap one arm around my waist as he turns for us to walk back toward the banquet hall. "This year is going to be something special for my girlfriend," he says in a smart-ass tone.

"Oh yeah? How's that?"

"Because she gets to spend an entire year with me by her side," he smiles.

"And how are you going to start this new year?" I ask, curious to what he'll say.

"With a nap," he laughs.

"That sounds like a wonderful idea," I reply.

"Do you need to go back down to your office?" he stops me to ask.

"Yeah, just to get my coat and bag."

"Want me to come with you?" he asks.

"That's up to you," I shrug.

"How about I go get the car from valet and get it warmed up for our drive," he suggests.

"Use those connections to get us out of here quick," I wink, which causes him to laugh again.

"I'll do my best babe. Meet you in the portico?"

"See you there," I say before kissing his cheek gently and turning to disappear down the back employee hallway.

14

Once I reach my office, I find Klarissa also there grabbing her coat. Thankfully she's too tired to ask me any more questions. We're nearly silent as we walk down toward the lobby together. Klarissa already ordered for an app service to pick her up at the side employee entrance, but she walks to the lobby with me as she waits for her driver to arrive. We part ways once we see Jared making small talk with someone working in valet while standing next to his blue Camaro.

"Have a good evening, Ms. Franklin," the valet says as I approach, "Mr. Wright," he adds before he walks away to return to his duties.

"Shall we?" Jared says, taking my bag and holding my door open for me to climb into the passenger seat.

"We shall," I reply with a smile.

He closes the door then drops my bag into his back seat before climbing into the driver's seat. "You're still okay with staying at my place in the city tonight?" he checks with me.

"Of course," I reply. "I can't wait to see where you live." This will be the first time he's ever taken me there. I'm sure he wanted to properly clean up his bachelor pad before having me over, and it never worried me. Now though, I'm wide awake with curiosity about what's in store.

"It's nothing special," he notes before driving out of the portico and into the city.

"It's yours, so it's special to me," I say feeling way too cheesy. I laugh before saying, "Wow, that sounded super cheesy." I cover my face, wanting to hide the embarrassment of not only saying it out loud, but then calling myself out.

Jared laughs as he reaches over to try to pry my hand away from my face. "I think that was adorable."

"I'm not adorable! Oh man, can we just forget that ever happened or something?"

"Definitely not! That is going down in the date diary, for sure."

"Oh crap," I say, feeling a bit defeated. How could such an embarrassing moment be noted as a memory of interest?

"Don't make it sound like a bad thing," he teases. "You have an amazing boyfriend to start the new year off with, so things can't be that bad."

"I guess you're partially right."

"Partially?"

"I do have an amazing boyfriend," I reply, feeling my cheeks turn red as I speak the wonderful truth aloud for the first time. Boyfriend. I like the sound of that.

* * * * *

Jared pulls his car onto one last side street before parking along the front of a strip of condominium type homes. "This is home," he says gesturing to the door closest to where he parked.

"You must have paid top dollar for this bachelor pad," I admit before either of us exit the car.

"I got a good deal on it," he shrugs.

"Those secret connections of yours?" I ask.

"Something like that," he says before exiting the car and making his way around to open my door. "I don't know about you, but I'm exhausted."

"That party took all of your energy, didn't it?" I tease as he closes the door and quickly grabs my bag from the back seat, refusing to let me take it from him as we walk up to the door.

"The surprise guests took a lot," he admits without further explanation. What is it about Mr. Berlusconi that worries Jared so much? Without the warnings from Jared, I'd only seen him as an obnoxious rich guy who flaunts his money. "Welcome to my not so bachelor, bachelor pad," he jokes as he opens the door for me.

"Hmm, it seems relatively normal," I admit, looking around for red flags. His home is neat and organized, as I would have expected from the dry and monotone version of him that I originally met.

"What were you expecting?" he asks curiously as he places my bag down on the nearby couch. He moves further into the room to deposit his wallet and keys into a tray near the kitchen.

"I'm not entirely sure, to be honest," I admit, still wondering what secrets lie within these walls.

"Let me show you to the bathroom upstairs so you can change," he says, picking my bag back up and reaching out for me to take his hand. He smiles as he takes mine and leads me upstairs, pointing out different things as we go. "I'll give you a minute," he says as he steps into his closet across the room while unbuttoning his shirt. He disappears around the corner before I close the bathroom door.

I quickly change out of the dress and feel much better back in normal comfortable clothes. I also feel much warmer in my fleece pajama pants and loose fit sweatshirt. I quickly brush my hair and gather up my belongings before walking back out into the bedroom. As soon as I open the door, I see Jared closing his closet door. He turns and smiles at me in his equally comfortable looking plaid pajama pants and long sleeve henley style shirt.

"How about some hot chocolate and a movie before bed?" he asks, clearly wanting to spend some more time together before we turn in.

"Sounds wonderful," I admit. "I feel so much better already just from getting out of that dress."

"I don't know how you women do it," he laughs as he walks over and places his hands on both sides of my face, looking directly into my eyes as he smiles. "I'm so glad that you came into my life, Amazia."

"Yeah, I am pretty amazing, aren't I?" I joke, hoping I didn't ruin his moment.

He laughs in response, "That you are." He slowly leans in to gently kiss my lips until the kisses grow more passionate by the moment. He does not generally give in so easily to kissing me. I usually need to nudge him into going for it. He moves one hand to the back of my neck, twisting his fingers into my hair. His other hand moves to my lower back, where he gently pulls me in closer. We stay in the moment for what feels like forever, before we finally release one another to come up for air.

He places his forehead against mine, and we both breathe heavily. The tension between us has only risen more and more over the last few weeks, but neither of us is willing to break our promise to take things slow. I know more than anything that Jared is afraid of crossing some magical line that he thinks exists in the early part of relationships. More than anything, I don't want anything to come between us, so I don't push him or the subject. We just let everything happen in its own time. The level of respect he has for this situation is overwhelming, and I like him even more for the boundaries that he has set for himself.

"Thank you for agreeing to be my girlfriend," he whispers.

"Of course, babe. Why wouldn't I agree?" I ask intrigued by his wording.

"I just never thought I'd be in this place, with anyone," he admits.

"Well, you never have to worry about that again," I say, lifting his chin so he'll look back at me.

He leans back to look at me, searching my eyes for something. "Do you really mean that?"

"I really do," I admit, surprising even myself at the honest feelings inside of me.

Jared smiles back at me in a way I never imagined possible when I met him. His eyes are so bright and full of happiness in this moment, and I want to capture this moment forever. "How about that hot chocolate?" he asks, letting me go again to lead me back downstairs.

*   *   *   *   *

Jared puts in the movie "New Year's Eve," an older romantic comedy, as he whips up some steaming hot, hot chocolate for us. Once he's done, he carries the mugs in and places them on the table in front of us. He wraps his arm around me and pulls me closer, holding me tight as we wait for the hot chocolate to cool down enough to drink. I look over at him and he smiles brightly at me again, a side of him I brought out from the deep dark depths of his soul. I made him this happy. I'm not sure what's so special about me or how I did it, but I did.

I snuggle close to him again after we finish our hot chocolate. He pulls me in close and I turn over to lean against his chest, snuggling up closer than ever before. He gently rubs my back and brushes back my hair as we watch the movie. Over time, I feel my eyes closing as I fight to keep myself awake, but the exhaustion is trying to take over.

15

I feel myself trying to blink my sleepy eyes awake as the light starts to shine through a nearby window. I breathe in, wondering what time I slept to. It feels like eight or nine. I turn my wrist over to check the time on my watch. 8:20, that was a good guess. I look around to check for the light source, feeling a bit disoriented in this room. What day is it? New Years Day. Oh, wait. That means last night was New Years Eve! I stayed at Jared's for the first time.

I remember cuddling on the couch last night as we watched a movie. I also remember feeling really tired. I must have fallen asleep, but this isn't the living room. I begin to realize that this is Jared's bedroom as I look around more. I gently roll over, realizing I'm tucked into the covers of his bed. As I turn over, I see Jared still sleeping on his half of the bed. He's sleeping on his side, facing me. He looks so peaceful as he breathes deeply in his sleep. I roll over onto my back and look up at the ceiling for a moment before I hear Jared stir. He moves closer and wraps an arm around me, pulling me closer to him as he leans over and kisses my cheek.

"Good morning, girlfriend," he says.

I can't hide the smile that grows across my face. "Good morning, boyfriend."

"I sure do like the sound of that," he says as I roll to face him. "How'd you sleep?"

"Good, I think," I admit.

"You think?" he asks in a teasing voice.

"Well, considering the last thing I remember was watching a movie downstairs, I'm not entirely sure," I offer as an explanation.

He laughs, "Yeah, you fell asleep. I didn't want to wake you, so I carried you up here and tucked you in. I hope that's okay. We didn't really discuss sleeping arrangements beforehand," he looks nervous as he explains.

"This is perfect," I admit, not being able to hide my feelings. I love that Jared would never cross a line and I genuinely know I can trust him.

"I didn't cross any lines or do anything wrong, did I?"

"Not at all, babe," I smile before leaning in to kiss him. He kisses me back, growing more passionate by the second before he pulls back to look into my eyes.

"You'd tell me, right? If I ever did anything to approach a line I shouldn't cross?" he asks.

"You're never going to cross a line," I say, knowing he won't.

"But if I did, you'd tell me?" he asks with genuine concern in his eyes.

"Of course, I would. I know how important that is to you. If you ever do anything to approach a line, I'll tell you. Promise."

"Amazia, I...."

"You what?" I ask, wondering what he was going to say.

"Nothing," he smiles and shakes his head. "I'll tell you later."

"Babe!" I say, wanting to know what he was about to say.

"I just have something to ask you, but not until after breakfast. I know how much you need your morning coffee first," he says before rolling out of bed and heading down to the kitchen.

"Men," I whisper to myself before rolling out of bed to follow him.

By the time I make it downstairs, I can hear Jared moving around in the kitchen. I look around at the condo in the daylight as I look for any detail I missed last night. I never went into the kitchen, so I'm most curious about what his bachelor pad kitchen is like. As soon as I enter the kitchen, I smell the aroma of fresh coffee in the air. I look around and find Jared removing a coffee mug from a k-cup brewer and turning to hand it to me. "Morning coffee, check," he says as he hands me the cup.

"You own a coffee machine, but don't drink coffee?" I ask, curious to why he has one.

"I own this brand-new coffee maker because my amazing girlfriend needs coffee in the morning to function, or so she says," he explains with a smile.

"Coffee is a morning necessity," I admit before taking a sip. "And my amazing boyfriend not only knows of my coffee needs, but apparently also knows how to make it perfectly."

"I've been taking notes," he jokes as he begins to make breakfast.

* * * * *

After breakfast, I shower and change while Jared cleans up from cooking. I was surprised to see a fully functioning kitchen, with real plates and utensils. That's something you don't always see with a previously single guy. Though, based on what he's told me about himself, he never imagined himself with someone. When I go back downstairs, I ask if there is anything I can do, but he says he has it all handled. He hands me his smart TV remote before kissing me and going upstairs to shower and change himself. I take the time to snoop through his Netflix and Hulu history, curious to what kind of shows and movies he tends to watch. I'm surprised to see a wide variety in his previously watched list, which only adds to his mysterious side.

"Stalking my Netflix history?" he asks as he comes back downstairs.

"Something like that," I admit.

"Find what you were looking for?" he asks as he plops down next to me on the couch.

"Just a continued mystery," I shrug.

"You mean, I'm not an open book?" he asks.

"Only when it comes to your feeling towards me."

"Isn't that the truth," he laughs.

"So, tell me something."

"Like, what?"

"Something I don't know," I turn to look over at him.

He turns to look back at me, looking down as if nervous about what he might say.

"Jared, whatever it is, it can't be that bad."

He smiles and glances up. "This isn't necessarily bad. I just don't know how you'll feel about it."

"Okay. Let's start with the topic," I gently push, seeing he is worried about this conversation.

"I want to be honest about something I have. I want to know how you feel because I don't want it to make you uncomfortable or worried. I want you to always feel safe and secure, especially around me," he starts, looking up as he continues. "What are your feelings or opinions on guns?"

"Guns?" I ask, not sure I had any idea what he was about to talk about. "Well, my family didn't own any growing up. I've never been around them or had first-hand experience with them. So, in all honesty, I don't know anything about them."

"Do you have a negative opinion on them?"

"I guess I'd say I'm neutral. I don't see an issue with them. I just don't know enough about them to have an opinion," I explain.

"Are you comfortable with them being around?" he asks.

"I think so," I shrug.

"I don't want you to feel uncomfortable knowing that I own some."

"I trust you."

He smiles. "I'm glad that you do. I hope you know that I'd do anything for you. I don't want the fact that I own guns to scare you away though."

"It's going to take more than that," I laugh.

"That's good to know, but I have a follow up question."

"Okay."

"Do you want to learn how to shoot one, so you could maybe one day have your own, for protection?"

"I don't know," I reply, feeling hesitant. I don't know anything about guns. Doesn't that mean I probably have no business owning one?

"I don't want you to feel obligated. I just want you to be safe. Part of that is me hoping you'll have one if you ever need to protect yourself, but mainly, I want to be sure you feel safe while with me and guns are present," he shrugs.

"I'd probably feel better if I knew more about guns. I mean it when I say I know nothing about them. Maybe we start with the basics and see how it goes."

He smiles, "I can work with that." He reaches forward and wraps his hand around mine. "Are you sure you're comfortable with guns being around? If not, we can avoid spending time here at my place for a while."

"That isn't necessary. I like your place, and I trust you. I know you'll keep me safe."

"This is New York City though, so hopefully one day I can convince you to have your own, for when I'm not around to protect you."

"Yeah, there was that one creep from work we all used to worry about. Some of the staff was worried about seeing him outside of work. Nothing ever came of it though."

"What creep?"

"His name was Seth. He doesn't work there anymore anyways. He was demoted one day then took off in the middle of an event the next."

"The Berlusconi wedding?" Jared asks.

"Yeah, actually. It was. That was why I was originally asked to stay and help the night of the rehearsal dinner."

"The night you hit me with the door," Jared reminds me.

"Yeah, that one," I laugh.

"Well, you don't have to worry about Seth anymore. That was taken care of."

"What do you mean?"

"I'm pretty sure Mr. Berlusconi is the reason Seth left in the middle of the event. He didn't like his attitude."

"You think Mr. Berlusconi got him fired?"

"Something like that. He has pull everywhere he goes. If the Berlusconi family wants something, they get it."

"Is that part of why you felt the need to warn me about them, back then, during the wedding weekend?"

"There are a lot of layers to that family. My involvement with them is complicated and maybe even messy," he looks down, clearly thinking about what else he wants to say.

"Why did you want to keep us a secret from them?" I gently push, hoping for some explanation as to why he's so weird around them if I'm around.

"I just didn't want you to get mixed up in their drama," he says shaking it off, pretending like nothing about this conversation is bothering him. I can see right through him.

I decide to let it go for now. I can see something is haunting him about the topic, but I won't push him. "We just need to check the guest list before we decide to go to any more parties," I tease, trying to lighten the mood.

"Probably a good idea," he lightens up. "On a side note, don't we have a date with a Christmas tree?"

* * * * *

Jared drives us out to my house in Connecticut shortly after breakfast. He knows that I've made it a tradition to pack away everything Christmas on New Years Day. Jared agrees with my timing, since he clearly loves Christmas and wants to celebrate through the New Year. That wasn't the case with my family growing up. Instead of having a holiday dinner together, we would clean up any signs of Christmas on the evening of Christmas day before we were allowed dinner. My parents were possibly worse than the grinch himself when it came to holidays and celebrations.

Jared makes us hot chocolate as we make our way through the house, putting away the ornaments and tree first before packing up everything else. Jared didn't bother to decorate his place this year since he was spending more time at my house. He said that next year we'll combine all of our Christmas stuff to be sure it looks like Christmas threw up all over my house instead of just the living room. I like that he's already talking about next Christmas together. We've only been dating for a few short weeks, but everything feels so perfectly aligned. Maybe it's a dream come true, but what if there is something else waiting for us. What if the fairytales about to end. I'm just waiting for shit to hit the fan.

16

The next morning at work Klarissa won't leave me alone. She's full of energy and full of even more questions about Jared. I deflect most of them by telling her to get to work. Thankfully, there are a few minor issues in the lobby, which briefly gets me away from her. I offer to take the lobby issues just to get a break.

"I know what you're doing," she says as I leave the office.

"Just doing my job," I reply in a smart-ass tone before the door closes behind me.

The issues in the lobby were so minor that the front office managers could have fixed it, if they had any experience and knew how. January is always a rough time for the front office. Lots of part time helpers for the holidays are laid off on January first. A lot of the more experienced staff is promoted to any openings in the hotel as they start training again for newly filled full time slots.

Klarissa meets me in the lobby to help me train the new front office managers in a few simple steps to take when they run into issues. Klarissa is our expert at the rooms control software, while I'm better with room blocks specifically. Together we give the new managers a crash course in troubleshooting. I take two of the managers to teach them about troubleshooting room blocks, while Klarissa takes the other two for general room control issues. I show the managers how to not only double check room block notes, but to also lock out front desk staff from making unauthorized changes. I use the example of the Berlusconi wedding while showing the managers how to properly control those situations before it gets out of hand. I also show them how to directly chat with me if they have any questions or concerns.

After going through everything, Klarissa and I trade groups to teach the same thing to the other managers. Once we're done, they all have a more thorough understanding of basic troubleshooting that they should be able to do without calling us. We do remind them that it is never a bad thing to call and ask questions. We also explain that if they even think they messed something up, they should contact one of us immediately to check. Again, I use the Berlusconi wedding as an example of how one small change brought on hours of extra work to make the room block work for all family requests. Thankfully, the front office agent who made those mistakes was let go during the post-holiday layoffs.

Klarissa and I were about to go back to the office when I hear Amanda's voice. "Amazia!"

I turn and see Amanda coming towards me at a hurried pace. She's followed by two other females, talking behind her as they walk.

"Amanda! Happy New Year!" I say. I haven't seen her at all this year.

"What?" she asks seeming thrown. "Oh, right. Umm, we'll catch up about all that later," she says quickly before the two people following her catch up. "Klarissa, can I speak to Amazia alone, please?"

"Sure thing," Klarissa shrugs before looking back at me. "I'll see you back in the office."

Once Klarissa leaves down the staff hallway, I turn back to Amanda. "What's going on?"

Amanda looks nervous as she introduces the people behind her. "Amazia, these are detectives that need to speak to you about a case."

I look over at the two females behind Amanda. "What type of case?"

One reaches her hand out, "I'm Detective Katherine Thomasina, this is my partner Detective Lillian."

"Amazia Franklin," I say as I shake her hand.

"They're looking into Seth," Amanda whispers, looking around her like it's some big secret.

"Okay. What about him?" I ask the detectives.

"Did you have any negative history with him?" Detective Lillian asks gently.

"I saw him in the halls occasionally," I shrug, not sure what they're looking for.

"Did you take part in the sexual harassment claims against him?" Detective Thomasina asks in a more direct and somewhat rude tone.

"I heard about them, but no. I never had that type of a run in with him," I explain.

"But you did have a run in with him?" Detective Thomasina pushes roughly.

"We just need to know as much as we can about him," Detective Lillian explains in a much kinder tone.

"He was a bit of a creep. He was always trying to catch me alone to ask me out. It didn't matter how many times he asked, I always said no," I admit.

"But he never crossed a line with you?" Detective Lillian asked, looking curious.

"No, never," I continue. "Though, if I'm being honest, I think he was always more afraid of me than I was him. I think standing my ground made a difference. I heard about some of the claims against him and I was a little surprised. I never thought he had it in him, but I also know that some women really don't know how to stand up for themselves and say no."

"When was the last time you saw Seth?" Detective Thomasina asks as she flips through her detective notes, looking for something.

"The afternoon of the Berlusconi rehearsal dinner, just before the staff broke for dinner break." I look over to Amanda, "What weekend was that? The week before Thanksgiving?"

"Funny you mention the Berlusconi wedding," Detective Lillian says. "They were here the last time you saw Seth?"

"He disappeared before the rehearsal dinner," I reply.

Detective Thomasina looks up from her note pad, "You remember that detail very distinctly. Why is that?" she sounds suspicious as she asks.

I laugh, "Well, I got roped into helping banquets that evening for the rehearsal dinner." I glance to Amanda, "Amanda really does owe me for that weekend."

"She's not wrong," Amanda replies with a nervous laugh.

"And how well do you know the Berlusconi family?" Detective Thomasina pushes.

"Not at all," I explain. "I spoke to them some throughout the weekend. I made some room changes in the room block to better accommodate all of their requests. Nothing out of the ordinary customer service."

"But someone reported you to be the one who escorted the bride to the ceremony," Detective Thomasina asks in an accusatory tone. "Is that true?"

"It is," I reply vaguely. "Is there a reason that's a big deal?"

"And what does this have to do with Seth?" Amanda adds.

Detective Thomasina slams her notebook closed. "Just trying to find out the real reason Seth went missing."

"What she means to say," Detective Lillian interrupts, "is that we are putting together a timeline for the weekend he went missing, and we don't want to miss any details. Sometimes the most minute details are what breaks a case."

"But why the focus on the Berlusconi family?" Amanda asks.

"We can't comment on an ongoing investigation," Detective Thomasina starts.

Detective Lillian interrupts her again, "Their presence here could all be a coincidence. The problem is the Berlusconi family doesn't trust outsiders easily. They seemed to trust both of you far more than would be considered normal for them." She turns to me before continuing, "And the fact that you spent alone time with the bride just before her wedding, makes you a person of interest when it comes to the family."

"But you don't think I had anything to do with Seth, do you?" I ask.

"We thought you had motive," Detective Thomasina explains. "But if you weren't part of the harassment claims, then it appears you might be a dead end."

"Is that a good thing?" I ask, feeling concerned that I'm a person of interest in his disappearance.

"I don't think you have anything to worry about," Detective Lillian explains. "I'd be sure to steer clear of the Berlusconi family if they return." She looks at Amanda before looking back over at me, "One more thing, why didn't you accept their invitation to get a room on the family?"

"I stayed with Amanda that weekend, in her suite," I explain with a shrug.

"Even though the family offered you your own room?" Detective Lillian gently pushes.

"To be honest, if Amanda hadn't already had a room, I'd have gone home for the evening. In the end, it felt safer to accept their offer rather than turning them down," I explain.

"It felt safer?" Detective Thomasina asks in a smart-ass questioning tone.

"That family creeps me out," I laugh, trying to be casual about my answer. I also want to be sure to leave Jared and his warnings out of it.

"You're not wrong about that," Amanda adds, also nervously laughing.

"I think we have everything we need from you," Detective Lillian says to me before turning to Amanda. "Thank you for your time, we can see ourselves out from here."

The two detectives turn and walk towards the portico together. They begin discussing something before leaving, Detective Thomasina looking back one last time as they exit the doors.

"What in the hell was that all about?" I ask Amanda.

"Shit if I know," she replies before looking at me. "I felt like they were interrogating me all day."

"How long have they been here?" I ask.

"They were waiting for me in my office when I got here today. The hotel manager already printed out copies of the room block lists and other accommodation requests they had made before I got in. Apparently, they had a warrant and everything."

"Shit, what for? This can't just be about Seth," I continue.

"They wouldn't say officially, but I think they're assuming Seth is dead. They said his family reported him as missing a few weeks ago, but they're investigating all angles," Amanda explains.

"That's suspicious," I state plainly.

"I mean, I won't miss Seth. He was shady as fuck though."

"I'm glad I don't have to dodge him in the hallways anymore, but I figured he just ran off and found a new job," I shrug.

"Maybe he did," Amanda says.

"Or maybe he didn't," I add, remembering what Jared said about Seth yesterday.

*   *   *   *   *

After Amanda heads back to the conference center, I walk back towards my office, thinking about what Jared said last night. Jared knows the Berlusconi family. He worked for them that weekend. He also mentioned that I wouldn't need to worry about Seth anymore. When I asked, he was vague when answering if the Berlusconi family had anything to do with it. Now, I'm wondering if they did. Those detectives sure seem to think so. What if Jared knows more? He was serious about the warnings. He wanted me to stay away from the Berlusconi family. He wanted our relationship to be a secret from them. But, why?

I shake it off and try to pretend like the secrets don't bother me. Jared has been nothing but honest with me. He's been protective from the start, even before we went out on a date. He was honest about the guns in his house and wanted to be sure I still felt safe with them around. Though, I'm sure I've been around them before without knowing. In New York City, I'm sure he's been armed plenty of times in the past. The point is, he has given me no reason to second guess him or his intentions. Maybe he knows more about Seth or maybe he doesn't. The point is, I trust him. It doesn't make me any less curious about what happened to Seth.

* * * * *

Later in the afternoon, just before packing up for the evening, my phone rings. "Ms. Franklin," I answer, not expecting a call.

"Ms. Franklin, this is Detective Lillian, we met this morning."

"Oh, right. What can I do for you, detective?"

"Well, I have a quick question I was hoping you could help me with."

"I can try. What's it in regard to?"

"A room reservation from the Berlusconi wedding. We have copies of all of the accommodations and room blocks, but there is a discrepancy we're wondering about."

"Okay. Give me one second to log in and I can see what it says on my end," I say, pausing while I get logged in. I quickly go back to history and open the Berlusconi room block file. "Okay, got it. What reservation are we looking for?"

"Well, there are several together. They were added the day of the rehearsal dinner. One is a suite, and the other are five separate rooms listed together."

"Added the night of the rehearsal dinner?" I ask, remembering a last-minute change. "Oh, wait...," I pause while opening the accommodations list. "Right. Here in the accommodations, Mr. Berlusconi requested a last minute add of 5 room for the rehearsal dinner band."

"And how is the suite related to that addition?" she asks.

"If I remember correctly, the band manager had requested, through Amanda, that the band either be moved closer to the banquet hall or have a separate room available near the banquet center."

"And were you able to accommodate them?"

"Let me check," I start while looking through the room reservations. Of course, I remember all of this, as it was for Jared. I want to be sure I say exactly what the room system says to cover my ass. "It looks like I noted that there was not availability to move all five rooms, so we added a single suite near the banquet center for the band to come and go as needed."

"Are those notes linked to the suite or the room reservations?" the detective asks suspiciously.

"They are noted in the accommodations file for the room block. I made a section for last minute band addition and noted all requests as well as follow ups. Amanda made the proper requests through Mr. Berlusconi to be sure an added suite was okay for the band. The band agreed to the accommodations."

"Oh, I see that now. I was looking at the wrong page. And what name were all of these rooms places under?" she asks.

I click through several room files to be sure they are all the same. Of course, I put them all in and know exactly what they say, but best to play it safe and not give away that I know more than I am offering up. "It looks like they were…"

I start, pausing to continue clicking through, "all under the band manager's name. Mr. Jared Wright."

"Are you sure?" she asks.

"Yeah. I mean, that's what all of the room reservations state."

"Can you see who registered all of those rooms?"

"Well, I added them to the room block reservation. There were some errors by the front desk that threw off some of the room block requests by the family. I made sure to take charge of any room changes and additions to be sure no further issues arose."

"Did you meet this band manager?"

"Yeah. I was in the lobby working on the initial room block issues when he checked the band in."

"Did you see him later that evening, at the rehearsal dinner?"

"I believe he was in the green room when I delivered the band meals after their set," I reply vaguely.

"So, he's a real person?"

I laugh, "From what I remember, yes. Is there something I'm missing here?"

"No, no. We've just been trying to track down the band members. The band itself doesn't seem to exist," the detective drops breadcrumbs.

"Yeah, they played pretty well, but they seemed a disorganized mess otherwise."

"Really?"

"Yeah, reminded me of a group of young college kids who play for fun, but have no real ambitions."

"You think the Berlusconi family hired a small band?" she asks, sounding surprised.

"I think Mr. Berlusconi hired them to please his daughter, not because it was his choice."

"That's a valid point. I'll look into it. Thank you, Ms. Franklin."

"Anytime," I reply just before the detective hangs up on me. "Okay…. Bye."

"What was that about?" Klarissa walks in to ask while she's putting on her coat.

"Those detectives again," I shrug.

"Now what?"

"Asking lots of questions about the Berlusconi wedding," I stand, grabbing my own coat.

"I thought they were investigating Seth's disappearance?"

"Me too," I reply, wondering if they really think Mr. Berlusconi had something to do with it, or not.

17

Jared was busy working the week after New Years. The last time I saw him was when he dropped me off at work the same morning the detectives came to the hotel. He said he didn't want to stay away for the next few days, but he might be out of town for a few jobs. He texted occasionally throughout each of the days to say he missed me and to simply say he was thinking about me. Each and every one brought a smile to my face, knowing that he cares enough to reach out and check in.

I didn't bring the detectives up right away. In fact, part of me wanted to wait until I saw him in person again. Jared called every night before I went to bed to see how my day was and to say goodnight. I considered bringing up the detectives in several of those phone calls, but always decided it wasn't the time or place. A week later, Jared was coming back to town, and I couldn't wait any longer.

"Some detectives came by the hotel asking questions about the Berlusconi wedding," I send in a text.

My phone instantly rings, his number showing up on my screen.

"Hey, babe," I answer calmly.

"What kind of questions?" he asks sternly, using his monotone voice.

"They claim they're investigating Seth's disappearance. They said they're looking into all possibilities and asked a lot about what happened that weekend."

"And what did you tell them?"

"Nothing they didn't already know," I shrug, wondering what has him sounding so worked up.

"Do they think the Berlusconi family had anything to do with it?"

"I don't think so. They just seemed curious about the timing of his disappearance."

"They following that angle?"

"No, I think they believe he took off after getting demoted from all of the harassment accusations from staff members."

"You're sure?"

"Yeah. They were making a big deal about talking to all of those employees when they came back yesterday. Apparently, they were all questioned about their last interaction with Seth before he disappeared."

"They think one of them had something to do with it?"

"Maybe."

"Were you questioned?"

"No, babe. I never had any reason to report him. They only talked to me about room reservation questions, nothing out of the ordinary."

"That's good."

"Are you, okay?" I ask, curious about his tone.

"Yeah, babe. I was just worried about you. I was afraid something had happened while I was gone."

"Nothing happened. Just business as usual."

"You're sure?" he asks, sounding gentler now.

"I'm positive. I would have told you if anything happened," I explain.

"You promise?" he asks, sounding his happier self again.

"One hundred percent, promise," I smile as I reply.

"Hey, it's time to go," I hear a male voice say in the distance.

"Babe, I've got to go," Jared whispers in his gentle voice. "I'll see you tonight for dinner?"

"Can't wait," I admit, feeling the butterflies in my stomach wake up at just the thought of seeing Jared again.

"Miss you," he admits.

"I miss you too. See you tonight," I say before he hangs up.

"Miss you," Klarissa teases in my doorway, clearly eavesdropping.

"Shut up!" I say, throwing a pad of Post-it notes at her face.

"Hey, now. What did the Post-it notes do to you?" she jokes as she picks them up and throws them back.

"They didn't hit you the first time," I joke as I toss them back onto my desk.

"Mister perfect coming back tonight?" Klarissa asks, sitting in the chair by my door.

"He is," I say, trying not to smile too brightly while she's watching.

"Date night?" she pushes.

"He's taking me to dinner, so yes," I admit.

"Does he have a brother? Or a cousin?" she asks for herself.

I laugh, "No, and I wouldn't let you torture them if he did."

"Hey! What did I ever do to you?" she asks, crossing her arms angrily.

"It's not what you did to me," I answer. "It's what you did to all those men you've dated."

"They just weren't worthy of my time and affection," she replies.

"That's what you're going with?" I joke.

"Anyways…" she says, changing the subject. "Coffee break?"

I check my watch, knowing I have all day to kill and nothing to do but wait for the day to end. "Yeah, why not. I have nothing else to do today anyways. I haven't had a day this clear in a long time."

"I know, right?" she laughs while standing. "I thought this job was going to be less busy than the front desk when I took it."

I stand and follow her to the back hallway to go up to the coffee shop just down the block from the hotel. "Well, if the front desk staff does their job right, then our job is much easier."

"Good thing we taught all those new managers the right way," she says brushing off her shoulders.

CLEANUP CREW | 161

"Yeah, I think that really did help," I suggest as we go to spend an hour wasting time in the coffee shop.

"Amanda!" I say, seeing Amanda in the employee hall, not far away.

"Hey, Amazia, Klarissa. What are you gals up to?" she asks while stopping to wait for us to catch up.

"About to go waste an hour or so at the coffee shop," Klarissa explains.

"Care to join?" I ask.

"I'd love to! Slow day?" Amanda asks.

"Thankfully, yes. You?" I return question.

"Not a banquet in sight for the next few days. I'm almost bored," she shrugs.

"Perfect timing for a nice long coffee break," Klarissa says, stepping between us and roping her arms through ours so we're all three walk down the hallway towards the exit.

* * * * *

"You not heading out yet?" Klarissa asks as she dons her coat.

I glance down at my phone to check the time. "Almost."

"I'm surprised you didn't take off early after such a slow day," she admits.

"I'm waiting for Jared to pick me up."

"Oh, right! Date night," she teases.

"I'll come in later another day this week, or duck out early, I don't know yet."

"Smart move," she says leaning up against the door frame.

"What?" I ask, as she leans against my door frame looking suspicious.

"How long have you two been dating now?"

"I don't know, almost two months I guess," I reply with a shrug. "Why?"

"You're just so smitten. It's adorable," she teases.

"Jealous?" I joke back.

"Entirely," she admits before standing up straight to leave. "Have a great night. I'll see you tomorrow."

"See you tomorrow," I wave as she heads out.

* * * * *

Jared promises a casual meal, and he almost keeps the promise. The atmosphere was nice and casual. Everyone is dressed casually, but the food is far from casual. I'm not sure Jared knows how to date someone without bringing them out to a fancy dinner. Not that I'm complaining either, but I'm just happy to not have to change into a dress every time we go out. I like to get all fancy once and a while, but I also like to just go out and be us.

We get a comfortable booth at the restaurant. Jared slides in next to me instead of across, stating he missed me too much to sit so far away. He keeps his arm around me the entire time until our food arrives. He even eats with his left hand to avoid elbowing me, what a gentleman. The butterflies in my stomach flutter the entire time, making it difficult to eat. I'm so glad Jared's back in town. I didn't realize how much I'd miss him. To say our relationship has grown over the few short weeks is an understatement. I really like, and I might even love him, though I don't dare to say it out loud. It's definitely too early for that.

After dinner, we walk around the block before returning to the car, just chatting and catching up while we walk hand in hand. We're about to head back toward the car when Jared's phone rings.

"Sorry, babe," he says, looking at the phone screen. "Crap, I have to answer this." He lets go of my hand and kisses my cheek before stepping away to answer the phone. "Yeah."

I can only hear a muffled voice, so I can't make out anything that they're saying.

"Wait, right now?" Jared asks, sounding angry about the timing of something.

More muffled talking.

"There isn't anyone else? I'm kind of in the middle of something," his angrily whispers back.

More muffed talking, which seems to grow more intense, though it's difficult to tell.

"Yeah, I understand. That's it for tonight though. You know I just got back to town. I can't keep running around on fumes."

More muffled talking.

"Fine. What's the address?" he pauses. "I'm heading there now. Give me forty minutes to get there and clean it all up."

More muffled talking.

"Oh good. They should be out of my way before I get there, right?" He pauses to listen. "Well, tell them to hurry up. I want them out of there before I arrive." Pause. "Because this is enough of an inconvenience without them holding me up." Pause. "Alright fine, but I'm not letting this turn into an all-night event." Pause. "Yeah, yeah. I'm on my way." He hangs up the phone and looks irritated about the call. He takes a moment to breathe and calm himself before he slides his phone into his pocket and turns to me.

"Everything okay, babe?" I ask as he steps back toward me.

He quickly reaches out and takes my hand back into his. "Yeah. Just need to make a pit stop on the way back home." He's trying to hide how frustrated he is. He's also back to his monotone work voice.

"Work?" I ask, intrigued.

"Yeah. Last minute job they need done immediately" he admits vaguely.

"I can always take the train back home and you can meet me back there once you're done?" I start to suggest.

"No way, babe," he stops, turning me to face him as he wraps his arms around me. He takes a breath before continuing in his gentle, caring voice. "I've been waiting impatiently all week to get back to you. One little job isn't going to ruin our night." He leans in and kisses me passionately on the lips, leaning further into me as I gently place my hand on his cheek, pouring all of the emotions I'm feeling into the kiss. After a few moments, he pulls back, both of us catching our breath as he leans his forehead down to mine. "I'll take care of the job quick, then we can find a way to snuggle the rest of the night."

"Promise?" I joke.

"Oh, one hundred percent, babe," he smiles down at me, leaning back to kiss me quick before taking my hand and beginning to walk back to the car.

18

Jared pulls up in a back alley behind an old warehouse. Snow has begun to fall as he parks the car. He hands me the keys before climbing out. "Keep the car running so it doesn't get too cold."

"You know how much I hate the cold," I smile.

"That, and I need you to stay in the car," he says, looking me in the eyes but using his serious voice.

"You actually visiting your other girlfriend in there?" I joke.

"No way. You're the only girl for me," he says leaning over to kiss me. "Call me if you need anything, okay?"

"Will do babe," I reply with a smile before he opens the door.

"Lock the doors," he instructs before closing his door and pointing.

Once I hit the lock button, he smiles and jogs toward the building. He walks up to a random door on a raised dock, clearly knowing exactly what door would be unlocked. "Not his first rodeo," I whisper to myself as I look around for any sign of anyone else in the area. This alley is a bit sketchy looking. I wonder what kind of a job Jared is doing in a place like this. He did say something about cleaning something up, I wonder what that means.

I try not to think on it too much, knowing if I overthink, I'll create a whole crazy story. I pull out my phone and check the weather. I didn't think it was supposed to snow today. Sure enough, the forecast has completely changed and they're now predicting an inch of snow in the city and over five inches back home in Connecticut. Looks like it'll be better to stay at Jared's tonight after all.

I hear a buzzing sound and notice Jared left his phone in the car. "Oh crap," I say, reaching over to pull it from the cup holder. "Call me if you need me? What do I do if you left your phone in the car?" I ask myself. I glance down at my watch and wonder if Jared is close enough to receive a text on his watch.

I shrug and wait for his phone to stop ringing to try and send a text. "Babe? You left your phone in the car." I hit send and wait, hoping to get a reply.

After a few minutes with no response, I put his phone back in the cup holder and shrug. Hopefully nothing happens out here. I look around again, suddenly feeling like this isn't a great place to be without him. I suddenly feel so alone. I send one more text, hoping maybe he moved closer by now.

"Babe, if you get this on your watch please respond. You left your phone out here."

Again, a few minutes goes by with no response. I go back to scrolling through the news on my phone. A few minutes later, Jared's phone begins to ring again. I glance at it, noticing an unknown number on the screen. Maybe it's just a telemarketer. The phone eventually sends the call to voice mail, but immediately starts ringing again. The same unknown number flashes on the screen. I pick up his phone and look, wondering why this unknown number keeps calling. As soon as the phone sends the call to voice mail, it begins to ring again, for a third time in a row. The fourth time it happens, I start to worry that this call is important enough to not wait.

I feel anxiety building in my chest as I try to decide what to do. Jared told me to stay in the car, right? So, clearly, I should listen and stay in the car. What if this call is important to why he's here. Since I have no idea what he's doing, I can't determine if this call could be important. What I do know is, his phone rarely rings. This isn't some scammer or telemarketer. This is important for some reason. I've tried texting him, but it clearly isn't reaching his watch. Clearly, he isn't getting notifications about this phone number calling him repeatedly, or he'd come get his phone, right?

Shit. What to do? I look down at the keys to the car. He left them with me so I'd leave the car running so I wouldn't get cold. But I could also use these keys to lock the car if I have to run inside to find Jared. My heart is racing as the phone rings again, for the fifth time, from the same number. I'd feel better ignoring his directions to stay in the car, than to answer this strange phone number. Maybe if it was a saved contact, I'd answer it, but this could be about anything really. Fuck it. I'm going in.

I unbuckle my seat belt, reach over to shut off the car, grab his phone and keys, and climb out of the car. I quickly close the door and lock the car before zipping my coat up further and jogging up to the dock. Once at the dock, I climb the stairs and am thankful for the awning blocking the snow from reaching up here. I walk forward towards the door that I saw Jared enter through, having no idea what lies on the other side. My anxiety builds and my heart races. This is a really stupid idea. I should have just stayed in the car.

I reach forward to grasp the door handle, wondering if I should turn back to the car. The phone rings again, pushing me forward even more. I take a deep breath and pull the door open as the phone stops ringing. I quickly slide inside as the door quietly closes behind me. Just inside the door is an empty and wide-open room. There is enough light to see all around me, but I don't see any signs of anyone. I look around to try to figure out where Jared might be. I can hear something in the distance. I walk forward slowly trying to figure out which way the sound is coming from. As I cross the room, I can see a light moving from the far right ahead of me. I slowly head that direction, trying not to make a sound as I move.

I start walking faster as I see someone moving in a room just ahead. As I'm about to round the corner into the room, the phone rings again. The loudness of the ring makes me jump out of my skin; I continue on trying not to make a sound other than the phone I can't stop. I walk forward towards the light, moving faster. I can see the shadow of someone moving towards me, and I hope it's Jared as I feel my heart racing even faster, if that's at all possible. I feel like my heart is about to beat right out of my chest as my anxiety grows with every step I take, and every ring of the phone.

I round the corner at the same time as Jared. I feel relief rush over me as I step into the room and it's him that I walk up to. "Jared," I say sounding breathless. I hold up his phone, "Your phone wouldn't stop ringing. I didn't know what to do since I couldn't call you. I tried to ignore it, but someone has called you like six times now." I hand over the phone, but Jared doesn't look happy. In fact, he looks like the serious and emotionless version of him, but worse.

"You should have stayed in the car," he says in the driest tone I've ever heard from him. He doesn't immediately reach for the phone which makes me suspicious. He looks stern and maybe even confused as to why I'm in here right now.

The phone rings again and I jump. "Shit, this phone," I say as I hold it out to Jared, hoping he'll take it now.

He reaches forward and roughly takes it from my hand. He looks at the screen and looks angry when he notices the number. "Don't move," he says to me before he answers. "What?" he barks into the phone.

I feel like I'm holding my breath as I wait for Jared to respond to whoever is on the phone. He is looking past me and avoiding eye contact. He feels so cold and emotionless as I watch him listen to whoever is on the phone.

"Well, that's unacceptable," he barks again. "You can't call me last minute then put me in a situation like this." He pauses to listen, clearly growing more frustrated by the minute. "Then get your ass down here and clean this shit show up yourself." He moves the phone away from his face and hangs up. He holds it in a death grip for several moments while taking several deep breaths. He closes his eyes for several moments as if that will help. I'm not sure if he's trying to calm himself down or lower his anxiety. In reality, this is a different person than the Jared I know, and I don't know how to react. I should have stayed in the fucking car.

After several agonizingly long moments, Jared slides the phone into his pocket, stands up straighter, and glances my way before glancing all around the room behind me. "You should have stayed in the car," he says in that dry tone again, but he isn't yelling, and he doesn't sound angry.

"I know. I'm sorry. I'll go back," I start as I go to turn around. The problem is, as I step to turn away, I see past Jared for the first time. The room behind him is large and well lit, which is exactly how my mind is able to capture the pure horror in only a second. "Jared..." I say in shock, as my mind tries to process.

Jared doesn't make a move. In fact, he's frozen still as if he can't move. His demeanor remains serious and emotionless as my anxiety reaches a whole new level as my mind races, trying to process the room in front of me. There is blood everywhere. It looks like a scene from a horror show or something. My mind cannot process it fast enough, but I can tell there is at least one body on the floor in the middle of the room, and possibly another on a raised surface at the far end of the room. I try my best to not focus on it, but it's too late. My mind is racing and Jared is just standing there.

"Is that..." I start, unable to form words. "What the hell did I just walk into. I should have stayed in the car. I knew it was a bad idea to come in here, but that phone. Your phone was blowing up. Like literally one call was sent to voice mail, and the phone was already ringing again. It was crazy. It was going to drive me crazy," I ramble as word vomit continues to spill from my lips while Jared just stands there. "I should have listened. I should have stayed in the car. I can't stop seeing what I'm seeing. I can't turn around and turn back time, right? Is that possible? Time travel? Because if it is, I really need to rewind and listen to the voice inside of me yelling at me to stay in the fucking car."

"Listen," Jared finally says in a dry tone without moving.

"Listen? Are you going to talk to me like there isn't a dead body on the floor right behind you?"

"Two."

"Jesus Christ! Did you really just... What the fuck is wrong with me? I'm literally standing here arguing with a wall about, well... I'm arguing with myself. Maybe I'm just losing my mind, right? None of this is real. I've been in a coma and this is some alternate reality, right? Because I know I didn't just walk into some crazy murder scene. You're not a murderer, right?"

"I'm not a murderer," is all Jared responds with. His tone is still dry, but he's serious and I really want to believe him that he isn't a murderer. I mean, if he was, wouldn't I already be dead too? He makes no move to comfort me or try to explain. It's like he's frozen from my reaction.

"That is a dead body though, well two apparently. And that is a shit ton of blood, so like, what in the fuck did I just get myself into," I continue to stumble over random words that I cannot even process as they fall from my mouth like water over a raging waterfall. I feel my fight or flight systems kicking in as I automatically start to step backwards, away from the room and away from Jared.

As I take a few steps back, Jared finally moves, slowly following each step I take. As my steps move faster, I try to get away, but Jared catches up. He tightly grabs both of my upper arms, but not tight enough to hurt me, just enough to stop me. He stays there a moment, waiting for me to look up at him, but I can't. "Look at me," he whispers. His tone is still dry, but also pleading as if the good Jared is fighting to get out.

"I…" I start to say I can't, but he gently shakes my shoulders so I'll look up at him. When I meet his eyes, I can see the kind and gentle Jared hidden deep down behind this dry and serious mask he has on.

"Listen to me Amazia. Right now, I cannot be the person that I am around you. I know that doesn't make sense, but I can't hold you in my arms and comfort you right now, like you need. Trust me when I say I want to, but I can't at this moment. I promise to explain everything later, but right now I have to be a different person. I have to do my job. I cannot protect you from this right now. I need you to trust me and listen to everything I say. This is the only way to keep you safe right now. You shouldn't be here, but you're here now and I can't erase that. I have to do my job or it'll put you in danger too. Do you understand?" he is pleading for me to trust him, which is difficult with a dead body on the ground next to us. I want to ask a million questions. I'd probably start with, 'Did you kill him?', but I know from his tense tone and the grip he has on my arms, that this isn't the time or the place.

"Yes," I whisper out, unable to speak clearly as I stare into his eyes, searching for my Jared, knowing he's in there somewhere.

"Tell me that you understand," he pushes.

"Don't freak out. Listen to what you say. Do what you say. Yes, I understand," I reply in as monotone of a voice as I can muster as I try to hide my fear, my tears, and my emotions right now.

"Can I trust you to go back to the car and wait for me?" he asks.

"I don't know," I answer honestly.

He drops his hands and sighs heavily. He wipes a hand along his face in deep thought as he looks around as if he's going to find a solution. "I don't want you in here watching this," he whispers seeming frantic to find a solution. "Can you just go sit back in the car and warm it up until I'm done? I promise I'll explain everything, later."

"Later?" I laugh. Yup, I'm losing my mind. I'm laughing.

"Amazia..." he starts.

"I can't even comprehend what is going on," I admit with a laugh.

"I want you to go safely sit in the car while I finish up working, then we can both get out of here," Jared instructs.

"Okay, fine," I start. "I'll go sit in the car and try to act like nothing happened," I say with a shrug. I go to turn around and leave, but before I can, there is another voice coming from the opposite direction.

"Jericho?" an unknown male's voice yells.

Jared looks terrified at that voice or the name, I can't immediately tell which. Who the fuck is Jericho? Is it one of the dead guys? Meanwhile, Jared stands up straight and the look on his face makes the hairs on my arms stand up at full alert. He'd warned me to stay away. He warned me that I never wanted to know about the rest of his life, but I fell too hard to stay away. I'm not sure who Jericho is or who the voice looking for him is, but clearly Jared is uneasy about it.

"Shit," is all Jared says before it's too late. "Just play along," he instructs at the last moment before the voice makes an appearance.

"Ah, Jericho, there you are," the unknown voice enters the bloody room from the door at the opposite end. The unknown male makes eye contact with me before looking up at Jared. "And who is this fine lady?"

"Recruit," Jared explains in his dry tone. "Isn't going too well," he says while side eyeing me.

"Looks a bit disturbed," the male says, looking me over. "The boss that desperate these days?"

"I think he's just stretched thin, especially with all of these last-minute work orders," Jared continues.

"Do we need to take care of her first?" the male asks with a shrug.

"No need," Jared says. "She's on her way back out." He turns and looks at me, tossing his extra set of car keys at me. "Go start the car and warm it up. I'll be out in five to ten."

"Yes, sir," I reply sternly, trying my best to play along. I avoid eye contact with the unknown man as I turn and leave the same way I came in.

"She at least a decent chauffeur?" the male asks as I walk away.

"Hardly, but she listens, so that's a start," Jared replies, still sounding in character.

"Not sure what happened to the crew that was supposed to get the bodies for you," I hear the male explaining.

"Yeah, it definitely put a speed bump on my clean up," Jared says, sounding annoyed.

"Well, I'll take the bodies and your trash. That way this place is emptied out before anyone comes looking for trouble."

"I appreciate that," Jared says.

"What about the girl?" the male asks.

"I'll deal with her later," is the last thing I hear Jared say before I walk out onto the dock and jog out to the car.

I run back out to the blue Camaro, noticing the snow is coming down even harder now. I quickly climb into the car and slam the door closed. I turn on the car and crank up the heat, trying to warm my body as well as my soul, which feels frozen and broken right now. The radio automatically starts as a song comes on that is all too fitting for what just happened.

19

As I sit in the car waiting for Jared to come out, I can't hold in the tears any longer. The song doesn't help, but I listen to the entire thing as tears gently stream down my face. I used to love that song, but suddenly it seems to have too dark of a connection to my life. I'm sitting here in his car, as if there was no bloody murder scene right inside of the warehouse doors. Am I next? Or am I just going to run right back into Jared's arms even though this lie is something we can't move past. What the hell does he do for work?

I start to think about all of his warnings about the Berlusconi family. I think about what he said about not having to worry about Seth anymore. I think of how he immediately called me when I said detectives were sniffing around the hotel. Are these all warnings signs? Were these all giant red flags that I ignored? Or am I just over exaggerating everything right now. I mean who wouldn't? That was literally a murder scene, right? And Jared acted like there was nothing odd about the whole thing. Is this what he does? Is he some kind of hit man?

I think I've hit my breaking point. My heart cannot take this anymore. I can't shut off my brain. I can't stop overthinking this entire thing. This is the end, right? But if I end it with Jared, does that mean I'm next on their hit list? I can't take the pounding in my head any longer. I reach over and open the car door, immediately climbing out to try to get some air, except I run straight into Jared.

"Shit," I say through tears.

"Get back in the car, Amazia," he says gently, but still in the dry tone from earlier.

"Just bury me and get it over with," I plead through the tears I can't stop.

"What are you talking about?" Jared asks, reaching out to grab my hand, but I pull away.

"Don't, Jared," I say as I stumble to the side to try to get away, tripping over something on the ground.

Jared catches me before I fall into the slush forming along the ground. "Amazia, stop trying to get away from me."

"Why should I do that?" I yell. "Is this entire thing over? Have you been fake as hell with me this entire time that we've been together?"

"Take a breath and get in the car," he demands.

"Take a breath," I laugh. "I can't even think straight right now."

"I know," Jared says sternly. "That is why you need to keep quiet and get in the car right now."

"Everything is up in flames. My entire life. My entire existence. My everything is you, it's all about you. So, how can I just ignore what happened inside and get into your car? Huh? How does that make any sense?"

"It makes sense in the middle of New York City at night," he explains.

"That's your answer," I laugh again as I try to pull my wrist from his hand.

He lets go and paces nearby for a moment before continuing. "How the fuck did everything get so messed up in one night," he says to himself.

"Care to explain any of that?" I ask, looking for something to convince me I shouldn't run for the hills right now.

"It's not what it looks like, not really," is his vague answer.

"Because that sentence explains *so* much," I reply at a whisper, trying to hold in the next round of tears trying to breach the surface.

"I didn't kill anyone. That's not what this was. That's not who I am," he vaguely explains. He sounds less dry and more like the Jared I know as we go.

"So, you just show up at crime scenes for fun?" I shrug.

"I show up where I'm told to," he stops pacing to reply with a shrug.

"And do what exactly?"

"Make it disappear," he shrugs again, clearly not knowing what to say.

"Wow, that explains so much and makes me feel so much better," I go to walk away again.

"Don't walk away."

I stop walking, waiting to see what he says next.

"Get back in the car."

"You think demanding I get back in the car is going to work right now?" I turn to him to ask.

"I think that keeping you safe is going to work. Get in the car, Amazia. Please," I can hear a slight pleading in his voice, but that doesn't convince me.

"You should have told me," I start, feeling the tears pouring out as the next round begins as I feel my head begin to pound with a headache from crying so much.

"I know," he whispers.

"What else are you hiding?"

"Nothing."

"How can I even begin to believe you right now?"

"Just listen and get in the car."

"Are you going to make me disappear too?"

"What? No. Never. It isn't like that."

"Isn't it though? I know too much. Isn't it time to get rid of me next?" I'm spinning, both mentally and physically as I feel myself losing my grip on reality.

"That isn't how this goes."

"I'm a mess. I can't even think straight right now. Where are we?"

"Get in the car."

"Again with the get in the car shit."

"Babe, listen to me," he says, stepping in front of me and putting both of his hands on my shoulders again and shaking me gently until I look back up at him. "I know you're upset.

I know you're scared. What I need from you right now is to let me get you home safely."

"Jared… right now… I just can't be here," I force out.

"I know. I get it. Once I get you home, I will leave you alone if that's what you want. What I am not going to do is let you wander around New York City alone in this condition."

"Jared," I start, unable to form words as I feel everything around me spinning.

"Amazia, listen to me. Get in the car," he is gentle but stern. He is back to using his voice that he reserves just for me. I can't deny the fact that the voice alone pulls me back into him, but I stop myself. "I have to get you home safe. I can't let you walk away from me out here, alone."

"Just bring me to the subway, I'll be fine," I say, knowing that's not really what I want either.

"Hell no."

"I'll be fine," I try to argue. It's a lie, I'm a mess and we both know it.

"You are an amazingly strong and independent woman, but I am not leaving you alone right now. You might not want to admit it, but you're freaking out right now. You have the right to freak out and be upset and confused and whatever else you're feeling, but you don't need to wander anywhere alone while you try to process."

"Process?" I ask, wondering how he could think I'd be able to process any of this.

"Yes, Amazia. You need time to process, and you can't do that wandering the city."

"Maybe," I reply, trying to consider what he's saying. "But it's snowing. You can't drive me all the way home in the snow."

"Don't worry about the snow. Let me get you home. Once I know you're safe, I will leave you alone if that is what you want."

"Fine," I say, realizing I'm not going to win this argument. Plus, I'm covered in snow and it's freezing out here. And let's be honest, I don't know if I'd make it home easily right now. I'm feeling confused and dizzy. I have no idea where I am or if this is all just a bad dream. I fell in love with an evil spirit, didn't I?

Jared lets go of my shoulders and gently grasps one of my hands to hold me up and lead me back to the car. As we approach the car he stops and turns me in front of him. "Babe…" he says.

I look up at him curiously.

"Don't give up on me so easily," he pleads gently.

"I can't make any promises right now," I admit, looking away from him.

"Let's get you back in the car. You're freezing cold," he says as he steps up to the door and opens it for me. Once I climb in, he makes sure I buckle my seat belt before he closes my door.

As he walks around the front of the car, I hear him trying to curse under his breath. "Fuck." He stops outside the driver's door and wipes his face one last time before climbing in.

"Jared?" I ask as he drives away from the warehouse. "Who do you work for?"

"Usually," he pauses, "the Berlusconi family," he admits.

"Who was that guy who showed up?"

"Another private contractor."

"Private contractor," I repeat then laugh.

I can see Jared glance over at me, but he doesn't say a word.

"What exactly is your job?"

"That depends on the day."

"What exactly was your job, today?"

"To clean up."

"Like the bodies?"

"No. That isn't my job."

"Is that why you were so mad when I walked in there?"

"No, not really."

"Then, why?" I ask glancing over at him for the first time.

"Doing this job means I need to turn off any emotions. I was already upset that this last-minute job was ruining our night. Then, I show up to find it wasn't even ready for me. Now, I was stuck doing double duty and you were out in the car waiting. I was terrified that I shouldn't have brought you. I figured it would be a quick in and out, but I hadn't even started yet when Anthony showed up."

"What is Anthony's job?"

"He just takes off the trash."

"What trash?"

"Any trash from the clean-up."

"So, this is like a whole long complicated process?"

"Something like that."

"And you don't usually deal with the bodies?"

"No."

"But you do this often?"

"Too often, yes."

"Every job?"

"Not that often."

This conversation is going nowhere, and my headache is getting much worse. I must give myself away by grabbing my head, because Jared looks over as I make a pained face and rub at my forehead.

"What's wrong?"

"I'm just overwhelmed and have this killer headache, which isn't helping."

"Close your eyes, try to concentrate on your breathing."

I laugh, "Yeah, because that is going to magically make everything better."

"Do you want me to bring you home and then leave?"

"I don't know what I want," I admit.

"Amazia, I need you to tell me if you want me to stay or go."

"Why does it matter?" I ask confused at his questioning.

"I've always told you I won't cross any lines with you. If you want to be alone to process and make a decision, then I will do whatever you need."

"I can't answer that question right now, Jared. I don't think I can even process who I am right now. I just went from thinking I loved you, to walking into a murder scene that will forever haunt my dreams."

"You thought you loved me?"

"What?" I ask, realizing what I must have said. "No, not like that," I lie. Shit, what an idiot.

"Just close your eyes, rest your head back, and breathe."

"I think I just need a few good hours of sleep."

"Maybe an entire night's worth," Jared suggests.

"Something like that," I say as I feel myself drifting off.

"How about this snowstorm?" I hear him ask before I must have fallen asleep.

20

I blink back crusty eyes, reaching up and feeling how swollen they are. As I rub my eyes, I remember the reason, all of the crying last night. The fuck happened last night? It all comes rushing back, the phone ringing off the hook, me walking into the warehouse, and the bodies. I roll over and look around and find no sign of Jared or anyone else. How the hell did I get home? I remember interrogating Jared in the car while he drove me home. I must have fallen asleep. I remember my head throbbing from a headache as we left the warehouse.

I throw on a hoodie over my clothes I'm still wearing from yesterday and search to find my phone. I see my bag on the dresser nearby and quickly check my phone and realize I'll never make it to work on time. I look at myself in the mirror and quickly realize that these puffy eyes are not going away anytime soon. Fuck it. I'm calling out. I dial my boss's number and explain I'm not feeling well and I'm going to use a sick day to be sure I don't bring anything contagious in. He's grateful and hopes I feel better soon. That was the easiest thing I'll deal with today. I turn on the shower and quickly shower off and change before venturing downstairs to see if I'm alone or not.

Once I make it downstairs, I can feel a silence that is only possible if I'm alone. I smell coffee though, and step into the kitchen to investigate. Once I walk in, I discover a note next to the full coffee pot. I pick up the note and look around, wondering if Jared waited for me to get up before he left, or if he brewed the coffee a while ago.

> Amazia,
> I don't know where to begin. The truth is, I never knew how to tell you about what I did for work. It's not exactly conventional. Once you helped me find my heart and my soul, I was afraid to tell you. I figured you'd hate me and never let me back in. Now you know, and I know that I may never get you back. Please give me a chance to really explain and show you that I'm the person you think I am.
> -J

"Men," I whisper before throwing down the letter and making a cup of coffee. I take my mug over to the couch and curl up under a blanket as I sip on the coffee. I think of last night and try to process any of it. So, he doesn't kill people, but he helps clean up after someone else kills people? Does that even make sense? This is usually done for the Berlusconi family. So, does that mean the warnings about the family are real? Does the family really have mafia connections like the hotel staff spread rumors about? And what about those detectives showing up and asking me questions about my connection to the Berlusconi family while they claimed to be investigating Seth's disappearance.

Yesterday was such a happy evening. Jared came back from being away for work for several days. Now I wonder what kind of work he was doing exactly. It's true what they say, the monsters really do come out at night. Is Jared one of them? Is he a monster? I always knew there were monsters in the world. Moving to New York City all alone felt like I was walking around with monsters creeping in the shadows everywhere that I went. Last night, I was in one of those shadows. Whether I was involved or not, I was at that crime scene. I was a shadow lurking around in the night.

Thinking about last night brings up a lot of mixed feelings. Walking into that warehouse ruined the night and forever ruined my opinion of the Berlusconi family. But with Jared, I feel like I can't just leave him behind. What if I take him back? What if I give him a chance to fully explain? Maybe we live happily ever after, and maybe he fucks up my entire life. Do I care? I can't stop thinking about him. I don't even care if he's a monster to some extent. He can fuck up my life as long as I get to keep him as mine in the end. Isn't that how true love works?

* * * * *

I take the rest of the day to catch up on cleaning and organizing around the house. I try my best to keep Jared off of my mind for most of the day. I consider reaching out several times. I even type a few text messages, but quickly decided against them, knowing I'm not ready to talk to him yet. My mind isn't thinking straight yet either. I need to make a decision about what I want and what I need before I try to confront him with what ifs.

Shortly after lunch, Klarissa texts me. "Are you okay?"

"Was just feeling under the weather this morning. Wanted to stay home and be sure I wasn't contagious or anything," I stretch the truth.

"Oh! Did you forget to tell Jared? He sent you flowers to work."

"He did?"

"Yeah, they're gorgeous," she sends with a photo of a dozen beautiful white and burgundy roses. "Doesn't the color symbolize something?"

Yes, the white ones are for innocence, and the burgundy for devotion, but I'll keep that to myself for now. "Maybe. I don't really know."

"Well, if you don't come in tomorrow, I'm stealing them."

"I'll be there tomorrow."

"Suit yourself," she sends before following up with, "And feel better soon!"

I don't dare ask her to send a photo of the card. I can only imagine what message he might have written on there. It may seem innocent, but I don't want to give Klarissa any reason to start harassing me about Jared all over again. Jared sending me flowers is enough to make my heart skip a beat, even under the current circumstances. Now I just need to wait and see what the card says so I can decide what to do next. Until then, I have snow to shovel.

I grab my coat, hat, gloves, and scarf and am about to wrap up in my layers when I look outside and notice that my driveway and sidewalk are already clear. I drop the hat and gloves on the table as I walk to look out of the front window. Not only is my property done, but also Mr. Brownstone's property next door. "Jared," I whisper to myself, knowing he's the only one who would have done this or paid someone to take care of it. I know this because he's the only person in the world, other than Mr. Brownstone himself, that knows I always take care of both properties when it snows.

I decide to go check on my neighbor since I'm already dressed for a walk outside. I walk over to Mr. Brownstone's door and knock. He quickly answers, "Amy!" he yells.

"Hey, Mr. Brownstone!"

"What can I do for you?"

"Well, I just came over to check on you. See if you needed anything."

"No, I think I'm alright. That nice young fella did a great job taking care of the place this morning."

"Oh, did Jared take care of everything himself?"

"The boy with the Camaro?" he asks.

"Yeah, that's Jared," I smile.

"He did around both of our front doors and around the cars. He hired some other young fella to finish the rest while he rushed off to work in the city this morning. Or at least that's what he told me."

"Well, I'm glad he was able to help us out," I smile gently. "You sure you don't need anything?"

"I am sure. Thank you, Amy!" he says as he waves and closes the door.

After I walk back to my house, I look out to the street, noticing the neighbors all working hard to clear the snow in their yards. "Is that asshole trying to win brownie points or something?" I ask myself. As I walk back inside, I kick myself for even thinking negatively. I know Jared isn't trying to win brownie points. He's helping because he genuinely cares. Knowing this warms my heart, but almost makes it ache as I try to decide what I'm supposed to do next. I can't just forgive him for lying to me, right? But does love conquer all? Would he even have me back after the way I reacted? Is Anthony going to run his mouth about someone else being at the warehouse? Is that going to get Jared into trouble? Will he be, okay?

* * * * *

The next morning, I get up and leave early. Part of me wants extra time after the recent snowstorm, but deep down, I just want to read the card that Jared sent with the flowers. I can't imagine what he'd say that he hadn't said in the note he left me at home.

As soon as I get to the hotel, I make a B-line for my office. I stop to hang up my coat and log into my computer before snatching the card from the flowers. I lean in and smell them, letting the fragrant flowers help calm my nerves. I open the card and hold my breath while reading:

A mazia,

I'm not sure how to fight for you but know that I'm not going to give up on us. You are my everything. If I knew how to do this, I'd do everything possible to get you to trust me again. I know it won't be easy, but please consider giving me a chance to explain.   - Jared

It's handwritten in his own writing. He obviously wanted the message to be private and didn't trust the flower company to get it right. Clearly, he's trying. I'm just not sure what I'm supposed to do in this situation. I meant it when I said I thought I loved him. I really wish I hadn't said that out loud to him, but I was definitely off my game that night. I remember the headache was so overwhelming that all I wanted was to close my eyes and sleep. I'd even go as far as to say it was a migraine which came on fast. The problem is, I don't know if the nausea was from the headache or the dead bodies.

I decide that the best thing for me to do is to sleep on it a few more times. I need a few days to consider what I want to do and more importantly, what I want to say to him. One way or another, we can't leave things the way we did. I don't want to let him go. I don't want to leave behind the best relationship that I've ever had in my life. I feel more comfortable around him than I ever did with my own family growing up. Granted, my family may not have been the best judge of what feels normal. The point is, I feel like Jared is a part of me. He is the piece of my heart that was missing. Him being around has filled a void that I never even knew existed. Something about our meeting was meant to be, and I cannot deny that.

Once I make the decision to forgive him, I remember the bloody scene that I walked into in that warehouse. Our evening had gone off wonderfully until he got the phone call for a last-minute job. I should have stayed in the car. Shit, I should have talked him into dropping me off at his place until he finished his job. Either would have saved me from a bloody murder mystery memory that I can never forget. Now I wonder what Jared really does for work, but even more, I worry that Jared and I might be in danger given that I wasn't supposed to be there, and I was seen. I'm not sure how the Anthony fella fits into everything, but I can bet it isn't good. He didn't seem super suspicious in the moment, but I'm sure he could sense my emotions were heightened during our encounter. I was able to hold back the tears until I made it to the car, but I'd bet my face said it all. I usually have a decent poker face, but I was too shocked to even try to control my facial expressions.

I don't even remember what really happened. I remember turning to leave before my brain processed what was going on in the room behind Jared. I remember rambling, a lot. Though, I really have no idea what it was that I said. I know I was freaking out. Surprisingly, it didn't freak Jared out. He stayed his cool, calm, dry, monotone, emotionless self the entire time. I do remember him approaching me at some point to say he wanted to comfort me, but he couldn't in that moment. I'm not entirely sure what he meant. Like, could he physically not comfort me because of what he was doing for some reason, or was it emotional. Maybe it was like an actor who can't break the fourth wall. Maybe Jared knew that if he broke down to his kind and loving self, that he wouldn't be able to turn back on his emotionless self to get the job done.

My phone dings. I reach into my pocket, pulling it out to reveal a text from Jared. "Did you make it to work okay today? I was worried when you didn't make it yesterday."

I smile then find myself biting my lip. Am I supposed to smile since he cares? Am I supposed to be creeped out that he knew I wasn't here? "I did," is all I reply.

"I'm sorry I hurt you. There is no excuse for lying."

"I just need some time," I reply honestly.

That was the last I heard from him for the next two days.

21

Two days later, I decide that I'm done over thinking everything. I'm off of work today and if I'm going to sit around at home and think some more, it's going to get me nowhere. No matter how many times I think about the two different ways this can go, I always end up back at the same outcome. It won't be easy. I won't get over it easily. It'll hurt for a while. But in the end, I know that I have to do what's right for both of us. I have to talk to him and set things straight. I have to talk to him about what he needs to do so that I can give him a fair chance.

I'm not sure I even know what a fair chance is. What I do know is that I can't keep circling around in my head with my decision. The lies are a problem, yes. The thing is, I don't think he kept it from me because he wanted to lie. I think he truly kept it from me to protect me. I keep thinking back to the hotel and the Berlusconi wedding. Even then, before Jared and I knew one another, he warned me. He told me to keep my distance. He told me to avoid the Berlusconi family. He told me to keep our distance, so the Berlusconi family didn't see us together. That part is beginning to make sense, at least with the small amount of information that I know.

In reality, I need to talk to Jared. I need to ask more questions and talk some things out. I want him to tell me everything, but I doubt he can. I want him to share what he can with me. I want him to share enough that we can move past this and get on with our lives, and our relationship. I don't want to give up the best thing I've ever had. I don't want to let Jared go. I can't let him go. He would take too much of my heart with him and I'd never recover. I honestly think it would be an even worse outcome for him. That's why I have to do something.

I grab my phone and start typing out a text. I write several drafts before I finally decide on something simple. "Do you have time to talk?"

After several agonizing moments without a reply, I toss the phone down on the counter and cross my arms. How is he not responding right away? Isn't he waiting for me to reach out? Maybe he gave up on the thought that I would. Either way, I'm expecting an answer. I try not to let myself get worked up over one text not being answered. Maybe he's working. Working. Now I'm back in that warehouse, looking behind him at all of the blood. I shake it off, knowing that reliving that moment in my head is never going to help anything.

I pick my phone back up and try another message. "Are you home?"

Again, I wait, but no response. I toss my phone back down on the counter and make my way upstairs. I'm just going to get dressed and ready for the day in case he decides to answer and I have to go into the city to talk to him.

After I get ready, I go back downstairs to find no missed messages. "What the hell?" I ask myself, feeling frustrated. I finally worked up the nerve to reach out, and he isn't even responding. I look around and notice that my house is a bit of a mess. I haven't really been in an upbeat mood the last few days. I left coffee mugs and dishes in the sink, dirty. I haven't folded the laundry or the blankets on the couch. I definitely didn't make my bed this morning either. I sigh, knowing I need something to do to pass the time while I wait. I decide to clean up all of these things and get the house back in order in case he's up for talking but wants to come here. If he hasn't responded by the time I'm done, then I'll try to reach out again.

When I'm almost done, I stop by the kitchen to check my home. Still nothing from Jared. I pick up the phone and call him, determined to get an answer out of him. The phone goes right to voicemail. His phone never goes right to voicemail though.

I type one more text. "Just tell me that you're alright…"

I toss my phone back down and decide to finish cleaning up before I let myself check the phone again. Once I finish up, I grab a bottled water, chug it, and reach over to check my phone. Still nothing. Nope, I'm not waiting any longer. I grab my purse and my keys off of the nearby table, slide on some sneakers, and grab my winter coat and scarf before racing off toward the front door.

* * * * *

Enough is enough. If he isn't going to respond to me, I'm going to confront him face to face. As I pull up outside of his condo, I notice his blue Camaro parked outside and know he must be here. I take a long deep breath and brace myself for what I might find before working up the nerve to go to the door.

As I make my way up the steps, I feel the anxiety building in my chest. It's a mix of worry about what I'll find, worry he doesn't want to see me, fear about what he's involved with, and the normal butterflies I get around him. It's overwhelming. Once I reach the door, I reach out and force myself to knock. I feel myself holding my breath while I listen for movement inside. At first, he doesn't answer and I hear no sign of movement. I knock again, with more force as my anger begins to build on top of the anxiety, thinking he is ignoring me on purpose. I knock obnoxiously a third time, without stopping until I hear him unlocking the door from inside. When he finally answers the door, I immediately notice that he looks terrible.

He looks like he hasn't showered in days. He looks disheveled and so unlike his normal self. His hair is a mess like he just rolled out of bed. His clothes look equally rumpled and askew. He's holding a bottle in one hand as he holds the door open with the other. He looks to be using the door to hold himself up more than to hold it open. He lets go of the door and struggles to remain standing.

"Well, shit…" he says, realizing it's me.

"Are you drunk right now?" I ask as he turns to walk back into his condo.

"I think that's what this feeling is," he replies in a slurred speech.

"But you don't even drink," I say without thinking. I follow him inside, deciding his walking away from the door was implied he wanted me to follow him inside. Although, it might be because he needs to sit down before he falls over. Either way, I walk into his condo and close and lock the door behind me as I go.

"You're right," he says before throwing himself down on the couch. "I don't drink. This isn't like me."

I walk over to the couch, unsure of what to say next. I stand in front of him, cross my arms, and stare at him. "What are you doing?"

He tips the bottle in his hand up as if looking through it. "I see a story at the bottom of this bottle."

"What story is that?" I ask, intrigued. I reach out and gently take the bottle from him.

"A good one. Great ending. Something I wouldn't expect or even deserve," he says slowly, stumbling over his words.

"Is the story about you sobering up?" I ask in a smart-ass tone, knowing he probably won't remember anyways.

"After that!" he replies loudly.

"I can't talk to you while you're like this," I say, turning to leave. I forcefully put down the liquor bottle on a nearby table as I go. I came here to finally have this conversation, but clearly now isn't the right time.

"But... No! Amazia, wait. Don't you leave me, Amazia. I need you," he pleads.

"You can't need me in this condition," I turn back to him and gesture towards his current state. "There is no place in your life for me while you're in this state," I say, trying to hide the sadness from my voice. "I came here to talk, but you clearly aren't ready to."

"But I do need you. You're my everything, Amazia," he stands awkwardly, as if he's trying to move like normal, not remembering how utterly intoxicated he is right now.

"Let's talk about this after you sober up," I say, turning again to leave.

I don't make it far before Jared runs up to grab my arm, as gently as expected from someone this drunk. He's more forceful than he means to be as he stumbles into me. When I turn to look at him with surprise in my eyes, he looks unsteady and possibly even nauseous. Before I can say anything he practically yells at me, "You're going to marry me, and we're going to have a family and live happily ever after away from all of this!" Jared demands this of me in as sturdy of a stance as he can manage. He looks serious as he says it.

"Jared..." I whisper, feeling my emotions getting the better of me as I become more overwhelmed in the moment. I almost feel breathless as the anxiety causes my heart rate to rise even more.

"Amazia, just tell me you love me," he pleads quietly.

"Not like this," I manage to choke out.

"But you do, right?" he looks genuine, but I can't take much more of him in this state.

"Call me when you're sober and ready to talk," I reply quickly as I practically rip my arm from his grasps before I run to the door.

"Amazia! Wait!" I hear him yell after me, but I quickly close his door to deter him from following me outside. I run out to my car, quickly turning it on to warm it up. I'm so glad I decided to drive my car here. I quickly put the car in gear and begin to drive away before my emotions get the better of me or Jared makes it outside. I don't look back as I drive away. Hopefully he'll forget this ever happened. What did I expect to walk into? At least I know he's alive. If he wants to have a serious conversation, then he needs to take it upon himself to get his shit together first.

22

It's been twenty-four hours since I left my house to go check on Jared. I'm off of work again today, but I can't stop thinking about the drunk Jared I found yesterday. He doesn't even drink, so why the intoxicated state? Was it because of me, or something else entirely? Is he lying about that too? I think back to his condo. It wasn't trashed or a mess. It was only Jared himself that was a mess. Though, in reality, with how long it took him to answer the door, he was probably upstairs in his bedroom. Maybe that's where everything looks trashed. For now, I need to find a way to clear my head.

I grew up land locked in Arkansas, but I had the lake. The house I grew up in wasn't full of holiday spirit and happy family moments, but it was on the lake. I remember the day I closed on the sale of it, I stood on the back deck looking out over the water. Since moving to Connecticut, I never once walked on the beach like I planned to when I picked this house. Of course, right now, in the middle of winter, it probably isn't the best idea. It also sounds perfect as I try not to think about Jared, especially after the condition I found him in yesterday.

I bundle up in all of the heavy layers that I can find before deciding to walk down to the beach. Why I don't drive is beyond me, but now that I'm here, it isn't so bad. My body heat from walking has warmed me up enough to not feel like an icicle as I slowly walk through the sand, kicking it as I go. The tide changing and the movement of the water means the sand is snow free. I try to imagine what the beach might be like in the summer. It doesn't get super-hot in New England for summer, but anything is better than this freezing air coming off of the sound at my face. I dip my face down into my scarf every once and a while, breathing out to warm up my face before exposing it back to the outside air.

I'm lost in deep thought of what the beach would be like in the summertime, as my mind quickly turns to what it would be like to walk on this beach in the summer with Jared by my side. I find myself smiling at the thought before quickly realizing the likelihood of that daydream coming true is slim to none after the interaction we had yesterday. I hoped that he'd sober up and call me by now, but clearly that isn't in the cards. Is that really how our relationship ends? Can we really end with a bloody murder and then a drunken mess?

Before I can think too much on the subject, I hear someone nearby clear their throat. It can't be. I quickly tell myself that it can't be him and to not get my hopes up. Then, I turn to look and am thrilled to see how wrong I am. Walking up to me is Jared. He is looking down and doesn't try to make eye contact, looking embarrassed. Maybe he remembers some of what happened yesterday. Maybe he remembers how he acted when he was drunk.

I continue walking, no longer kicking sand as I go. Jared walks closer before trying to match my steps, walking next to me in silence. The butterflies in the stomach lift off and take flight as I try to figure out what to say. I try to keep my breath steady as I prepare to speak. It takes me several minutes of walking in silence to work up the nerve to ask, "Are you feeling better?"

He takes in a deep breath before replying, almost like he's surprised I broke the silence. "I am," is all he says.

I need to just get to the point and not draw this out for too long. "Why are you here?" I ask after several more moments of silence.

He laughs before saying, "Getting right to the point."

I stop, looking over at him, not understanding why this is funny. "Yes, Jared. I'm getting right to the point. What else do you want from me?"

He looks hurt by my tone, and I instantly feel terrible. "I'm sorry. I just want you to know that I'm sorry." He looks away after he says it. I'm not sure if he's embarrassed or upset.

"Jared," I start. I pause to consider my reply carefully. "Why are you here?" I ask gently, watching him for his reaction.

"I need to explain what happened. I thought that the alcohol would help somehow. I thought it would make me feel better or make me forget. I realize now that alcohol doesn't solve any problems, it just suppresses them for a short time."

He pauses, still looking away from me and out into the water. "What I'm trying to say is that I'm sorry for drinking and I'm sorry for how I acted and I'm sorry that you had to see me that way and I'm sorry that I never told you the truth and I'm sorry for..."

I interrupt his obnoxiously long run on sentence, "Jared."

"Amazia?" he responds without looking.

"Jared, look at me," I say gently, wanting to reach out and touch his face, but thinking better of it for the moment.

He hesitantly looks over at me, looking worried as he does. In fact, he looks terrified. "Without you I couldn't think straight. The alcohol only made it worse, and I regret every single drop."

I can't deny the feelings I have for Jared. His statement about regretting every drop of alcohol only helps remind me of why I like him so much. Love isn't a walk in the park. It isn't a walk on the beach either. "I still get butterflies in my stomach when you're around," I admit.

"Amazia, I can't lose you," he says turning, looking deep into my eyes.

"After everything," I start, pausing to find the right words. "After everything that happened, after everything that I saw, I'm definitely... confused."

"That's to be expected."

"I don't want to lose you either, Jared."

Jared steps closer and reaches out to take my hand but waits for me to accept his hand before pushing me. "I'm sorry for lying about my job, and I'm sorry for drinking, and I'm definitely sorry for yelling at you about marriage and everything when I wasn't thinking clearly. I was just terrified of losing you."

"I know," I reply as I step closer into him.

He gently wraps his arms around me and hugs me close. I can feel the raw emotions rising in both of us as we stand there in each other's arms for several long moments. The warmth shared between us almost makes me forget about the ice-cold wind blowing off of the sound. "I wish we could leave and never come back," he says.

"But…" I wonder what the but is.

He pulls back, looking at me from an arm's length away. "Mr. Berlusconi doesn't let people go that easily," he says sternly, almost in the dry tone of the Jared I originally met.

"What does that even mean?" I ask in a pleading tone.

"There is so much I've been wanting to tell you," he admits with sadness in his eyes, a sadness I've never seen before.

"Then tell me," I push gently.

"What if it scares you away for good?"

"I'm not going anywhere," I admit.

He smiles brightly with tears in his eye. "I wouldn't even know where to begin."

"Would the beginning be too much to ask?" I laugh.

"Maybe," he laughs in reply. "At least for right now. It's kind of a long story."

"Then, what are the highlights?" I ask as I start walking back towards the parking lot.

"I work for Mr. Berlusconi, off the record," he admits.

"Doing what, exactly?"

"Cleaning up messes," he vaguely answers.

"Like the other night?"

"Just like the other night."

"Is that your only job?" I ask, remembering how he said he worked several small jobs.

"Not exactly. All of my work is for Mr. Berlusconi or one of his connections."

"And Mr. Vittori?" I ask, wondering how he fits into all this.

"He is very much like me. He works for Mr. Berlusconi. He's been with him for a very long time and pretty much goes everywhere with him."

"Why didn't you want them to know about us?" I have always been curious about that.

Jared sighs and stops walking. "You remember how I told you that I was complicated. How I didn't feel any real emotions before you?"

I nod.

He looks over at me before continuing, showing raw emotions as he does. "They hired me because of my lack of emotions. They knew I could handle the work without having feelings for what they were doing. They also knew that I'd never love someone; someone I'd have to lie to and keep secrets from."

"So, you didn't want them to know about me because you didn't want them to know that your emotions changed?" I ask, putting the pieces together.

"That was a large part of it, yes."

"And the other part?" I ask, reaching out to wrap my arms around his waist as I step in closer, trying to make him feel more comfortable as he continues to be deeply honest.

"I was afraid that they'd pull you in," he admits as he wraps his arms around me and pulls me closer.

"What do you mean?" I ask, looking into his eyes and feeling confused.

"I was afraid that they'd find a way to get you to work for them, if they knew about us."

"Why would they do that?"

"Well, with how fixated Mr. Berlusconi was on you during his daughter's wedding, I was suspicious. The way he acted and the way he constantly requested you was similar to how he generally grooms people to one day work for him."

"So, he tests them out to see if they're compliant?"

"Partly. He also tries to learn as much as possible about them. He likes to exploit any weaknesses. He tries to find something you want to lure you in."

"And you honestly think that was his plan for me?"

"I'm still curious to know if that was his reason for being at the New Years party."

"Didn't he ask you to work for him that night?"

"Yes, which threw me because he usually only invited me when there is something worth cleaning up."

"So, then why that night?"

"I honestly don't know. I asked for the night off and told him it was important to me. It took some convincing, but he gave in because I never ask for anything like that."

"Why me?"

"I'm not sure about that either."

"Why do I have to be good at my damn job?"

"For me it wasn't you doing the job."

"I know, I know. It was my charming personality," I tease.

"Something like that," he jokes back.

"You can't just conform to society and be normal, can you?" I ask in a joking tone.

He sighs before replying, "I'm never gonna be good enough for you. I can't change who I am, it's just too late to go back and rewrite history. I can't go back to before I got tangled up with the Berlusconi family... *We* can't go back," he explains.

"And I'm not asking you to."

"I know I ruined everything. I didn't tell you the whole truth and nothing will ever make the lies okay. Losing you means I'd lose everything. I'd do anything to get you to trust me again. I'd do anything to help prove to you how I feel. I'd do anything."

"I'm willing to give you a chance, Jared. I can't lose you either," I admit. "I want to trust you, I really do. I know this is complicated and I will have plenty more questions, but when it comes to you and me, I trust you completely. I know you'd never do anything to intentionally hurt me."

"I'd understand if you wanted to run away and say we're not meant to be. I can never go back to before you. You've changed me. You've awakened my soul somehow."

"I don't want to go back either. That was why I came to talk to you yesterday. I took my time to weigh my options and consider what I really wanted. In the end, I always came to the same conclusion. You are my heart and my soul," I admit, feeling deeply honest about my feelings for the first time in my life.

"I'm not who you thought I was, and I get that. I wanted to hide the truth, not because I wanted to hide anything from you, but because I didn't want you to see that side of me."

"I'm here for you, both sides of you. The good, the bad, the messy, and the secretive. I'm all in, Jared."

"I never expected you to say that after everything," he says before pulling me in to a gentle kiss. He pulls back shortly after to lean his forehead against mine and just holds me close. We stay there for at least a minute before he pulls back and lets me go. He reaches down to take my hand and begins to lead me back towards the parking lot. "Let's get you warmed up."

We walk hand in hand in silence for several moments while I work up the nerve to ask another question. "What's your real name?" I ask, remembering a different name being called back in that warehouse, when Anthony arrived.

"Jared is more of a nickname," he avoids the question.

"But, legally...?"

"Jericho," he shrugs.

"Do you hate it?" I ask.

"Kind of," he laughs as we walk up to his car. He opens the door for me to climb in, already running and toasty warm inside.

23

Jared brings me back home where he makes hot chocolate and forces me to go upstairs and take a hot shower. He says that I was outside alone for too long. He told me that taking a hot shower wasn't optional, so I gave in. I was truly in need of a shower anyways. He also told me to be sure to get dressed to leave. He wouldn't tell me anything else, but I went along with it.

When I get back downstairs, I start to question him more about his story. He explains that everything he said about himself and his family is true. He lied about his name for two reasons. One is because he hates it, and the other is because he avoids it since Mr. Berlusconi calls him by his legal name. I ask him more about what he does, without asking specific questions about what I walked in on the other day.

"Listen, I know you can't tell me everything," I say as I sit on the couch next to him with one leg tucked under me. I'm facing him as he does the same to face me.

"I don't hurt anyone," he says with a shrug. "That is not my thing, like at all. I just clean up things that are caused from someone being harmed," he says it slowly then immediately looks like he regrets his wording. "God, that sounded awful," he says, covering his face.

I reach out and take his wrist, gently pulling his hand from his face. "Babe. Don't hide."

"But what I do… it's awful," he admits, looking over as he lowers his hand.

"I can't deny that," I laugh, letting go of his wrist.

He smiles, "You're not scared?"

"Oh, I'm terrified. I'm terrified of a lot of things."

"Are you terrified of me?" he asks in a serious tone.

"No. I trust you completely," I say while I look him deep in the eyes.

"Even now that you know what I really do for work?" he asks.

"Is it really the mafia?" I ask.

"Yeah. Sorry," he shrugs.

"That's terrifying. But, yes, I still trust you. Maybe not the Berlusconi family, but you I trust."

Jared leans in slowly. He reaches his hand up and gently rubs my cheek with his thumb, making my heart skip a beat. He gently rubs his thumb over my lips before leaning in to passionately place his lips onto mine. He moves his hand back up and into my hair to pull me closer as our passion increases. Moments later, he pulls me over to him so I'm straddling him on the couch. The butterflies in my stomach take off all at once as he moves both of his hands to my hips. His mouth opens as our tongues explore one another's mouths. While I get lost in my exploration of Jared's smooth tongue, he gently grasps the lower hem of my t-shirt and pulls it up and over my head.

We break apart just long enough to look into one another's eyes. He looks deep into mine as if he's searching for permission. I don't dare give him an answer as I lean forward and return my lips to his. This time I lean in further and force his lips apart. I make the split-second decision to return the favor and pull at the lower hem of his shirt. We break apart as I slide his shirt over his head. In return he begins to kiss my neck and work his way down. He leans over, laying me down on the couch as he leans over me, continuing to kiss along my neck and collar bone. I find my fingers wrapped in his hair as he slowly makes his way lower.

He pauses along the top of my bra, trailing several gentle kisses along the top edge before leaning up to place his lips back on mine. This time much gentler than the moments earlier. After a few kisses, he leans down against me and leans his head against my shoulder. "Babe, I can't..." he whispers.

"I know," I admit, wishing I was wrong.

"What? How?" he asks, leaning up to look down at me.

"Because I know you'll never cross the line with me... at least, not until it's the right time."

"You really do trust me?"

"I really do," I admit.

"And you're okay with my obsession to never cross any lines with you?"

"It's one of the reasons I love you," I admit.

"You love me?" he asks, smiling ear to ear.

"I do," I smile, feeling my cheeks flush at my admission, biting my lip to hide my embarrassment.

"I love you, Amazia Franklin," he says, leaning in to gently kiss my lips again. Once he pulls back, he looks down into my eyes again.

"What are you doing to me, Jared?"

"What am I doing to you?" he jokes. "You're the one who found a heart inside of this frozen soul."

"And you thought you'd never love someone," I say before leaning up to kiss his cheek as I reach for his shirt, handing it back to him.

"I definitely never imagined I'd love someone amazing like you," he says returning the favor.

"The best is yet to come," I joke as I climb out from under him and slide my shirt back on.

*   *   *   *   *

Jared and I decide to venture out for an early evening dinner in town. We google the best spot since he isn't familiar with the area. Of course, that was after he gave me a hard time for not knowing all about the town that I live in. Let's be honest, other than when I was looking for a place to buy with the realtor, I haven't done much in this town except live in my house. I spend all of my time in the city, working.

Our dinner is rudely interrupted by a phone call. Jared looks down at his phone and his demeanor immediately changes. He ignores the call and sends a quick text back.

"Who was it?" I ask curiously.

"Mr. Vittori," he admits, looking upset.

"What does he want?" I ask at a whisper.

"I don't know. I told him I'd call after dinner."

I smile, knowing he's doing that for me. "Hey," I say reaching out and putting my hand on his. "Try not to over think every little thing right now. It's the only way we're going to survive this whole thing, together."

He smiles and does his best to take my advice. "What did I do to deserve such an amazing girlfriend?"

"I'm still trying to figure that out," I tease.

After dinner, Jared waits until we're in the car to call Mr. Vittori back. Jared looks upset as he listens to whatever he has to say. "But what specifically did he say?" Pause. "Do you think we need to worry?" Pause. "When is he going to tell Berlusconi?" Pause. "That soon?" Pause. "And we have no idea what else he knows?" Pause. "Yeah. I understand." Pause. "I really appreciate the heads up, man." Pause. "Alright. Yeah. Bye." He hangs up the phone and sighs heavily.

"Babe, what's wrong?"

He looks over at me, "Just a complication from the other night."

"At the warehouse?" I ask.

"Yeah. The guy, Anthony… he told Vittori you were there."

"Was he mad or something?"

"No. He called to warn me… to warn us. Anthony plans on telling Mr. Berlusconi all about it at their next event together."

"And when is that?"

"Tonight," he admits.

"Oh, great!" I say, feeling defeated. "So, what do we think that means for me? And for you?"

He sighs heavily. "We go on business as usual. Hopefully nothing comes of us. Vittori said he'll let me know what he hears tonight."

"Why did he warn you?" I ask curiously.

"He told me, when we were out of town together, that he saw a clear change in me. He knew I was happier, and he put the pieces together that you were the reason. He said he wouldn't tell anyone, but since we were already seen at the New Years party, he knew it was only a matter of time before Mr. Berlusconi said or did something about it. He promised to give me any heads up he could."

"Do you trust him?"

"I do. He's had my back plenty of times over the years."

"Well, let's hope that nothing comes of it."

"What you said," he jokes as he puts the car in gear and begins to drive us back to my house.

* * * * *

The next morning, Jared and I get up super early so he can drive me into the city. He has an event he has to go to with the band from the Berlusconi wedding, but he insists on driving me to work first.

"I thought you didn't actually work with the band?" I ask as we approach The Rush.

He laughs, "I don't. They work for Mr. Berlusconi, like I do. Apparently, I did so well at the wedding that I'm unofficially their day of event manager for any other event they go to."

"That sounds better than cleaning up messes," I shrug.

"Yeah, well... sometimes there are messes where that band goes," he admits, sounding disappointed.

"So, they... work for him, work for him?" I ask.

"Yeah," he admits before looking over at me. "They're multi-talented, I guess you can say."

"Interesting," is all I come up with as Jared parks in the portico of The Rush. "Thanks for the ride," I smile at him.

"Anything for you, love," he says before he climbs out and walks around to open my door.

"Always the gentleman," I tease as I climb out of the car.

"Only for you," he teases back as he closes the door. "Have a good day. I'll miss you," he says before pulling me into his arms, hugging me tight.

"I'm sure I'll be bored all day," I say before he pulls back to look at me. "It'll give me plenty of time to think about you," I smile.

He leans in to kiss me, only holding back because of our audience. "We're being watched."

I glance over and see the valet staff all looking our way. "They're just jealous," I shrug.

"I bet they are," he leans in and kisses me one last time before letting me go. "I love you, Amazia," he says with a gentle smile.

"Love you too," I smile before I turn to walk inside. I glance back as Jared opens his door but stops to watch me walk inside. I blow him a kiss as I step into the lobby.

24

The workday goes off as planned, nice and boring. Klarissa has the week off for some family reunion back home. She didn't want to go, but I talked her into it. The hotel is light for the next few weeks. There are plenty of conferences coming and going, but most do not have room blocks or room specific requirements. Most of our work is managed by the front office during slow weeks like this. I have lunch with Amanda to discuss upcoming room blocks. We decide to have it as a working lunch together so we can both leave an hour early today.

After work, I use the staff exit to head towards the subway. I'm not looking forward to the ride home today. I'd much rather spend my evening with Jared, but his event is going to last late into the evening hours. He offered to drive out to my house afterwards, but I told him we'll plan something tomorrow instead. I'll probably crash early tonight if I'm stuck home alone.

As I step out of the staff door, there is a strange vehicle parked nearby. It's stopped at the curb between the staff door and the crosswalk towards the subway. Something about it rubs me the wrong way. I decide to walk the opposite direction and walk around the block to get to the subway instead. While walking, I pull out my phone and text Klarissa about the car, knowing she'll be interested in the possible hotel gossip. She doesn't immediately reply, so I slide my phone back into my pocket just as I round the corner, walking right into a very tall person.

"Oh! Sorry," I start to say as I feel something slide over my head, covering my face, obscuring my vision. "What the hell!" I yell, trying to kick out at the person who has already wrapped an arm around me, practically carrying me towards the street. "Put me down!" I yell as I'm lifted into a nearby vehicle. "Well, shit," I say to myself under my breath.

"Just sit quietly," the male says as he ties my hands together behind me. Next, he pushes me into a seat and buckles me in. "Let's move," he says to someone else just before the vehicle starts to move.

"Where are you taking me?" I ask.

"What about sit quietly don't you understand?" the male asks in an annoyed voice.

"Apparently, the quiet part," I mumble to myself.

We drive through the city for approximately twenty to thirty minutes before we finally come to a stopping point. Even with the busy city traffic, we could be almost anywhere by now. Someone unclips the seat belt before grabbing a hand full of my coat and pulling. "Come on," he says as he drags me out of the vehicle.

"Geez, take it easy," I say as I fall out of the vehicle and onto the ground.

"Maybe you should learn how to walk," the male says in a smart-ass voice.

"Maybe I should watch where I step. Oh, wait! I can't fucking see," I reply, knowing I probably shouldn't be such a smart-ass with my mystery kidnappers, but what the hell.

"Come on," the male says as he grabs under my arm to help me up before ushering me forward. We walk fifty-two paces before he lets go to push my shoulder down. "Sit."

I cringe as I go down, thankfully landing on the chair. "Cozy," I whisper to myself.

I sit here in near silence for hours. I lost track of time around thirty minutes in. I can hear the male pacing nearby for part of the time before he finally sits down somewhere. After an incredibly long wait, I hear a cell phone buzz. Next, I hear the male walking towards me.

Moments later, someone pulls the hood off my head, revealing a large empty warehouse room. Great, this is the type of place they apparently like to kill people in. I look over and don't recognize the man standing nearby. I can see the hood in his hand, so he clearly is the one who pulled it off of my head. The skin on my wrists continues to chafe as I try to wiggle my hands free.

A few moments later, the door at the end of the room opens and Mr. Berlusconi walks in, followed by another man I've never seen before. I should have known this was all his doing. Well, at least Mr. Vittori isn't here to kill me, right?

Or did Jared say he's more like him? Maybe Mr. Vittori is part of today's cleanup crew. As Mr. Berlusconi gets closer, he's smiling like a perfect customer service employee would.

"So, this is how it ends?" I ask as Mr. Berlusconi walks up to me.

He laughs, "Oh, don't be so dramatic." He looks over at the male behind me and directs him. "Untie her."

The man comes over and silently cuts the rope holding my hands behind me. I immediately start rubbing my wrists to try to rub away the rope burn pain. Otherwise, I don't try to move or stand up. Clearly Mr. Berlusconi wants to talk or I'd already be dead.

"I'm the one being dramatic?" I ask, not caring if my smart-ass attitude shows. The man has already kidnapped me. Does he expect me to act like a princess after that?

"Well, thinking this is the end sounds a bit dramatic; don't you think?" he asks as he pulls up a chair to sit in front of me. He sits backwards on the chair to face me.

"Why am I here?" I ask directly.

"Just to talk," he says without a care in the world.

"And you don't think kidnapping me was the most dramatic way to have a conversation?"

He looks to be considering my words before he replies. "I guess you have a fair point there. The problem is, I like being dramatic when I can. I don't often get the chance to put on such a dramatic production."

"Oh, really?" I ask, intrigued.

"Can you think of a dramatic production?" he asks, clearly testing me.

"Your daughter's wedding was quite the show," I answer, covering.

He laughs, "And my daughter sure did love you. Did you know that?"

"No, sir. I wasn't aware of her feelings," I stretch the truth.

"So, tell me about your boyfriend."

"What about him?" I ask, knowing he's testing me again.

"How are you and Jericho doing?" he's reaching.

"We're doing fine. Why do you ask?" I try to turn the tables.

"The thing is, another associate reported that Jericho had a helper on a recent job," he pauses, waiting for my reaction. "The way he described them, it sounded an awful lot like you."

"When was this so-called job? I've never been with Jared while he's working."

"What about the wedding?" he lights up, thinking he caught me in a lie.

"Well, we didn't know each other back then," I shrug it off.

"Right..." he says, still looking for a way to get information from me.

"What did you and Jericho do the night he got back to town?"

"You mean a few days after New Years?" I ask, knowing exactly what he's talking about.

Mr. Berlusconi only nods in reply.

"Umm, let me think," I start, pretending to have to try to remember. "Jared picked me up from work, we went out to dinner, and on our way home he got a phone call. Said he had a job to finish up, but it wouldn't take long. He was going to drop me off at his condo, but I said to just go straight to the job and I'd wait in the car until he was done."

"And is that what happened?" he leans forward to ask.

"Yeah. I mean, some guy he works with saw me in the car. Came over to ask if I was lost or needed anything."

"A man?"

"Yeah. Tall guy, kind of squirrely. Said his name was Andrew or Anthony, or something like that," I shrug. "Why are you asking about him?"

"He's the one claiming you were with Jericho," Mr. Berlusconi looks at me like he believes every lie that I'm stretching.

"Well, I was with Jared that night. That doesn't explain why you kidnapped me and tied me up."

"Amazia Franklin. You are a very interesting woman."

"Me? How so?" I laugh at him.

"First off, you act like you know why Jared goes by a different name," he's testing me again.

"He hates his legal name. Why should he go by Jericho, when he absolutely hates it?" I shrug it off. Score one for me.

"Okay. Next question. What was he doing for work that night?"

I shrug again. "I have no idea. He said it was a quick task bunny gig. I don't think I asked any more questions about it."

"And you just trust him to pick up a random job in the middle of date night?"

"Gotta do what you gotta do to make a living," I shrug again.

"But you don't struggle for money," he's reaching here. He's trying to dig up my past.

"No. Not really."

"Old family money?"

"Deceased family money. Does that count?"

"So, they were wealthy?"

"No, not exactly. I just sold everything off and moved across the country," I answer, trying not to tell anything too personal or revealing.

"Moved across the county?" he asks, looking genuinely surprised.

"Yeah. I've only lived in New York City for a little over a year," I shrug, wondering why this has him so interested. What could make such a simple fact about me pique his interest that way?

"Amazia... where did you move from?"

I wonder if I should answer him, but it's not like he wouldn't find out if I kept it from him. "Arkansas. I moved here from a small town in Arkansas."

"Interesting," he says as he pulls out his cell phone and begins an aggressive text. He continues texting for what feels like forever until he finally hits send and puts his phone away. "What did Jared tell you?"

"About...?" I ask, pretending to not know what he's asking.

"What he does for us?" he gets right to the point.

"Like, the time he was a band manager?" I play dumb and I think I'm really pulling it off.

"Something like that."

"I feel like I'm missing something here. Either that or I have no idea why I was kidnapped and interrogated," I do my best to be convincing. In reality, I'm worried enough to not have to act that part out.

Mr. Berlusconi stands and begins to pace in front of me. He looks to be contemplating what he says next. "Okay," he says as he continues pacing. "Maybe Jared told you and maybe he didn't. What I do know, is that now... you're roped in through your connection with him. So, one way or another, you're a part of all of this."

"Part of all of, what exactly?" I ask, trying not to sound as terrified as I feel.

"The Berlusconi family has certain standards. To keep all of those intact, we have a large number of employees. Some are full time while others are more of an under the table type of employee."

"You're saying that Jared works... under the table?"

"Precisely," he stops pacing for just a moment before beginning again. "Some of my under the table employees know a lot more about my family and my business than even my top full-time managers."

"That sounds odd," I continue to play dumb.

"You really have no idea what I'm talking about?" he stops to stare at me.

I shrug, "I really don't think I do."

"Jericho didn't tell you?" he looks serious.

"Since I have no idea what you're talking about, I'm going to say… no."

"Just let it be known that if you're called upon, you will be required to do as you're told. You are just as much a part of this as Jericho is now."

"I'm still not sure what that means," I smile awkwardly.

"Go home. Ask him what I'm talking about. If he doesn't tell you, I will." Mr. Berlusconi turns to the man who's holding the hood that was previously on my head. "Lorenzo, go ahead and drop her off at Jericho's front door." Mr. Berlusconi walks away without any further explanation. "We're not the bad guys Amazia. Just remember that," he looks back to say before he exits the room.

As soon as he leaves, the man behind me comes back up, quickly throwing the hood back over my head. "Keep your hands to yourself so I don't have to tie them back up," the man says grumpily before forcing me to stand by grabbing my upper arm and pulling me up.

25

I'm not sure where the warehouse was, but after getting into the vehicle, we drove for over an hour before we finally reached our destination. The male pulls the hood off my head as we stop on the side of the road. I can tell by looking out of the windshield, that we're on Jared's street.

"Here is your cell phone and your backpack," Lorenzo says, handing me back my phone and pushing my bag over to me.

"That's it?" I ask.

The male shrugs, "I just follow orders."

"And those orders were...?"

"To drop you off here at nine o'clock P.M."

"Specific," I mumble.

"You have several missed calls and texts to attend to," he says gesturing toward my phone.

I look down and unlock the phone, finding a few messages from Klarissa and a lot from Jared. There are also twenty-two missed calls, all from Jared. "Shit..." I whisper to myself before pulling up missed calls to dial his number.

"I'd appreciate it if you could exit the vehicle first. I don't want to be caught in the crossfire," Lorenzo shrugs while opening the door for me.

"Lucky you," I say as I climb out and onto the sidewalk just down from Jared's door. I hit the call button as soon as my feet hit the sidewalk.

"Just the messenger," he says before slamming the door and driving away.

"Amazia! Where are you? Are you okay? I've been worried sick!" Jared rambles as the vehicle drives away.

"I'm okay. Are you home?" I reply vaguely. I want to know if I'm about to be stuck out here alone in the cold before I say anything.

"I'm two blocks away, why?" he asks, sounding concerned.

"I'm here," I reply.

"At my house?" he asks, sounding surprised.

"It's a long story."

"Babe... tell me what's wrong," he sounds gentle, but demanding.

"Can I just wait until you get here?" I ask, looking around, wondering if anyone is watching.

"Are you sure you're alright?" he asks, sounding concerned.

"I will be once you get here," I say as I walk towards his front door.

As I approach the door, I hear a car pulling up and know it's his even before he says, "I'm just about there."

I sit on the front step before he pulls up and parks. He immediately climbs out and runs around the car toward me. Once he has eyes on me, he hangs up the phone and I do the same. I tuck my phone into my coat pocket and watch as Jared runs up to me, looking scared, which I've never seen before.

"Where have you been?" he asks, pulling me up to standing and looking me up and down. He looks to be going over me inch by inch, head to toe.

"Can we just go inside?" I ask, feeling like we're still being watched.

"Are you okay?" he tries to look me in the eye, but I glance around us instead of making eye contact.

"I am now that you're here," I admit.

Jared places his hands on my cheeks to try to get me to look at him. "Babe, you're freezing," he says before quickly dropping his hands and pulling his keys from his pocket. He grabs my right hand and pulls me with him towards the door. Once he unlocks it, he quickly pulls me inside and locks the door behind us. He takes my bag and places it on a nearby chair before helping me get my coat off. He tosses my coat onto the chair with my bag before tossing his down with it. He gently wraps me in his arms, and I finally give in and make contact.

"It's been a long day," I admit.

"What happened after work?" he asks as he searches my eyes. "You said you were leaving then went silent."

"I didn't have my phone," I vaguely say, not wanting to admit what happened to him.

"Come on. Let me make you something to warm you up. You're still freezing." He takes my hand and leads me to the kitchen. He switches on the light and lets go of my hand only to brew a cup of hot water. When he turns, he looks down and notices the marks on my wrists. "Amazia!" he reaches down and grabs my wrist, pulling it up to inspect it. "What the hell happened?" He looks into my eyes, trying to read my mind.

"It was nothing, really," I shrug it off.

"This isn't nothing," he grows harsh.

"Mr. Berlusconi has a flare for the dramatics," I admit.

"What did he do to you?" he ask, pulling my arm without knowing, clearly growing frustrated enough that he doesn't notice his death grip on my arm.

"Babe. I need you to take a breath first," I try to calm him.

"Not until you tell me what he did to you," he demands.

"I'm fine. Nothing happened to me. But... I need you to breathe and loosen your grip," I gently say.

He looks down and notices his death grip and immediately lets go. "Shit, babe! I'm sorry! Did I hurt you?"

"I'm fine," I say as I reach up with my other hand to rub his cheek and try to calm him.

"I would never forgive myself if something happened to you," he says, leaning into my hand. He reaches up and covers my hand with his.

"I'm perfectly fine. He just wanted to talk," I begin to explain.

"With your wrists tied together?" he asks angrily.

"He didn't exactly invite me over for tea," I joke, but clearly Jared isn't up for humor.

"What did he want?"

"To ask about the night Anthony saw me."

"And what did you say?"

"That I was in the car and some guy said he knew you and asked if I was lost."

"Did Berlusconi believe it?"

"I think he did," I shrug.

"Did he hurt you in any way?"

"No," I admit, looking into his eyes to convince him.

"Babe…" he leans in, placing his forehead on mine as he gently wraps his arms around me, folding me into his arms. "I'm never letting you out of my sight again."

"You can't protect me twenty-four hours a day," I tease.

"Watch me," he sounds determined.

"I played it off like I know absolutely nothing about what you do," I continue.

"And he believed you?"

"Sure seemed like it."

"Then what?"

"He said to call you and ask you. He said that if you didn't tell me, he would," I shrug.

"Did he say anything else?"

"That one way or another, I'm roped in because of my relationship with you."

"Shit," he whispers.

"What do we do now?"

"I don't know," he says, pulling away gently before reaching for the cup of hot chocolate and handing it to me. "Come on," he says, leading me to the couch. "Do you need anything from home?"

"Umm, no. I mean, I can manage without going home," I shrug.

"You're more than welcome to stay here tonight."

"Are you giving me a choice?" I ask in my teasing voice.

"Kind of," he smiles. "You can stay here or we can both go to your house."

"We can stay here," I smile.

"Good. Easier to keep an eye on you here."

"What are we going to do about Mr. Berlusconi? I can't say you wouldn't tell me anything. I definitely don't want to hear his explanation."

"I'm sure he'd try to convince you that he did nothing wrong."

"He already said for me to remember that he isn't the bad guy," I shrug.

"How does he think he's not the bad guy?"

"Mental illness?" I joke.

"Maybe," he laughs. "In all seriousness, we need to figure something out." He sits in deep thought for a moment. "Amazia, with you I can't simply control how I feel. I never had emotions like this before and I can't turn it off when you're around."

"Okay."

"The night that you walked in on me working… I couldn't go to you. I couldn't wrap my arms around you and comfort you like I so desperately wanted to."

"Because you were afraid to turn it on," I state, understanding what he's getting at.

"Exactly. If I turned on the side of me that cares so deeply for you, I doubt I could have turned it off to finish the job. There is no way I could do my job with a love filled energy, that wouldn't feel right."

"I understand that."

"I needed to finish that job. There is no turning back once you're assigned a task. There is no getting away from a job that Mr. Berlusconi lines up for you."

"What does that mean for me?"

"I want to tell you to lace up your shoes and run. You can't give him an inch or he'll take a mile."

"But I can't run as long as I'm with you."

"He'll tear us apart, Amazia. I can't lose you, not like that. Don't give him a chance."

"He can't tear us apart. I won't let that happen."

"You're my one last shot here, my last shot at redemption. You're going to save me."

"I wouldn't say all that," I joke.

"I want to get out, but I can't. I *can* keep you out of it. You can escape it still."

"I'm not going anywhere or doing anything without you."

"I so badly wanted you to be my escape, but I can't figure out a way to break out. I'm dying to get out and be with you without all this extra drama and nonsense. I'm a hostage to the Berlusconi family. Don't become a hostage too," he pleads.

"I'm a hostage as long as I'm with you."

"That's why I have to get you out."

"No, babe. I'm standing my ground. I'm not giving up on you and I'm definitely not giving up on us that easily."

"It'll be dangerous."

"And I have you to protect me."

"I couldn't protect you today," he looks down.

I reach over and gently lift his chin with my hand. "I'm fine. No one hurt me."

"But your wrists!"

"Unnecessary complication. I shouldn't have been pulling at them so hard to try to break free."

"Don't say that. You did the right thing by trying to fight your way out."

"I know, that's not what I mean. If I wasn't fighting them, you wouldn't see a mark on my wrist. I did that to myself."

"This isn't your fault."

I interrupt him. "I know. I'm just explaining that you did nothing wrong. I trust you and I know you'll do everything you can to protect me."

"I love you too much to lose you," he says with passion in his eyes.

"I promise, I'm not going anywhere," I whisper as I climb over closer to him.

"I'm going to hold you to that," he whispers, pulling me onto his lap.

"I hope you do," I whisper as I lean down, gently placing my lips on his as he wraps his arms around me to pull me in closer.

He returns my kiss, gently at first, then suddenly turning more and more passionate until I again feel his tongue exploring mine. His hands gently explore as we continue, until he gently breaks off, pausing to catch his breath.

"Amazia?" he asks.

"Yes, babe?"

"Can we move this upstairs?" he whispers.

"Yes, please," I whisper back just before his lips crash back down on mine.

He stands, lifting me up with him. I wrap my legs around him to keep from falling. Jared carries me upstairs and gently sits me down on his bed. His hands slide down to the bottom of my shirt before he lifts it up over my head. Our lips only part a moment before I reach up to pull his lips back down to mine. After a moment, he leans me back onto the bed, following me as I go. He hovers over me; his lips never leave mine until he moves them down to my neck before exploring further.

After several moments, he pauses again. He leans up so he can see my reaction when he asks, "Is this okay?"

"More than okay," I admit.

He smiles gently and brings his mouth back up to mine. "I love you, Amazia," he whispers before he begins to line kisses down my neck again, as he continues to explore further.

26

I wake up to find Jared's arm wrapped around me, holding me close. As soon as I blink my eyes open, he tightens his grip. "Good morning, beautiful."

"Good morning, love," I reply while rolling over to face him.

"You sleep, okay?" he asks, searching my eyes for something.

"Amazing. You?"

I watch surprise in his eyes at my answer. "Amazing huh?"

"Yeah," I lean in and kiss him.

Shortly after Jared and I shower and get dressed for the day, we meet in the kitchen, where Jared has my fresh cup of coffee waiting for me.

"That t-shirt looks better on you," he says as he hands me the coffee cup.

"I'm not so sure about that. It looks pretty hot on you," I tease.

A moment later, Jared's phone rings. "It's Vittori," Jared says before answering and putting it on speaker for me to hear. "What's up?"

"What the hell happened last night?" Vittori sounds frustrated.

"Wait, was he not there?" Jared covers the phone to whisper to me.

"No," I whisper as I shake my head.

Jared looks perplexed by that news. "Were you not there with Berlusconi?" he asks, even though he now knows the answer.

"I was on another assignment," he replies vaguely.

"Then what do you know?" Jared asks.

"Nothing! Absolutely nothing! He kept everything from me. What did he do?" Vittori asks.

"Well… he kidnapped Amazia," Jared says with a shrug.

"What the hell! Where is she? Is she okay?" Vittori starts to question, sounding surprisingly concerned.

"She's with me, now. She's okay," Jared smiles gently at me.

"Did Anthony tell Berlusconi about his run in with her?" Vittori asks.

I nod in confirmation.

"Yeah, he did," Jared relays.

"Did he hurt her?" Vittori sounds mad.

"No," Jared wraps an arm around my shoulders and pulls me into his side. "Few rope burns on her wrists, but she's okay otherwise."

"Shit, Jericho. I'm sorry. I promised to keep you in the loop."

"No, no. This isn't your fault. He figured you'd tip me off. He knows us too well," Jared explains.

"He's probably testing me now," Vittori suspects.

"Likely. You need to lay low and pretend you know nothing extra about Amazia," Jared instructs.

"I'll do my best, but I'm on a mission to deliver a message," Vittori explains.

"What kind of message?" Jared asks, glancing at me in a curious way.

"I'm on my way to tell Amazia that Mr. Berlusconi requests a meeting with her, tomorrow."

"Where?"

"The Rush."

"She's calling in sick," Jared says, shrugging to me for validation.

I nod, taking out my phone and texting my boss that something came up.

"I'll try to act surprised when I get there. Probably a good idea, calling out."

"Well, I doubt she can go the entire day with these rope burns without someone getting suspicious," Jared says while holding up my wrist to inspect it.

"You know he'll tell me to use you to get to her, to deliver the message?"

"I'd bet on it," Jared acknowledges.

"Your house?" he asks.

"We'll go to Amazia's, in Connecticut. Get her out of the city for the day."

"Good idea. I'll meet you guys out there after lunch," Vittori explains before hanging up.

"He knows where I live?" I ask.

"I told him how far away I was a few times he tried to call me for a job while we were out there," Jared explains.

"So, Mr. Berlusconi knows too?"

"Likely, but not necessarily."

"He seemed very interested in the fact that I only recently moved out here," I remember.

"What do you mean?"

"He asked about money. He insinuated that he thought I inherited old family money. When I said it was just deceased family money from selling all their things before moving to New York, he perked up. He seemed surprised at the revelation. Then he asked where I moved from. I was worried I shouldn't say, but at that point I had no idea what his intentions were. Once I said Arkansas, he pulls out his phone and started to text someone."

"That's odd."

"I have no idea why it interested him so much."

"Me either," Jared says, looking in deep thought.

"What are we going to do about this meeting?"

"We'll see what else Vittori has to say, and then we'll go from there."

"I can't avoid it, can I?"

"No, but you can avoid going alone," he says, pulling me into a hug, wrapping one arm around my lower back, and the other cradles my head down onto his shoulder.

* * * * *

Once rush hour dies down, Jared drives us out to my house. Once we get there, Jared does a sweep around the house, looking for anything out of place. He also checks on all of my window and door locks, to be sure they're all in working order.

"Is this all really necessary?" I ask.

"One hundred percent," he answers sternly.

"Should I just stay with you for a while, or something?" I ask.

He stops what he's doing and looks over at me, surprised. "I wouldn't want you to give up your own space."

"I'm not saying I'd give this place up, just yet."

"Then what are you saying?" Jared asks curiously.

"This place is pretty far from the city, our jobs. It isn't the most convenient place to go to and from right now, under the current circumstances," I shrug.

"It is harder to keep an eye on you while you're out here alone," he agrees.

"Would it be crazy to suggest?" I ask, not wanting to bring it up completely.

"Amazia," he says as he comes closer, reaching out to wrap me in his arms. "Would you move in with me?"

"Are you seriously asking, or just because I'm in danger?"

"Oh, I'm seriously asking. I already looked up how to ask. I was just waiting for the right time."

"Is it the right time, now?" I wonder out loud, remembering last night.

"Now or never," he teases.

"I'd love to move in with you," I admit, knowing its true, even if I'll miss this place.

The doorbell rings.

"Ugh, Vittori has terrible timing," Jared teases, kissing my lips before letting me go to answer the door. "Come on in," I hear Jared say after he opens the door.

"Hey, Amazia," Vittori says with a wave as he walks into my living room.

Jared makes his way back over to me and protectively wraps an arm around me. "You here to deliver a message?"

Vittori laughs, "As you know, Mr. Berlusconi requests Amazia's presence tomorrow."

"Sounds fun," I mumble sarcastically.

"What do you think we need to expect?" Jared asks.

"Anthony told Berlusconi that he saw Amazia at that warehouse. I can only assume that's why he wanted to talk to her alone yesterday," Vittori explains.

"But why the theatrics?" Jared asks.

"That's what I said," I add in.

"My best guess," Vittori shrugs, "is he wanted to scare her or both of you."

"Into doing something he wants?" Jared continues.

"Probably," Vittori confirms.

"Did Berlusconi believe what Amazia told him?"

"He said she was waiting in the car the whole time. He thinks Anthony went out to confront her to cause some trouble."

"So, he believed me?" I ask.

"It looks like it," Vittori says.

"How do we know?" Jared asks.

"Because Anthony is no longer employed," Vittori says looking suspiciously at Jared.

"I see," Jared replies, understanding something that isn't being said aloud.

"Why weren't you there, yesterday?" I ask Vittori, wondering why Berlusconi's right-hand man was absent from a meeting with me.

"I thought my assignment last night seemed odd, for me. He never sends me out to stake out a possible hit unless it's with him. That being said, I went along with it and didn't question it. Then, I received a text to drop it and meet Berlusconi at his house first thing in the morning. He sent another text that said I needed to find someone to hack into some Arkansas records."

"Arkansas?" I ask.

"Does that mean something to you?" Vittori asks me directly.

I glance up at Jared before looking back at Vittori. "That's where I lived, before I moved here, a little over a year ago."

"Curious…" Vittori says, looking in deep thought.

"Any idea what the connection is?" Jared asks.

"Not yet, but I'll look into it. I know he wanted some family records. I'm not sure if it's connected or not. Could be a coincidence."

"Do you know who was with Berlusconi last night?" Jared asks.

"Yeah. New office guy named Colt," Vittori says.

"Colt replacing you?" Jared jokes.

"I sure hope not," Vittori laughs. "But if that's the case, I guess you'll find out after the fact."

"Yeah…" Jared replies awkwardly.

"Sorry," Vittori says while glancing over at me. "Didn't mean to bring that up."

"It's okay," I admit, trying not to think about the bloody warehouse again.

"Listen," Vittori starts. "We're all in a tight spot here. Clearly, Berlusconi doesn't trust me to not tell you what's going on," he says to Jared. "He might just be covering his ass by bringing Colt in, but we gotta be smart about all this."

"Any suggestions?" Jared asks.

"Honestly, no. I have no idea what the safest decision is. We need to be sure we all stick to the same story," Vittori starts. "What don't I know?"

"We met at the wedding, but we didn't start talking until I ran into her outside of the hotel a week or so later," Jared starts.

"And I made it clear that I stayed in the car that day at the warehouse" I shrug.

"And Berlusconi thinks you don't have any idea what Jericho really does for the family?" Vittori asks.

"Yeah, but he said if Jared doesn't tell me, he will," I reply.

"What are we gonna say you told her?" he asks, looking back and forth between the two of us.

"If you came in here today, to deliver your message, and I asked what this was all about... what would you say?" I ask.

"Shit," he says scratching his head before crossing his arms. "Jericho?"

"Well obviously she knows the truth. So, I guess we'd tell her that the Berlusconi family pays me to help cover up evidence against them?" Jared shrugs.

"That's a good start, but she'd have to know the details," Vittori shrugs.

"Okay... I tell her about what happened inside the warehouse. Since Berlusconi asked her about that night, I'd explain how I was just supposed to clean up, but whoever was supposed to collect the bodies never showed up. That's why we were still there when Anthony showed up and got suspicious of her being in the car."

"You okay with that?" Vittori asks me, looking for me to break or something.

"Yeah. I mean, I'm not giving up on Jared that easily," I reply, hugging him closer.

"You know he's going to count her as in now, right?" Vittori asks Jared.

"Yeah. He warned her about that yesterday," Jared admits.

"She doesn't have a choice now," Vittori adds.

"I get it," I admit, making sure he understands how serious I am about staying.

"If something goes bad between you two... that doesn't change anything with the Berlusconi's," Vittori continues.

"We get it," Jared says, pulling me closer.

"Alright," Vittori says before looking over at me. "Be at the house tomorrow at noon."

"The house?" I ask.

"Jericho knows where to go," he nods toward Jared.

"I'm going to talk to him first," Jared adds.

"And I'll do my best to listen in," Vittori steps up. "We're in this together now, all of us. We just can't let Berlusconi know." Vittori steps up and Jared lets me go to shake his hand before seeing him out.

After Jared closes and locks the door, he turns to me as I say, "And so it begins."

"Let's pack up some necessities and get back to the city," Jared says, picking up a box and handing it to me.

"You grab the coffee, I'll grab some of my stuff," I joke.

"Oh, I'm not letting you out of my sight. We're both going upstairs to pack your stuff," he teases.

"Suit yourself," I joke as I turn and walk toward the stairs. Once on the first step, I glance back at him and see him smiling as he follows me.

27

The next morning, Jared lets me sleep in while he makes breakfast. Once he's finished, he comes upstairs to wake me. "Wake up sleeping beauty," he whispers as he lays on top of the covers next to me.

"What time is it?" I ask as I roll over towards his voice.

"Almost nine," he says while gently brushing the hair back off of my face.

"What? Really?" I ask while my eyes open suddenly.

"Yes babe. You clearly needed your beauty sleep."

"Shit," I say, sitting up. "Good thing I called out of work already for today too."

"Don't sweat it babe," Jared sits up with me and reaches out to hold my hand, bringing a smile to my face. "What's wrong?"

"What?" I ask, not realizing I was in a daze.

"Is something wrong?"

"Oh! No. I'm just overthinking everything."

"You're worried about your meeting with Mr. Berlusconi," Jared states without question.

"Obviously," I admit with a shrug.

"I'd be concerned if you weren't scared."

"I'm more worried about you," I explain.

"Don't worry about me. I'm going to protect you no matter what."

"I'm just worried something will happen to you."

"You can't get rid of me that easily," he teases. "In all seriousness, I'm going to talk to Berlusconi myself first. I'll see if I can figure out what he wants from you."

"Any idea what it might be?"

"No clue. I really wish I did, then maybe we could prepare."

"At least I'll have you," I smile.

"At least you'll have me," he repeats with a smile before leaning in to kiss me. "Get dressed. Breakfast is getting cold."

*   *   *   *   *

Jared drives us to Mr. Berlusconi's house, or at least one of them. I'm happy to learn that none of his family currently resides at this residence. I was worried that I might run into the daughter and have to explain to her why I was there visiting her father. Jared talks me into staying in the car for a short time, until he has the chance to talk to Mr. Berlusconi on his own.

I wait impatiently in the car for what feels like an hour. I glance at my watch and realize it's only been ten minutes. I shrug and decide ten minutes is all that was necessary. I climb out of the car and make my way inside, the same way that Jared went. Once inside, I follow the right hallway until I hear Jared's voice nearby. I follow it to a door, and gently lean closer to try to hear the conversation going on inside.

Mr. Berlusconi is the one talking as I reach the door. "Jericho, you know why I picked you. I picked you because you had no emotions and were so dry. You had no feelings which meant you could not hurt anyone. You would not have to lie to anyone. I chose you because you would not love anyone; and now all of this with Amazia has changed everything."

"I'm still a human being!" Jared argues. I'm surprised to hear him getting into a heated debate with Mr. Berlusconi, after all of the warnings he's given me.

"I guess so. A human being who finally grew a heart. Are you going to grow a conscience next?"

"Maybe..." Jared replies awkwardly.

"Have you already begun to?" Mr. Berlusconi asks suspiciously.

"Not for the work I do," Jared replies sternly. There is an awkward pause between them. Without being able to see, I suspect they're either both giving each other the stare down or avoiding eye contact with one another altogether.

"You know I would have paid you to be at that New Years party," I hear Mr. Berlusconi start back up, jumping to the first time he saw Jared and I together, as a couple.

"I was not going to step away to do a job for you while I was spending time with her," Jared quickly replies.

"And you know what...? I don't hate that for you. I'm glad to see she's pulled something out of you. Something that I did not think could possibly exist within you anymore," Mr. Berlusconi continues.

"Well then, leave her out of all this," Jared practically demands.

"You know I can't do that, especially with what she knows now," Mr. Berlusconi's voice is calm as he gives Jared his answer.

The next thing I know, I'm jumping in the air as someone whispers in my ear, "Are you enjoying the show?"

"Geez, you scared the crap out of me," I admit at a whisper.

"Maybe if you weren't eavesdropping, you'd be more aware of your surroundings," Mr. Vittori says as I turn to look at him.

I fight back the urge to roll my eyes at him, remembering Jared's early warnings about the Berlusconi Family. It's probably safe to think that those rules apply to Mr. Vittori as well, at least in this setting. Jared may trust him, but I'm not as trusting of him just yet.

Mr. Vittori steps closer to the door before he says, "We might as well just go in. It's not like he's going to hide anything from you now. You know too much."

"Is that a threat?" I ask.

"No, that's a promise," Mr. Vittori says with a charmingly evil smile. After several moments he steps into the doorway and motions for me to proceed ahead of him.

"Why is everything always so complicated," I whisper, more to myself than anything.

"You have no idea how complicated it really is," Mr. Vittori whispers back, almost like he's revealing his true feelings on the subject. I begin to glance back but quickly stop myself as I see Jared and Mr. Berlusconi notice Mr. Vittori and I walking up.

"Ah, Amazia! What wonderful timing," Mr. Berlusconi starts. "Jericho and I were just talking about you," he sounds delighted, as if the said conversation was going well for anyone but himself.

"She was waiting outside," Mr. Vittori says, keeping my eavesdropping a secret. Maybe he's on our side after all. "Didn't think it was worth making her wait, given the... circumstances," he says while nodding towards Jared.

"No, no. That's probably best," Mr. Berlusconi agrees. "We should have just asked them to meet here together."

"Isn't that what we were just discussing?" Jared dares to ask.

"And I think I made it very clear," Mr. Berlusconi says in a final tone while looking at Jared. After a long beat, he looks back to me. "Though, I only think it's fair if we let Amazia make her own decision on this matter."

"Are you actually going to let her choose?" Jared asks as calmly as I think he can manage.

"Of course," Mr. Berlusconi begins, "because I know she'll make the right choice." He looks over at me with a smile which looks genuine, almost like a politician posing for a camera. After a moment he looks away and begins to walk towards the back door. "Vittori, be sure they exit the property safely before we head out to our next meeting," he says as he leaves the room.

"Yes, sir," Mr. Vittori says, waiting for Mr. Berlusconi to leave before making a move or saying a word. Once he's gone and the door closes, he glances at me before looking over to Jared, "You know this isn't going to end the way you want it to."

"That's what I'm afraid of," Jared replies, seeming more casual with Mr. Vittori.

"You're stuck now, both of you. You're better off to just accept it and move on," Mr. Vittori suggests to Jared. "At least she knows what she's getting into."

"Does she?" Jared asks, glancing at me briefly before quickly looking down and away.

"She knows more than we did. And… she has you," Mr. Vittori adds gently.

This interaction between Jared and Mr. Vittori is strange. Their guards are down some since Mr. Berlusconi left the room. They seem to genuinely trust each other, at least to some extent. It's also clear that Vittori doesn't want to talk openly in this house. "Can we just drop this for a minute," I say without thinking.

I watch them both turn to look at me, surprised I spoke up. Mr. Vittori waits for me to continue, and when I don't, he looks to Jared. Jared looks torn, maybe even hurt. He also looks like he's trying to hide it. The problem is, if he never really had emotions or feelings like this before, he has no idea how to hide them or control them either. After several moments, he collects himself and comes over to my side and gently wraps on arm around my back, "I'm sorry, Amazia."

"Don't be sorry, just… I don't know… stop talking about it as if I'm not standing right here."

"She was eavesdropping outside," Mr. Vittori gives me away.

"Why didn't you tell Mr. Berlusconi that part?" Jared asks. I can feel his arm tense around me as he waits for Mr. Vittori's answer.

"I didn't lie," he shrugs. "Maybe left out part of the truth, but I would never get caught in a lie around here," he evades Jared's actual question.

"But, why?" Jared gently pushes.

"You're the closest thing I have to an ally around here, Jericho. I won't put myself on the line for you if it came down to me or you, but I'd rather have you on my side in this shitty world we're both stuck in…" He glances over at me briefly before adding, "We're all stuck in."

"So, you're saying that one way or another, I don't really have a choice?" I ask.

"I'm saying that you do have a choice," Mr. Vittori begins. "You get to choose your involvement level. You can either be involved and follow whatever direction you're given, or… you can be involved through Jared."

"Like by association?" I ask.

"Something like that," Mr. Vittori shrugs.

"Either way, there is no turning back," Jared says gently. "I don't want you involved in any of this…"

I interrupt, "Jared, I know that, but we can't turn back time. I should have listened to you. I should have stayed in the car, then none of this would have happened."

"That's not entirely true," Mr. Vittori chimes in. "Things were already in motion back on New Years Eve."

"Seeing us together at the party sealed our fate?" Jared asks.

"I'm afraid so," he admits. "Now, if it makes you feel any better, Mr. Berlusconi has had his eye on her since his daughter's wedding. One way or another he was going to find a way to employ her."

"Why can't I be shitty at my job?" I whisper under my breath to myself, but they both hear me.

"No good deed goes unpunished my friend," Mr. Vittori says.

"I'm short on good deeds," Jared says to him.

"You have a decision to make," Mr. Vittori says as he motions for us to head towards the front doors. "I say you consider the options and consequences and go from there."

"Do you really think we have any choice?" Jared asks as we walk to the front of the building.

"I think you get to choose her level of involvement," he repeats. "I'd choose to keep her disconnected as much as possible. Let her only be connected through your relationship."

"And you think that'll work?" Jared asks.

"I honestly have no clue. Your guess is as good as mine. No one has been in the situation before, at least not during my time working for him," Mr. Vittori admits. "What I do know is that Amazia interests Mr. Berlusconi. That in itself should help keep her safe. He also really appreciates you, Jericho, and all that you've done for him over the years. I wouldn't take that lightly."

"Thank you," Jared says, letting me go to shake Mr. Vittori's hand before Mr. Vittori goes back inside to lock up.

Jared reaches out for my hand, gently taking it and walking me towards the car. "We need to keep you as far away from all of this as possible."

"I just don't know if he's going to let me," I admit, my brain feeling overwhelmed with a decision I can't possibly understand the consequences of.

"We're sure going to try, Amazia," Jared says as we get to the car. "Whatever happens, I'm going to keep you safe. Don't you ever forget that."

"I know," is all I can reply as he wraps his arms around me, holding me close for a few moments before releasing me to open the car door for me.

I climb in and wait for him to come around and start the car.

28

The next week goes by without a word from Mr. Berlusconi. Even Jared admits that he hasn't heard from him at all either. Jared has been working for several other connections, but not directly for Mr. Berlusconi, which is unusual. Jared tried to reach out for Vittori this morning to figure out what's going on, but he didn't answer. I wonder if Vittori has called back since Jared dropped me off at work. It's been a busy week at The Rush. We have several different conferences in house, and it's been complicated the entire time. From room block changes, to a burst pipe in the last available room in one section, to the conferences overlapping, it's been insanely busy. Klarissa and I have been working at the front desk and with housekeeping to help run everything. I haven't even seen her much this week.

Things finally slow down around lunch time. It is the last day for two of the conferences, and both of those have large end of the week events in different ballrooms. Most of the conference guests are in the ballrooms, keeping them out of our hair for most of the day. I text Klarissa to meet me for lunch in the staff cafeteria once she's free. I grab my tray and eat, looking around for her, and I'm still not seeing her anywhere. I check my phone just as a text comes in from her saying, "Get to the front desk ASAP. You have a visitor."

"Shit," I whisper aloud to myself, unsure of who it might be, but having my suspicions. I clear my tray and pull out my phone while on my way toward the front desk. I text Jared, "I have a mystery visitor at the hotel," before sending Klarissa a follow up text of, "Who is it?"

"Any idea who?" Jared replies.

"No clue. Klarissa didn't say who, just that I had a visitor," I reply, followed up the shrugging emoji.

"Be careful. Keep your phone on you," he replies, sounding paranoid and protective even through written word. Maybe it's just because I know him, but if he's worried, I'm worried.

"I'm on my way to find out who it is. They're in the lobby," I send to Jared just before I step out of the employee doors and right into someone standing on the other side.

"Oh, sorry," I begin as I slide my phone into my back pants pocket and look up to find a familiar face.

"Amazia! Just who I was looking for," Mr. Berlusconi beams at me.

I look for Vittori, but don't see any sign of him. "Mr. Berlusconi, what are you doing here?" I ask, trying not to sound as freaked out as I suddenly feel.

"I came to see you, of course," he replies as if I should have been expecting him.

"What can I do for you? You having another event that we need to prepare for?" I ask, not sure what he could want from me while I'm working.

"I'm here about a different type of employment," is all he says, looking serious, as if I'm supposed to read his mind.

"Is this something we really need to discuss here?" I ask at a whisper.

"Well, I've been waiting for your answer," he begins noting the face I'm making. "Though, I'm guessing Jericho hasn't been passing on the messages I sent."

"What messages?" I ask, suddenly wondering if Jared has been hiding something from me.

"Maybe Vittori forgot," Mr. Berlusconi whispers under his breath before taking his phone out and glancing through it for a moment before looking up. "Yup, that's my fault. I double booked him earlier this week." He looks up at me as if I'm supposed to understand what that means.

"I'm sorry, is there something I need to know?" I ask, feeling as confused as ever.

"Coffee?" he asks, gesturing toward the front doors of the lobby.

"I'm not so sure that's a great idea," I reply hesitantly.

"It's just coffee in the coffee shop on the end of the block," he explains. "Text Jericho and tell him where we're going if that helps."

"I'm not so sure that will be helpful," I admit.

"He's protective of you. I like that."

"Do you?"

"Of course, I do. Amazia, I'm not sure what he's told you about me or about what he does for my family, but I'm not the bad guy here."

"Are you saying that Jared is?"

He laughs, "Of course not! Jericho is one of the good guys."

"Then what are you saying?" I ask, determined to get to the bottom of what I'm supposed to infer about this conversation.

"Can we go for that coffee now?"

"I can't just leave in the middle of my workday," I throw in.

"I'm sure you can make an exception for a working coffee break."

"So, you are planning another event?"

"Not exactly."

"Amazia! There you are," Amanda walks over, clearly out of breath. "I've been looking everywhere for you!"

"Amanda, what's wrong?"

"The evening performance for the realtor conference just canceled, stuck in Iowa in a snowstorm. And, then there is the..." she begins, but pauses as she looks over and realized who I've been talking to. "Oh, Mr. Berlusconi. What are you doing here?" she looks back and forth between the two of us.

"Good afternoon, Amanda. I'm sorry to hear your day isn't going as planned. Perhaps I can be of assistance?" he replies.

"I'm sure these problems are below you, sir," she says, sounding unsure of herself. I myself wish she hadn't said such a harsh thing to him.

"You'd be surprised at what I can assist with in a pinch," he replies to Amanda. "Isn't that right, Amazia?" he turns to me.

"You betcha," I say awkwardly, trying to sound enthused.

"Know a band that can play tonight on short notice?" Amanda questions.

"As a matter of fact, I believe I do. Excuse me for just a moment to make a phone call. What time is the performance?" he asks while pulling his phone back out.

"Band goes on at six," Amanda replies.

"Give me a moment," he says before stepping away towards the portico while dialing a number.

Once he's out of earshot, Amanda comes closer to whisper, "What is Mr. Berlusconi doing here, and why are you talking to him?"

"I was called to the lobby for a visitor," I shrug. "I still have no idea why he's here."

"After those detectives came snooping, I'm not exactly trusting of him and his family," Amanda admits.

"Were you trusting of them before?" I ask.

"Maybe... No, you're right. I was just terrified of them, there's a difference."

I laugh, "You got that right," I reply while pulling out my phone and quickly texting Jared while Mr. Berlusconi is out of sight.

"Do you think he'll actually have a band here tonight?" Amanda asks, trying to find him outside among the crowd of people coming and going.

"There is no doubt in my mind," I admit. I slide my phone back into my pocket and look around, wondering when he'll come back.

"What is going on with you… and Mr. Berlusconi?" she asks.

"That's a long story that I couldn't even begin to explain. I've just crossed paths with him a few times since his daughter's wedding and I can never seem to distance myself enough," I admit, while remaining as vague as possible.

"Well, stay clear if possible. He seems like bad news," Amanda says.

"Says the one taking advantage of his connection to a local band," I joke.

"Okay, after tonight, stay clear," she laughs.

"Deal."

"Is he doing this out of the kindness of his heart, or is there something he wants?" Amanda asks as Mr. Berlusconi enters the doors across the lobby from us.

"Oh, he definitely wants something," I whisper to her before he's close enough to hear.

"Great news, ladies! I've got you a band for tonight," Mr. Berlusconi says as he approaches us.

"You're kidding?" Amanda asks, looking shocked that he really pulled it off.

"No ma'am, I don't kid. And even better news, it's someone you two both know," he continues.

"The band from your daughter's wedding?" I ask, already knowing the answer before he asks.

"How'd you know?" Amanda asks me.

"Lucky guess," I shrug, but inside my brain is turning, trying to figure out his angle here.

"They'll be here at four to set up and be ready to play at six," Mr. Berlusconi explains.

"Great! And what can I do for you, to return the favor?" Amanda asks hesitantly. "Are you planning another event here at The Rush?"

"Not at the moment," he replies to her before looking at me. "Amazia will take care of paying me back, don't you worry."

"You can get back to it, I know you have a lot to do," I tell Amanda, releasing her from this awkward moment.

"I really do," she replies, looking like she doesn't want to leave me alone. "Sorry. Thanks again Mr. Berlusconi! See you later Amazia," she yells back as she heads towards her office.

"Are you staying to help with the event?" he asks me.

"Most definitely not," I reply, not wanting to fall for whatever trap he's setting.

"That's good. Over working can really be exhausting."

"What is it that you want from me?" I ask him frankly.

"Like I've said before, I'd like to employ you."

"Even though I clearly already have a job?" I ask as I gesture around.

"This is more of a part-time thing," he casually explains, as if he isn't asking much of me.

"And if I say no?" I dare to ask.

"Then there will be consequences."

"Another threat?" I ask, staring at him and refusing to back down.

"Of course not, Amazia. You already know you're stuck with me, one way or another. Now, you can come to the coffee shop and discuss the long-term plan with me, or I can let someone else decide for you," he says matter of fact. He isn't taking no for an answer.

I stand there contemplating my options. I don't want to go, but it's the middle of the day, he approached me at work with tons of cameras, I can tell Jared where I'm going, and I frequent this specific coffee shop enough that I'd feel safe. I guess it's better than him kidnapping me again. "Fine. Let me grab my coat from my office," I say as I go to step past him toward the far employee door.

"And be sure to text Jericho, so he knows where you are," he says in a suspicious tone.

* * * * *

As soon as we enter the coffee shop, the barista nods my way, knowing my order already. I follow Mr. Berlusconi to a small booth along the front windows facing the street. He picks up the coffee menu on the table and looks through it in silence. A minute later, the barista delivers my usual order. "Here you are. And for you, sir?"

He looks up from the menu, looking inconvenienced by the barista's timing. "Coffee. Black."

"Coming right up," the barista says in a bright tone before disappearing behind the counter to retrieve his coffee.

"Why are we here?" I ask.

"Getting right to business, I like it," he says as he puts down the menu and looks my direction for the first time since we arrived at the coffee shop.

"Let me be honest here, I'm not interested in what you like," I dare to speak the truth. I'm not going to let him run my life and I need to be clear about it.

"Ah, and the true Amazia comes to the surface," he says before pausing as the barista comes back with his coffee.

"Can I grab either of you a bagel or pastry?" she asks.

"No, thank you," I kindly say. She heads back to the counter then.

"Clearly, you would like for me to get to the point of our meeting," he begins before pulling a few papers out of his inner pocket. "Now that you know what you're involved with, I hoped you'd come here willingly for a private conversation."

"Better than being kidnapped from work again," I reply in my best smart-ass tone.

He chuckles to himself before unfolding the pages and looking them over. "That was merely a scare tactic," he says without looking up from the paperwork he is looking through.

"I know you have a flare for the dramatics, but that has nothing to do with why I'm here right now," I admit, confused by the casual tone he has taken.

"Do you understand that you shouldn't cross me?" he asks, again without looking up.

"Isn't that implied?"

He peeks up over the paper and raises a brow at me. "Well, yes, but I have to be sure you understand before I explain why you're here."

"I understand. I'm not trying to risk anything. I get it, I'm stuck with you one way or another," I shrug as I admit the obvious.

"Good," he says while turning the paperwork over for me to look at.

"What is this? What am I looking at?" I ask as I glance through the photocopied papers of what seem to be a police report.

"A few police detectives have been sniffing around," he begins and pauses for my reaction. I glance up, knowing exactly who he's talking about. "They seem to think I had something to do with a recent disappearance."

"Did you?" I stare at him as I dare to ask.

He quickly looks away to avoid my question. "They asked for copies of some of my financial documents from the weekend of my daughter's wedding. They are apparently wanting to check them against copies from the hotel," he glances at me again to gauge my reaction. "The problem is, they found discrepancies that I didn't expect."

I glance through more deeply, trying to figure out what it is I'm supposed to find on these pages. "I'm not sure I'm following," I shrug.

"My travel agent was stealing from me," he leans forward to say.

I lower the papers to the tabletop and glance up at him. "And is said travel agent still a problem?" I ask in the most casual way possible.

Mr. Berlusconi simply laughs at me.

"What?" I ask, confused at his reaction.

"She's alive and well. She's just… no longer employed."

"That doesn't seem possible," I add suspiciously.

"You really think I'd be dumb enough to clean up that mess while the detectives are watching me?"

"Well, no, but…" I lose any train of thought I had, wondering if she's going to live much longer. "Is this why I'm here?" I finally ask.

"She was booking extra rooms for every trip I made. She was paying for the hotel expenses in cash, then canceling the room at the last minute, and taking out the refund in cash to pocket. The paperwork always said the original cost of rooms before the cancellation. That's how she slipped money past my bookkeeper for years."

"Years?" I ask, shocked that someone had the balls to steal from the Berlusconi family.

"Right?" he jokes as if we're old friends.

"What does all of this have to do with me? Is this about the files from the hotel, or something?"

"Amazia, you only did your job by providing the hotel paperwork to the detectives. I know you weren't trying to get involved, but now that you've taken an interesting interest in Jericho, you're kind of, well… stuck," he shrugs.

"But how does any of this," I gesture towards the papers, "have to do with me?"

"You're going to take her place."

"Come again?" I ask, not following.

"Remember when I said I wanted to employ you? In reality, I've been trying to find a good job for you since you helped my daughter out before she walked down the aisle. Then, you dating Jericho was a complication I was concerned about. Now, not only do I like the two of you together, I also have the perfect job for you."

"You like Jared and I being together?" I ask, not believing him.

"You've brought a whole new part of Jericho to the surface. And, in reality, I can easily keep my new travel agent safe with him nearby," he shrugs.

"Your new travel agent?" I ask before I put the pieces together. "Oh. You mean me."

"Will you?" he asks.

"Do I have a choice?"

"That's a very complicated question."

"What about the person I'm replacing?"

"She's off limits, for now."

"And, Jared and I?"

"What about you?"

"Are we off limits?"

He laughs, "I guess that depends on you." There is a brief pause before he becomes serious. "Just take the job, Amazia. Vittori or I will contact you when I need travel arrangements made. He'll provide you with all of the financial information you need and all you need to do is book the accommodations. I'm sure you could handle that in your sleep."

"So, you're saying that if I accept this job… Jared and I are safe… as long as we don't become idiots and cross you in some way?"

"Something like that," is all he says with a devious smile on his face.

"Jared isn't going to be happy about this."

"You don't need to tell him," he shrugs.

"Not a chance. I'm not keeping secrets from him."

"Probably the best choice. We were all surprised you stuck by him once you figured out he had been lying to you."

"He wasn't exactly lying, just masking the whole truth," I reply before regretting making an excuse for Jared.

"Same difference."

"Are we done here?" I ask, really needing to get back to work before someone notices I'm still gone.

"As long as you agree to take the job, I see no other reason to keep you from your full-time employment."

"You're taking this job thing seriously," I laugh.

"It is a job, Amazia. Part-time, sure. But I compensate my employees well, as Jericho can attest to."

"I'm not doing it for the money."

"I know. You're doing it out of love."

"I have a job that pays me just fine," I say as I stand.

"You won't even need that job once you realize how well I compensate my employees. Trust me, Amazia."

"Trust is difficult, especially considering you haven't always requested a meeting in such a professional manner before."

"Amazia," he says as he stands, "I really like this smart-ass version of you. I'm glad you finally feel comfortable enough to show me your true self."

"It's important that my employers see the side of me that isn't hidden under my fake customer service voice."

"I'll be in touch," he says before dropping money on the table for our coffees. "Domenic will walk you back to the hotel," he says, gesturing to the man at the next table.

"Domenic?" I ask as the male rises.

"Did you two not meet at the wedding?" Mr. Berlusconi asks.

"Not that I recall," I admit, not recognizing him as he stands and turns towards me.

"Amazia, this is Domenic. Domenic, this is Jericho's girlfriend, Amazia."

"Pleasure," I say in a smart-ass tone, trying hard to not roll my eyes at the introduction.

Domenic only nods.

"And I'm supposed to let some stranger walk me back to work?" I ask Mr. Berlusconi.

"He's on the payroll. You'll be fine," he shrugs before he walks past me towards the exit.

"That's it then?" I ask.

"I have a band to meet up with," he replies before disappearing out onto the street.

"Shall we?" Domenic says, gesturing towards the door.

"I guess," I reply under my breath as I step through the door.

We walk back to the hotel in silence, Domenic just a step behind me, acting almost like a body guard. It really only creeps me out. It would have been different if Vittori was here instead. Part of me wonders if Vittori isn't here because Berlusconi knows he'd have warned Jared about the meeting. Oh shit, Jared. He's probably about to lose his mind that I haven't checked in. I go to pull my phone out of my back pocket to text him as we approach the hotel portico.

I'm about to unlock my phone when I hear his voice coming from just outside the lobby doors. "Amazia! There you are!"

I look up and am surprised to see Jared jogging over to me. "Jared. What are you doing here? I was about to text you back," I barely finish saying as he wraps his arms around me, holding me close. "Jared, I'm fine."

He pulls back and looks me up and down. "Are you sure?"

"Babe," I say in a serious tone, "I'm fine. Honestly."

He looks behind my shoulder and notices Domenic. "What are you doing here?" he looks confused as he asks. I turn to look at Domenic before he can answer.

"Was told to walk her back to the hotel," Domenic replies vaguely.

"Where's Vittori?" Jared asks.

"On another assignment, up state," Domenic answers dryly.

"Up state?" Jared sounds surprised.

"That's what I'm told, sir," I'm surprised to hear Domenic address Jared in such a way.

"Thanks for getting her back safely," Jared says in an odd tone.

"Yes sir. See you tonight?" he asks.

"No. I declined tonight's assignment," Jared replies.

"Lucky you. Must be nice having such connections to the boss," Domenic adds.

"Luck has nothing to do with it," Jared replies in a dismissive tone.

Domenic only nods before turning to walk away from the hotel.

"What was that about?" I ask.

"Can you get off work early?" he asks.

"That depends," I admit, waiting for more information.

"I want to be as far away from the hotel before the band gets here, and I'd prefer to explain Domenic's choice of words once we're back home and alone."

"Let me run down to the office and get my backpack and clock out."

"I'll be waiting by the car," he says before kissing my forehead and letting me walk into the hotel.

29

Jared drives us home, in silence. It isn't awkward, but it is unusual. It appears as if he is thinking deeply about whatever is on his mind. Once we're home, the silence continues until we walk inside. I put my backpack on the floor inside the door just before he puts his hand on my shoulder to turn me to face him. He looks serious as he looks deeply into my eyes. "What happened today?"

"Berlusconi wanted to talk," I reply vaguely.

"And you left the hotel with him?" he asks.

"I didn't think I had a choice," I admit.

"You probably didn't," he admits, looking down.

"I knew the coffee shop, Amanda had seen me talking to him, and I was able to text you. I felt it was better to go with him than to give him a reason to kidnap me again."

He looks up then, surprised at my words. "Babe," he begins.

"He wanted to show me documents that prove that someone was stealing from him," I blurt out.

"What? Who?"

"Some woman that was booking his hotels for him."

"What does that have to do with you?" he asks, sounding suspicious about the connection.

"He wants me to take over the job."

"He's trying to make you work for him," he replies as a statement of fact.

I nod.

"You can't do it," Jared replies.

"Like I have a choice."

"What about the woman?"

"She's alive, for now. The only reason Berlusconi figured it out was because of the detectives looking into Seth's disappearance."

"How so?"

"They found the financial discrepancies between the hotel receipts and the official books Berlusconi had."

"He can't kill her while the police are snooping around," Jared understands.

"Exactly."

Jared looks back up at me. He puts his hands on both of my arms and says, "Tell me that you're alright, Amazia. Look at me and tell me you're alright, please."

"Why wouldn't I be?" I ask, feeling confused.

"Berlusconi and Domenic. They took you away from work, away from safety, and what? Did they threaten you?"

"There were no threats. And when it comes to Domenic, I didn't even know he existed until we were leaving the coffee shop and Berlusconi announced that I had an escort back to work."

"Really?"

"Yeah. I thought it was weird. Who is he?"

"Domenic?" he asks.

I nod.

"Come sit down," he says, leading me to the couch before he continues. "Domenic works for Berlusconi, obviously. He's never been much of a fan of me. That's why I'm not sure why Berlusconi let him walk you back to the hotel, unless it was some kind of secret warning for me."

"Why would you say so?"

"I'm not sure. It could be nothing, but with this family, you never know."

"Jared, can I ask you something?"

"Of course, babe."

"And you'd answer honestly?"

"I'm never keeping a secret from you again."

"What did Domenic want to imply when he said you had connections to the family?"

Jared sighs before answering, "It's something I should have told you sooner. Don't be mad."

"Babe, whatever it is, it's okay."

"I just promised, no more lies. I don't want you to lose your trust in me."

"I won't. I promise."

"Remember when Berlusconi said he chose me because of my emotionless state? He chose me because he knew I'd never love anyone?"

"Yeah, I remember my eavesdropping," I laugh at myself.

"I lost my family when I was young. After that, I didn't have a home for a long time. I bounced around, a lot. When I was in high school, I was adopted, out of nowhere. I never even met the person who adopted me. I thought the whole thing was strange, until I learned more about the situation."

"I'm confused. What are you not saying?"

"Mr. Berlusconi adopted me when I was sixteen."

"Why?"

"I don't know why he chose to adopt a teenager. He chose me because of my lack of emotions. Someone tipped him off. I'm not sure if it was someone in the system or in the school system, but he adopted me to test me. Once I showed no sign of emotions, he began to tell me more and more about his business."

"His crime business?"

Jared nods. "He told me enough to scare me into staying. I was a frequent runaway before then. I never ran from his house, too many people coming and going at all hours."

"So, when Domenic said you have connections, it's because Berlusconi partly finished raising you?" I ask.

"Something like that," Jared admits, looking down and away from me.

"Jared," I say as I reach out and take his hand.

"I'm sorry," he whispers.

"You have nothing to be sorry for."

"I just feel like I lied to you."

"Because you didn't tell me the whole truth behind your history with Berlusconi? Come on. Nothing changes between us."

He looks up and looks surprised. "Doesn't it, though?"

"No," I reply, looking seriously at him. "Nothing that minuscule will change how I feel about you. We're in this together babe, the good and the bad."

"Til death do us part?" he asks as a joke.

"Something like that," I laugh in reply.

"Let's hope it doesn't come to that," he returns to his serious tone.

"Berlusconi said he likes us together," I shrug.

"Really?" he sounds intrigued.

"Yes, really. It caught me off guard too. Though… it makes more sense now, knowing he adopted you," I tease.

"It wasn't a loving family, or anything like that," he replies.

"But," I start, tilting his chin so he'll look back at me, "that isn't how your life has to be."

He reaches up and gently runs his fingers through my hair before holding my face and looking into my eyes. "We can be different. We can create the perfect, loving family."

"Then we will," I reply.

"You promise?" he asks with a smile on his face.

"Whatever your heart desires," I smile back before he leans in and kisses me gently.

"What have you done to me?" he asks as he leans his forehead against mine.

"I haven't done anything, babe. You're just being your true self."

"Maybe you were meant for me," he adds.

"I think you came into my life, just when I needed something positive to believe in," I admit.

He leans back so he can look down into my eyes. "The same goes for you. I never thought I'd be happy. I never thought I'd fall in love."

"Was it worth the wait?" I tease.

He smiles one of the biggest smiles I've ever seen on him, "One hundred percent." He leans in and kisses me passionately as we let the day fade away so we can simply enjoy one another's company.

30

I was looking forward to sleeping in on my day off, but I was rudely awakened by the sound of a doorbell. I groan and roll over to find Jared is already missing from bed. I throw off the covers, slide on a pair of sweatpants and a hoodie, quickly brush my teeth, and head downstairs to see what Jared's up to. On the way down the stairs, I can already smell the freshly brewed coffee that he always makes just for me. I really don't understand how he functions without caffeine.

As I reach the bottom of the stairs, I can hear two voices coming from the kitchen. I begin to approach, quickly realizing I recognize both voices; it's Jared and Vittori. I walk around the corner and into the kitchen just as I hear Vittori say, "He keeps sending me out of town."

Jared looks up and smiles when I enter. "Good morning, beautiful," he says as he opens his arm to hug me to his side, kissing my cheek as he does.

"Morning," I smile back.

"Amazia," Vittori nods hello.

"Vittori," I nod back. "What are you doing here so early?" I say as I move away from Jared to pour myself a cup of coffee.

"Officially, I'm here to drop off your company credit card," he says, sliding an envelope across the counter toward me as I stand next to Jared again, across from Vittori.

"And unofficially?" I ask, glancing at the envelope, but otherwise ignoring it.

He glances at Jared who nods, as if giving him permission to speak his mind. "Unofficially, I'm here to ask you what the hell you were thinking."

"Excuse me?" I ask, feeling confused as I glance back and forth between Jared and Vittori.

Jared reaches his arm up to rub my back and comfort me. "He's asking why you agreed to work for Berlusconi after we said we wanted to keep you distanced from everything."

"Because he really gave me an option to say no," I say defensively.

"Babe, no need to be defensive," he turns towards me, still rubbing my back. "Excuse Vittori's demeanor, he's just upset at the outcome here." He steps closer, wrapping his arm around my shoulder and pulling me close again.

"He's not wrong," Vittori says under his breath.

"Well, then, you didn't have to be an ass when you asked me."

Vittori laughs, "I'm sorry."

Jared laughs next, "Did she really just get you to apologize?"

"Yeah, I guess she did," Vittori admits to Jared.

"Is this some inside joke that I don't understand?" I ask, looking up at Jared.

"Something like that," Vittori replies. "You know you've changed Jericho for the better, right?" he asks me.

"That's what people keep telling me," I admit, looking down.

There is a moment of silence as I see Vittori glance at Jared in a questioning way.

"Apparently, Berlusconi likes Amazia and I being together," Jared says with a shrug.

"That's an interesting twist of events," Vittori admits.

"You're telling me," I add in. "At least he didn't kidnap me this time."

"I just don't understand why he keeps sending me out of town every time he wants to talk to you," Vittori thinks out loud.

"He probably knows you'd tell me," Jared adds.

"You're probably right, but why bother keeping it secret, unless there is something else that we don't know yet," Vittori continues.

"That's the mystery, isn't it?" Jared wonders.

There is a long silence as the three of us are left to our own thoughts. Before anyone comes up with anything, Vittori's phone rings. "Well, speak of the devil himself," he says, showing us Berlusconi's name and number on the screen. He swipes to answer, "Vittori." There is a moment while he listens to whatever Berlusconi has to say. "Yes, sir. Just delivered it myself," he raises his eyebrows at us as he listens. "Understood. See you there," he says before hanging up. "Guess that means I better head out before he figures out that I'm still here."

"Did he mean for you to deliver this personally?" Jared asks, holding up the envelope.

"Probably not," he shrugs, "but, I don't want everyone knowing that Amazia has been staying here with you. And, I don't trust anyone enough to stop by here," Vittori admits.

"Well, thank you. I appreciate the judgment," I reply.

"Yeah. I don't like that Berlusconi has Domenic around again," Jared adds.

"I feel the same way. That guy always rubs me the wrong way," Vittori continues.

I feel myself begin to laugh, then try to cover it up. "I'm sorry, but for either of you to say that someone rubs you the wrong way, is kind of hilarious."

Jared and Vittori laugh with me. "She has a point," Jared says.

"That she does," Vittori agrees. He sips the last of his coffee before placing the mug in the sink. "Well, thank you for the coffee. I better be on my way to meet Berlusconi."

"Thanks for coming by yourself," Jared says again as he walks Vittori out.

I sip my coffee while Jared lets Vittori out and locks the door before coming back into the kitchen. He walks up behind me and wraps his arms around me, pulling me close and kissing my hair. "You sleep, okay?"

"Yeah, I think so," I smile, leaning back into his arms.

"Are you okay?" he asks, after a moment of silence.

I turn and look up at him. His arms loosen, but he keeps his hold of me. "Yeah, just not thrilled to be working for Berlusconi."

Jared reaches over and grabs the envelope, ripping it open and pouring the contents out next to us on the counter. A credit card, a key, and a folded-up paper fall out. "Looks like you get a key to the mansion too."

"Something else I don't want," I say as I reach over to pick up the folded page. I unfold the 3x4 inch piece of paper and see a short, handwritten note. "Use it well. Ask Jericho and Vittori any questions you have," I read aloud.

Jared rolls his eyes, "He really is putting the three of us in a sinking ship together."

"You think we're in a sinking ship?" I ask.

"I sure hope not. It just seems odd; the way Berlusconi is going about everything. Keeping Vittori separated from anything that has to do with you, secret meetings with you. I don't know, it all just seems odd, even for Berlusconi," Jared admits, appearing in deep thought.

"Do you have any jobs today?" I ask, pulling him back to the present.

"I do not," he smiles down at me.

"Then how shall we start our day?" I ask with a smart-ass smirk on my face.

"Oh, I have some ideas," he says as he pulls me close and begins kissing me passionately. Gone are all the worries plaguing us as we relax into one another.

31

A week has gone by since Vittori handed me the key to the mansion, or at least that's what Jared calls it. In reality, it's a key to the house Jared and I met Berlusconi at a few weeks ago to discuss my involvement in the Berlusconi family. I haven't had to use it yet, but apparently that is the drop location for any accounting paperwork that cannot be sent electronically. Although, with my job at The Rush, I can get most of the paperwork sent digitally to Berlusconi's accountant with just a basic knowledge of the rooms control systems. I set up a separate e-mail address for any reservations I've had to make for Berlusconi.

So far, I've only had to book a few overnight rooms for Vittori when he goes out of town. Every time he leaves town, I expect a surprise meeting from Berlusconi, but it's clearly all been just a test. Then, Berlusconi shows up at the hotel, again.

"Amazia!" he says as he walks into my office.

Klarissa stands up from her desk and looks at me confused. I shake my head at her and she sits back down, watching us carefully as Berlusconi closes the door behind him. He walks over and takes a seat in front of my desk.

"Why don't you just invite yourself in?" I say in a smart-ass tone, not bothering trying to hide my annoyance as I continue typing on my computer.

"Nice Ivy Matthews painting," he says as he settles into his seat.

"Don't you remember sending it here?" I ask in an uninterested voice.

"You've impressed me so far, Amazia."

"How's that? By booking a few simple hotel rooms and sending verified financial documents before check-in and after check out so you can tell they clearly match?" I ask as I refuse to look up from my work on the computer.

"Amazia," he says, waiting for me to stop what I'm doing and acknowledge him.

I finish typing the sentence I was on before crossing my arms, sitting back in my chair, and looking at Berlusconi. "Can I help you with something?"

"It's pay day!" he says in a happy voice.

"And you had to come down here, barge into my office unannounced, just to tell me that?" I continue to sound as annoyed as I feel.

"Amazia," he says leaning forward in his chair. "You still don't get it, do you?"

"Get what?" I ask, not sure where he's going with this.

"You passed all my tests," he explains.

"And?"

"You get to live!" he says in a celebratory voice.

"Oh boy!" I say, turning back to my computer.

He laughs, "Amazia, I'm kidding."

"Hilarious," I reply while continuing to type my report.

"Okay. I can tell when I'm overstaying my welcome," he stands. "Enjoy your first paycheck," he says, tossing a fat envelope onto my desk.

"What is that?" I ask, looking back and forth between him and the envelope.

"Did Jared not tell you how payday works?" he asks curiously.

"I guess I figured you'd just let the men deal with it."

He laughs again, "I like you, Amazia. I really do."

"Hope to keep it that way," I say under my breath.

"Have a good afternoon. I hope you enjoy your evening with Jericho. I hear he has a big night planned," he says as he walks to the door.

"What? Did you give him a job?" I ask, glancing over to him.

"No. He asked for the night off," he shrugs. "Bye," he waves as he opens my door and walks away, disappearing around the corner.

I quickly snatch the envelope from the desk, tossing it into my backpack before anyone can see it.

"What was that?" Klarissa asks, leaning against the door frame.

"I don't even know," I sigh and shake my head.

* * * * *

After work, I'm surprised to get a text from Jared saying he's waiting outside. I clock out and head to the lobby, walking through to the portico where I see Jared chatting with his favorite valet employees. Once they see me, they point me out to Jared who turns and smiles at me. He shakes the hand of the guy he's been chatting with and comes over to kiss me, "Hey babe."

"Hey," I reply. "Why did you decide to pick me up?" I smile.

"Well, I'm taking you out."

"Right now?" I ask.

"Only if that's okay?" he says reluctantly, sensing my tone.

"Do I get to change first?" I ask.

"Whatever you heart desires my love," he says, holding the passenger door open for me.

We return home so that I can change out of my work clothes. It's still winter in New York, so I throw on a pair of warm jeans and a dressy sweater, so I'll fit in no matter where he's planning to take me. He hasn't said anything and is keeping it a mystery. The thought of what Berlusconi said in my office comes to mind. He said that Jared had a big night planned. What did he mean?

"Ready babe?" Jared comes into the bedroom to check on me, bringing me back to the present.

"I am," I turn and smile at him after I check my hair one last time.

Jared drives us to the Marriott Marquis on Broadway, where of course he has a valet service already waiting on our arrival. I know there is a restaurant on the 48th floor, but I've never been there. I can only assume this is where he's taking me. Jared holds open every door that an employee doesn't on our way to the elevator. Once he hits the 48th floor button, I know we're on the way up to The View Restaurant and Lounge. The Rush doesn't have a restaurant with a view, and this view is supposed to be fantastic.

As the elevator doors open, we are greeted, again, by someone expecting us. "Jared and Amazia?" she asks with a smile.

"Yes, ma'am," Jared replies kindly.

"This way," she says, leading us toward a private table away from the other guests currently dining. "Here we are. Your server will be out with your wine and appetizer shortly," she says before walking away.

"You always prepare for everything, don't you?" I ask.

"I sure do try," he admits as he pulls my chair out for me.

"What's the special occasion?" I ask, not wanting to wait and see what he has in store.

"I just thought we needed a good date night," he begins. "The last few weeks since the holidays have been busy, and honestly stressful. First, Berlusconi sent me out of town, then he took you to a meeting without asking, then he's trying to get you to work for him…. It's been a lot. I wanted a good date night like when I first took you out. We deserve it."

"And it's apparently payday," I add in.

"Yeah, I noticed your payment wasn't included with mine, like I expected it would be."

"Berlusconi delivered it himself."

"To The Rush? While you were working?" he sounds surprised.

"Sure did. Barged into my office unannounced and everything," I admit.

"Here we are," the server says, delivering an appetizer and pouring us each a glass of wine from the bottle he brought to the table. "Any changes to your original plan?" he asks Jared.

"No sir," he answers. The server nods to Jared before disappearing into the back room. "That's very unusual," Jared admits.

"I didn't think it was customary of him," I shrug.

"For now, let's try not to think about that or the Berlusconi family at all," Jared suggests.

"Yeah. He said you asked for the night off," I add, watching to gauge his reaction.

Jared laughs, "Of course he'd say something."

"What's the big deal?" I ask, not sure what's so funny.

"I rudely told him to leave us the hell alone tonight," he laughs again.

"No, you didn't!" I say in a shocked voice.

"And, you know what he said?" He continues once he sees me shaking my head, at a loss for words. "He said, 'You're starting to sound like a smart-ass like that girlfriend of yours.' Can you believe it?"

"Geez Jared, what happened to not poking the bear?" I ask.

"It's more complicated than that," he admits.

"Well, I want to hear all about it, but not until we finish this fantastic date night without any more thoughts of the Berlusconi family."

He raises his wine glass, "I'll drink to that."

"Cheers," I add, picking up my own glass and drinking.

*   *   *   *   *

We finish dinner and dessert without another word about the Berlusconi family. Jared is full of smiles and laughter all night, which is beyond happier than I've ever seen him before. I can't tell what's different about tonight, but I don't dare ask, with fears of ruining the moment. After dinner, Jared helps me put my coat back on before we make our way back down to the street where I'm surprised to already see Jared's car parked out front and ready to go.

"At least now I understand how you have all these connections," I joke as he opens the passenger door for me.

"Not complaining, are you?" he teases.

"Maybe, maybe not," I reply just before he closes the door and walks around to the driver side.

"Well, I am going to take advantage of every connection I can to spoil my amazing girlfriend whenever possible," he says with a smile on his face.

"You seem really happy today," I note, wondering how he'll reply.

He looks over at me and in the eyes. "I am, Amazia. I'm really happy," he says before putting the car in gear and driving away.

"What's next?" I ask, trying to figure out which direction he's heading.

"You want me to spoil the surprise?" he asks.

"Maybe just spoil the location?" I reply hesitantly, not really wanting to spoil his surprise date night.

"We are going to Top of the Rock."

"The observation deck?" I ask.

"That's the one."

"You bought out the entire space, didn't you?" I ask, guessing that he doesn't want a crowd.

"You know me so well," he teases back at me.

We both laugh as he drives towards Rockefeller. The only thing that interrupts our laughter is Jared's phone ringing. We both stop laughing and glance at each other before he reached down to pick up his phone. He instantly looks concerned.

"Who is it?"

"Vittori," he says, sounding a mix of concerned and confused. He glances at me before he answers, "What's up?" There is a brief pause before Jared starts talking over him. "Slow down! Slow down. Vittori, shut up for a second." There is pause until Vittori stops talking long enough for Jared to get a word in. "What happened?" There is a long pause while Vittori explains something to Jared. "Okay, okay. Stop! Where are you?" Pause. "Fine. Stay put. We're coming to you," Jared says then immediately hangs up on Vittori.

"Change of plans?" I ask sadly.

He glances at me and smiles sadly, "Change of plans."

* * * * *

When Jared parks next to Vittori's car at the back of another warehouse, my heart rate picks up, wondering what we're walking into. "You coming?" he asks as he shuts off the car.

"Why not," I say as a statement, getting out of the car with Jared.

We can see Vittori sitting on the back dock, waiting for us by the stairs. "Thanks for coming," he says as he stands up, looking disheveled compared to his normal self. "I didn't want to interrupt your special night, but I didn't know who else to call. Who else I could trust."

"It's okay. We can get back to our night after. Now, tell us what we're looking for," Jared pushes him to get to the point.

Vittori opens the door to show us in while he explains. "I came in as the cleanup crew for the night, but I can't find the weapon anywhere."

"No one else was available?" Jared interrupts him to ask.

Vittori stops to shrug, "I was told you had the night off and to just deal with it myself instead of bothering you."

"Berlusconi told you to just deal with it yourself?" Jared asks, sounding like he doesn't believe it.

"I thought he was kidding, but then he asked if I was going to hit the road or not, so I left and came here."

"So, what's missing?" I ask, looking around for a mystery item.

"The murder weapon. The knife," Vittori admits, avoiding eye contact with me.

"Are you sure no one else was here?" Jared asks.

"I've walked through twice with no sign of anyone or anything," Vittori continues.

"Who else is on the crew for this one?" Jared asks.

"No one. Just me, and well, now you two, technically," Vittori runs his hand through his hair, looking frustrated.

"Where's the body?" Jared asks.

"Already taken care of," Vittori confesses.

"Did you ever see the knife?" Jared speaks up, trying to get to the bottom of where the weapon went.

"Come to think of it, no," Vittori stops and looks back at Jared. "What if I'm freaking out about this for nothing?"

"It isn't likely. It wouldn't follow the protocol to not leave the weapon behind. Who ran the hit?"

"Domenic," Vittori states.

Jared pauses for a moment, looking surprised. "Berlusconi put him on a job already? He just got back from wherever he's been."

"Your guess is as good as mine," Vittori shrugs.

"I hate that guy, but he follows protocol. That knife has to be here somewhere," Jared says before looking around at the office file boxes surrounding us. "Amazia," he starts before tossing me a pair of leather gloves, "go through these boxes, carefully. Be sure the knife didn't end up stashed in here for some reason."

I nod, pulling on the gloves and digging through the boxes.

"We'll go check the rest of the warehouse," Jared says to Vittori. "Hopefully we can solve this mystery quick."

"Sorry to interrupt your big night," Vittori apologizes again.

Jared glances at me to gauge my reaction to Vittori's choice in words. It does seem suspicious that both Berlusconi and now Vittori have made a comment about tonight being a big and important night. "Come on," Jared pushes Vittori out of the office and into the rest of the warehouse.

I shrug off whatever Vittori was hinting to as I go through all of the exposed boxes first. I doubt Domenic would have moved around all of these boxes to hide a knife deep within them. Wouldn't that defeat the purpose of having a cleanup crew?

Suddenly, I feel the atmosphere in the warehouse change. The hair on my arms instantly stands up and I feel a negative presence enter the room. Before I can really process the odd feeling, I hear three distinct gunshots. I immediately abandon my search through the boxes and turn to run towards the sound. Probably not the best idea. Jared would definitely be mad at me for running towards gunfire, but I need to find him and make sure he's alright.

As I run out onto the open warehouse floor, I see a body lying on the ground in the middle of the room. I try to run that way, but Vittori runs up to me from another direction, wrapping his arms around me, and holding me back. I feel myself screaming Jared's name as I try to run towards him. Vittori's grip is too strong and he's not allowing me to advance towards Jared. I can hear Vittori saying something, but I can't make out the words as I continue to scream Jared's name without another thought in my mind. I swear I see another person leaving in the direction Vittori came from and begin to panic even more. What happened in here? Is Jared alive?

At some point, I calm down enough for Vittori to only keep one hand on me. He uses his other to make a phone call. I can only assume that he called Berlusconi to help clean up the mess he created. Everything happens in a blur. The ambulance and fire truck arrive together. They all rush in and begin working on Jared. I can hear the sound of his heartbeat as they hook him up to their Zoll monitor. I close my eyes and focus on the steady beating of his heart as Vittori continues to refuse to let me go near him. "Let them work," I remember him urging me once the paramedics arrived. Once the ambulance leaves with Jared, Vittori walks us outside and instructs me to get into Jared's car so he can drive us to the hospital. I don't question why we're taking Jared's car. I don't question why the police haven't arrived to ask us a million questions. I just sit quietly, feeling numb as my body and mind try to process what the hell just happened to my perfect date night.

32

I remember Vittori leading me through the hospital to a waiting room where he practically forced me into a chair, so I'd stop pacing the hallway. He tries to talk to me a few times, but I never hear the words that he says. I'm numb and my mind is foggy. That is until I see Mr. Berlusconi step off of the elevator. I don't even remember standing and running up to him. My first conscious thought is when Vittori tries to pry me away from Berlusconi as I slam my hands into him repeatedly.

"This is your fault!" I yell while still trying to swing at Berlusconi, but Vittori has picked me up and pulled me away from him.

"Amazia, calm down," Vittori urges me. Once I finally settle, he puts me down and releases his hold on me.

"It's okay Vittori," Berlusconi says, looking defeated himself.

Vittori steps up and stands next to Berlusconi, preparing to put himself between us if I decide to attack him again. This is the first time my mind is processing how Vittori looks. Not only are his clothes disheveled, they are torn and dirty. There are clear cuts, scrapes, and bruises that weren't there before, covering his arms and face. Clearly, he was in a struggle of some sort at the warehouse before I heard the gunshots.

"I know you're upset…" Berlusconi starts but I interrupt him.

"This is your fault!" I yell. "You either did this or caused this or something!"

"Amazia, listen," Vittori starts.

"I've got this," Berlusconi says to Vittori before looking back at me. "Amazia, trust me when I say that I had nothing to do with this. I gave Jared the night off to spend with you. I'd have no reason to drag him into any of this."

"I don't believe you," I spit out at him before turning and walking back to the waiting room chairs, throwing myself back down into the same one I was sitting in before. I sit there for hours before Vittori comes to sit next to me. "Any word?"

"He's still in surgery," he answers.

"At least that means he's alive," I whisper.

"Amazia, do you want me to bring you home?" he asks.

I laugh, "I don't even have a home without Jared."

"I mean… do you want me to bring you home to shower or change or anything?" he's trying to be friendly, even though it's odd. He's Jared's friend, not mine.

"No," I shake my head and look away, not wanting to make eye contact or show the tears burning at the edges of my eyes.

Vittori gets up and walks away, moving to the nearby room Berlusconi is working from. I can see two other people in the room now discussing something with him. I turn away from them and curl up in the chair, trying my best to not think. At some point I must fall asleep.

* * * * *

I wake up to find a hospital blanket wrapped over me in the uncomfortable waiting room chair. I try to sit up, pain immediately shooting through my back from the position I slept in. I try to stretch, but it only makes it worse.

"Morning," I hear Vittori say. He's sitting two chairs over from me, flipping through a book. He reaches over to the table in front of him to grab a Dunkin Donuts coffee cup and hands it to me. "Coffee?"

"Thanks," I say, reaching to take the coffee from him. He clearly left to shower and change. He's sitting here now in a fresh pair of blue jeans, a black t-shirt, and black leather jacket. His hair is full of gel, looking perfectly placed unlike last night. "Did we get any news?"

"He's out of surgery and in a room down the hall," he vaguely answers.

"Is that all you're going to tell me?" I ask in a smart-ass, grumpy tone.

"Oh, are you going to talk to us now?" he puts down his book and looks over at me. That's when I realize he said 'us'. I look around and find Berlusconi sitting on the other side of me, also reading a book of some kind.

"Yeah, I guess so," I answer, not really sure what I did to piss him off.

"She was just in shock," Berlusconi adds in. "She didn't mean to throw punches and blame us for what happened," he never looks up from his book as he talks.

"Well, maybe a little," I shrug.

"Jericho is stable," Berlusconi continues, putting down his book to look at me. "He still hasn't woken up though. They aren't sure when that'll happen."

"Can I go see him?"

"Yeah. You ready?" Vittori stands up to ask.

I stand up and follow him without saying a word.

"You want me to go in with you?" Vittori asks.

"No. I'll be okay," I glance up at him and see worry on his face.

"I'll give you a few minutes," he steps back and gives me space as I place my hand on the door handle, taking a deep breath before walking in.

Seeing Jared attached to all of the different equipment is overwhelming. The heart and blood pressure monitors are bright and lead to all of the different lead wires that are attached all over. The other side of the bed has all of the meds and fluids they are pumping into him through the multiple IV's I can see in his arm and hand. Otherwise, he looks at peace as he sleeps, gently tucked in under the hospital blanket.

I make my way over to his side, gently reaching out to hold his hand. I feel the tears trying to breach the surface as

I try to come up with the right words to say. "I'm here babe. You're gonna be alright. Just rest now and I'll be here waiting for you when you wake up. I love you," I finish as I lean down and kiss his cheek. I swear I feel him squeeze my hand back, but I may have just imagined it. I pull up the rolling stool from the nurse's desk and sit by his side, holding his hand and wishing he'd wake up.

I sit there with him for at least an hour or two before Berlusconi and Vittori interrupt my silence. "Are you going to admit that this is all your fault yet?" I ask Berlusconi.

"Amazia..." Vittori begins but is interrupted.

"Vittori, it's alright. Let her speak her mind. She isn't wrong. This wouldn't have happened to any of you if I wasn't a part of your lives."

"At least you understand that this is your fault," I whisper under my breath, wondering how much of this Jared can hear. "In all seriousness, do you know who did this?" I glance over at him.

"Friends of the victim? Maybe they followed him there?" Vittori guesses.

"No. That isn't likely. I doubt it was anyone outside of the inner circle," Berlusconi voices.

"Then who?" I ask.

"I think I have an idea," Mr. Berlusconi says before disappearing from the room.

I go to follow him, but Vittori stops me. "Let him go."

"What? Why? He didn't tell me anything!" I yell at him.

"Let him do his thing. If I know him, he's going to try to make sure his suspicion is correct before he tells either of us anything. He isn't going to falsely accuse anyone. He will know facts before he will tell us anything."

"And why do you think you can trust him?" I demand.

"Because Jericho is like a son to him. Jericho means a lot to him and his family. I know that's hard to understand and it isn't my story to tell, but Mr. Berlusconi cares deeply for Jericho and his well-being."

I make my way back to the side of the hospital bed to sit back down next to Jared. "I know about their history. That's what makes this all worse. Why did Berlusconi let this happen?"

"Even Berlusconi can't control everything, no matter how hard he tries."

"Suddenly you're defending him?" I ask.

"That's complicated," he admits, but leaves it at that.

33

A few days go by with little to no change in Jared's condition. Once a day Vittori brings me back to Jared's place to change and do whatever needs to be done to keep life moving. The first time we went back to Jared's, Vittori parked and left his Camaro there. I never asked why Vittori did that. Vittori also took care of Jared's personal items from the hospital, keeping them safe and secure. You'd think there was a diamond in his personal effects that was worth money or something the way Vittori was so protective of them.

Shortly before lunch, Vittori returns with take-out for us, knowing the hospital food is awful, no matter how hungry you are. We eat in silence, breaking the rules and eating in Jared's room. We don't talk much other than the details about the day. At some point, he gets a text message that seems to intrigue him.

"What is it?" I ask curiously.

"Someone is coming to pick you up," he answers.

"Me?" I ask confused.

"Yeah. Berlusconi says he has figured out who was trying to harm Jared," Vittori explains.

"And I have to go somewhere to find out?" I ask, not sure where this is going.

Vittori shrugs, "I guess. I can't understand why Berlusconi wouldn't let me help him look into this one."

"Seriously? He's keeping you out of it because you're a part of this package deal. He knows he needs to keep you separated from his investigation. He wants results almost as badly as we do."

"He really does care about Jericho, you know." Vittori has told me this before, but I don't understand why he thinks this is true.

"Why do you always say that?" I ask.

"Because it's true."

"If you say so."

A minute later Domenic walks into the room, "You ready to go?"

"Wait. You?" is all I can say, looking over at Vittori for help.

"You can trust Domenic to get you where you're going," Vittori urges gently. "Berlusconi sent him for a reason. Just… trust that."

"Alright," I reply hesitantly before standing up and grabbing my coat. "I'll be back shortly," I whisper to Jared before kissing his cheek and turning to follow Domenic to his vehicle.

Domenic pulls up outside of an abandoned warehouse and my stomach immediately sinks. "Get out," he says as he himself climbs out. I sigh and reluctantly follow. My stomach turns as I close my door and look around. Domenic is already walking towards the warehouse, and I rush to keep up, not wanting to be left alone, even if the alternative is to be with Domenic.

As we enter the back door, the squeaky hinges announce our arrival. I can hear it echo throughout the giant tin can shell of a warehouse. I begin to think the worst is about to happen. I can sense something negative in the air. Domenic doesn't seem to feel the same evil in the air, and I can't figure out why. Was this all a lie? Is Berlusconi going to take me out? Did Jared or I do something wrong, without even knowing?

We round a corner where I can see Mr. Berlusconi standing behind an old, worn, rusted metal table. "What shall I do with her?" Domenic asks.

"Wait, what?" I ask, looking back and forth between the two of them, feeling the panic rise inside my chest.

Mr. Berlusconi steps around the table, clearly carrying something in his hand, but it's on the opposite side of him, and I cannot see what it is. He continues to walk around the room and arching towards where Domenic and I are standing. I take my eyes off of Berlusconi long enough to see Domenic is smirking at me as if he has won some secret game, I know nothing about. As I glance back towards Berlusconi, I see him raising his arm. In his hand, I can clearly see what he's holding. His arm continues to rise as his trigger finger moves to the trigger of the Glock in his hand.

I blink as I watch the hand rise, pointing directly between Domenic and myself, or so I thought. I hear the gun shot and hold my breath. I wait, wondering if it's over. I've been squeezing my eyes shut, but I finally relax and open them, letting out a breath as I realize there is no pain or odd sensation rushing through me. I look over and see Domenic on the ground, dead, with a single gunshot wound to the head.

I look away, not wanting to see anything else about the wound. What I did process will already be seared into my brain forever. I try to calm myself, feeling myself hyperventilating as I try to put together what just happened. Before I can clear my head, I feel a hand on my shoulder, and I jump back. I look over and see Berlusconi holding his hands up, no longer holding a gun.

"Amazia," he says gently. "It's okay," he says as he holds his hands up in a surrender type fashion. I realize that his hand was the one that touched my shoulder before I jumped back.

"What the hell," is all I'm able to get out before I tense up again.

"Listen, I'm sorry you had to see that," he gently begins.

"Did you just..." I begin, pointing at Domenic, without looking.

"He had to think he was bringing *you* here to die," Berlusconi begins slowly. "It was the only way to keep him from getting suspicious."

"Suspicious of what?"

"That I figured out what he was up to."

"I'm sorry. Can you start from the beginning? Or like, just get to the point where you kill me too?"

"Amazia, relax. I'm not gonna kill you," he says, looking confused at my assumption.

"Then why am I here?" I ask, feeling on the edge of a breakdown. I have no idea what the hell is going on anymore. I want to be back at the hospital with Jared. "Is this about Jared?"

"It's about you and Jericho. What happened to Jericho was not what was intended that night."

"What do you mean?" I ask, feeling even more confused as we go.

"Jericho was not the target," he says before pausing, looking like he doesn't want to admit what comes next. "Amazia, you were the intended target that night."

"What? Why?" I can't believe what I'm hearing.

"It's a long story and I promise to explain everything, but right now, we need to go."

"Go where!?" I yell.

"Back to the hospital," he says. He takes a deep breath and pauses before adding, "Jericho is awake."

"What?" I perk up at the news. "Then lets fucking go!" I turn to leave before realizing I have no idea how I'm supposed to get back to the hospital. I turn back to Berlusconi who points behind him towards another door. I go to walk past him but stop, looking at the gun tucked into his waistband.

"I know this is hard to believe, especially given the circumstances of what just happened, but you're safe with me."

I glance back toward Domenic, without really looking. "How am I supposed to believe that?"

"Jericho is like a son to me, whether you want to believe it or not. I'm not sure that I'm capable of love, but if I was, I'd love him like a son. Which means, you're like a daughter to me." He looks sincere, but I don't have time to judge that right now. I have to get back to the hospital, back to Jared.

I shake my head and walk past Berlusconi and run out of the warehouse. Once I'm on the side dock, I see his car down below. He exits behind me, making a phone call. "It's done. Send in the cleanup crew." There is a pause before he says, "No. He's not available for a while," I glance back and see him watching me as he talks in code. He nods before hanging up his phone and walking down the stairs to the Black BMW X7 Dark Shadow Edition. "Come on, get in."

I'd prefer to find another way back to the hospital on my own, but I know this is the fastest way to get back to Jared. I roll my eyes and climb into the passenger seat, quickly buckling up as Berlusconi floors it, speeding all the way back to the hospital.

34

Berlusconi and I get off of the elevator to find Elena Berlusconi waiting for us in the elevator lobby. "Dad! There you are," she says, running over to hug him. "I've been wondering where you were hiding," she says as she lets him go and looks over at me. "Amazia," she starts, coming over to hug me too. "I'm sorry to hear about Jericho. Are you alright?" she lets go to look at me.

"As alright as I can be, I guess," I shrug, surprised by her appearance at the hospital.

"Amazia," Mr. Berlusconi interjects, "why don't you go see him. I'll be in, in a moment."

I nod silently, glancing at him and Elena one last time before walking down to Jared's room.

"What are you doing here?" he asks Elena as I walk away.

"Why didn't you tell me about Jericho? You know he's like a brother to me?" I hear her ask as I turn the corner and can no longer understand their conversation.

As I reach his door, it is slightly ajar. I can hear Jared and Vittori talking at a whisper inside. "Do you, have it?" Jared asks.

"Yes. I made sure it was in your personal effects and secured them right away," Vittori replies.

"And... Amazia? Is she okay?" Jared asks as I push the door open.

"She's perfectly alright," Vittori smiles at me. He stands up, "I'll give you two a minute."

Jared reaches up and pats his arm, "Thanks man."

Vittori nods at him and walks towards the door. He pauses to put his hand on my shoulder, "He's gonna be alright," he whispers to me before exiting the room, closing the door behind him.

I can feel the tears filling up my eyes, but I can no longer contain them as I walk over to Jared's side. He's sitting up in the bed now and his color is already much better now that he's awake. "Jared..." I force out, but my voice cracks before I can say anything else. I look down at his hand, avoiding eye contact.

"Amazia, it's okay. I'm okay," he says, reaching his hand out to take mine.

"Don't strain yourself," I whisper, getting closer so he doesn't have to reach for me.

"Hey, look at me," he says, squeezing my hand to get me to look.

I take in a deep breath and try to stop the tears, wiping them off of my cheek before looking up and into his eyes. As I do, I see so much love and happiness in his eyes, even given the circumstances.

"I'm fine. I promise," he says in a serious tone.

"You're not fine," I laugh at him.

"But I will be," he looks deep into my eyes like he's trying to force me to believe him.

"How can you be so sure?" I ask.

He smiles up at me, "Because I love you too much to leave you behind."

"Babe," I whisper before leaning in and holding his face in my free hand. "I love you, too," I lean in to kiss him on the lips, feeling more love than ever as our lips connect. The tears continue to stream down my face as I feel all of the emotions that I've been bottling up for days release. After several moments, I pull my lips away and rest my forehead against his. "Don't you ever scare me like that again."

"I promise to do my best to dodge any future bullets," he teases.

"That's not funny," I stand up again to look down at him.

"Sorry, babe," he apologizes as we hear the door opening.

We both look over to see Berlusconi and Vittori stepping in. I wipe the tears off of my face again as I sit in the chair next to Jared that I've been sleeping in for days and keep a strong hold on Jared's hand.

"How are you feeling?" Berlusconi asks Jared.

"Better than I should, given the number of new holes in my body," Jared jokes.

Berlusconi looks shocked by Jared's joke. Maybe Jared really has changed more than I was aware of. "Well, that sounds like good news, I think," Berlusconi looks back and forth from Jared and Vittori, assessing the situation.

Vittori tries to hold in a laugh while standing on the opposite side of the bed.

Berlusconi stands at the foot end of Jared's bed and leans on the foot rail as he continues. "Are you up for a... discussion?" he raises his eyebrows as he watches Jared for his reaction.

"This seems serious?" Jared replies in a questioning tone.

Berlusconi glances at me, causing Jared and Vittori to follow suit. Berlusconi looks back at Jared to admit, "Domenic is dead."

"Wait, what?" Vittori asks sounding panicked as he looks back and forth between Berlusconi and myself. "I just let him leave with Amazia a few hours ago!"

"I know, and that was the plan," Berlusconi explains.

"What am I missing?" Jared asks us.

Berlusconi looks to me.

I sigh and look at Jared. "The night we went to help Vittori, the night you got shot, the shooter wasn't after you."

"You're saying it was targeted?" Vittori asks me.

"There's a reason you couldn't find a weapon. They wanted you to call for backup," Jared comes to an understanding, putting the pieces together.

"Who took care of that hit?" Vittori asks Berlusconi.

"Domenic," he answers plainly.

"And it was a setup?" Jared asks.

"Yes," Berlusconi replies, leaving out the most important part.

"If Jared wasn't the target, then who was?" Vittori wants the answer to the missing piece of the puzzle we've laid out.

Berlusconi and I look at one another. I nod, knowing he's waiting for me to acknowledge the elephant in the room. Berlusconi looks to Jared and answers, "Amazia was the target."

"Why?" Vittori asks, shaking his head in confusion.

"Where was Domenic these last few years?" Jared asks, knowing there is more to the story.

"Last few years?" I ask.

"Domenic moved away a few years ago," Vittori explains to me. "He only returned to New York within the last year or so."

"He moved back last winter, after an incident," Berlusconi vaguely answers.

"On a job?" Vittori asks.

"Sort of," Berlusconi shakes his head.

"Where was Domenic?" Jared asks again, getting suspicious of something.

Berlusconi looks to me again. "I didn't have time to tell you anything else," he says to me.

"Whatever you have to say to me, can be said to them. I trust Jared and Vittori. They need to know as much as I do," I reply, not knowing anything about what Berlusconi is about to reveal or how it has to do with me.

Jared squeezes my hand in response to my words, bracing us both for whatever comes next.

Berlusconi sighs and looks down. "For the last few years, Domenic has lived, and worked, in a small town in Arkansas." He looks up to me, then Jared to watch for our reactions.

"Isn't that where you moved here from?" Jared asks me.

"It is," I reply, not putting the pieces together. I look to Berlusconi, "Does that have something to do with why I was his target?"

"Domenic was your brother's best friend, before he died," Berlusconi admits the truth.

"But my brother isn't dead. He's still alive," I reply in a confused voice.

"Are you sure?" Berlusconi asks, looking confused.

"I'm positive. I pay for his long-term care," I explain.

"Long-term care?" Vittori asks.

"Yeah. He's in a specialized memory care facility. He hasn't been the same since the car wreck that killed my father and uncle. He survived, but hasn't been able to function normally since," I explain. I try to avoid Jared's eyes, knowing this is all new to him as well. I never told him about my brother.

Jared squeezed my hand in response, trying to show he's with me. "When was the wreck?"

"A year and a half ago," I answer, looking around as everyone's face changes. They seem to have come to a realization that I can't "Why are you all making that face?"

"What was your uncles name?" Vittori asks, looking for the last piece of a puzzle that was lost for an eternity.

"Antonio Barry," I reply, looking around at all of them as they clearly understand something I don't. "What aren't you guys telling me?"

"That was no accident," Vittori reveals when no one else does.

"What are you talking about? My brother was drunk and wrecked into them; both of their cars flipped. My father and uncle were out trying to find him, but he ran them off the road before they could stop him from driving," I begin to ramble.

"Amazia," Jared says gently, trying to stop me from spiraling. "Antonio Barry wasn't his real name. His name was actually Antonio Barone, and he was in hiding for over twenty years."

"What? What are you talking about? What does that even mean?" I ask looking around at all of them.

"It means we need to go see your brother, before it's too late," Vittori says.

35

I've never been on a private jet before now. I have to admit, it's a much less stressful way to travel. The last time I was in Arkansas, I was packing up that last of my things to drive to Connecticut to officially move into my new house. I sold most of my family's things before closing on the sale of their house. I didn't even bother to visit my brother one last time before leaving, and now I'm wondering if he's really as far gone as the doctors told me. I'm second guessing everything.

"You, okay?" Vittori asks as he sits down across from me on the plane.

I look up, realizing I've been staring off in deep thought for a while. "Umm, yeah. Just a lot going through my head," I admit, feeling more comfortable around Vittori since spending so much time with him at the hospital.

"I'm sorry Jericho can't come with us, but I hope you know you can trust me."

I smile at him, "I do." Vittori has opened up around me too, making me question him less. The cuts and scars along his arms and face have mainly healed. The only one still noticeable is the long laceration down his right arm. He told me that when Domenic attacked them, he still had the knife he murdered the hit subject with. Vittori said he was barely able to get it and the gun from him before I ran through the warehouse. He also shared how mad he was at himself for not realizing who it was sooner.

"Jericho did say that he should be able to go home once we get back from our trip," Vittori adds, trying to cheer me up.

"He's probably better off in the hospital for a few more days while we're gone. He's more likely to actually do his physical therapy while someone is making him," I admit.

Vittori and Berlusconi both laugh, knowing I'm right.

It's only the three of us taking this trip. Berlusconi didn't want to trust anyone else with the news that Antonio Barone was indeed alive and in hiding for twenty years. Berlusconi shared some information about when Uncle Tony used to work alongside him in New York City back in the day. Antonio paid a lot of money to hide any relation to his sister once she got married and officially had a new name. He created a new identity for her entire family. He changed all records of her maiden name so that she could live safely with her new family without anyone ever being able to find her if something went sideways. When he got on the wrong side of a rival Sicilian mafia, he fled the city and went into hiding.

When Antonio ran, he changed his name to Antonio Barry and moved in with his sister, Alessia. Although, her new name was Alicia Franklin, my mother. Antonio tried to keep a normal job and even joined the city council when I was a young child. I helped fill in those blanks for Berlusconi as he was figuring out the entire timeline. It appears that Domenic's father had a hunch about Antonio's whereabouts, so he sent his son to Arkansas under a different surname and enrolled him in a nearby high school to the one that Matteo and I were at. It was Matteo's junior year when he decided to start going by Matthew because he hated his legal name. Once he did, he joined a recreational basketball league where he made more friends than he ever had at school. That was when he started to keep secrets. I never met his friends from basketball, but apparently that was where Domenic met my brother and got him involved in an illegal drug trade.

My brother was never the same after he graduated high school. He dropped out of college before even finishing his first semester. My uncle and him were always arguing about something. My father never understood why Uncle Tony was so protective and angry at Matthew, but now I understand why. My father never knew the entire truth about why Antonio changed their names. My mother never shared the entire truth with him about the mafia her brother was a part of. She was afraid it was going to put them in danger if he knew. When she died of a sudden brain bleed my senior year, my father got into a lot more arguments with Uncle Tony. I never understood what they were constantly arguing about until now. They were not only arguing about Matthew's behavior, but also about the consequences his involvement with drugs could mean for the entire family. I remember my uncle yelling about if anyone found out who they were, they'd all be in danger. I always brushed it off, not wanting to get involved, but maybe this is part of the reason why my parents were never ones to carry out fun family traditions.

"Earth to Amazia," Berlusconi teases.

"Huh? What?" I ask, coming back to the present.

"I said, we're about to land," Berlusconi repeats.

"You sure you're ready for all of this?" Vittori asks.

"As ready as I can be," I admit, not knowing if I can handle any of this, especially without Jared to keep me sane.

* * * * *

Of course, Berlusconi has a professional driver pick us up from the private airfield not far from my childhood home. He's not on Berlusconi's payroll, so we only take a short drive with him to a private car rental service. Berlusconi rents us a blacked-out Dodge Durango and Vittori loads all of our bags while Berlusconi fills out the rental paperwork.

I hear my phone ding, and I look down to find a text from Jared, "Miss you."

I reply, "Miss you too."

"Jared?" Vittori asks.

"Yeah," I smile, putting my phone back into my pocket.

"Did you know he tried to sign out AMA to come here with you?" Vittori asks as he closes the back door of the Durango.

"What? No. I didn't know. Why would he do that? He needs to recover first."

"That's exactly what I told him so he'd stay. That man really loves you. He would do anything to be here with you, including signing out of the hospital too early."

"You were able to talk him into staying?"

"It wasn't easy," he laughs, "but yeah."

"Thank you."

"In return, I promised I wouldn't let you out of my sight. So, maybe take it easy on me?"

I laugh, "Sounds like a plan."

"Ready to go?" Berlusconi asks as he exits the business.

"All set," Vittori answers, holding the back door open for me to climb in.

Once we're all inside, Berlusconi says, "Here goes nothing."

*   *   *   *   *

Berlusconi drives us to the memory care facility where my brother is staying. He hired a doctor to accompany us and check into Matthews medical records since the crash. Once we're all alone in my brother's room, the doctor finally speaks freely.

"These documents are inconclusive," the doctor begins.

"What does that mean?" I ask.

"Some of these documents are fake. Other documents are slightly altered. In reality, this entire file is a big lie to hide what's really going on," the doctor looks at Berlusconi as he stops.

"You can speak freely. Mr. Vittori and Ms. Franklin are trusted allies," Berlusconi explains.

The doctor sighs heavily and pulls out one single sheet of paper. "I performed a secretive drug test on Mr. Franklin's current state. I cannot explain his state before or immediately after the vehicle accident as those documents have all been altered. I can tell you with absolute certainty that his current state is completely medically induced through the use of ketamine."

"Ketamine? I don't recall that being in any of the medical paperwork I've seen or signed over the last year or so," I speak up.

"That's because it isn't authorized for this type of long-term use. Someone is drugging your brother, probably to keep him quiet," the doctor continues.

"Can it have effects on him and his memory because of the long-term misuse?" Berlusconi asks.

"It's possible, but only time will honestly tell. It depends on his state before the ketamine was used to put him in such a disassociated state."

"How soon can we get him transferred to a facility that you, or someone you trust, runs?" Berlusconi asks.

"As soon as I turn in the paperwork," he says handing a copy to me. "I just need a family authorization. I already have a transport ambulance on standby outside. I don't trust leaving him here, in case someone is watching, especially with our sudden and large presence."

"Smart call," Vittori adds.

I sign the paperwork and hand it back to the doctor, trusting that Berlusconi did all of this to help my brother. "Now what?"

"Now, we wait and see how he responds," the doctor advises.

We hang around until Matthew is transported away from the facility. The doctor said it'll likely take several days for him to get any results. He said it'll be a slow process of getting him back to a normal state. He will be running a number of tests and trials as he comes around before reporting anything back to us. We decided to keep Mathew's new location a secret from everyone, including us, in case someone figures out why we transferred him. I tried to send them my billing information for the account the money for my brother's care comes out of, but Berlusconi refused to let me use my money.

I argued that the money I put aside for my brother's care was actually the money my father and uncle left for me. Berlusconi explained that it was likely money left over from what he gave my uncle before he ran to hide. Either way, Berlusconi is paying for my brother's care now and I just need to deal with it.

Berlusconi drives us to a steakhouse half way between the facility and the airport. We sit and have dinner while we wait for our return flight to arrive at the nearby airstrip.

"So, this is where you grew up?" Berlusconi asks, trying to make small talk.

"It is," I vaguely answer.

"Is all of this information about your family overwhelming?" Berlusconi asks.

I sigh, "That's a loaded question."

"Bet you never thought you'd find a connection between the Berlusconi family and yours," Vittori laughs.

"Definitely not, especially after all of Jared's warnings about you guys," I admit, then regret my word choice.

"Warnings?" Vittori asks and Berlusconi looks just as curious.

"Well, he was concerned about your interest in me during the weekend of Elena's wedding," I shrug.

"He didn't want you involved, even back then?" Berlusconi asks.

I nod in response.

"But you two didn't start seeing each other until sometime after the wedding, right?" Berlusconi continues.

"Correct," I admit honestly.

"He clearly had a thing for her the first time he saw her in that hotel lobby," Vittori adds between bites.

"Wait, what?" Berlusconi questions him.

"Just something he said that weekend, about having a strange feeling that he didn't understand," Vittori continues.

"About her?" Berlusconi asks.

"Well, he didn't say anything specific, but looking back, that's the only thing that makes sense," Vittori adds.

"Curious," Berlusconi begins. "Maybe if I had opened up to him more when he was a teenager, he would have been different, like he is now."

"Like he is now?" I ask.

"Amazia, ever since you came into his life, he's been a different person. I've never seen him this happy. He's smiling and carefree. I've never seen anything remotely like that from him," Berlusconi explains.

"What do you think Domenic wanted with Amazia?" Vittori changes the subject.

"I still can't figure that out," Berlusconi admits. "Maybe he realized that she might figure out why her brother wasn't getting better. Especially once I showed him that she existed."

"What do you mean?" Vittori asks.

"He never knew about Amazia's whereabouts. He didn't cross paths with her during the wedding since I kept Domenic off site. It was the day I met her for coffee that I had him come with me."

"When you sent me out of town again?" Vittori asks.

"Yeah. I didn't think I could trust you to keep quiet about Amazia. I knew you'd tell Jericho what was going on."

"So, instead you let Domenic realize who she was and where she moved to?" Vittori accuses.

"Well, clearly I didn't know about the connection," Berlusconi admits.

"Why did he and Jared not get along?" I pipe up to ask.

"Domenic was always jealous of Jericho. He was jealous of his high school years living with my family. He was jealous of the jobs Jericho was getting over him. He was jealous of how good of a job Jericho did. You name it, Domenic was jealous," Berlusconi explains.

"And when Domenic saw Jared outside of The Rush when he walked me back that day, he hated me even more," I put together.

"Probably drove him to create that plan to kill you," Vittori says.

"Lucky for us, he failed," Berlusconi adds.

"Cheers to that," I joke.

Vittori and Berlusconi laugh as we finish dinner and take a late-night flight back to New York City.

36

Just before we land back in New York, Vittori wakes me up to prepare for us for touchdown. I'm reminded of how nice it is to fly on a private jet when we pull up to the private hanger. We're able to instantly get off and right into the vehicle waiting for us.

I'm surprised to see Lorenzo holding the door open for me. "Ms. Franklin," he nods at me.

"You've met Lorenzo?" Vittori asks.

"He's the one who kidnapped me for Berlusconi," I smile a smart-ass smile at him.

"My apologies, ma'am," Lorenzo says.

"Just following orders," I imitate him, causing Vittori to laugh as he climbs into the front passenger seat ahead of me. I'm surprised to see Berlusconi climbing into the other backseat before Lorenzo climbs back into the driver seat.

"Where to boss?" Lorenzo asks Berlusconi.

"You need to stop anywhere before going back to the hospital?" he asks me.

I shake my head, eager to get back to Jared.

"Back to the hospital," Berlusconi instructs.

Berlusconi drops me and Vittori off at the hospital. I didn't expect Vittori to accompany me back upstairs, "You're coming?" I ask as he gets out of the vehicle with me.

"Can't leave you alone," he jokes. "Jared might kill me."

I laugh, "Facts!" We have to enter through the Emergency Room to get into the main hospital as it's only 4 A.M. here. The security staff is already pretty familiar with Vittori and Berlusconi coming and going at all hours, so we have no trouble getting through. Once we're alone in the elevator, I ask the question that's been on my mind all day. "Is Berlusconi in the drug smuggling, or gun smuggling business, or something?"

Vittori only laughs at me.

"What's so funny?" I ask, shocked he's laughing at my question.

"You think that because your brother got mixed up in drugs, that means Berlusconi is too?" he asks in a joking tone.

"Isn't the mafia known for drug trafficking, or something?"

"It's way more complex than they portray in TV shows or even the news."

"So, no to the drugs?" I try to get a straight answer.

"No. We don't have any ties to drugs or smuggling or anything like that."

"Then why do people end up dead?"

"Crossing the Berlusconi Family," he shrugs.

"I'm lost," I admit.

"You've heard of the Sicilian Mafia, right? The one that your uncle got caught up with?"

"Yeah, kind of," I shrug.

"They're the ones who have a group in New York City trafficking drugs. Your uncle tried to stop them from selling in an old neighborhood he covered. He was in charge of protecting that street from such criminal organizations, and the Sicilians wanted him dead, so he ran."

"So, if the Berlusconi's don't traffic drug, what do they do?"

"We charge people for protection. We help political figures buy voters, maybe some occasional extortion," he continues until I interrupt.

"Kidnapping, murder?" I questioningly add to the list.

"Those are generally rare, unless someone crosses the family, or someone who works for the family."

The elevator doors opens and we need to be more cautious of our word choice. "So, Domenic was working for the Sicilian's?"

"That's the best we can gather."

"So, are they going to be mad that we... took care of him?"

"Only if they find out."

"Won't they be suspicious?"

"Maybe, but we got it cleaned up before anyone would know."

"Are you part of the same cleanup crew that Jared is?"

"Sometimes yes, sometimes no," he says as we stop outside of Jared's room. "We all have something we take care of personally or in groups. It does mean more of us coming and going from the same place, but it also means we're really good at what we do. Jared, for example, is the best at cleaning up any mess left behind."

"And you?" I ask, hesitant to even ask.

"Bodies and weapons," he admits.

"Really?" I ask, feeling surprised.

He laughs, "Yeah, but I rarely get involved unless I have to."

"How'd you get that privilege?"

"Berlusconi needed a new right-hand, and Jericho turned it down, so he asked me next."

"Why would Jericho turn it down?"

"A mixture of reasons. Mainly, he wants to distance himself from Berlusconi and the family. He never really wanted to join the family business, but when the Berlusconi family adopted him, he felt he had no choice. He wanted to just do his cleanup job and live his life. Berlusconi kept finding other ways to bring him in and keep him involved, but Jericho wanted nothing to do with Berlusconi himself."

"That's complicated."

"I told you, it's way more complicated than you can imagine."

"One last thing," I pause, waiting for him to let go of the door handle. Once he does, I continue. "What does Berlusconi mean when he says that you aren't the bad guys?" It's the question that's been bothering me since the day Berlusconi had Lorenzo kidnap me.

Vittori shrugs, "We don't go out to cause trouble. We don't go looking for reasons to," he pauses to look around, "to take people out. In reality, we avoid it whenever possible. But we also can't look soft if someone does dare to cross the family."

"You're almost like the nice mafia," I laugh.

"Hey, look at it however you want to, but just don't cross Mr. Berlusconi and you'll be fine," he finishes before opening the door to Jared's room.

Jared is sound asleep when we walk in. Vittori quietly goes over to talk to the person Berlusconi left keeping watch up. He quickly stands to whisper with Vittori before nodding and headed out. Vittori comes over and asks, "Need anything?"

"No," I shake my head. "I'm going to try to get some rest before the morning nurse rounds."

"Get some rest. I'll tell Leo to hangout nearby in case you need anything before I return," he says as he heads toward the door.

"You need to rest too," I add before he opens the door.

"I'll rest when I'm dead," he teases as he opens the door.

"Be careful what you wish for," I joke back as he leaves.

I gently lean in and kiss Jared on the cheek before I move my chair closer to the bed. I climb into my favorite uncomfortable chair and wrap myself in the warm hospital blanket and quickly fall asleep.

* * * * *

"I figured you'd prefer a real breakfast," I wake up to Mr. Berlusconi's voice.

"I'm over the runny hospital eggs, that's for sure," Jared replies as I open my eyes and stretch.

"Good morning, sleepy head," Berlusconi jokes as I throw off the blanket and stand to stretch.

"Good morning to you too," I say in a smart-ass tone.

"Someone's in a snarky mood this morning," Berlusconi teases.

"How are you not exhausted and cranky yourself?" I ask.

"I napped in a comfortable bed instead of that awful chair."

"Cheater," I say, rolling my eyes.

"Babe!" Jared warns.

"Don't worry Jared," Berlusconi jokes. "Amazia and I are friends now. You don't have to worry."

"What exactly happened in Arkansas?" Jared asks suspiciously.

"Good news!" Vittori busts in with a huge smile on his face.

"You've won the lottery?" I ask in my cranky, smart-ass tone.

Vittori rolls his eyes before announcing, "I got your discharge papers!"

"Really?" Jared asks, sitting up in bed.

"Really! You finally get to go home," Vittori says tossing the pages onto the table over the hospital bed.

"Thank god!" Jared smiles. "I really just wanna sleep in my own bed."

"Me too," I groan as I try to stretch out the knot in my lower back.

"You mean, you wanna sleep in my bed?" Jared teases.

"Same difference," I roll my eyes again.

"What did you guys do to make her so cranky?" Jared asks.

"Maybe she's just feeling needy?" Vittori jokes.

"Okay, Okay," Berlusconi interrupts. "Enough of that talk. I don't want any unnecessary images in my head."

Vittori, Jared, and I all laugh at Berlusconi's awkward outburst.

"What?" he asks, looking around at all of us. "You're practically my kids. I don't want to think about what you guys do during your off time."

"So, dead bodies are fine, but not what consenting adults do in their personal time?" I ask in a serious tone.

"She has a point," Vittori adds while eating from his own breakfast container.

"Is that mine?" I ask, ripping my breakfast from Vittori's hand.

"Oops, sorry," he apologizes before looking at Jared. "Who pissed in her cereal this morning?"

"That's what I keep asking," Berlusconi says under his breath.

"Oh, wait! I know," Vittori says before disappearing into the hall for a minute. He returns a few moments later with a cup carrier full of Dunkin Donuts coffee. "Here you are," he says, handing me my cup before he takes his or Berlusconi's out.

"Ah, should have known," Berlusconi says, taking his own. "She runs off of caffeine."

"One thing I'll never understand," Jared adds.

"Weirdo," Vittori and I say in unison.

37

Vittori brings back a duffle bag with a change of clothes for Jared once the doctors officially release him. He insists on getting dressed on his own, but finally lets me help when he struggles getting his shirt and hoodie on without help. He rolls his eyes at me when I tell him to quit being stubborn. He's allowed to ask for help while he continues to recover.

Vittori waits for us in the hallway as Jared refuses to use the hospital required wheelchair to leave. I'm not sure if he already told the nurses that it wasn't going to happen, or if Vittori paid them off. What I do know is that he insists on walking out with me and Vittori like a normal person, so we let him. When we exit the elevator into the basement level valet parking garage, I'm not surprised to see Lorenzo driving Berlusconi around in his BMW.

"Where's my car?" Jared randomly asks.

"I parked it at your place right after the incident," Vittori answers.

"Shit. Can't believe I didn't think about that until now," Jared looks surprised he forgot all about his precious car.

"I think fighting for your life was a little more important," I add.

"I guess," Jared laughs as he gently climbs into the back seat, sliding into the center so I can sit next to him.

Vittori climbs into the opposite side and secures his seatbelt before tapping on Lorenzo's seat, "Hit it."

Berlusconi is typing away on his phone in the front passenger seat nearly the entire ride to Jared's condo from the hospital.

"What are you writing up there? A book?" I ask a few blocks away from our destination.

"Just replying to an email with your boss," he says casually.

"You're what?" I lean forward, trying to see.

"Relax," he says, locking his phone and putting it away. "I was forwarding the doctor's notes excusing you from work to take care of Jericho."

"What doctors note?" I ask.

"The one I created and got the doctor to sign," he shrugs.

"You have no shame," I state.

"Hey," he turns to face us. "What happened to Jericho was unexpected and traumatic. I only used that to be sure you got time off without repercussions. I took care of all of that while you were busy taking care of him."

"That's how my boss found out I was taking the time off," I come to the realization, never knowing how Klarissa found out I was taking a short leave.

"You were a bit distracted," Berlusconi shrugs.

"Remember the first day when she wouldn't even talk to us?" Vittori jokes.

"Or when she wouldn't stop hitting me?" Berlusconi jokes back.

Jared's eyes grow wide at that. "You did what?" he asks me.

"Relax, Jericho," Berlusconi says as we pull over in front of Jared's residence. "She was upset that you were hurt, and she thought it was my fault. I understood and I took it."

"Holy shit, Amazia," Jared looks at me. "What ever happened to not poking the bear?" he asks in a serious tone, but his eyes are teasing me.

"We better get these two inside before they start having a lovers quarrel," Vittori jokes.

"Haha, real funny," I roll my eyes as I open my own door before anyone else can get to it.

"I really like her for you, Jericho," Vittori teases.

"What the hell happened while I was in that hospital," Jared asks as he slowly climbs out of the SUV.

"Realization that life is short," Berlusconi offers while rolling down his window.

"So, what's next?" Jared asks him.

"You, taking some time off," he replies.

"What? Seriously?" Jared sounds shocked.

"Son, you took three bullets only days ago. You deserve some time off," Berlusconi reaches out and holds Jared's shoulder as if he's trying to make him understand.

"There'll be plenty of work for you once you're all healed and have graduated from physical therapy," Vittori jokes.

"When did you become such a smart-ass?" Jared asks him.

"I guess I spent too much time with your girlfriend," he shrugs and smiles at us.

"Come on," I try to change the subject. "Let's get inside before you pass out from shock of how everyone is acting."

"Oh, before you go," Berlusconi stops us. "We'd like for you two to come by for dinner tomorrow night."

"We?" Jared asks.

"Molly, Elena, and myself," he answers.

"We haven't had a family dinner in years," Jared shrugs.

"Again," Berlusconi pauses for a moment, "we're reminded that life is too short. I know I haven't always been the most caring person in the world, but I want to be sure I do everything to keep my family together. And that includes you Jericho, and your lovely… girlfriend, Amazia." He looks at me strangely when he pauses before saying girlfriend. I really have no idea what the pause means, but it's a bit odd.

Jared looks to me before accepting Berlusconi's offer. I nod in agreement. "What time do we need to be there tomorrow?" he asks, sounding reluctant.

"Dinner is at five," Berlusconi says as he closes the window of BMW.

"We'll be there," Jared replies.

"You two go enjoy some alone time together," Vittori teases before climbing into the BMW himself.

"Jackass," Jared whispers under his breath.

"What's wrong with you?" I tease.

He smiles, "Nothing. Just Vittori has been giving me a hard time since the hospital."

"Well, let's go inside and get you settled back in your home," I say, ushering him towards the door.

"Our home," he says, stopping to look into my eyes.

"Our home," I smile back at him.

Before I can say anything else he leans in and kisses my lips, reaching forward to hold my hand in his. I kiss him back before pulling back and clearing my throat. I shake the keys in my opposite hand and glance toward the door. Jared groans but lets go of my hand so I can unlock the door and let us in.

*   *   *   *   *

"What am I supposed to wear to family dinner?" I ask, frantically tossing my clothes out of the closet as I worry about what to wear.

"Babe, why are you so worried about what to wear? It's not like you're meeting any of them for the first time."

"Well, this is the first time I'm meeting Molly and not serving her dinner," I add, looking for a proper excuse.

"And you spent the afternoon with Elena before her wedding, so it's not like you don't know her some."

"And she was at the hospital the day you woke up."

"Really?" he stops to ask.

"Yeah. She was there when Berlusconi and I got back from dealing with Domenic."

Jared doesn't immediately say anything. Instead, he makes his way over and reaches out to grab my arm, pulling me away from the closet to talk. He looks serious as he looks into my eyes, "And how are you dealing with being there for that?"

"What? Domenic?"

He nods, rubbing my arm gently.

"I mean… It was awful, but I was so glad it wasn't me, that I pushed most of it from my mind I guess."

"Do you wanna talk about it?" he asks, reaching his arms around me and pulling me close.

I shake my head, "No. I'm fine."

"Are you sure?" he pushes gently.

I smile, trying to help prove it. "I'm sure."

"Promise you'll tell me if it ever becomes too much?"

"Promise," I smile.

He leans in and kisses me as he cradles the back on my neck, gently pulling me closer. His kisses deepen as I feel the passion between us rising once again today. I find myself wrapping my fingers through his overgrown hair as his lips leave mine to kiss his way down my neck.

"Babe?" I say, interrupting our moment.

"What is it?" he asks between kisses.

"We have to get ready for dinner."

He sighs against my collarbone, "Party pooper."

"Yeah, that's me," I shrug as he leans up to kiss my lips one last time before letting me go.

"I know you didn't want me to stop," he teases.

"Of course I didn't!" I practically yell at him. "I've been impatiently waiting for you to recover."

He smiles, reaching up to brush a lock of hair back behind me ear, "Wear the dress."

"What?" I ask as he turns to walk away.

"Wear the blue dress, to dinner."

"Dinner is that fancy?" I ask in shock.

"Sometimes, on special occasions."

"What have I gotten myself into," I whisper to myself as I pull the dress off the hanger in the closet.

I take over the bathroom to finish getting ready while Jared changes in the bedroom. When I step out, I find Jared buttoning up a collared shirt. "Ah, that's why you didn't need help. You, cheater you," I tease.

"Just trying to look the part," he admits. "You ready?" he asks as he pulls on a jacket.

"No time like the present," I admit as he holds his arm out for me to take. "Why thank you, sir," I tease in a flirty voice.

"Anything for you, my love," he smiles.

"I really wish you were allowed to drive," I say as we reach the bottom of the stairs.

"Why? So you could stare at me the entire drive?"

"Partly," I tease back. "And, because you know where we're actually going."

"We're going to the house in Greenwich. That's where they're living currently."

"Why didn't you tell me they have a place in Connecticut?"

"Babe, they have a place pretty much everywhere," he laughs.

"Right… Damn rich people."

He laughs at my response, "Come on."

As we step out of the condo, we find Vittori waiting for us at the curb. "It's about time," he teases.

"What are you doing here?" Jared asks.

"Escorting you to dinner."

"Really? He's making you work tonight?" Jared pushes.

"Actually, he invited me to dinner, but I declined."

"Why?" I ask.

"It feels too personal, eating with the family. Plus, Elena's husband isn't going to be there, so it really is just the family, along with Amazia, of course."

"All the more reason to stay," I add, hoping for another neutral party.

* * * * *

As soon as we sit down for dinner, I realize just how rich these people really are. There are different servants for every part of dinner. There is even one who is simply in charge of beverages. Every time you take a sip, it's practically refilled on the spot.

"So, you're Antonio's niece?" Mrs. Berlusconi asks.

"Yeah," I start. "Quite a surprise when I discovered that my family is connected to all of you."

"That was some surprise!" she continues politely.

"I'm really glad you stayed with me the morning of my wedding, especially now that we know what Domenic is capable of," she rolls her eyes towards her father.

"I had no idea that he and his father were working with the Sicilians," Mr. Berlusconi admits, looking at her seriously, as if to tell her to drop the subject.

"Where is your husband?" I ask, changing the subject easily.

"He's away on business in California for a few days," she smiles.

"Does he travel often?" I dig.

"A few trips here and there. Sometimes it's more frequent than others," she vaguely replies.

The evening continues with countless small talk. I zone out for most of it, feeling Jared's discomfort at the family table. I glance over at him to try to gauge what's bothering him, but he hides it well, smiling along with everyone else as the evening goes by. After dinner, Mr. Berlusconi, Jared, and I retire to his study to talk.

"Why did you really ask us here?" Jared asks.

"Well, I wanted to lay some things out on the table," Mr. Berlusconi replies.

"Like what?" Jared follows up.

"About your adoption," he begins.

"What about it?" Jared asks, looking confused.

"I know you were going through a lot. You know that I picked you out of everyone because of how quiet and damaged you seemed."

"Thanks for the reminder."

"My point is... I chose you because I thought you'd be helpful in the long run. And for years, you proved my point perfectly. You were able to handle anything I threw at you, because you didn't process emotions and feelings the way most people do. I always thought that was a good thing. You could never be hurt by the emotions that arise when someone threatens the ones you love. I thought it would keep you safe. In reality, it was just a waiting game for you. Once you let Amazia into your life, you changed. I knew there was something about her when you mentioned your interaction with her in the hotel lobby. You never really cared enough to notice anyone… until Amazia. She helped us out that weekend in more ways than one."

"Why were you there, by the way?" I ask Jared. "Like, why were you really there?"

Jared looks down for a moment before looking up at Berlusconi, who nods.

"Remember you were asking about Seth?" Jared starts, waiting for me to acknowledge before continuing. "I was there to clean that up."

"That's why you knew Seth wouldn't be a problem again," I think aloud.

"Wait, you had a problem with him?" Berlusconi asks, sounding irritated.

"Not really. I handled it. It wasn't an issue with me," I shrugged it off.

"He was greedy and cocky," Berlusconi starts. "It wasn't until the day before the rehearsal dinner that Elena was able to identify the man who tried to rape her six months ago."

I reach up and cover my mouth in shock.

"That was when I was called in, along with the band, to work the wedding," Jared adds in.

"So, you guys..." I cannot get out the words.

"It wasn't an unbiased call in any way," Berlusconi admits. "But it was justified."

"That's... Wow..." is all I can get out.

"My point in bringing this up," Berlusconi tries to get the conversation back on track, "is to say what's been on my mind. I told Amazia some of this a few days ago, but I wish I had done things differently once we adopted you."

"What do you mean?" Jared asks.

"Molly and I were discussing it, and we both think that we could have made you feel more like a welcome part of the family."

"You welcomed me just fine. You took me in and cared for me instead of leaving me in the system when it was determined I had no living relatives."

"Yes, but we didn't make sure you felt like part of the family. I know it doesn't seem like it, but you are like a son to me. Maybe I should have realized it sooner, but you almost getting killed, brought my life full circle for me. I should have made you feel like a son as soon as you arrived here."

"I'm not sure how that would have gone over," Jared shrugs.

"Yeah," Berlusconi laughs, "you were a pretty grumpy teenager." After a brief pause, Berlusconi glances at me before continuing. "I'm wondering now, though, if you might have broken out of your shell sooner if we had been more welcoming. Either that, or maybe Amazia was necessary in your life, but I'll never know if I could have made a difference sooner. My point is, I never thought you were capable of being this happy and carefree. Molly and I want you to come around and be a part of this family again. Elena agrees. She wants you to be around when they start a family. She wants you to be Uncle Jericho and all that entails."

Jared doesn't react at first. He's sitting there trying to process.

"And, we wouldn't mind have Amazia around more either," Berlusconi adds, bringing a smile to my face.

After an extended silence, Jared stands up. "Alright," he says while looking up.

"Alright?" Berlusconi asks for clarification.

Jared shrugs, "Why not give it a chance?"

Before Jared can react, Berlusconi pulls him into a hug, looking awkward, like they both have no idea how to hug one another. I try to stifle a laugh as I watch their awkward connection.

"Okay, Okay," Jared says, patting Berlusconi's back before pulling away awkwardly.

"That was…" I start, looking for the right word and finding it as soon as they both look at me, "mortifying." I try to hold in a laugh, but lose it once I see them laughing too.

"Was it that bad?" Berlusconi asks.

"Possibly worse," I laugh out.

"At least you're still my smart-ass," Jared says, wrapping an arm around me back.

"Was she always like this?" Berlusconi asks.
"Oh, I was," I answer for myself.
"I just warned her not to be like this around you," he adds.
"Well, that worked really well," Berlusconi jokes.

38

Two days after dinner with the Berlusconi family, I decide to go back to work, but it's short lived. Klarissa tries to catch me up on everything going on. We look through all of the reservations and room blocks she's created to check for errors. She did a great job with my unannounced absence, and she held down the fort. I was in the middle of telling her as much when my phone begins to ring with an unknown number displayed on the screen.

"Why does this number seem familiar?" I wonder out loud.

Klarissa looks over and shrugs, "It's a Connecticut area code. Better answer it."

"Hello," I answer, looking at Klarissa as I wait for the voice to identify themselves.

"Is this Ms. Franklin?" a male voice asks.

"This is...?" I reply in a suspicious tone.

"This is Sergeant Bradfield from the Stamford Police Department. Do you have a moment to speak with me?"

"Yes sir," I reply, feeling worried and confused.

"Do you still reside on Shippan Avenue?"

"I still own the residence, yes. I haven't been out there in a week or so."

"And are you familiar with your neighbor, Mr. Brownstone?"

"Yes, sir. Is he alright?"

"Are you able to come by the house or the station for a quick word?"

"I mean, I could, but I'm at work in the city at the moment. Would be at least an hour until I could be there. Do you need me to head back to Stamford?"

He sighs, "Ma'am, I hate to tell you this over the phone, but Mr. Brownstone was found deceased in his residence this morning."

"What? What happened? He was doing fine the last time I was out there," I begin to ramble.

"We're still investigating and I cannot comment further at this time. Several neighbors advised us that you were the only person in the neighborhood that he regularly spoke with, is that correct?"

"Yeah, umm, I used to check on him every few days. I took care of the snow in front of both of our places all winter. He is… was… he was a nice man."

"I would like for you to come out here after work, if you don't mind, so we could ask you a few more questions."

"Of course, I will be on my way shortly," I reply before hanging up.

"What happened?" Klarissa asks.

I put the phone down briefly and look up at her. "My neighbor, Mr. Brownstone. He's dead."

* * * * *

As soon as I get off the phone, I pack up my bag and clock out. I walk out of the employee exit, leading towards the subway station to get back to Jared's as fast as possible. I should have probably called him before leaving, but my mind is racing and I didn't know what I should do first.

Shortly after stepping out onto the sidewalk, I hear a male's voice yell, "Amazia! Amazia, wait!"

I stop, thinking the voice is familiar. I turn slowly to see Lorenzo running up to me from the other end of the block. "Lorenzo?"

"Hey! Where are you going?" Lorenzo asks, stopping in front of me, clearly out of breath from his short jog.

"Back to Jared's," I answer before pausing to check on his condition. "Are you, okay? You look like you're having a heart attack or something."

He stands up straight and adjusts his jacket, "Yes, ma'am, I'm fine. Just don't run well in the cold. Hurts my lungs."

"And why were you running?" I question suspiciously.

"Is your car here?" he asks.

"No, I took the subway," I admit.

"That's what I thought. Come on, my cars down the street. I'll drive you back to Jared's."

"It's fine, really. I can walk to the subway and then…" I start but am interrupted.

"Amazia. I can't let you take the subway, Berlusconi's orders. Please don't make me go against that," Lorenzo pleads.

"How do I know I can trust you?" I ask hesitantly.

"Look," he says, pulling out his phone and finding a message before turning the phone to me and placing the phone into my outstretched hand. "Vittori sent it this morning. Berlusconi was worried when you came to work and didn't take a car. He doesn't want you on the subway, alone, until we know for sure if Domenic was working alone or not."

"Okay. Fine," I say handing back the phone, "but no word to Vittori or Berlusconi about me leaving early or going to Connecticut until I tell Jared."

"Connecticut?" Lorenzo asks.

I give him a death stare. Didn't I just say I have to tell Jared first.

Lorenzo raises both of his hands in defense. "Shit, sorry. Just going to drive the car and keep my mouth shut." I'm not sure who Lorenzo is more afraid of, Berlusconi or me.

On the way, I text Jared that I'm coming home early and will be there soon. He replies right away asking if everything is okay. I reply that I'll explain when I get there, but we need to leave shortly after I arrive. He replies that he is getting dressed and will be waiting for me.

As soon as Lorenzo drops me off at the house, I see Jared looking out the window. He rushes to greet me at the door. "Why did Lorenzo drive you home? Is everything okay? Are you okay?"

I raise one hand to stop his rambling. "Don't worry I'm fine," I say before leaning in to kiss his cheek and squeeze past him to get inside where it's warm. "Apparently Berlusconi doesn't want me traveling to and from the hotel alone. Lorenzo was hanging around outside in case he caught me coming or going on my own."

"Really?" Jared sounds surprised.

"I was confused too. He showed me a text from Vittori to standby at The Rush. I didn't have time to complain or argue."

"Why? What's wrong?"

"Remember Mr. Brownstone? My neighbor in Connecticut?"

"Yeah, older fella? I shoveled his driveway when I did yours."

"That's the one," I start, not wanting to admit what I learned. "He's dead. A Sergeant from Stamford Police Department called to inform me. He asked that I head out there, if possible, to speak with him. Said that all the neighbors said I was the only one he ever talked to."

"And you're going?" he asks me as I set my bag down on a nearby chair and pick up my car keys.

"Yeah. I figure it'll be good to check on the house too. It's been empty since before you got... well you know... your incident," I awkwardly avoid the shooting word. "You coming?"

"Of course, babe. I'll go anywhere you need me to," he smiles and reaches out to take my hand.

"Come on," I say, heading for the door.

"Should I call Berlusconi and Vittori?" Jared asks. I'm not sure if he's looking for permission to tell them or checking to see if they already know.

"Tell Vittori first. I told Lorenzo to keep my leaving work early quiet until I could tell you what was going on."

"You told Lorenzo?"

"No. Just told him I had an errand to run."

On the way out of the city, Jared talks to Vittori first, filling him in on the development. Jared explains that we really don't know anything about his death or if it was suspicious yet. We just wanted him to know where we ran off to. Vittori says he'll fill Berlusconi in as he is about to pick him up.

"He said to call him ASAP if the Sergeant mentions foul play or anything suspicious," Jared says to me after hanging up. "They're going to look into it either way, but they want to know if they need to be worried."

"You really think it has something to do with the family?" I ask as I drive into Connecticut.

"I'm not sure, but I don't think we should simply rule it out either."

"Great," I say, trying to process what else could possibly happen this year.

"Hey," Jared starts, reaching over and resting his hand on my leg. "Don't overthink anything."

"Kind of hard not to, especially if something terrible happened to Mr. Brownstone... If he was harmed because of me... It's not like he chose for me to purchase the house next door to him while unknowingly running away from my past."

"Okay, you have a point. Let's just not jump to that conclusion until we know more."

"Okay. I will try," I glance over to him and smile, trying to keep my thoughts calm for the rest of the ride.

* * * * *

As I pull down the street, I notice a large number of police vehicles present near my house. There is a police line and an officer standing by a block away. I roll down my window as I pull up next to him. "Afternoon ma'am. Streets closed."

"I'm here to see Sergeant Bradfield. My name is Amazia Franklin. I live next door to the deceased," I explain.

"Oh, right. Hang on," he says before stepping away and talking into his radio. After several long moments he steps back up to my window. "Okay, I'll hold up the tape. You can drive down and park in your driveway like normal. Sergeant Bradfield will meet you there."

"Thank you," I say as I roll up my window and drive under the police tape, pulling into my driveway and putting the car in park before anyone walks up. "This is awkward."

Jared shrugs, "Guess we knew what we were in for."

"Did we though?" I ask as I reach for the door handle and step out. Jared follows my lead and does the same.

Jared and I meet at the back of the car as we see someone walking over from Mr. Brownstone's yard. "Ms. Franklin?" he asks as he approaches us.

"Yes, sir," I reply, shaking his hand once he extends it.

He looks at Jared suspiciously.

"Jericho Berlusconi," Jared says, holding his hand out for the Sergeant to shake.

I try to hide my surprise at the name he uses with the police. "My boyfriend," I add, giving the Sergeant the connection to why he's here.

"Did you also know the deceased?" he asks Jared.

"I met him once, a few weeks ago after a snowstorm. I got up early to shovel our driveways before leaving for work in the city," Jared answers.

"And you spoke to Mr. Brownstone?"

"Yes, sir. He came out to ask who I was," Jared laughs at the memory. "We spoke for a brief moment before he said he was glad to see a man taking care of things for Ms. Franklin for once, instead of her doing everything herself."

"Yes," the Sergeant adds, looking through his notes. "Several of the neighbors stated that Ms. Franklin often took care of shoveling both yards as well as many summer yard tasks as well."

I shrug, "Was just being a good neighbor."

"Some of the elderly in our community really need a kind neighbor like you," the Sergeant says while still flipping through notes. He takes out a pen and finds a blank page before glancing up at Jared and I. "Let me go ahead and get this out of the way. Where were you both on Sunday evening?"

"Sunday…" I start. "That was almost a week ago."

"Six days," the Sergeant says.

"At the hospital," I reply, knowing this is a great alibi for us, but then wondering what Jared will think.

"The hospital?" the Sergeant asks, looking for more details.

"Oliver Wolcott Medical Center, in the city," I continue.

"The entire day?" the sergeant replies, taking notes as he continues to question us.

"I may have left for an hour or two to go home to shower and change," I finish.

"Home? As in here?" he asks pointing at my house.

"OH! No. Home as in Jericho's home," I reply, using the name he used, trying to be careful to follow his lead. Though I really wish he would speak up.

"And where were you on Sunday, Mr. Berlusconi?"

"The hospital," he answers vaguely.

"The same one?" the sergeant asks in an annoyed tone.

"Yes, sir."

"Did you leave at all?"

"No, sir. I was admitted at the time."

"Admitted?" he asks, looking up at Jared.

"Yes, sir. I was recovering from an incident," he replies vaguely, giving Sergeant Bradfield reason to be suspicious of Jared and the circumstances.

"I don't want to pry, but I have to ask; what kind of incident?" he asks.

I feel myself holding my breath, but I try my best to not show how nervous I feel with this line of questioning. Jared must know what he's doing here. He must have plans for if this ever happens on a job. Are his hospital records sealed? Can Mr. Berlusconi hide what happened to him?

"I was shot, sir," he admits plainly.

"Oh, I'm sorry to hear that," he sounds sincere, but also looks at Jared with more suspicion in his eyes. "Are you recovered?"

"No, sir, not fully. I've only been out of the hospital a few days. This is my first time out of the house since leaving the hospital, but Amazia didn't want to come out here alone. I'm not even cleared to drive yet or lift weight or anything really."

"Well, you look well for someone who was shot recently," the sergeant continues questioning, masking it as caring for his situation. "I took a bullet once, worst pain. Where were you hit?"

"Abdomen, three times; although, one was more of a graze, I guess. Somehow missed all my major organs and got into surgery fast. I'm pretty lucky to be alive and standing here right now," Jared is so relaxed in his answers.

"Three times? Wow, who did you piss off?" the Sergeant laughs, but still taking notes.

"Tried to help a shop owner get rid of a prowler. Didn't know he had a gun, or I'd have left it to the professionals," Jared answers, gesturing to the Sergeant.

"Usually that's the best solution, especially in New York City," the Sergeant says, satisfied with Jared's answers. He looks back to me, "When was the last time you were home. Here, home," he adds gesturing toward my house.

"Umm, about two weeks ago, maybe. Everything has been a bit of a blur since Jericho's stay in the hospital. I don't think I could tell you how many days passed when I was sleeping in a chair in the lobby or his room."

"Is there a reason you haven't been home?" he's reaching.

"Jericho and I had been discussing moving in together. I didn't want to let go of this place yet, but we decided to mainly stay at his place in the city, since we both work in the city. It was wasting a lot of extra commute time, going back and forth to see one another," I admit.

"I can understand that," Sergeant Bradfield says as he takes a few more notes and closes his notebook. "My wife lived and worked in the city when we first met. Going back and forth was a real bitch. Thankfully it all worked out in the end for us. You should probably hang onto this place until you know for sure what you guys want to do long term. Not easy to get a nice suburban house like this so close to the city and the sound."

"That's good advice. Thank you," I smile kindly.

"Well, I really wanted to get those questions out of the way to help clear you as a possible suspect, but if your story checks out about the hospital, then clearly neither of you could have been here at the time of Mr. Brownstone's passing."

"He was such a kind person," I add, looking down, sad at the loss. "Did he become ill? We never talked about his medical situation or anything."

"It's an active investigation, so I can't divulge much. What I can say is that this is being investigated as an unwitnessed death, with possible foul play involved."

"Foul play?" Jared asks, sounding as shocked as I feel. "Who would want to harm an elderly man?"

"Unfortunately, it doesn't look like a simple case of natural causes," the Sergeant says before pulling his phone from his pocket to answer a call. "I've got to take this. Are you planning on staying the night out here?" he questions as he points towards the house.

I look at Jared who shakes his head slightly so I know for sure how to answer. "No, sir. We plan on checking on a few things before heading back to the city."

"That's fine. I don't see any reason to further question you. You two be safe going home, and good luck on the rest of your recovery," he says as he answers his phone and walks off towards Mr. Brownstone's house.

Jared nods at me and we silently make our way into my house. Thankfully, the heat has been working fine because I'm freezing. Between the cold weather and the odd line of questioning, which I wasn't prepared for, my nerves got the best of me. I close and lock the door before rubbing my hands up and down my arms in an attempt to warm myself up.

"Shit!" Jared whispers before pulling out his phone. He texts someone before looking up at me and realizing my posture. "Babe. What wrong?" he asks while sliding his phone back into his pocket and coming over to me. He takes over rubbing my arms.

"Just freezing all of a sudden," I admit with a weak smile.

He turns and pulls a blanket off the nearby couch. He comes back over and wraps the blanket around me before pulling me in. "Come here," he wraps me into a hug, rubbing my back to warm me up as he cradles me against him. "Better?" he asks as he pulls back enough to look into my eyes.

"Much," I smile up at him. "What do you think happened?" I ask, sadness clear in my voice as I imagine all of the terrible things that might have happened to Mr. Brownstone.

"Shh, shh," Jared tries to stop me. "Don't think about it. We don't know that it had anything to do with us."

"But he said," I start.

"He was vague and he wants you to break and give him something that he doesn't need to know."

"Do you think he's suspicious?"

"He's definitely suspicious. He seemed to believe our alibi easily. We just need to be sure it all lines up when he looks into it."

"And, is your name at the hospital Jericho Berlusconi?"

"It is… it was," he shrugs.

"Is that your last name?" I ask, realizing I don't know what it is, legally.

"That's complicated," he shrugs. "Just like I go by Jared instead of Jericho, Berlusconi is the name I use with the family. Anything medical or legal is Berlusconi."

"So, you have like two identities, or something?" I ask.

"Or something."

"If Berlusconi is Jericho's last name, then is Jared's Wright?"

"Whatever I want it to be," he shrugs again. "I just tell Vittori and he takes care of any identification I need."

"Seriously?" I ask, feeling surprised at this revelation.

"It's how we can work so many different jobs when around the family without anyone catching on or finding a trend. Like, when I was the band manager, Jared Wright. I've used that one ever since, but legally I took on the name Berlusconi when I was adopted."

"What was your birth name?"

"Jericho Ryan Castelluccio."

"That's a mouthful," I laugh.

"You're telling me. Berlusconi was an improvement."

There is silence between us for several moments while my mind wanders back to Mr. Brownstone. "Do you think he suffered?"

"I sure hope not," he replies. He must see the emotions rising to the surface. As soon as the tears reach my eyes, he pulls me in close, cradling my head against his shoulder as they begin to flow uncontrollably. "It's okay babe. We're going to figure out what happened."

"What if it was my fault?" I whisper through the tears. "What if he was killed because of me? How am I supposed to live with that?"

"Let's take it one step at a time, babe. We don't know for sure if this had anything to do with either of us. It could all be a big coincidence."

39

Once I shed all of the tears that I can, Jared helps me do a quick walk through around the house. We check bathrooms and air filters, as well as making sure there isn't anything in the kitchen which needs to be tossed. There are definitely things in the fridge that could go, but we decide we'll come back within the next week or two to clear it out. That way our trash isn't suspicious for the police surrounding the area.

I grab a duffle bag and pack a few more of my things to take back to Jared's with us. Jared continues to check that nothing seems amiss in the house as I grab one last hoodie from my closet and zip the bag. He comes back into my bedroom when he hears the zipper.

"Ready to go?" he asks.

"I am," I smile, tossing the strap over my shoulder.

"Here, let me," Jared starts to reach out.

"Oh, no, no, mister," I smile. "You can't lift anything until your doctor allows it."

"Yeah, you're right. Thanks, babe," he smiles, but looks defeated. He doesn't like feeling helpless.

"Hey, I just want you to recover as fast as possible. I need you back to one hundred percent," I say, stepping closer. "I need my fierce protector back on the job."

"He's still on the job," Jared whispers back slowly.

"Not the way that I *need*," I whisper back sensually before rising on my tip toes to gently press my lips against his.

"Well," he says as he reluctantly pulls back, "let's get back home so we can continue this."

"So, we can be alone rather than a house surrounded by police and detectives?" I ask.

"So that we can be somewhere I know is safe," he explains. "I can't protect you alone. In the city, we have help."

"Since when can't you protect me?"

"Since those three bullets tried to take me out," he shrugs.

"Good point. Let's go."

*　　*　　*　　*　　*

We leave without any of the officers making a big deal out of it. The same officer who raised the tape earlier, raises it again so we can leave. Although I can see several neighbors out watching, no one else tries to contact me or stop us from leaving.

As soon as we leave the area, Jared takes out his phone to call Berlusconi directly. He puts it on speaker phone, "Jericho?" he answers.

"Hey. You're on speaker. Amazia's with me."

"This doesn't sound good."

"The investigators are looking into the deceased as an unwitnessed death with possible foul play, to use their words."

"Any idea the nature of the death?" Berlusconi asks.

"They didn't give anything away," Jared shrugs as he responds.

"They get alibis from you two?"

"He did. They know we were both at the hospital."

"You used your Berlusconi name with them, correct?"

"Yes, sir. I did."

"Good. I'll make some calls and take care of the hospital and the Stamford Police Department. You two heading back to the city?"

"Yes, sir."

"Good. Vittori is going to meet you at your place. There will be two others on watch at all times around you two until we can get to the bottom of this. You got a room Vittori can crash in?"

"Yeah. We'll figure it out."

"Okay," Berlusconi says, sounding worried as he pauses before continuing. "Drive safe and keep your eyes peeled. If whoever this is wanted you two back in Connecticut, there is a chance they're watching or following."

"I hope that isn't the case, but I'll keep an eye out."

"See you two tomorrow," Mr. Berlusconi says before disconnecting.

* * * * *

When I pull up to Jared's, I see Vittori stepping out of his own vehicle to meet us.

"He's been here waiting for us," Jared says as he unbuckles his belt and reaches for the door handle to get out onto the sidewalk.

I follow suit and exit the vehicle. I grab my duffle from the backseat before following Jared to meet Vittori half way to the door. "Hey," I say as I walk up.

Jared puts his arm around my back and continues their conversation. "They don't seem suspicious about us or that it might have anything to do with us."

"Foul play, though?" Vittori asks. "Maybe they were just trying to see how you'd react."

"It's possible," Jared adds. "Either way, he knows we were both at the hospital during the suspected time of death. As long as Berlusconi can cover up the reason behind the shooting, then we should be good."

"What exactly does 'cover it up' mean?" I ask.

"Normally, in a shooting, the police would be called to the hospital," Vittori starts. "Berlusconi had to create a cover story and be sure it stayed out of police reports. He has a doctor at Oliver Wolcott Medical Center on our staff. The only reason we had to bring Jericho to the hospital itself is because of how bad off we thought he was."

"How bad off I was," Jared corrects. "Even the doctor said that if you hadn't brought me in, I probably wouldn't have made it."

"Good call," I add with a smile.

"It was difficult to decide while you were screaming at me the entire time," Vittori jokes.

"Rude," I say before walking away towards the front door.

"Babe!" Jared yells and runs up behind me.

"She was yelling… a lot!" Vittori adds as he follows us inside.

"Maybe now's the time to keep that to yourself," I hear Jared whisper to Vittori.

"What? She can take it," Vittori replies.

*　　　*　　　*　　　*　　　*

First thing in the morning, I stir as soon as I feel Jared sliding out of bed. "Come back to bed," I groan.

He crawls back over and kisses my forehead. "It's time to get up, love."

"But I don't wanna," I groan again, pulling the covers up higher.

"Come on," he pushes in his sweet voice. "Get dressed and I'll make you some coffee."

"You sure know the way to my heart first thing in the morning," I tease.

"Don't you know it," he says before kissing my cheek and crawling off the bed.

I open my eyes and roll over towards him. He smiles when he sees me watching. He pulls a pair of jeans from his dresser and slides them on before disappearing into the bathroom to brush his hair and teeth. He still really needs a haircut. It's definitely been too long. I watch when he comes back out and crosses the room to the closet to try to find a shirt. As he goes, I can see the new scars still healing all over. The most healed is the graze along his right side just along his ribcage.

There are two other larger scars on the front of his abdomen, along with several smaller incision marks along his side, abdomen, and his flank from the multiple surgeries he went through those first two days. He steps back out of the closet and looks at me watching him. He pauses and says "What?" with a smile before pulling his shirt on, clearly in some pain while doing it.

"Just watching you," I smile back at him.

He comes over to my side of the bed and leans down as I roll over to face him. "Checking out all my new scars?" he teases.

"Something like that," I admit.

He sits on the side of the bed. "I'm fine. You know that, right?" He sounds so serious as he leaves behind his joking voice, and almost sounds like the old Jared I originally met.

"Hey," I start, sitting up. "What's wrong?"

He looks over and smiles.

"Don't use that old monotone, emotionless voice on me," I try to tease but in a more serious tone than normal.

He laughs, "I'm not trying to. I'm sorry. I just don't want you to worry."

"Of course I'm going to worry. That's part of relationships. I love you and don't want anything bad to happen to you." I reach over and rub his arm.

"I love you too. I just don't want this to make you live in fear. I'm going to take care of you. And I'm going to keep you safe, even if it means I need a little extra help for now."

Right on cue, the doorbell rings. "Saved by the bell," I joke.

"What?" he asks as he stands.

"Never mind. Pop culture is lost on you sometimes," I tease as I toss the cover aside.

He leans down and kisses my lips gently. "I'll go get your coffee started while you get dressed."

"Any idea who's here?"

"It's Berlusconi."

"How do you know?" I ask, wondering if he checked his phone already or something.

"I just do," he smiles as he steps out into the hallway, closing the door behind him as he goes.

*   *   *   *   *

After I get ready for the morning and am dressed, I make my way downstairs, following the smell of the coffee as I go. I can hear Jared, Vittori, and Berlusconi chatting in the kitchen as I make my way toward the kitchen. As I round the corner, I see all of them sitting at the round kitchen table.

Jared gets up as soon as he sees me to fill a cup of coffee to hand to me. "Hey," he says as he kisses my cheek and ushers me to the table as I take the coffee cup from him.

"Did you get more details from Stamford?" Vittori asks Berlusconi as I sit down.

"I did… and it isn't great news."

"He was murdered?" Jared immediately asks.

"Looks like it," Berlusconi answers. "They said that there was a lot of trauma," he vaguely answers, glancing over me as he does.

"He was tortured," I state, knowing what Berlusconi doesn't want to say. Jared rubs my back to try to comfort me as we both come to the realization that whoever tortured my neighbor, was probably looking for me.

"Do we still think she's the target?" Vittori asks.

"It's the only thing that makes sense," Berlusconi admits. "The good news is, they believe your alibi stories and are no longer looking into either of you in any way, not even as a possible connection."

"That's a small relief," Jared speaks up.

"What's our game plan?" Vittori asks.

"Well, I'm relieving you of any upcoming assignments. You're going to stay with Amazia," he tells Vittori.

"What about Jared?" I ask, already worried enough about his recovery.

"Someone will be with him at all times too, but we all know you trust Vittori. If Jericho can't be the one keeping an eye on you, I want it to be someone you trust," Berlusconi explains.

"You're probably going to get sick of seeing me around," Vittori shrugs.

"I think it's a great plan," Jared adds.

"Do I get to choose who we can have on the exterior coverage?" Vittori asks.

"If you wish," Berlusconi willingly gives in. "It'll be best if you know and trust whoever is out here. I'd suggest rotating though, so it doesn't get noticeable."

"Do we think this has something to do with Domenic?" Jared asks.

"It's possible," Berlusconi throws his hands up as if he's at a loss. "Stamford has no suspects or leads in reference to Mr. Brownstone. I guess that's probably good for us. I thought Domenic moved back here alone. Either someone from his family knows the truth about Amazia, or someone moved here with him from Arkansas. I really have no idea at this point."

"Is there anyone else this could be about? I mean, what if it isn't about Amazia?" Vittori asks.

"If we're being honest?" Berlusconi starts, only continuing once Vittori nods. "Any of us could be the target. They could be trying to use Amazia to get to any of us. The Sicilian Mafia might have gotten word from Domenic about our connection to her. Someone who lost an election might have figured out we were involved. Someone might want to run one of the neighborhoods we watch. The possibilities are endless if we go that route."

"Is there anyone else that you personally pissed off when you adopted me?" Jared randomly asks.

"What do you mean?" Berlusconi asks, not following.

"Domenic hated me because you adopted me. I know Domenic's connection to Amazia is through her brother, but when he came back and saw us together, it couldn't have helped. It's had me thinking, what if Amazia isn't the original reason that any of this happened?"

"You think it has to do with you?" Berlusconi asks Jared.

Jared shrugs, "Just a possibility. What if me getting shot was completely intended? What if it really was me that they were after?"

"Where is this coming from?" Vittori asks.

Jared laughs, "All those hours alone in the hospital room when you guys went to Arkansas."

"Well, let's not overthink anything," Berlusconi says, standing and pushing in his chair. "We're going to get to the bottom of it. In the meantime, we're going to keep both of you safe and we're all going to watch our backs."

"Copy that," Vittori replies for all of us.

"I've got a lot of scheduling conflicts to deal with, so I'm heading back to my office. Let me know if you need anything."

"Thanks Dad," Jared surprises me by saying. Mr. Berlusconi even pauses for a moment in surprise. Vittori turns and stares at Jared in shock.

"Love you guys," Berlusconi shocks me even more by saying as he reaches the front door.

"What… the… fuck… just happened?" I ask.

"I think we died and this is purgatory or an alternative universe… or something," Vittori replies to me.

"What?" Jared looks back and forth between me and Vittori.

"Umm, you called him Dad, dude. Then he said he loved you," Vittori explains with a still shocked expression.

"Yeah. It's not the first time. Just the first time in a very long time," Jared says, looking down at the table to avoid eye contact with either of us.

"You guys have a strange connection. I swear I'll never understand," Vittori says as he gets up to refill his coffee cup.

40

A few days pass without incident. Vittori brings me to work every morning and hangs out in my office with me for most of the day. Occasionally he leaves to retrieve us something to eat, but there is usually someone else on property keeping watch for anything suspicious. Jared has been stuck in the house most days. Lorenzo comes by to bring Jared to and from physical therapy as needed.

On Wednesday, I'm typing away on my computer when an email dings in my work inbox. Moments later, I see Vittori sit up while looking at his phone. I hold my breath as I change tabs to my email and see it's from Amanda. The subject line says "Meeting room request approved." I didn't request a meeting room. I go to immediately reply, but am stopped when I notice "Berlusconi" in the body of the email.

"Berlusconi's on his way here," Vittori speaks up.

"Yeah. Apparently, he requested a private meeting room," I add as I turn my computer monitor towards him.

"How'd you know that?" Vittori sounds surprised.

"Amanda forwarded it to me. His request states that my presence is requested. She sent a calendar invite and everything."

"I guess whatever he's coming to tell us, he trusts that The Rush is a secure location to discuss it in."

"What about Jared?" I ask, checking my phone for any missed messages.

"Berlusconi is having Lorenzo pick him up and bring him here."

"Isn't this overkill? Why not just meet back at Jared's after I get off work?"

"Maybe he thinks it's time sensitive," Vittori shrugs as he stands.

"Where are you going?" I ask.

"I'm going to go clear the meeting room, get a key from Amanda, and make sure it's secure other than our single key."

"I can request a lock out code for the room. That way she can have it ready when you meet her."

"Even better," he smiles. "Call me if anything happens or you need anything. Do not hesitate," he reminds me like he does every time he leaves the room, even just for bathroom breaks.

"I will. Promise," I roll my eyes once his backs to me.

A minute after he leaves Klarissa comes and leans against the door frame. "What's with the protective detail?" she asks in a smart-ass tone.

"You waited all week to ask?" I reply without looking up from my computer.

"Well, he doesn't often leave you alone long enough for me to pry," she answers.

"Jared's boss just wants to be sure Jared and I are safe until the police can catch whoever shot him," I admit with a slight twist to the real story.

"Are you that worried? I thought it was a wrong place, wrong time kind of thing?"

"It was, or at least we think so. His boss is rich and has the resources, so why not let him use them. Vittori and I already spent a lot of time together when Jared was in the hospital, so it's not too awkward."

"Well, if you ever need rescuing from your office or something, just email me," she winks at me before going back to her desk.

My phone dings just as I'm about to get back to work. It's a text from Jared. "Heading to you with Lorenzo."

I reply, "I know."

He replies, "Don't leave your office until one of us comes to get you, okay?"

I reply with an eye roll emoji. A moment later I send, "Yes, babe," following by the kissing emoji.

He only replies with several laughing emojis.

* * * * *

An hour later, Jared walks into my office to retrieve me for the conference room. Lorenzo isn't far behind but is keeping his distance as he feels out of place in the back employee hallways. I'm pretty sure that Vittori and Berlusconi paid off the security staff by now or something. Maybe they already worked for Berlusconi since Elena's wedding. Either way, no one ever tries to stop them. Shit, I've seen security shake Vittori's hand and make small talk. We walk the most direct route to the conference room by staying in the employee halls until we're close to the room.

As we exit the employee halls, we see Vittori and Berlusconi standing outside the private room with Amanda and two others I don't know, but recognize from Elena's wedding. "Amazia!" Amanda comes over to Jared and I. "Glad you got my email. I wasn't sure if you already knew about this meeting."

"I did," I smile my customer service smile at her.

"Well, I'll leave you to it," she says handing me the key card. "This is the only key. Last four of my phone number is the lock out code."

"Perfect," I smile as I take it from her.

She immediately ducks into the back employee halls and leaves the area.

"Shall we?" Berlusconi asks as he gestures towards the room.

I step up and scan the keycard before putting in the last four of Amanda's phone number. The door unlocks and I open it. Vittori takes the door from me, holding it open for the rest of us to enter. Jared pulls out a seat for me to sit before he pulls the chair next to me closer and sits. I look around and see that it's only myself, Jared, Berlusconi, Vittori, and Lorenzo in the room. The other two stand guard outside. Lorenzo closes the door and stands guard on the inside. It's likely he was chosen because I know him, but this still feels rather strange.

"So, why are we here?" Jared gets right to the point.

"I didn't think this should wait," Mr. Berlusconi says, looking around at all of us. "We're actually waiting on one more person to arrive, but we can start." He pulls a folder out of his briefcase and sets it on the table, sliding it over to myself and Jared. "This is a copy of the false police and autopsy report for your father and uncle."

"False report?" I ask, not sure I want to look at that folder at all.

"Yes. It basically says that they were killed on impact in a vehicle collision involving a drunk driver in vehicle number two," Berlusconi continues.

"What's the catch?" Jared asks.

Berlusconi pulls another folder out of the briefcase and slides it towards Jared and Vittori. "This is a copy of the original, and real report."

Vittori reached forward and opens the folder where he and Jared can skim through the details. I look at Berlusconi to avoid looking at the folder. "This tells an entirely different story," Vittori says as he flips through.

"How do we know this is the real report?" Jared asks.

"Two reasons. One, the writer of the fake report works for the Sicilian's," he stops without telling us the second part.

"And the other reason?" Jared pushes.

Like clockwork there is a knock at the door. Berlusconi stands, continuing as he walks to the door, "Secondly, I have a witness."

I think everyone in the room holds their breath as Berlusconi moves towards the door. Who is knocking? Who is the witness? Berlusconi knocks a pattern on the door, waiting for a specific pattern to be repeated back before he pushes the door open. I'm about to pass out from holding my breath. I feel my lungs screaming for fresh oxygen as my pulse increases to a noticeable rate. Jared reaches over and holds my hand as if he's trying to calm me down, but it doesn't work.

"Hey," Mr. Berlusconi says to whoever is outside of the door. "Thanks for letting me send someone to escort you here."

"Why the whole production?" the voice of a male asks from the hallway.

"Why don't you come in and see," Mr. Berlusconi says, stepping out to hold the door open for our visitor.

It doesn't hit me at first as the male steps into the room from the hallway. He is instantly familiar, but my brain tries to deny the reality of the situation. Then, he looks around the room. As soon as his gaze lands on me, my brain catches up. I stand up without a thought, tears filling my eyes as I whisper through them, "Matteo?"

"You know I hate that name," he laughs at me.

I practically push the chair over as I run over to hug him. My brother, back from the dead, well not the dead, but close to it. "Is it really you?" I ask after I pull away.

"Afraid so sister," he says looking down at me. He pats my head like he always used to, knowing how much I hate it.

"Is that for calling you Matteo?"

"Pay back is a bitch," he laughs.

"How is he walking around?" Vittori asks first, having met Matthew when he was a bit more of a vegetable.

"This is the brother?" Jared asks. I turn to him and notice he's standing up.

"Okay, okay," Berlusconi tries to reel us all in. "Everyone sit down. We have a lot of discuss."

I roll my eyes, which causes Matthew to open his eyes wide in what looks like fear. "What?" I whisper to him.

"You can't do that," he whispers angrily.

"What? Roll my eyes?" I ask in a normal voice.

"Amazia!" he replies, before realizing that everyone else in the room is laughing at us. "What's so funny?" he asks everyone with a bit of snark in his tone.

"Let me introduce you to your sister," Vittori jokes.

"I don't get it," Matthew adds.

"We're all well aware of her eye rolling," Berlusconi explains. "Now, Matteo, please take a seat."

"Sir, please call me Matthew," he asks of Berlusconi as he pulls out and sits in the chair between him and Vittori.

"Don't count on it," Jared says under his breath.

"Jared!" I warn as I sit down next to him.

Berlusconi decides to cut us off by introducing everyone. "Obviously, Amazia and Matteo know each other. Matteo, this is Jericho, and this is Vittori," he gestures to them as he makes introductions. "This is Amazia's brother, Matteo, or apparently, Matthew," Berlusconi rolls his eyes as he says it.

"How are you feeling?" Vittori asks. "After being, for lack of a better term, a vegetable for the last year or so."

"Strange, honestly," Matthew starts. "It doesn't feel like I lost all that time, but at the same time I feel very... odd, I guess."

"You walking already seems impressive," Jared adds.

"Yeah. They kept me moving while I was still... out of it, so that seemed to have helped. As soon as they woke me up, or whatever you want to call it, they forced me up and out of bed. Said the sooner I got up, the sooner I'd be able to walk on my own. I didn't understand until I tried to take a step and realized my body didn't want to respond."

"He's been in physical therapy throughout the day for the last several days, getting to where he could talk and travel here," Berlusconi adds.

"Why didn't you say anything?" I ask.

"One, I wanted the answers about your dad and uncle first. Secondly, you've been a bit busy since everything happened with your neighbor," Berlusconi explains gently.

"Your neighbor?" Matthew asks.

"Long story," I answer, not wanting to waste time on that story.

"We'll fill you in later," Jared tells Matthew, prompting Berlusconi to continue.

"I got the copies of both reports on your father and uncle's wreck. I saw the clear discrepancies, but it was hard to pull fact from fiction, until I called and asked to speak to Matteo... Matthew."

"Really?" Jared asks.

"What?" Berlusconi questions.

"Never mind," Jared shakes his head, clearly upset that he's already calling Matthew by his preferred name.

"Anyways," Berlusconi pauses for a moment to try to catch Jared's eye, but Jared refuses to look up. "I got the doctor to set up a video chat so I could talk to him and get his side of the story."

"I mean, I had no idea who you were. I also really had no idea how much time had passed," Matthew adds.

"So, what did you have to say?" I ask, not wanting to wait any longer for answers.

"You don't know?" Matthew asks me, sounding shocked.

"The story I was told, is that you were drunk and out of control. Dad and Uncle Toni went to find you before you tried to drive. You crashed into them, killing them both, and suffering brain damage yourself."

"That's not what happened at all!" Matthew sounds upset at the realization.

"And until recently, I had no reason to question that story," I admit.

"Why did you move?" Matthew randomly asks.

"To start a new life. A life away from tragedy. A life away from the town who blamed you. A life away from the memories of a basic life that meant nothing to me as long as you were a vegetable and everyone else was gone," I practically yell at him, trying to hold back tears.

"Hey, hey," Jared says taking my hand under the table. "Take a breath," he says gently, squeezing my hand until I calm down some.

"Sorry," I whisper to everyone without making eye contact with Matthew again.

"How did you get caught up in…" Matthew begins to ask, unable to finish.

"The Berlusconi family?" I ask.

"Well… yeah," Matthew says, glancing at Berlusconi for his reaction.

"Coincidence," Berlusconi answers. "She just happened to be working at this hotel when my daughter got married here just before the holidays."

"But you continued to stay in contact? Why?" Matthew asks me.

I look at Jared, but don't answer my brother.

"I wanted to hire her. I had Vittori look into her and see if we might have a reason to hire her for something," Berlusconi says. It's the truth, just not the entire truth.

"So, you tried to hire her, before you knew her connection to Uncle Toni?" Matthew asks.

"Right?" Berlusconi laughs. "I mean, I never imagined she had any connection to me, let alone your family."

"You agreed to work for him? Without knowing what you were getting into?" Matthew asks me.

"It's way more complicated than that," is all I say.

"And she knew what she was getting into," Vittori adds for us.

Matthew gives Vittori a strange look before looking back at me. "Then how did you guys make the connection?"

"Well," Berlusconi pauses, likely deciding on where to start. "Domenic tried to kill Amazia but shot Jericho... Jared... instead. From there, we were able to do some digging and figure it out."

"Domenic worked for you though, didn't he?" Matthew asks.

"More like a double agent for the Sicilians," Vittori answers.

"Shit! Really?" Matthew asks.

"Yeah. That's why your father and uncle were killed," Berlusconi begins. "Domenic tracked them down for the Sicilians. Once he got close enough and found a way for it to look like an accident, he struck, hard and fast."

"The Sicilians covered it up?" Matthew asks.

"They did," Berlusconi adds. "I'm afraid that looking into your condition and then transferring you, drew a lot of attention from them."

"Do they know we're here?" Matthew asks.

"We think so," Vittori joins in. "We think they might have been the ones who killed Amazia's neighbor. We think they were looking for her."

"Were you home?" Matthew asks.

"No. I haven't been staying there. My house is all the way out in Connecticut. It's a long commute." I know I'm being vague, but I'm not sure how to break the news to Matthew that Jared is my boyfriend.

"Is this why we're meeting in a hotel conference room instead of elsewhere?" Matthew asks.

"I wanted this to happen as soon as possible. I also didn't want Amazia to miss another day at work. There have been far too many sick days here lately," Berlusconi says.

"Were you sick?" Matthew asks.

"No. When Jared was in the hospital, I stayed there with him," I answer, avoiding eye contact.

"Where do we stand now?" Matthew asks.

"Amazia and Jared have around the clock protection. Vittori has been spending his time wherever Amazia is. He's been staying at their place in the city and accompanying her to work daily. I'd have preferred to have Jared do it, but he's still recovering," Berlusconi partially explains.

"Three bullets will do that to anyone," Jared jokes.

"Three? Where?" Matthew sounds in disbelief.

"Abdomen," Jared shrugs. "One was just a graze though."

"Damn," Matthew says, staring at Jared in awe.

"What are we doing about Matthew?" I ask Berlusconi.

"He'll be staying at the mansion with Lorenzo and myself. We're getting someone to continue his physical therapy at the house until we can get him a new identity."

"New identity?" Matthew asks.

"You can't go walking around as Matteo Franklin anymore. He died of long-term complications from the accident," Berlusconi shrugs.

"What about Domenic?" Matthew asks.

"Dead," I immediately answer.

"How?" Matthew asks, looking around.

"He was a traitor and needed to be taken care of," Berlusconi answers for everyone.

"I still can't believe he killed Dad and Uncle Toni," Matthew looks down, still trying to process everything.

"Apparently he played his part well," I add. "He made you think he was your friend and he kept himself out of sight so no one from the family could grow suspicious of him."

"I'm sorry I wasn't there to warn you, to protect you," Matthew says, trying to catch my eye.

"I have plenty of people to protect me," I admit as I look around the room.

"You know what all of this is, right?" Matthew asks.

"No, Matthew. I'm completely naive to everything," I say with an eye roll.

He looks at Berlusconi who only smiles in response to my eye roll. "She's a special case," he says.

"I never wanted you to be a part of this. Uncle Toni and I said we'd do everything to keep you separated from his mafia past."

"But you were involved, and you didn't tell me anything."

"Only to protect you!"

"Yeah, because that worked out so well."

"You're the one who moved to New York City!"

"As if I knew any better!"

"Matthew. Amazia," Berlusconi starts to get our attention. "Both of you drop it for now."

"Yes, sir," I reply out of habit, realizing that's the first time he's ever talked to me like I was his child. He's definitely treating us differently now that he knows who our uncle was. Jared squeezes my hand again under the table. I squeeze it back to thank him for trying to comfort me.

"For now, we need to figure out who is after you two," Berlusconi nods to Jared and I. "We have to figure out if the Sicilians are after you, or just Domenic's family."

"Do the Sicilians still want revenge on our family, for whatever my uncle did back in the day?" I ask.

"It's possible, but I think it's more likely to be specifically targeted," Berlusconi starts.

"What does that mean?" Matthew asks.

"I think Domenic's family needs to be looked into," Berlusconi continues. "Them hunting down Antonio was strange. It's not something that the Sicilians would have planned or allowed. They'd have sent someone to go in and quickly take them out. They wouldn't play the long game."

"So, we think someone related to Domenic is who's coming after us?" Jared asks.

"Who sent Domenic to begin with?" Vittori asks.

"That's what we need to figure out," Berlusconi says.

41

Berlusconi's phone rings. He checks the screen before standing up and heading towards the door. "I need to take this. That's all I have to share for now," he says as he ducks into the hallway.

"Well, this was informative," Vittori says while standing to stretch.

"You're just used to being with Berlusconi and in the know sooner," Jared teases him.

"Yeah, you're probably right," Vittori laughs.

"Amazia?" Matthew tries to get my attention.

"Hmm?" I ask, as I look up at everyone.

Matthew stands and walks around the table. I stand and back up to Jared, wanting to feel him close to keep me calm. "Can we talk about this?" Matthew asks.

"It's just a lot right now. I never thought you'd come out of that state," I admit.

"I'm sure that was difficult, especially with what happened to Dad and Uncle Toni," Matthew looks down, looking for words. "I just don't want to leave you alone again."

"I'm not alone," I reply quickly, causing Matthew to look up at me suspiciously.

"If you haven't been staying at home… Where have you been staying?" Matthew comes to the realization and asks.

I glance back at Jared who nods at me before I look back to Matthew and continue. "Matt, Jared is my boyfriend."

"Nice to meet you," Jared says, holding out one hand to shake Matthews.

Matthew reluctantly takes it, "Jared?"

"I go by Jared. My legal name is Jericho."

"That's…" Matthew starts, unable to find a good word.

"Terrible?" Jared asks.

"Yeah," Matthew laughs. "That's way worse than Matteo."

"It really is," Jared laughs back.

"So, you've been staying with him?" Matthew asks.

I nod as Jared wraps his arms around me, pulling my back closer to his front so we can both continue to face Matthew.

"And you recently got shot, three times?" Matthew asks.

"Yeah. That's another long story though," Jared starts.

"It was Domenic," I add in to keep Matthew from thinking it isn't safe for me to be around Jared.

"Amazia," Matthew starts, rubbing his face in thought. "I just want to be sure you're safe."

"I'm safe. Jared will keep me safe. Vittori isn't taking his eyes off of me while we're out. Berlusconi has others keeping watch. I'll be fine," I explain to my brother.

"Are we gonna be, okay?" Matthew asks.

"What do you mean?" I ask.

"I don't want you to hate me or distance yourself from me because of what I kept from you."

"Matthew, it's way more complicated than that."

"Exactly," Matthew replies, looking around at myself, Jared, and Vittori.

"It'll take time, but we'll figure it out," I say as Berlusconi comes back in the room.

"Ready to go?" he asks Matthew. Lorenzo nods and steps out into the hall, waiting for Berlusconi and Matthew.

"I love you sister," Matthew says.

"Love you too," I reply with a weak smile.

He nods at Jared and walks towards the door, leaving an awkward silence in the room.

Berlusconi breaks the silence, "Vittori, let me know when you're back at Jericho's… Jared's, would you?"

"Yes, sir," Vittori replies. Once Berlusconi leaves, Vittori turns back to us. "Now that was strange."

"You're telling me," I say, stepping away from Jared so we can all get out of that room.

"You ready to head home?" Jared asks.

I glance at my watch before answering. "Yeah, I just need to grab my bag and clock out."

"Let's go," he says, taking my hand and walking with me back towards my office.

"I'll meet you at the car," Vittori says as he pulls out his phone.

Once Vittori is gone and we're in the employee halls, Jared pulls me to a stop. "Are you okay?"

"I'm fine," I try to answer.

"Amazia, look at me," he says waiting for me to make eye contact. "Are you really, okay?"

"I don't know," I admit.

"It's okay if you're not. This is all a lot to take in."

"I never thought he'd talk again, let alone be normal again," I admit.

"Do you trust him?"

"What? Why would you ask that?"

"Do. You. Trust. Him?" he asks with a pause following every single word.

"I don't know," I admit, looking down.

Jared uses his hand to gently grab my chin and force me to look back up at him. "It's perfectly okay to be unsure, babe."

"But he's, my brother."

"A brother who lied to you for years."

"You lied to me."

"That's not entirely the same."

"I know. I'm just unsure about it all."

"Are you unsure about me?" he asks, looking deep into my eyes.

"I am very sure about you, about us," I admit.

"Because I love you so much. I just want you to be safe and to be happy."

"And I want those things for us, too."

"Love you," he says before kissing my forehead. "Come on. We need to get your stuff so we can get back home," he winks at me as he takes my hand and leads me towards my office again.

"Tell me more," I tease back.

* * * * *

Once I get my stuff from my office, Jared and I meet Vittori in the portico. The valet rushes over yelling for Jared, asking him where's he's been. He even jokes that he was worried when I was also missing for over a week. He admits that he didn't want to bother me and ask, in case something had happened between us. We assure him that we are both fine. He seems to finally relax when Jared tells him that he'd be back to driving and stopping by in no time.

Once we all load up into Vittori's Cadillac Escalade, I can't help but tease him about the obnoxious vehicle choice. "Hey, Vittori. I've been meaning to ask, why in the world would you want to own an Escalade?" I ask from the back seat.

"This isn't my personal car," he admits while shifting into gear and pulling out of the portico.

"Berlusconi's?" I ask.

"One of many official vehicles," Vittori answers.

"Isn't that like a flashing neon sign saying, 'here we are!' to whoever's after us?"

"She has a point," Jared adds with a shrug from the front passenger seat.

"Maybe you're right, but I simply follow orders," Vittori confirms. "On a side note, I'm starving."

Jared laughs, "We need a traditional Friday evening meal." He doesn't say anything else until Vittori and I both glare at him, waiting for him to explain.

"Pizza, obviously," he shrugs as if we should have known.

"That's so random," I joke.

"You're not in Arkansas anymore, Amazia," Jared teases.

"And I'm not Dorethy, either."

Vittori only laughs at us. "I'll grab a pizza pie on the way back."

After stopping to pick up the pizza, Vittori drives us back to Jared's where we arrive in time to see a switching of the guard outside. Vittori and Jared recognize whoever is covering the night shift. Jared simply nods to them while Vittori hands me the pies and walks over to talk to them. I follow Jared inside, carrying dinner into the kitchen.

A few minutes later, Vittori comes inside, locking the door behind himself. "Berlusconi must be worried now that Matthew is awake and in the city."

"Why do you say that?" Jared asks as he pulls out some plates for everyone.

"Spencer, Vincent, *and* Oliver are keeping watch tonight," Vittori admits. Sadly, this means nothing to me.

"Damn," Jared sounds impressed. "That's a solid crew."

"I'm gonna sleep like a king tonight," Vittori jokes.

"Maybe that's why he really did it," Jared shrugs.

"I'm sure that may be a part of it, but I think he's worried with Matthew here," Vittori replies as he grabs a slice and begins to eat.

"If they're all here, who do you think is with him and Matthew?" Jared asks.

Vittori shrugs, too busy chewing to answer.

"Hopefully someone worth a shit, if he's worried about Matthew being here," I grunt under my breath.

"They'll be fine," Vittori tries to reassure me. "Berlusconi isn't going to put himself in any danger. If he was worried about being with Matthew, they wouldn't be staying at one of his properties."

"Yeah, they'd be in some low-end hotel hiding out," Jared confirms.

"I still can't believe he's alive, like really alive," I admit out loud.

"I thought it was a bit of a shock learning he was being drugged into that state back in Arkansas," Vittori adds.

"Was Berlusconi ever able to track down who was paying the facility to keep quiet about it?" Jared asks, piquing my interest.

"He found ties to Domenic, but not a direct link," Vittori confesses. "He was still trying to figure out the missing link when I was last with him."

"What about Domenic's father?" I ask.

Jared shakes his head. "We thought so too, but we tracked his financials first. Never found anything concrete."

"If he's involved, there is no paper trail. He's either being smart by using off-shore accounts, or he simply has nothing to do with it," Vittori shrugs.

"I don't like mysteries," I admit, before finishing off the crust I've been holding onto.

"We'll get to the bottom of it," Vittori adds as he reaches for another slice.

"For now, we just go on living day by day," Jared says.

"Berlusconi will get to the bottom of it," Vittori continues. "And he'll keep Matthew safe in the meantime."

"This is so complicated," I say without thinking.

"Didn't I warn you?" Vittori laughs before taking another bite.

42

Another week goes by without incident. Vittori continues to accompany me to work and anywhere else I go. I keep my schedule light and my travel to a minimum for Vittori's sake. I know he's just doing his job and that he and Jared are friends, but it feels unfair to force him to practically live with us these last few weeks. He never complains, but I'm sure he'd like to go home and sleep in his own bed at some point.

Today, Lorenzo is going to accompany me to work so that Vittori can drive Jared to a doctor's appointment at the hospital. Since the Stamford Police Department still has an open investigation into the murder of Mr. Brownstone, Berlusconi wants to be sure everything is documented as it should be. Instead of having Jared met the doctor in his unlisted office, he meets him during a scheduled appointment through the follow-up system. At this point, it's all about the documentation, but a few scans at the hospital could also be helpful in confirming the success of Jared's recovery.

Jared wants to get back to a semblance of normal. He wants to drive again and feel free to do as he wants, when he wants, without protection. Even if he's released back to his normal, he likely won't be fully active for several more months. Though, it still seems a miracle that he's alive. At least, that's what I think every single time I see him shirtless. I try not to stare at his scars, both new and old, but it shows how strong he is. It shows what he was able to survive.

"Amazia," Klarissa says as she steps into my doorframe.

"Yeah?" I look up, expecting her to ask a question, but she looks unsure of herself. "Lorenzo," I say, grabbing his attention.

He looks up from his computer, "Yes, ma'am?"

"Could we have a minute?" I ask, hoping he can sense some girl talk needing to be had.

"Of course," he says while standing. "I'll go grab some coffee from the lobby." He excuses himself past Klarissa before he disappears down the back hall.

Klarissa steps into my room and closes the door behind her. The door softly clicks closed as she steps forward while holding a folder in one arm. Her other hand remains in place, pressing her palm into the door as if it won't stay closed on its own if she lets go.

"Klarissa... what is it? What's wrong?" I stand and go over to meet her. I feel myself second guessing the decision as I begin to roll my chair toward her. Something is really off about that way she's acting, the way she won't look up at me now that we're alone. "Klarissa, come sit. Talk to me." I gesture toward the chair Lorenzo was sitting in as I roll my chair from around the desk to join her.

She nods and begins to step towards the chair slowly. Once she gets there, she sits, placing the folder on her lap, but she doesn't look up. She doesn't speak.

"Klarissa... the suspense is kind of killing me here..." I admit, as I feel sweat trickle down my back as my pulse quickens. The front of my hair line warms as perspiration forms, one drop rolling down towards my eye.

"I had a sister," she whispers under her breath.

"Wait, what?" I ask.

She hands me the folder without any further explanation. I take it and flip through the first two pages, finding the key details. "I don't understand. Where did you get this?"

"Remember those detectives that came asking about Seth?"

"Yeah, the two females?"

"One of the days you were off, they came back. They got DNA from all of the females who accused Seth of any harassment."

"Wait. Since when did you accuse him of anything?" I ask, surprised at the admission.

"It was when I was first hired. It really doesn't matter. Nothing happened," she brushes it off as not important. "I only agree to let them take my DNA because it would distract them from you not being here."

"Were they asking about me? Why didn't you ever tell me?"

She shrugs, looking embarrassed. "They were talking a lot about your connection to the Berlusconi family. Apparently, someone brought it to their attention that you were with the bride before the wedding. Something about the whole thing seemed suspicious to them, for someone who doesn't work for them."

"What does that even mean?" I ask, confused at what exactly we're talking about.

"They never said anything else once I agreed to give my DNA."

"Have they been back?" I ask.

"Not until today, when they dropped this off," she gestures toward the folder.

"What did they say?"

"That I was cleared in the mysterious disappearance of Seth, but that I needed to know the truth about what else they found."

"Where is this from?" I close the folder to ask.

"A murder, five years ago. Probably a serial killer but it's never been solved."

"If you had a sister… how come you didn't know?"

"They said that my mother, or my father, or both, might be kidnappers. They said the girl's parents had lost more than one child. They said my entire life might be a lie."

I reach out and pull her into my arms, hugging her close. I breathe a huge sigh of relief as my muscles slowly relax. I'm not sure what I was afraid of, but I was worried that Klarissa got rid of Lorenzo for a reason. I was worried that she was faking being my friend, just like Domenic had done to my brother. I was terrified that this was the end. I was terrified that she found her time to take me out and I was going to die right here in my cramped office deep within the employee halls of the hotel.

Lorenzo comes back with a coffee but stops at the threshold as he sees me embracing Klarissa. I nod to him that everything is fine. He takes a step back, but keeps the door cracked to hear if anything changes. I watch him roll a chair over to sit in, right outside of the door.

Eventually Klarissa lets go. She rubs the tears away from her face. "I think I need some time off," she whispers, sounding unsure.

"I'll put in a request. How much time do you think you'll take?"

"Honestly," she begins, pausing as if deciding if she's going to go through with whatever she has planned. "I might quit. I might pack up and move."

"Move?"

"Home. Well, to the place where I apparently was born and kidnapped from."

"That's a big decision to make on minimal details," I admit.

"You moved suddenly and seem to be happy," she shrugs.

"The situation is entirely different."

"I just need a fresh start after," she reaches for the folder, holding it up, "after this."

"Well, as much as I want to talk you out of it, I can't make this decision for you."

"I know. I just wanted you to know first, in case I don't show up next week."

"Please don't leave without telling me," I ask as she stands and goes to walk out. "Want to head out early today?"

"Can I expect a good reference from you?" she asks as she faces away from me in the doorway.

"Klarissa…" I start.

"Please Amazia."

"Yes. Yes, of course you can expect a glowing recommendation."

"Thanks," she says as she steps out of the office. She grabs her coat and her bag and disappears down the employee halls without another word.

"What was that about?" Lorenzo asks as he stands, watching her go.

"Complicated story," is all I say as we watch her go.

*   *   *   *   *

"How'd it go?" I ask Jared as soon as I step through the front door, seeing him and Vittori chatting in the living room.

Jared stands with a huge smile on his face, "Clear to drive and return to work."

"Return to work?" I ask in a standoffish voice as he approaches me.

"Nothing too dangerous and no heavy lifting," Jared answers as he steps up, wrapping his arms around me.

"That's better, I guess," I say, not wanting him to return to work too early.

He leans in and kisses me, pulling my thoughts away from me as I lose myself in his lips. After a few intense moments, Vittori clears his throat, bringing us back to the present. "Sorry," I whisper to Vittori as I feel Jared smiling as he pulls away.

"Anyways," Vittori says as he stands. "I'm going to go get ready."

"Ready for?" I ask, looking back and forth between him and Jared.

"We're having dinner with Berlusconi," Jared answers.

"With the family?" I ask nervously.

"No," Jared quickly answers. "Just us, Berlusconi, and your brother."

"Maybe a few other people standing guard," Vittori shrugs as he exits the room.

"Special occasion?" I ask.

"Just dinner," Jared says with shrug.

43

Vittori drives us to the same mansion that I have a key to. It's the same mansion that we met Berlusconi at after he kidnapped me. It's where Jared pleaded for Berlusconi to keep me out of everything. Berlusconi was too determined. It's where I first knew I could trust Vittori, when he decided not to give away my snooping. It isn't an entirely negative place. It's giant and looming as we approach. And dark... Why is it dark?

"Are you sure he said the mansion?" Jared asks Vittori as he must also notice how dark it appears.

"I'm positive," Vittori says in a concerned sounding voice as he pulls up on the street out front without entering the driveway.

"Is it ever that dark?" I wonder out loud.

"Never," Jared answers.

"Berlusconi would prefer to support the electric company and keep far too many lights on," Vittori adds.

"And they'd need light to prepare dinner," I add, feeling stupid for the random comment.

"Who was on watch?" Jared asks Vittori.

"Lorenzo, Spencer, Vincent, and Oliver," Vittori lists.

"Lorenzo?" I ask.

"Yeah, he came straight here after dropping you at home. He was supposed to work a few hours of overtime for the dinner," Vittori admits.

"Because of my brother?" I ask, glancing back and forth between the two of them to sense any reactions.

"Do you think he could be dangerous or something?" Jared asks in a concerned voice.

I shrug. "I honestly have no idea. I don't feel like I know him at all anymore. Everything I thought I knew about him was a lie."

"I think it was just an extra precaution while we were all five here together," Vittori begins. "Berlusconi wanted to be sure that if someone was after any of us, we were prepared."

"So, we still don't know who it is?" I ask.

"If they surprised Vincent, Spencer, and Oliver, there is no telling who this could be," Vittori answers, glancing at Jared.

"Those three are Berlusconi's…. most brutal men," Jared starts. "All former Navy Seals, too."

"Shit. Really?" I ask.

"They like the high paying contract work. They get to stay in the states, potentially keep an eye on their families, and Berlusconi provides good benefits for them," Vittori finishes.

"If someone got past the three of them, what is our plan?" I ask, knowing we need to do something.

"You're staying in the car," Jared turns to me to say.

"Hell no!" I instantly reply. "You're not leaving me alone and vulnerable in this car!"

"She has a point," Vittori agrees.

"I can't let you walk in there with us," Jared says.

"And you can't leave me out here alone!" I yell back.

"Okay, okay," Vittori interrupts. "Stop yelling."

"Sorry," I say in a defeated voice. At least I know Vittori is on my side.

"We need to approach, but quietly, and without being seen," Vittori starts.

"Okay," Jared straightens in his seat. "You're in charge. What's the plan?"

*   *   *   *   *

I'm not sure what I expected. I really wish I took Jared up on those firearm lessons because I'd feel better carrying a gun right now. Thankfully, I'm sandwiched between Jared and Vittori as we attempt to make our approach from the street. I follow Vittori's lead as he hugs the wall along the property line. We step onto the property near the road and make a long loop around toward the back. Once we're near the back corner, we are able to remain concealed as we walk through a line of trees.

As we approach, we notice no signs of life. There is no light coming from inside on this side of the house. It's hard to tell if the power was cut or not from out here. My eyes are finally adjusting to the darkness as we approach the house finally. We crouch outside a window.

After a moment, Vittori glances inside before returning to our level. "Nothing."

"Next," Jared says.

Vittori instantly moves on to the next room. "Nothing."

"Next," Jared replies again.

"I hear something," Vittori says as we all step up to the next set of windows. Vittori stands to look inside, clearly seeing something as he remains standing. "Someone's in there."

Jared begins to stand. I hesitate but follow their lead. As I stand completely, I can hear the voices Vittori heard. Before I notice anyone, I guess the windows we are at lead to Berlusconi's office. The voices are coming from the dining room across from the office. That's when I see Matthew.

"You thought it was the Sicilians?" an unknown female voice is laughing inside the house. "No sugar, this is completely personal."

"What do you have against me?" Matthew questions.

"You?" the female laughs again. "Oh sweetie, you really don't get it. I'm here to avenge my husband."

"Your husband?" Matthew sounds confused.

"Shit," Jared says as he watches from next to me. Matthew is tied up to a chair. The voice we hear must be coming from the female pacing nearby. We can only see through the single doorway leading out of the office. I can't see anyone else from this angle.

"I always wondered if you would remember all those things that I told you. I explained everything to you. You were just in that drugged up state," the female continues in a snarky voice. "It sure is nice to have people on the payroll in the medical field, isn't it?"

"You didn't answer the question," Matthew throws at her.

"We got married! Domenic and I," the female admits. "I really thought you'd remember me talking to you in that memory care facility. Me, pretending like I still loved you when the nurses came by," she continues in a smart-ass voice.

"Was anything you said or did true?" Matthew asks, sounding hurt at the new revelations.

"Where is Berlusconi?" Jared asks Vittori in a hushed voice.

"I still don't see any sign of him," Vittori replies.

"This is a bad angle," I add. Jared and Vittori both glance over at me as if they're surprised. "What?"

"Nothing," they whisper in unison.

"We'll talk about that little moment later," I say before looking back into the house.

"Matteo," the female pauses, stopping to lean down in his face. "It was all a lie."

"You knew Domenic all along?" Matthew sounds hurt as he asks.

"We fell in love at that rock show, the one I met you at. He was bringing you along to meet me, but then we decided to have a little fun. We didn't plan on fucking with you for so long, but you fell right into our plan to get close to you," the female continues.

"You told me you loved me!" Matthew's emotions are mixing between surprise and hate.

"Oh, baby," she says as she climbs onto his lap, straddling him, taunting him. "You were just a toy for me to play with."

Matthew tries with all his might to fight her off, but he's restrained against the chair too well. His arms are both tied behind him and his legs are secured to the legs of the chair.

The unknown female pulls out a knife from her waist and holds it up next to Matthew's face. "Better stop fighting me before I give you a reason to fight," she taunts in a sexual voice.

"We need to get in there," I say, worried for Matthew.

"No. *We* need to get in there," Vittori says, meaning him and Jared.

"We're not having this argument again!" I whisper angrily.

"Babe," Jared says placing a hand on my shoulder so I'll look at him. "We're not leaving you alone, but you have to listen. We do not know who else is here. We do not know how many people are inside. We don't know if Berlusconi, Spencer, Vincent, or Oliver are alright. We may walk into a trap. We may walk into a blood bath. I honestly don't know. But you have to be ready. You can't freak out. You have to focus."

"I understand," I reply while looking seriously into his eyes. We need to save my brother. We need to save ourselves.

"Why are you here?" I hear Matthew ask through gritted teeth.

"To kill the last of your family," she replies while twirling the knife in her hand.

"You already killed my dad and my uncle. Who's left?" Matthew asks, trying to trick the female.

"Oh, darling," she leans in closer, whisper into his ear. We can't hear what she says.

Matthews eyes go wide as she leans away, laughing loudly.

"Did you think I didn't plan this well?" she continues to laugh.

"Too bad Domenic wasn't as smart," Matthew dares to say, looking defiantly up at her.

She slashes the knife against his shoulder, clearly drawing blood as a large laceration forms. "Ooops, did I accidentally hurt you baby?"

"You're psychotic!" Matthew says through the pain.

"I'm going to make you watch as I tear your little sister apart, piece... by piece." She lifts the knife to Matthew's face and gently slides the blade along his skin. "Maybe I'll have my way with you one last time while I kill her."

"Shut your fucking mouth, you whore!" Matthew screams, clearly done with playing nice.

"That wasn't very nice," she teases just before she plunges the knife into Matthew's thigh just below hers as she continues to straddle him.

Matthew's scream drowns out our voices.

"Let's go," Vittori says as I cringe at the events unfolding inside.

"Stay focused," Jared whispers to me as he reaches for my hand before squeezing it as he nods for me to follow Vittori.

Once we walk away from the window, we can no longer hear their conversation. What we can hear are Matthew's screams as the female inflicts more pain or torture on him.

"We've got to get in there," Jared whispers to Vittori as they check every window they pass.

"Still no sign of anything," Vittori admits.

"She can't be alone. Can she?" I ask.

Jared and Vittori both glance at me before each other. They both shrug, looking unsure about what might be going on inside.

44

As we round the front corner of the house, my heart drops through my stomach as I feel myself about to vomit. In front of the house, on the front steps, are two lifeless bodies. I feel myself cover my mouth to stifle any cry or noise that tries to escape. Jared grabs my arm to stop me as Vittori approaches, rifle in hand and aimed toward the front door. He leans down and checks on the two bodies. He glances back at Jared and shakes his head.

"Who is it?" I whisper.

"Don't worry about that right now," he whispers. "We need to worry about the living. We need to get to Matthew."

I nod, unable to form words as he gently nudges me forward towards Vittori. As I get closer, I realize the front door is wide open.

"Stay behind me and keep cover," Jared whispers as he steps in front of me. He races up the steps to stand just outside of the wide-open door while Vittori provides us cover. I try my best not to glance at the dead bodies on the steps as we pass. Once Jared's in place, Vittori moves to the opposite side of the opening. Jared slowly pulls a knife from his waistband, handing it to me. He glances back and whispers, "Better this than nothing."

I nod, praying to God that I won't have to use this.

Vittori holds up three fingers, then two, then one. Moments later, he and Jared turn into the front door, weapons high and fingers on the trigger. Another scream comes from Matthew as we move further into the house. Still no sign of anyone else. With two bodies outside, Mathew in the dining room, at least two more people are unaccounted for. We reach the corner that will turn into the dining room.

Jared turns and mouths to me, "Stay here."

I nod, knowing I don't want to see what's on the other side of this door just yet. I back myself against the wall, holding the knife tightly in my right hand, just in case.

I watch as Jared nods at Vittori before they turn the corner, and all hell breaks loose. Clearly the female isn't alone, based on the amount of gunfire that erupts. It's almost deafening as I try to remain calm and keep an eye on my surroundings. I try to keep count of the shots fired, but there are just too many overlapping sounds. I also hear Matthew scream again, thinking the female must still be torturing him. I hear a physical struggle, then gunfire hitting glass, shattering something within the dining room. I try to sink back further into the wall, desperate to be invisible if someone runs by me.

"Behind you!" I hear Matthew yell through his pain.

"Shit," I hear Vittori say in a whisper. I can't tell if he's surprised, hurt, or something else. Shortly after, I hear another set of loud thuds, as if a physical assault is in progress between several people. I hear something metal crash to the ground, maybe a rifle. I hear a body thud into the ground shortly after.

"Vittori!" Jared yells, sounding like he's in a struggle. He can't be fighting someone. He isn't recovered enough for that.

I feel my pulse quicken even more, if that's even possible. I can't let Jared fight someone. I have to help! I take a deep breath and suck in all of the courage that I can muster and charge into the room, knife held high and ready. As I cross the threshold, I try to quickly take in the room. Matthew is tied to a chair at the far end of the room, alone. Vittori is on the floor, with someone on top of him, struggling with one another over a handgun. In front of me is Jared, now being thrown down to the ground by the female we saw earlier. Oh hell, no! I think as I race toward her and stab the knife into her shoulder as hard as I can. I should have aimed for a better place, because I instantly regret it as she turns to me with a pure look of evil on her face.

"You little bitch!" she says calmly as she stares at me as if all her rage is directed towards me and only me. I take slow and deliberate steps back as I feel her ripping apart my soul with just a look of death. I feel like she's slowly pulling my soul from my body, piece by piece.

"Amazia, run!" Matthew tries to shout but struggles to have enough breath.

I almost glance at him but know better than to take my eyes off of the female.

"I'm going to have fun tearing every single piece of flesh from your living body," she says as she reaches over her shoulder to rip the knife from her own flesh. She doesn't throw it to the ground. Instead, she twirls it between her fingers like a magician. "Or maybe I should make you watch me gut your brother first?" she says in a questioning tone. "Doesn't that sound fun?" she asks as she takes a slow step toward me. "Or maybe, I should finish the job Domenic started and finish off your boyfriend first." She smiles a wicked smile as she raises the knife and slowly turns towards Jared.

The next I see in slow motion as I hear myself yell, "No!"

The female turns as she raises the knife high, ready to strike as soon as she's facing Jared. At the same time, I see Jared reaching for something. I sure hope he isn't reaching for the knife that he gave me. That could be the difference between life and death right now. As the female is almost fully turned toward Jared, I hear a gunshot and see the man over Vittori slump down onto him. I sure hope that was Vittori killing him, but I don't have time to look. The female is about to swing her hand down toward Jared as Jared pulls something from his waist band on his left hip. He rips it out from under his jacket and points the black handgun up at the female just in time.

I hear the shot go off before my brain can process. The female continues to move toward Jared, making me wonder if he even got a shot off before she got too close. Bang, another shot. I hold my breath as the female continues to lunge toward Jared at the ground. Bang, a third shot just before the female lands on top of Jared, knife clattering to the ground next to them.

"Jared!" I yell, racing to pull the female off of him. As I run to him, I see Vittori rolling his assailant off of him. He's watching me as I rush to roll the body off of Jared, tears rushing down my cheeks as I can no longer contain my emotions. Vittori appears next to me and helps me roll the female over, revealing Jared underneath.

"What's wrong?" Jared asks in a sarcastic voice.

"Oh my god! Jared!" I practically yell at him as I throw my arms around him, pulling him close as he wraps his arms around me, holding me tight for a moment before releasing me. He sits up, still holding his handgun, and looks at Vittori. "Any sign of him?"

"Kitchen," Matthew replies weakly.

"Matthew!" I grab the knife and stand, remembering the torture the female was putting him through before we left the window. Vittori helps Jared up and they follow me to Matthew. I see them retrieving their rifles as I use the knife to cut Matthews hands and feet free. "Matthew. Matthew, look at me."

"Hey, baby sister," he says weakly, no longer able to hold his head up to me.

"Don't you give up, you piece of shit!" I yell at him, holding his chin up to check for more injuries.

"Don't fret little sister. It was worth it to save you," Matthew says with a weak smile.

"Well too bad for you, you aren't dying today," I feel myself say as I pray that I'm telling him the truth. I already lost him once. I can't lose him completely this time.

"Call 911," Vittori says while handing me his phone.

"Really?" I ask, surprised.

"He needs immediate medical attention," Vittori says. "Tell them you have a stabbing victim and don't answer anything you don't have to. Shit, hang up if you have to."

"Okay," I say, fumbling to dial 911.

"We're going to check the other rooms," Jared says.

"Keep that knife close," Vittori says as he and Jared walk towards the kitchen.

"What's in the kitchen?" I ask Matthew once they leave.

"Berlusconi and Spencer," Matthew weakly answers between breaths.

"Hold on Matthew," I say as I call 911.

"911. What's the location of your emergency?" a male voice asks.

"Oh shit. I can't remember. A mansion just outside of the city," I stumble over my words.

The dispatcher repeats a street number and address that they must have gotten from the GPS. "Does that sound correct?"

"Yes, yes. That's the right street. I think that's correct."

They ask a few more questions to verify the location before proceeding to, "Tell me exactly what happened."

"I have a 28-year-old stabbing victim, multiple stab wounds."

"Do you know who stabbed him?"

"Some female."

"Is the female still there?"

"Yes?"

"Does she still have a weapon?"

"No. She's… she's dead."

"Is the patient breathing?"

"Matthew," I say shaking him. "Yes, but barely."

"Is the bleeding under control?"

"No. Definitely not," I realize as I try to analyze the damage. "Stay awake Matthew. Don't you dare give up!"

"Do you have a clean, dry cloth, or towel?"

"Umm," I start looking around as I see Jared come back into the room with a few kitchen towels. "Yes. Yes, I do."

"Listen carefully so you do it correctly. Place the cloth over the bleeding wound and press firmly without lifting the towel to look."

"Okay. Okay, I'm doing it."

"Is the bleeding under control?"

"I don't know! There is so much blood coming from everywhere! Are they almost here?" I ask as I can hear the sirens drawing closer.

"They're almost to you. I need you to answer a few more questions before they arrive."

Jared leans forward and hits the mute button. "Just leave it open until the medics get here," Jared says as he crouches down next to me.

"Is Berlusconi here?" I ask.

"He and Spencer are... well they're alive."

"Do we need another ambulance?" I ask.

"No. Vittori is loading them into the truck."

"What, really?"

"Amazia," he starts, placing his hand on mine. "This next part gets complicated."

"Okay," I say, unsure of what's about to happen.

"I'm going to take Berlusconi and Spencer to our doctor's house before anyone gets here. Vittori will stay here with you. If anyone asks, you were coming to meet your brother for dinner and walked into this. Finding everything a mess. Vittori was patrolling the property when he killed the woman before she could kill you. Do you understand?"

"I.. I think so," I stumble.

"When in doubt, don't say a word. Pretend to be in shock and unable to focus. Once they move you to the police station, Berlusconi's lawyer will meet you. It will all be fine. Okay?"

"Yeah."

"Babe," he says, forcing my chin up. "I love you. It will be alright. I have to go before they get here. You've got this babe. You're okay. We're okay." I only nod as he kisses my lips gently before standing to run out the front door.

"Love you," I whisper, hoping he hears me before he disappears outside.

45

"Ms. Franklin, why were you going to the Berlusconi residence tonight?" a detective asks me in a cold, damp, interview room at the police station.

"I was going to have dinner with my brother," I admit.

"And when you arrived, you found a woman torturing him?"

I nod, not wanting to lie.

"And how did she die?" the detective continues, never looking up from their notepad as they scribble notes.

"The security guard came out of nowhere and shot her," I shrug.

"Is there anything you're not telling me?" the detective asks just as someone knocks on the door.

The detective opens the door in time for an unknown male to stroll in. "No more questions for my client without my presence."

"We were unaware that she needed a lawyer," the detective begins to reply.

"So, you admit to forcing her here without cause? You admit that you did not tell her she was allowed legal aid?" the lawyer throws at them.

"That's not what I meant," the detective replies.

"Come on, Ms. Frankin. We're leaving," he says as he strolls toward the door, waiting for me in the hallway.

I get up and follow him, avoiding eye contact with everyone else as I go. Once we're in the lobby, I see Vittori standing by with another lawyer carrying a briefcase. "We'll take care of this," the other lawyer says. "You get Ms. Franklin back home," he says to Vittori.

Vittori shakes both of their hands silently before gesturing for me to lead the way outside. I follow him toward a blacked-out SUV and climb into the passenger side door that he opened for me. Vittori goes around to climb into the driver's seat.

"What in the hell," I let out once we're alone.

"Tell me about it. This is a mess."

* * * * *

Vittori drives us to a warehouse along the water. Once he parks, we both climb out and I follow as he leads the way, into a side door off of a dock. As we walk in, we both stop dead as two people immediately hold guns up to us.

"Whoa, whoa," Jared's voice comes from behind them. "That's them."

The two immediately lower their weapons and go back to pacing near the doors.

"What are we doing here?" I ask.

"The cleanup," Vittori admits.

"But the detectives already saw everything back at the house," I say, feeling confused.

"Only what we couldn't clean up in time," Jared adds.

"Where's my brother?"

"At the hospital, in surgery," Jared answers.

"Why aren't we there?" I ask curiously.

"Once he's stable, our doctor will get him transferred so we can wipe his files. Until then, we have to wait. You can't be connected to him for this to work," Vittori explains.

"For now, we cleanup the bodies we were able to get out of there," Jared says, sounding unsure about me being here.

"You can wait in the car if you don't want to be a part of this," Vittori suggests.

"I'm fine," I admit.

"Amazia!" I hear a familiar voice.

"Berlusconi. You're here?" I ask, surprised to see him.

"Spencer and I needed some stitching up, but no one can take me down that easily," Berlusconi says, clearly in more pain than he's trying to let on. His right arm is currently in a sling, for example.

"Glad you're alive and well," I smile awkwardly.

"Jericho... Jared, can I have a word?" Berlusconi says. "Alone?" he asks as he glances at me.

Jared wraps his arm around my shoulder, pulling me close. "Anything you have to say to me, you can say it in front of Amazia."

I can see Vittori ducking into the next room along with the male I assume must be Spencer.

"Well, it's about the way I've treated you," he pauses glancing up at us as if he's unsure of himself. "I feel like I pushed you too far as a teenager. I pushed the fear of love on you. After you lost your family, and you lost everything you knew, I used that to be sure you'd never love anyone again. It not only kept you compliant, but it helped you get through the day without feelings. When you met Amazia, I saw the change in you, maybe before either of you even noticed. The night you arrived at the hotel for Elena's wedding, you were already different. That scared the living shit out of me, if I'm being frank. I was worried that if you developed feelings, that you would question everything that you do. You're not an evil person and that's why you were never able to kill anyone. You had that deep empathy, but you didn't feel it on the surface. My point is… I'm sorry for not letting you be a normal teenager. I'm sorry for hiding emotions and feelings below all of the pain you had suffered. Maybe you would have been a completely different person if I wasn't stuck in my ways, if I didn't ruin your chances."

"You didn't ruin me," Jared admits. "Losing my family broke me long before I met you. Being put into a disorganized system broke me in more ways. Going home to your house, with Elena and your wife is what saved me."

"Even if I turned you onto a life of crime?" he asks.

"Is it a crime if it's necessary?" Jared asks.

"Maybe you need to ask Amazia. Her opinion of you is what matters."

"I think life is way more complicated than a simple yes or no," I admit.

"See! I knew I liked her," Berlusconi jokes. "Now, come on. Let's not leave all the work to Vittori."

Jared keeps his arm around me as we walk into the next room where Vittori is sealing the top of several barrels. Inside are piles of items. It's someone's belongings, but I'm not sure if it's Berlusconi's fallen employees or the females. Once they're sealed, Vittori and Spencer roll them to the edge of the water and dump them in. There are a few holes in the sides so they sink faster, as well as several cinder blocks inside the top. I watch Spencer and Berlusconi go through some paperwork and casually toss it into a fire barrel occasionally. Once we're all done, we meet in the center of the warehouse.

"Where to?" Jared asks.

"The mansion is out of the question for a while," Vittori adds.

"I guess, the Manhattan apartment for now," Berlusconi suggests.

"Sounds like a good plan," Spencer adds in.

"Then Manhattan it is," Vittori agrees.

"You didn't run and hide from the cleanup," Jared teases me.

"This is a day in the life, huh?" I ask, making a joke to lighten the tension.

Everyone laughs as we make our way out to the vehicles. It's been a long day, and I can't wait to curl up next to Jared and sleep.

*   *   *   *   *

The next morning, after waking up in Berlusconi's Manhattan apartment, everyone gathers for a huge buffet breakfast prepared by Berlusconi's staff from the mansion. Thankfully, none of them were harmed when psycho bitch came gunning for all of us. Berlusconi was able to get all of them out the back door before it got dangerous. Of course, working for the Berlusconi family comes with certain risks that you have to be ready for.

Shortly after we all finish eating, Berlusconi walks in as he is hanging up from a phone call. "Good news," he says as he strides into the room and takes a seat at the head of the table. "Matthew is out of surgery and awake."

"Oh good," I say with a sigh of relief. Jared reaches over and takes my hand, squeezing it gently. I look over at him and return his smile before asking, "Do you know anything else?"

"Well," Berlusconi says between bites. "There was a lot of internal bleeding. He lost a Kidney and a lot of blood, but they were able to repair enough damage to make him stable. He's awake and responding well."

"What about the police?" I ask vaguely.

"Taken care of," Vittori adds.

"No record of the police being at the mansion. Once we get Matthew transferred from the hospital, all traces of his time there will disappear as well," Berlusconi confirms.

"What if those two female detectives get a whiff of this?" I ask.

"We'll cross that bridge if we have to," Berlusconi doesn't seem worried. "There is always a way to twist the truth or change reports."

"So, I'd guess his name isn't Matthew Franklin in the hospital?" I ask.

"Correct," Berlusconi answers then looks up as if he remembers something. "That reminds me, he'll need a new surname for his new identity once we get him out of that hospital. Since Matteo Franklin, for all intensive purposes, died back in Arkansas."

"You should let him make that decision," I shrug. "Or make the decision for him. Either way, I don't think he'll care."

"I'll ask him once we get him transferred to a facility we can monitor more appropriately," Berlusconi explains. "One of the doctors on our payroll is working on getting him transferred once he's stable enough to move."

"What about the rest of us?" I ask after a few awkward moments of silence.

"We go back to business as usual," Vittori shrugs.

"As if nothing else happened?" I ask, glancing back and forth between all of them.

"For now, either Jared, Vittori, or Spencer will still escort you to and from work. The rest of the day, you should be safe in The Rush. I'd also venture to say that you guys can all return home tonight if you want to," Berlusconi says with a shrug.

"I can stay a few more nights, just to be sure everything has settled down," Vittori adds, looking at Jared. "Only if you want me to. I don't want to overstay my welcome."

I glance to Jared and nod before he says, "Why don't you hang out for a few more days before you head back to your place?"

"Sounds like a plan," Vittori replies. "That way I can do all my laundry at your place before I head back to mine."

"Using me for my washer and dryer," Jared jokes.

"And the food," Vittori shrugs.

Jared throws a bagel at Vittori as they both laugh.

"One big, happy, family," I joke as I take another sip of my coffee.

46

A week later, everything is back to normal. Jared is still working on physical therapy but is back to working several small jobs for Berlusconi as needed. Vittori went back to his place last night, saying he thought it was finally time he gave us our space back. Matthew is still recovering in one of Berlusconi's homes with a full-time nurse and a daily doctor visit. Once he's ready, I told him he can move into my house until he decides what he wants to do. He doesn't know if he wants to stay in New York with us or move back west. Berlusconi is back to sending me travel destinations so I can manage those itineraries. Of course, I really can't complain with how well he pays me for just making some basic reservations.

I came back to work two days after the incident at the mansion, just a normal Monday for me. The catch was, Klarissa had cleared out all of her belongings. I was surprised at first, before remember everything she said about her twin and her possible kidnapper parents. I can't even begin to process what she found out about her life. If it was really all a lie, I might pack up and run away too. I just hope she made the right decision. This morning, I received my first reference call for her. I gave her a glowing recommendation and said that they'd be idiots to not hire her. Hopefully it's the fresh start she needs.

I spent the entire day interviewing for her former position. Most of the candidates are in-house applicants looking for a promotion. A few are employees from competing hotels nearby. In reality, I doubt I'll ever be satisfied with anyone other than Klarissa. She did far more than her job description by taking on extra jobs to act like an assistant to me rather than just another room control agent. I doubt I could ever teach anyone to do all of the extra work she did. For now, I'll have to settle for the most experienced applicant and hope for the best. At the end of the day, I have no idea what I plan to do, or who I plan to hire. I decide to leave it all behind so I can get dressed for tonight's date night.

Jared said that he wanted to make our last date night up to me, since Vittori so rudely interrupted, which turned into a whole bloody mess, literally. Jared said that he'd be coming from a job outside of the city, so he'd be meeting me at the restaurant. He was sending Vittori to pick me up, like he did most days since Berlusconi still won't let me travel to and from work alone. Once I'm dressed and ready, I pack my bag and check my phone just in time to see Vittori's text saying he's arrived.

When I walk out to the portico, I see Vittori chatting with the same valet that Jared made friends with. Part of me thinks he might secretly be on Berlusconi's payroll too, but

I never can tell for sure. Vittori waves goodbye to him before opening my door for me. "You look stunning tonight," he says before closing my door and walking around to the driver side.

Once he closes his door, I say, "The valet staff is going to start thinking I'm dating both of you."

Vittori laughs, "Not a chance. They all know how Jared feels about you."

"What is that supposed to mean?"

"Nothing," Vittori says, clearly not telling me something.

"I'm going to figure you out one day," I promise.

"Good luck with that," he says as he pulls out of the portico.

"Where are you taking me tonight, Mr. Chauffer?" I joke.

"You'll have to wait and see," he smiles as if there is more to tell than just where he is taking me.

* * * * *

Thirty minutes later, Vittori pulls up to Rockefeller Center. It's a well-known landmark in NYC, but also next to the spot that Jared took me ice skating just a few weeks ago. The ice rink is still open and full of people skating around. Vittori parks the car and exits before walking around to open my door.

"Here we are," he says as he holds a hand out to me.

"Here?" I ask as I climb out of the vehicle, looking around for Jared.

"Well, here is where we get out," Vittori smiles. "I'll bring you to Jared." He tosses the keys to someone standing nearby.

I'm unable to tell if it's a valet or a Berlusconi employee with just a quick glance. Vittori is already ushering me towards the strange entrance with the words Observation Deck above them.

"Where are we going, exactly?" I ask Vittori as we follow a man toward an elevator that is waiting for us.

"Jared's waiting for you at Top of the Rock," he answers once we step into the elevator.

The man we were following turns a key inside of the elevator and selects our destination, "Enjoy," he says as he steps back, leaving Vittori and I alone in the elevator.

"This seems sus," I joke to Vittori after a few moments of awkward silence.

"Why's that?"

"You're not letting me out of your sight, like you did when we didn't know who was trying to kill us."

"Well, it's nothing like that," he replies vaguely.

"Then what is it like?"

"You'll just have to wait and decide for yourself."

"Decide what?" I ask as the elevator doors open.

We step out into the lobby for Top of the Rock and look around. Vittori remains silent as he nods for me to walk down a hallway. The hallway has a few leather looking benches along the middle, and tall windows along the walls on each side, leading out to the observation deck. The entire area is nearly empty as we make our way down the hall. Vittori opens a nearby door, holding it open as he gestures for me to step through.

Once I do, I'm in awe as I see the beautiful NYC skyline from above the city. It's beautiful as the city turns to lights and the sun set glows in the sky all around us. Before I can fully analyze everything that I'm seeing, I see someone step up next to me.

"May I?" Jared asks, holding his arm out for me to link mine through.

I look over and focus my attention on him as I smile brightly, feeling my cheeks blush at the sight of him all dressed up in a sexy suit. "Yes, you may," I reply as I link my arm through his.

He leads us around the observation deck, pointing out where The Rush is, the direction his condo is in, the direction of the Berlusconi Manhattan apartment, and of course the mansion. He reminds me of the ice-rink down below, but I don't dare look over the edge. I'm not really afraid of heights, but I don't like the feeling like I'm about to fall while looking over the edge.

"The city is beautiful from up here," I admit as we look out over the railing. Jared's standing behind me with his arms around me as we look out together. The sunset was changing colors across the horizon when I first arrived, but is quickly fading into twilight as the city begins to glow from below.

"I'm glad you like it," Jared says quietly.

"Seems pretty deserted though," I admit, looking around. "Is this normal?"

Jared laughs, causing me to look over my shoulder at him. "Not exactly."

I look around again, trying to understand what he means.

He tightens his grip around me and takes a long deep breath, like he's preparing to say something. Finally, he breaks the growing silence. "Amazia, I can't begin to describe how much you've changed my life."

"I was also the reason you got shot," I whisper back, wondering why the skyline has suddenly made him talk about his emotions.

He laughs, "That doesn't count."

"If you say so," I joke.

"Anyways," he sighs heavily, "I wanted to bring you up here on our last date. You know, the night I got shot," he says in a teasing tone.

"That changed your plans a bit."

"It really did ruin my plans for the perfect date night." He pauses for several moments before continuing. "Dinner was nice, but it wasn't the part I was most looking forward to."

I think about asking what he's hinting at, but I am really at a loss. Why is he acting so strange right now? He keeps pausing dramatically, but I don't feel like he's doing it for effect. It seems like he's doing it out of nerves, but that isn't like Jared at all. Is that why Vittori had to escort me up here? Are they worried? Is someone else after us? Are we still in danger?

Before I can ask Jared any of these questions on my mind, he continues. "I was terrified of what would happen when my heart and my soul opened up to you. I didn't want anyone to find out, because I was afraid that it would put you in danger. I was selfish and followed my heart to pursue you. I felt such a pull towards you that I didn't understand. I'd never felt this way before and I had no idea what these feelings and emotions even meant. I acted on them a bit too much at The Rush during Elena's wedding weekend, and that scared me even more. What if Berlusconi found out? What would he do? But at the end of the day, I wanted you. And, thankfully, it all worked out, even if I couldn't keep you away from this life we live."

"I wouldn't change anything," I whisper back, making sure he knows I don't blame him for any of the complicated details that have come up since we decided to start seeing one another.

"I promised that I'd never keep another secret from you after you found out the truth about what I did. I didn't know how to tell you without scaring you off. In the end, you were thankfully too stubborn to let me go," he laughs. "The day you came to my door, pounding until I answered and proved I was okay, was what helped set me straight."

"You were quite drunk," I laugh, remembering how intoxicated he was.

"The first and the last time I got drunk. But when you left, it was like I lost a part of myself. I instantly dumped the rest of the alcohol and started to plan out how I'd get my life together and get you back. I would have to do something to win back your trust and your heart, and I wasn't going to give up."

"Lucky for you, I was already head over heels for you."

"Lucky for me, you're tough enough to stand up to Berlusconi."

"That too," I laugh at myself.

"You already know how much I love and care for you, but I wanted our date night to end up here. I wanted our date to end where you could look out over the city and see that our love is above the entire city. I wanted you to know just how strongly I feel," he loosens his grip around me.

"What are you saying?" I ask, at a loss. What does he mean that our love is above the city? Is this some metaphor I'm not catching? Wait, is metaphor the right term? Before I start to overthink, I realize Jared has let go of me. I turn, looking for the warmth of his arms. I look for his eyes, quickly realizing he isn't at eye level.

"Amazia," he says slowly.

I glance down, realizing where he went, and he isn't tying his shoe. I feel myself gasp as the entire moment moves in slow motion.

"You are the best thing that has ever happened to me. I hope that you'll do me the honor of being my wife," he starts.

I feel my hand fly over my mouth as I try to hide my shock in the moment. Oh no he isn't, I think to myself as I realize he is on one knee and holding something in his hand. He begins to slowly raise his hands together, opening a small box to reveal what's inside.

"Amazia Franklin, will you marry me?"

"Holy shit," are the words I whisper to myself, knowing he heard me as he laughs at my initial reaction. I look from the beautiful diamond ring, up to Jared's eyes, feeling my own begin to water. "Yes!" I finally answer, causing tears to escape my eyes.

Jared stands up, revealing a tear escaping his own eye as he pulls out the ring, reaching for my left hand, and slowly sliding the ring onto my ring finger. "I love you," he whispers.

"I love you too," I whisper back as tears continue to roll off my cheeks.

He puts his right hand on my cheek before bringing his lips crashing down on mine in a passionate kiss before pulling me into his arms. A moment later I hear cheers and applause around us, pulling us back from a moment. Jared pulls back and smiles as he rests his forehead against mine and whispers, "I hope you don't mind. I invited a few people."

I pull back and look around. I see Vittori, Berlusconi, Spencer, Lorenzo, Elena, and Mrs. Berlusconi clapping nearby, all holding champagne glasses. Vittori walks up to hand us each our own glass before turning towards everyone, raising his glass, and saying "To Jericho and Amazia!"

"To Jericho and Amazia!" everyone repeats before downing their champagne.

"All of this, for us?" I ask.

"No babe. All of this for you," he clarifies before leaning back in to kiss me again. This time he doesn't immediately pull away as everyone hoots and cheers us on.

Once we pull away, smiling at one another, I sense someone approaching. We turn and see Berlusconi and his wife walking up. "Jared," he emphasizes, "we are so proud of the man you've grown to be."

"And the beautiful woman you've chosen to be yours," Mrs. Berlusconi adds.

"Your brother wanted to be here," Berlusconi says to me. "Logistically it wasn't safe for him to be here, especially until we get his new identity into place."

"Thank you for telling me. It means a lot," I admit.

"He did give Jared his blessing though, before we set this whole thing up," Berlusconi admits. "Buying this place out a second time was a bit more complicated than the first time."

"The first time?" I ask, looking back and forth between Berlusconi and Jared.

"This was the plan, the night I was shot in that warehouse," Jared admits.

"That's why you were acting so odd and why Vittori kept making weird comments about your plans," I finally come to the realization.

"You really had no idea?" Vittori steps up to ask.

"Not a clue," I admit.

"And tonight?" Vittori asks.

"No idea," I laugh.

"You did good," Vittori tips his glass to Jared.

"Okay, okay," Elena breaks everyone up. "Let the love birds have some fresh air." She shoos her parents and Vittori away before turning to face us. "I can't wait to be at your wedding and be there for you the way that you were for me, even if you didn't really know me yet," she says to me, melting my heart a little.

"Thank you, Elena," I smile, knowing I'll always feel welcome in this family.

"No. Thank you for bringing a soul into Jared's body," she laughs.

"Very funny," Jared says.

"Dinner everyone," Berlusconi yells over out, gesturing for everyone to follow him to the buffet just inside the doors.

"Quick, let me get your photo with that beautiful ring before we eat," Elena says, moving us into the place she wants us to stand. "Engaged on three. One, two, three…" she says, taking probably a million pictures from every angle she can. "Okay, okay. I think I got one."

"One?" Jared teases.

Elena sticks her tongue out at him in a sibling tease before turning and walking to the buffet.

Jared holds my arms and turns me to face him. "Fiancé… I kind of like the sound of that," he smiles.

"Me too," I admit, not bothering to hide my smile.

"I love you."

"And I love you," I say before his lips crash down on mine again.

After a few moments, he pulls away and rests his forehead against mine as we each catch our breath. "We better entertain our guests."

"You're right," I admit. "Plus, we still have a lifetime together."

I smile as he releases me, taking my hand in his as we walk towards the buffet to join our family.

Bonus Chapter: Jericho

I finally got something worth fighting for. I got the girl, Amazia. She is amazing and I'm lucky to have her... well, I was lucky to have her. It's just like me to finally have a good thing before I went and fucked it all up. One night, one stupid mistake, and she's gone. I shouldn't have taken her there. I should have known better than to expect her to stay in the car. Curiosity killed the cat, and maybe it killed her too. What if Mr. Berlusconi finds out. I'm sure Mr. Vittori has already told him. Why did I think drowning myself in alcohol was going to help. I don't even drink.

* * * * *

Alcohol does nothing positive for my mood. Instead, it just makes me dizzy and sleepy. I try to force myself to stay awake as I find myself too confused to concentrate on Amazia and what I might have lost. There is no way she would have given me a chance if I was honest from the beginning. There is no way she would have understood. Now, there is no going back. Would she ever understand? Will she ever be safe again?

I tip back the bottle and drink more and more, trying to forget Amazia. Everyone says alcohol does that, but clearly, I have a tolerance or something because all I can think about is her. Her amazing smile and smart-ass personality are always on my mind. She's beautiful and witty and I never thought I'd fall so hard for someone. But my job is too hard for her to understand. She's not like me. She's empathetic and caring and wouldn't hurt a fly. Now she's seen something dark and evil. She's seen my involvement in something unthinkable.

I hear a knock at my door. Stupid door to door salesman. I take another swig and ignore them. Even if I wasn't drunk, I wouldn't want to deal with anyone right now. Another knock, a bit louder comes from the front door. They're persistent at least. A few moments later, a third round of knocking begins. This time it is loud and doesn't stop. Maybe it isn't a salesman. Oh shit, what if it's Vittori. I reach over to check my phone and quickly realize it's dead. I forgot to charge it the last two days while I was trying to drink away my feelings for Amazia.

I pick up the bottle and walk towards the door, feeling myself stumble and trip as I try to make it there. The sooner I get there, the sooner the pounding on the door, and in my head, will stop. "What do you want?" I angrily whisper to myself as I unlock the door to open it. The pounding on the door doesn't stop until I am pulling it open. I lean into the door to hold my balance and quickly realize that it isn't a salesman or Vittori. It's Amazia.

"Well, shit…" I hear myself say before I can stop myself.

"Are you drunk right now?" she asks, looking angry.

I quickly turn away and walk back toward the couch. The room is spinning too fast for me to stay standing. "I think that's what this feeling is," I reply, hearing my own slurred speech.

"But you don't even drink," she says as she closes and locks my door.

"You're right," I say as I fall back down onto couch. "I don't drink. This isn't like me."

"What are you doing?" she asks, standing in front of me with her arms crossed angrily over her chest.

I tip the bottle back to look into it, towards the secrets at the bottom. I need to look at something other than her. She's clearly angry with me and I can't bear the feeling of her hate. My heart aches just with knowing she's upset. "I see a story at the bottom of this bottle."

"What story is that?" she asks as she takes the bottle from me.

"A good one. Great ending. Something I wouldn't expect or even deserve."

"You sobering up?" she asks in the smart-ass tone that I love so much.

"After that!" I yell, unintentionally.

"I can't talk to you while you're like this," she puts the bottle down and quickly turns to leave.

If she leaves, she might not ever come back. I can't let her leave like this. I can't let her leave mad at me. I can't give up, no matter how drunk I am. "But... No! Amazia, wait. Don't you leave me, Amazia. I need you," I plead, begging her not to leave me behind forever. She can't give up on me.

"You can't need me in this condition," she turns to gesture to my current state. "There is no place in your life for me while you're in this condition," her voice cracks as she appears to be holding back tears.

"But I do need you. You're my everything, Amazia," I try to stand but my legs fail me. I push through and stand to try to get closer to her. I need to convince her to stay and give me a chance.

"Let's talk about this after you sober up," she says as she heads toward the door.

I stumble forward and reach for her arm. I grab her arm to stop her, but quickly feel sick and unbalanced. I should not have moved so fast. This is why drunk people can't drive. You can't even walk in this condition. How do people do this? I look up at Amazia and see surprise in her eyes. I feel nauseous as I wonder why she's looking at me this way. Then I glance down at my hand and see that my grip is far too tight. I do my best to let go without falling as I feel myself confessing my deepest desire without warning. "You're going to marry me and we're going to have a family and live happily ever after away from all of this!" Crap! I just yelled at her. And I told her she's going to marry me. What the fuck was I thinking? Oh, wait! I wasn't thinking. Stupid fucking alcohol. Why did I think this was a good idea? This is terrible. But I didn't think she'd come over here. I didn't think she'd ever want to see me again.

"Jared," she whispers.

"Amazia, just tell me you love me," I whisper, trying not to yell again.

"Not like this," she chokes out.

"But you do, right?" I ask while trying to make eye contact.

"Call me when you're sober and ready to talk," she says quickly as she turns away to leave.

"Amazia! Wait!" I yell after her, but she's already left, closing my door behind her. I go to the window and watch as she runs out to her car. She quickly starts her car and drives away without looking back. "Shit," I whisper to myself, feeling like I really messed it up this time.

I stumble back to the couch and search for my phone. As soon as I find it, I search for my charger and plug it in. While I wait for it to charge enough to power back on, I stumble to the kitchen and grab a bottle of water from the pantry. I chug the entire thing. Isn't this the way they tell people to sober up? Or is that to help drunk people throw up? Well shit, either should work, right? Several agonizing minutes go by before my phone finally powers on. It takes another few minutes for everything to load, including two days of missed calls and texts. "Fuck," I say as I scroll through noticing several missed calls from Mr. Berlusconi and a few texts from Vittori. I reply to those first, letting him know there were some technical issues with my phone. Vittori immediately replies that he was about to send someone over if I didn't reply soon. I sigh, realizing I dodged a bullet if he isn't angry.

I take a breath and try to focus as I open the missed calls and texts from Amazia. Nothing from her until this morning when she texts that she wants to talk. After a while she asks for me to just reply and tell her I'm okay, but my phone was dead. I couldn't receive her messages to reply. At least she cares enough to check on me. Is there still hope? Or did I fuck that up when she came over and found me like this? The thought alone helps sober me up enough to decide I'm done with the alcohol. I grab the bottle and quickly pour it down the drain before I get the stupid idea to finish it off. If there is any chance for me to keep Amazia in my life, now is the time for me to step up and make it count.

* * * * *

When I get to her house, her car is here, but she doesn't answer the door. I look into the window, but there is no sign of her. I listen quietly but hear nothing. I walk around frantically, looking into all of the windows for any sign of movement. Maybe she went into the city? No, her car would be at the train station. I run back to my car and drive a few blocks away to the beach. She once told me that she bought this house because she always liked the idea of being able to walk on the beach to think. As I approach, I can see her walking the beach in the distance. I park my car and run along the sidewalk to get as close as I can before making my way down to the sand.

She's walking slowly, with her hands tucked into her pockets for warmth. A thick winter scarf is wrapped around her neck, and she has it folded up so she can tuck her face into it to block the wind coming off of the sound. She looks bundled up enough, but her face is already red from the cold. She doesn't notice me as I slowly approach. She's kicking the sand and clearly in deep thought. As I get close, I clear my throat loudly to be sure she notices someone is close by.

She glances up to see who it is, almost as if she expected me. Her eyes light up when she sees me, but she quickly looks away. She continues walking slowly but stops kicking sand as she goes. I fall in step beside her and try to follow her lead. I don't want to say anything wrong. I don't want to ruin my one chance to make everything up to her. I'm not sure that I can ever make up for lying about my job. On top of that I have to make up for my behavior when I was drunk a few days ago.

After several minutes of agonizing silence, she breaks it. "Are you feeling, better?"

"I am," is all I can manage to reply.

"Why are you here?" she jumps to the point.

"Getting right to the point," I laugh, remembering this is one of many reasons that I love her.

She looks mad at me when she stops to say, "Yes, Jared. I'm getting right to the point. What else do you want from me?"

"I'm sorry. I just want you to know that I'm sorry." I look away, upset with myself for making a joke out of this intense situation we're in.

"Jared," she gently begins again. "Why are you here?"

"I need to explain what happened. I thought that the alcohol would help somehow. I thought it would make me feel better or make me forget. I realize now that alcohol doesn't solve any problems, it just suppresses them for a short time." I look out at the water as I try to avoid eye contact with her. "What I'm trying to say is that I'm sorry for drinking and I'm sorry for how I acted and I'm sorry that you had to see me that way and I'm sorry that I never told you the truth and I'm sorry for…"

"Jared," she interrupts my long-winded rambling.

"Amazia?" I don't dare look up at her as I try to catch my breath.

"Jared, look at me," she gently demands of me.

I hesitantly look over, feeling utterly terrified that this is it, the end. I decide to plead my case before it's too late. "Without you I couldn't think straight. The alcohol only made it worse and I regret every single drop."

"I still get butterflies in my stomach when you're around," she admits.

"Amazia, I can't lose you," I say, looking deep into her eyes to try to gauge her reaction.

"After everything," she pauses. "After everything that happened, after everything that I saw, I'm definitely… confused."

"That's to be expected."

"I don't want to lose you either, Jared."

I step closer to her, holding out my hand until she accepts it. "I'm sorry for drinking and I'm definitely sorry for yelling at you about marriage and everything when I wasn't thinking clearly. I was just terrified of losing you."

"I know," she replies as she steps in closer to me.

I gently pull her to me, into a hug filled with more emotions than I have ever felt. This is the only way I can share the emotions that I could not put into words if I was forced to. The feelings between us bring so much warmth to the ice-cold January afternoon. "I wish we could leave and never come back."

"But..." she begins.

I pull back to look at her as I say, "Mr. Berlusconi doesn't let people go that easily."

"What does that even mean?"

"There is so much I've been wanting to tell you."

"Then tell me."

"What if it scares you away for good?" I ask, genuinely scared she'll run and never look back.

"I'm not going anywhere," she admits, instantly stealing my heart.

I feel myself smile as I try to hold back the tear of joy that I feel creeping to the surface. I'm a man, I can't cry. "I wouldn't even know where to begin."

"Would the beginning be too much to ask?" she laughs nervously.

"Maybe. At least for right now. It's kind of a long story."

"Then, what are the highlights?" she asks as we turn to start walking toward the parking lot.

"I work for Mr. Berlusconi, off the record," I start slow.

"Doing what, exactly?"

"Cleaning up messes," I remain vague as I'm not sure what to say that won't change her mind about me.

"Like the other night?"

"Just like the other night."

"Is that your only job?"

She must remember that I said I worked several part time jobs. "Not exactly. All of my work is for Mr. Berlusconi or one of his connections."

"And Mr. Vittori?"

"He is very much like me. He works for Mr. Berlusconi. He's been with him for a very long time and pretty much goes everywhere with him."

"Why didn't you want them to know about us?"

I feel myself sigh heavily before I stop walking. "You remember how I told you that I was complicated. How I didn't feel any real emotions before you?"

She silently nods in response.

Admitting this scared me the most out of everything so far. "They hired me because of my lack of emotions. They knew I could handle the work without having feelings for what they were doing, but they also knew that I'd never love someone. Someone I'd have to lie to and keep secrets from."

"So, you didn't want them to know about me because you didn't want them to know that your emotions changed?"

"That was a large part of it, yes."

"And the other part?" she asks as she reaches out to wrap her arms around my waist.

"I was afraid that they'd pull you in," I admit while pulling her in closer.

"What do you mean?" she looks up into my eyes again.

"I was afraid that they'd find a way to get you to work for them, if they knew about us."

"Why would they do that?"

"Well, with how fixated Mr. Berlusconi was on you during his daughter's wedding. The way he acted and the way he constantly requested you was similar to how he generally grooms people to one day work for him."

"So, he tests them out to see if they're compliant?"

"Partly. He also tries to learn as much as possible about them. He likes to exploit any weaknesses. He tries to find something you want to lure you in."

"And you honestly think that was his plan for me?"

"I'm still curious if that was his reason for being at the New Years party."

"Didn't he ask you to work for him that night?"

"Yes, which threw me because he usually only invited me when there is something worth cleaning up."

"So, then why that night?"

"I honestly don't know. I asked for the night off and told him it was important to me. It took some convincing, but he gave in because I never ask for anything like that."

"Why me?"

"I'm not sure about that either."

"Why do I have to be good at my damn job?"

"For me it wasn't you doing the job."

"I know, I know. It was my charming personality," she teases.

"Something like that."

"You can't just conform to society and be normal, can you?" she jokes.

I sigh before replying, "I'm never gonna be good enough for you. I can't change who I am, it's just too late to go back and rewrite history. I can't go back to before I got tangled up with the Berlusconi family... We can't go back," I clarify.

"And I'm not asking you to."

"I know I ruined everything. I didn't tell you the whole truth and nothing will ever make the lies okay. Losing you means I'd lose everything. I'd do anything to get you to trust me again. I'd do anything to help prove how I feel. I'd do anything." I feel my heart ache as I test out these strong feelings for Amazia.

"I'm willing to give you a chance, Jared. I can't lose you either. I want to trust you, I really do. I know this is complicated and I will have plenty more questions, but when it comes to you and me, I trust you completely. I know you'd never do anything to intentionally hurt me."

"I'd understand if you wanted to run away and say we're not meant to be. I can never go back to before you. You've changed me. You've awakened my soul somehow."

"I don't want to go back either. You are my heart and my soul."

"I'm not who you thought I was, and I get that. I wanted to hide the truth, not because I wanted to hide anything from you, but because I didn't want you to see that side of me."

"I'm here for you, both sides of you. The good, the bad, the messy, and the secretive. I'm all in, Jared."

"I never expected you to say that after everything," I admit while pulling her in to a gentle kiss. I pull back and place my forehead against hers. We stay here for at least a minute before I let her go. I take her hand and start walking toward the car again as I use my other hand to start it with the remote start. "Let's get you warmed up."

We walk hand in hand in silence for several moments before she speaks up to randomly ask, "What's your real name?"

"Jared is more of a nickname," I answer to avoid giving her the honest answer.

"But, legally...?"

"Jericho," I shrug. I hate my legal name almost as much as I hate when Mr. Berlusconi uses it.

"Do you hate it?" she asks.

"Kind of," I admit as I open the passenger door for Amazia to climb in. She didn't run away and she didn't tell me to leave her alone. My heart may stay whole after all.

Thank You

This book I randomly wrote over two weeks. I'm still not sure how I did it. I was teaching full time and in school full time, yet this story randomly bloomed in my mind and demanded to be written. Amazia and Jared are very special characters to me. They touched my heart and took over this story and developed a romance that was not entirely planned for them. Through it all, I had friends and family support me. One of my former co-workers, Vaz, said, "Your other book was good, but this just hits differently." That was when I knew that this story was not just a side story to toss aside, but would be my first standalone. Many of the characters you met will show up again in their own standalone books, but that will be down the line.

Let me reach out now to thank so many people who have supported me. First off will be my amazing boyfriend who isn't a reader, but still deals with me wanting to read and write in every free moment I can find. My next shout out is to Ashley and Erica, my amazing editors this time around. Erica was worried that I'd be mad at her, but I needed every edit she found. Of course, this book is an independently published novel, and it is not perfect. Adults can mess up. No one is perfect. I try to teach my students this everyday. Therefore, my next shout out is to my students. Mainly my first year students who supported me through every publication that came out while I taught them (part 2 and 3 of the debut series) and pushed me to write more and share more stories with them. I want to thank my second year of teaching students who are currently making me laugh almost as much as my students from last year.

Please follow me on social media and check out my website for future notifications and updates:

Stefaniedidominzioauthor.com
Tiktok: @Stefaniedidoauthor
Facebook: Stefanie DiDominzio Author Page

Milton Keynes UK
Ingram Content Group UK Ltd.
UKHW021353011224
451693UK00012B/810